The Collected
Supernatural and Weird
Fiction of
Catherine Crowe

The Collected Supernatural and Weird Fiction of Catherine Crowe

Thirty-Five Short Stories of the Strange and Unusual Including the 'Evening Tales', 'The Swiss Lady's Story', The Dutch Officer's Story' and 'My Friend's Story'

Catherine Crowe

LEONAUR

The Collected
Supernatural and Weird
Fiction of
Catherine Crowe
Thirty-Five Short Stories of the Strange and Unusual Including the 'Evening Tales',
'The Swiss Lady's Story', The Dutch Officer's Story' and 'My Friend's Story'

by Catherine Crowe

FIRST EDITION

Leonaur is an imprint of Oakpast Ltd

Copyright in this form © 2018 Oakpast Ltd

ISBN: 978-1-78282-772-6 (hardcover)
ISBN: 978-1-78282-773-3 (softcover)

http://www.leonaur.com

Contents

Preface   7

First Evening   9

Second Evening   17

Third Evening   28

Fourth Evening   38

Fifth Evening   46

Sixth Evening   52

Seventh Evening   61

Eighth Evening   72

Appendix   78

The Italian's Story   89

The Dutch Officer's Story   105

The Old French Gentleman's Story   114

The Swiss Lady's Story   127

The Sheep-Farmer's Story   144

My Friend's Story   158

Night Side of Nature Fact or Fiction?   165

Preface

It happened that I spent the last winter in a large country mansion, in the north of England, where we had a succession of visitors, and all manner of amusements—dancing, music, cards, billiards, and other games.

Towards the end of December, 1857, however, the gaiety of the house was temporarily interrupted by a serious misfortune that occurred to one of the party, which, in the evening, occasioned us to assemble with grave faces round the drawing-room fire, where we fell to discussing the slight tenure by which we hold whatever blessings we enjoy, and the sad uncertainty of human life, as it affects us in its most mournful aspect—the lives of those we love.

From this theme, the conversation branched out into various speculations regarding the great mysteries of the here and hereafter; the reunion of friends, and the possible interests of them that have passed away in the well-being of those they have left behind; till it fell, naturally, into the relation of certain experiences which almost everybody has had, more or less; and which were adduced to fortify the arguments of those who regard the future as less disjoined from the present than it is considered to be by Theologians generally.

In short, we began to tell ghost stories; and although some of the party professed an utter disbelief in apparitions, they proved to be as fertile as the believers in their contributions—relating something that had happened to themselves or their friends, as having undoubtedly occurred, or to all appearance, occurred—only, with the reservation, that it must certainly have been a dream.

The substance of these conversations fills the following pages, and I have told the stories as nearly as possible in the words of the original narrators. Of course, I am not permitted to give their names; nobody chooses to confess, in print, that he or anybody belonging to him, has seen a ghost, or believes that he has seen one. There is a sort of odium attached to the imputation, that scarcely anyone seems equal to encounter; and no wonder, when *wise* people listen to the avowal with such strange incredulity, and pronounce you at the best a superstitious fool, or a patient afflicted with spectral illusions.

Under these circumstances, whether I have ever seen a ghost, myself, I must decline confiding to the public; but I take almost as courageous a step in avowing my entire and continued belief in the fact that others do occasionally see these things; and I assert, that most of those who related the events contained in the ensuing pages of this work, confessed to me their absolute conviction that they or their friends had actually seen and heard what they said they did. Some of the company related curious traditions and legends connected with their family annals; and these form the second part of this little book, which I hope may prove a not uninteresting companion for a Christmas fireside.

Catherine Crowe

15th October, 1858.

First Evening

"But there are no ghosts now," objected Mr. R.

"Quite the contrary," said I; "I have no doubt there is nobody in this circle who has not either had some experience of the sort in his own person or been made a confidant of such experiences by friends whose word on any other subject he would feel it impossible to doubt."

After some discussion on the existence of ghosts and cognate subjects, it was agreed that each should relate a story, restricting himself to circumstances that had either happened to himself or had been told him by somebody fully entitled to confidence, who had undergone the experience.

We followed the order in which we were sitting, and Miss P. began as follows:—

"I was some years ago engaged to be married to an officer in the regiment.

Circumstances connected with our families prevented the union taking place as early as we had expected; and in the mean while Captain S., whose regiment was in the West Indies, was ordered to join. I need not say that this separation distressed us a good deal, but we consoled each other as well as we could by maintaining a constant correspondence; though there were no steam packets in those days, and letters were much longer on their way and less certain in their arrival than they are now. Still I heard pretty regularly and had no reason for the least uneasiness.

"One day that I had been out shopping, and had returned rather tired, I told my mother that I should go and lie down for an hour, for we were going out in the evening, and I was afraid I might have a headache, to which I am rather subject; so I went up to my room, took down a book and threw myself on the bed to read or sleep as it might happen. I had read a page or two and feeling drowsy had laid down the volume in order to compose myself to sleep, when I was aroused by a knock at my chamber door.

"Come in," I said, without turning my head, for I thought it was the maid come to fetch the dress I was going to wear in the evening.

"I heard the door open and a person enter, but the foot was not hers; and then I looked round and saw that it was Captain S. What came over me then I can't tell you. I knew little of mesmerism at that period, but I have since thought that when a spirit appears, it must have some power of mesmerising the spectator; for I have heard other people who had been in similar situations describe very much what I experienced myself. I was perfectly calm, not in the least frightened or surprised, but transfixed. Of course, had I remained in my normal state, I should either have been amazed at seeing Captain S. so unexpectedly, especially in my chamber; or if I believed it an apparition, I should have been dreadfully distressed and alarmed; but I was neither; and I can't say whether I thought it himself or his ghosts I was passive, and my mind accepted the phenomenon without question of how such a thing could be.

"Captain S. approached the bedside and spoke to me exactly as he was in the habit of doing, and I answered him in the same manner. After the first greeting, he crossed the room to fetch a chair that stood by the dressing table; He wore his uniform, and when his back was turned, I remember distinctly seeing the seams of his coat behind. He brought the chair, and having seated himself by the bed side, he conversed with me for about half-an-hour; he then rose and looking at his watch, said his time had expired and he must go; he bade me goodbye and went out by the same door he had entered at.

"The moment it closed on him, I knew what had happened; if my hypothesis be correct, his power over me ceased when he disappeared and I returned to my normal state. I screamed and seized the bell rope which I rang with such violence that I broke it. My mother, who was in the room underneath, rushed upstairs, followed by the servants. They found me on the floor in a fainting state, and for some time I was unable to communicate the cause of my agitation. At length, being somewhat calmed, I desired the servants might leave the room, and then I told my mother what had happened. Of course, she thought it was a dream; in vain I assured her it was not, and pointed to the chair which, wonderful to say, had been actualy brought to the bedside by the spirit—there it stood exactly as it had been placed by him; luckily nobody had moved it I said, you know where that chair usually stands; when you were up here a little while ago it was in its usual place—so it was when I lay down—I never moved it; it was placed there by Captain S.

"My mother was greatly perplexed; she found me so confident and clear; yet, the thing appeared to her impossible.

"From that time, I only thought of Captain S, as one departed from this life; suspense and its agonies were spared me. I was certain. Accordingly, about a month afterwards, when one morning Major B. of the —— regiment sent in his card, I said to my mother, 'Now you'll see; he comes to tell me of Henry's death.'

"It was so. Captain S. had died of fever on the day he paid me that mysterious visit."

We asked Miss P. if any similar circumstance had ever occurred to her before or since.

"Never," she answered; "I never saw anything of the spirit but on that occasion."

"I have no experience of my own to relate," said Dr. W., "but in the course of my late tour in Scotland, I went amongst other places to Skye, and I found the whole island talking of an event that had just happened there, which may perhaps interest you. There was a tradesman in Portree of the name of Robertson; I believe he was a sort of general dealer, as shopkeepers frequently are in those remote localities. Whatever his business was, however, it frequently took him to the other islands or the mainland to make purchases. He had arranged to go on one of these expeditions, I think to Raasa, when a friend called to inform him that a meeting of the inhabitants was to be held on some public question in which he, Robertson, was much interested."

"'You had better defer going till after Friday,' said Mr. Brown; 'we can't do without you, and it's very possible you may not get back in time.'

"'Oh, yes, I can do all my business, and be back very well on Thursday,' said Mr. Robertson; objecting that if he waited over Friday it would be no use going till Monday. Brown tried to persuade him to alter his plans, but in vain; 'however,' said he, 'you may rely on seeing me on Thursday, if you'll look in, in the evening; as I would not miss the meeting on any account.'

"This conversation took place at an early hour on Tuesday morning. Immediately afterwards Mr. Robertson bade his wife and children goodbye and proceeded to the boat which left at eleven o'clock, having on board, besides himself, two other passengers, and two boatmen.

"On Thursday evening, Mr. Brown, who had been busying himself in fortifying and encouraging their adherents against the next day and had taken upon himself to answer for his friend Robertson's presence, as soon as he had finished business, set off to keep his appointment with the latter, anxious to ascertain that he was arrived.

"His anxiety was soon relieved, for on his way he met him.

"'Well, here you are,' said he, holding out his hand.

"'Yes,' answered Robertson, not appearing to notice the hand, 'I have kept my promise.'

"Upon that Mr. Brown introduced the subject of the meeting and mentioned the hopes he had of carrying the question, with which Robertson seemed satisfied; but as soon as possible turning the conversation into another direction, he began talking to his friend about his wife and children, and certain arrangements he had wished to be made respecting his property.

"His mind seemed so much more engrossed with these matters than the meeting, that little was said upon the latter subject, and Mr. Brown, having parted with him in the street, rather wondered why he chose such a moment to discuss, his private affairs.

"The next morning, at the appointed hour, the principal inhabitants of the place assembled in a public room at the Tun. Brown, who wanted to say a word to Robertson, lingered at the door; but as he did not come, he thought he must have arrived before himself, and went upstairs.

"'Is Robertson here?' said he, on entering the room.

"'No,' said one, 'I'm afraid he's not come back from Raasa.'

"'Oh, yes,' said Brown, 'he'll be here; I saw him yesterday evening.'

"They then discoursed about the matter in hand for some time, till finding the chairman was about to proceed to business, Robertson's absence was again reverted to.

"'I know he's come back,' said one, 'for I saw him standing at his own door as I passed last night.'

"'He can't have forgotten it,' said another.

"'Certainly not, for we spoke of it last night,' said Brown.

"'Perhaps he's ill,' suggested somebody.

"'Just send your man to Mr. Robertson's, and say we are waiting for him,' said Brown to the landlord.

"The landlord left the room to do so; and, in the meantime, they proceeded to business.

"Presently, the landlord re-entered the room, saying, that Mrs. Robertson answered that her husband had not returned from Raasa and that she did not much expect he would be back till night.

"'Nonsense,' cried Brown, 'Why, I saw the man yesterday according to appointment, and had a long conversation with him.'

"'I am sure he's come back,' said one who had spoken before. 'I was coming down the street on the other side of the way, and I saw him standing at the door with his apron on. I should have crossed over to speak to him, but I was in a hurry.'

"'It's extraordinary,' said the landlord; 'Mrs. Robertson declares he's not come.'

"Some jokes were then passed about the apparent defection of Robertson from his spouse, and the meeting concluded their business without him, his party being exceedingly annoyed at his absence, which they thought not fair to the cause.

"'He should have given us his support.'

"'I suppose he has altered his opinions.'

"'Then he had better have said so.'

"'It struck me, certainly, that he was rather lukewarm on the subject when I talked to him last night; but on Tuesday I saw him just before he started, and he said he would not miss the meeting on any account. I'll go and look after him and know what he means.'

"Accordingly, Brown proceeded to his friend's house, and found Mrs. Robertson and her children at dinner.

"'Weel, Mr. Brown,' she said, 'so your meeting's over.'

"'Aye,' said he, 'but where's Robertson? Why didn't be keep his word with us?'

"'Why, you see, I dare say he meant to be back—indeed, I know he did: but business won't be neglected, and I suppose he could not manage it.'

"'Do you mean to say he's not come back?' said Brown.

"'Sure, I do,' answered Mrs. R. 'Of course, he'd have been at the meeting if he had.'

"'But people saw him last night, standing at his own door,' answered the cautious Brown.

"'Na, na, Mr. Brown, don't you believe that,' said Mrs. R., laughing; 'they that say that had too much whiskey in their een.'

"The children laughed at the idea of anybody seeing their father when he was at Raasa, and on the whole it was evident, that if John Robertson had returned, it was unknown to his family. But what could be his reason for so strange a proceeding, and why, if he wanted to evade the meeting, had he needlessly shown himself at all? Why not really stay away from Portree?

"However, Robertson did not appear; and later in the day the landlord of the Tun said to Brown, as he was passing the door, 'You must have been mistaken about seeing Mr. Robertson; the boat from Raasa is not come in.'

"'Then he must have come over by some other, for I not only saw him but walked and talked with him. I can't think what he can mean by playing at Hide and Seek, in this way?'

"'It's very extraordinary,' said the landlord, 'for I am expecting a hamper from Raasa; and so, hearing from you that Mr. Robertson was come, I went down to inquire about it; but they declare no boat of any sort has come in these two days; the wind's right against them.'

"'I know the boat from Raasa is not come back,' said the porter; 'for I saw Jenny McGill just now, and she says her husband is not re-turned.'

"'Really, you'll persuade me that I'm not in my right senses,' said the perplexed Brown. 'If ever I saw Robertson in my life I saw him last night; I was going to call upon him, as he had asked me to do so before he went away; but I met him, not far from my own house; and what is more, he told me of a thing I did not know before, regarding a purchase he had made, and spoke of what he intended to do with it.'

"'It's most extraordinary,' said the landlord.

"'Eh, sirs,' said an old fishwife, who was standing by, 'I wish it may not be John Robertson's ghaist that ye saw, for the wind's sair agin them, and I'd a bad dream about Jamie McGill last night.'

"They all laughed; but this was the first suggestion of the sort that had been made; and though he would not confess it, Brown began to feel rather uncomfortable; the more so as several things were recalled to his memory that had not struck him at the time. He remembered that Robertson had avoided shaking hands with him, either on meeting or parting, as was his wont; he had even then been struck with the grave tone of his conversation, and with his choosing that particular moment for pressing on his friend's attention what did not appear to have any urgent interest at present.

"Then it occurred to him that he looked ill and sad—he had at-tributed this to fatigue; but now, putting everything together, he could not help feeling a considerable degree of uneasiness. He kept hovering about Robertson's house, and from that to the shore all day; went to bed at night quite nervous; and by the next afternoon the alarm had spread and become universal. It was not without cause.

"John Robertson never came back; the boat had been lost—how, was not known, as all onboard had perished. However, Mr. Brown took upon himself to be the friend and guardian of the bereaved family; and the information he received in that melancholy interview he was enabled to turn much to the advantage of their circumstances."

"A very remarkable story," said I.

"Yes," answered Dr. W. "very remarkable indeed, if true."

"And is it not true," I said, "remember, we are upon honour; I should think it a very ill compliment if anyone attempted to mystify us with an invented story."

"I did not invent it, I assure you," replied Dr. W.; "I give it you as it was given to me on the spot. If you ask me if I believe it, I can't say I do."

"Do you think the people who told you believed it?"

"They certainly appeared to do so."

"And did it seem generally believed?"

"I can't say but it did; but of course, one must have wonderfully strong evidence before one could believe such a thing as that."

"Granted; but unless you had seen the thing yourself, you cannot have stronger evidence of a phenomenon of that description, than that it was believed by those who had good reason to know the grounds of their belief. They were able to judge how far Mr. Brown was worthy of credit; and they had the advantage of having witnessed his demeanour at the public meeting, when he asserted that he had walked and talked with Robertson, at a time he could not possibly know if he was telling a lie, that the man would not sooner or later return to confute him. Besides, as far as we see, it would have been a useless and wicked lie, inasmuch as it was calculated to make the man's family very uneasy. His subsequent conduct does not at all countenance the persuasion that he was capable of such a proceeding."

"Certainly not; but you know the Scotch, are very superstitious."

"I can't agree with you; the higher and lower classes of the towns are exactly similar in that respect to the same classes of England. In all countries the lower classes are more disposed to put faith in these things, because they believe in their traditions and adhere to the axiom that seeing is believing. The higher classes, on the other hand, are carefully educated not to believe in such traditions and to reject the axiom that seeing is believing, if the thing seen is a ghost. Now

I freely admit, that our senses often deceive us, and that we think we see what we do not; everybody with the slightest intelligence has, I suppose, learnt to distrust his own senses to a certain extent; but why on one particular point we should reject their evidence altogether, I never could understand."

"You have heard, I suppose of spectral illusions?" said the doctor.

"Of course, I have, and admit their existence; but we have so many cases on our side, that doctrine will not cover, and it is so impossible for you to prove that any particular case of ghost seeing falls under that head, that it is no use discussing the subject. It complicates the difficulty I confess but can never decide the question. I was going to say, however, that the shopkeepers and middle classes of Scotland are anything but what you mean by superstitious—the class to whom Brown and Robertson belong, is the most hard-headed, argumentative, and matter of fact in the kingdom; and their religion, which is eminently unimaginative, so far from inducing a belief in ghosts, would have a precisely opposite tendency, because ghosts do not form an article of belief in either the longer or shorter catechism. In the remoter districts of the Highlands, the people are said to have more of what you would call superstition; but the same peculiarity is remarked in all mountainous regions; and as it has never been satisfactorily accounted for, we will not enter into the discussion now."

Second Evening

"After the doctor's story, I fear mine will appear too trifling," said Mrs. M., "but as it is the only circumstance of the kind that ever happened to myself, I prefer giving it you to any of the many stories I have heard.

"About fifteen years ago, I was staying with some friends at a magnificent old seat in Yorkshire, and our host being very much crippled with the gout, was in the habit of driving about the park and neighbourhood in a low pony phaeton, on which occasions, I often accompanied him. One of our favourite excursions was to the ruins of an old abbey just beyond the park, and we generally returned by a remarkably pretty rural lane leading to the village, or rather, small town of C.

"One fine summer's evening we had just entered this lane, when seeing the hedges full of wild flowers, I asked my friend to let me alight and gather some; I walked on before the carriage picking honeysuckles and roses as I went along, till I came to a gate that led into a field. It was a common country gate, with a post on each side, and on one of these posts sat a large white cat, the finest animal of the kind I had ever seen; and as I have a weakness for cats, I stopped to admire this sleek, fat puss, looking so wonderfully comfortable in a very uncomfortable position; the top of the post on which it was sitting, with its feet doubled up under it, being out of all proportion to its body, for no Angola ever rivalled it in size."

"'Come on, gently,' I called to my friend, 'here's such a magnificent cat,' for I feared the approach of the phaeton would startle it away before he had seen it.

"'Where?' said he, pulling up his horse opposite the gate.

"'There,' said I, pointing to the post, 'Isn't it a beauty; I wonder if it would let me stroke it?'

"'I see no cat,' said he.

"'There on the post,' said I, 'but he declared he saw nothing, though puss sat there in perfect composure during this colloquy.'

"'Don't you see the cat, James?' said I, in great perplexity to the groom.

"'Yes, ma'am; a large white cat on that post.'

I thought my friend must be joking, or else losing his eyesight, and I approached the cat, intending to take it in my arms, and carry it to the carriage; but as I drew near, she jumped off the post, which was natural enough—but to my surprise she jumped into nothing—as she jumped she disappeared! no cat in the field—none in the lane—none in the ditch!

"'Where did she go, James?'

"'I don't know, ma'am, I can't see her,' said the groom, standing up in his seat, and looking all round.

"I was quite bewildered; but still I had no glimmering of the truth; and when I got into the carriage again, my friend said he thought I and James were dreaming, and I retorted that I thought he must be going blind.

"I had a commission to execute as we passed through the town, and I alighted for that purpose at the little haberdasher's; and while they were serving me, I mentioned that I had seen a remarkably beautiful cat sitting on a gate in the lane; and asked if they could tell me who it belonged to, adding, it was the largest cat I ever saw.

"The owners of the shop, and two women who were making purchases, suspended their proceedings, looked at each other, and then looked at me, evidently very much surprised.

"'Was it a white cat, ma'am?' said the mistress.

"'Yes, a white cat; a beautiful creature and—'

"'Bless me!' cried two or three, 'the lady's seen the *White Cat of C.* It hasn't been seen these twenty years.'

"'Master wishes to know if you'll soon be done, ma'am? The pony is getting restless,' said James.

"Of course, I hurried out, and got into the carriage, telling my friend that the cat was well known to the people at C, and that it was twenty years old.

"In those days, I believe, I never thought of ghosts, and least of all should I have thought of the ghost of a cat; but two evenings afterwards, as we were driving down the lane, I again saw the cat in the same position, and again my companion could not see it, though the groom did. I alighted immediately and went up to it. As I approached, it turned its head, and looked full towards me with its soft, mild eyes, and a kindly expression, like that of a loving dog; and then, without moving from the post, it began to fade gradually away, as if it were a vapour, till it had quite disappeared.

"All this the groom saw as well as myself; and now there could be no mistake as to what it was. A third time, I saw it in broad daylight, and my curiosity greatly awakened, I resolved to make further inquiries amongst the inhabitants of C., but before I had an opportunity of doing so, I was summoned away by the death of my eldest child, and I have never been in that part of the world since. However, I once mentioned the circumstance to a lady who was acquainted with that neighbourhood, and she said she had heard of the White Cat of C. but had never seen it.

"But as you may not think this story very interesting since it only relates to a cat, I will, if you please, tell you another, in which I was concerned, although I saw nothing myself."

"We shall be very happy," I said, "but I am far from thinking your story wanting in interest, in fact, to me it has a very peculiar interest. There are few friends so sincere as the animals who have loved as, and none that I, for my part, more earnestly desire to see again. I have had two dogs, in my life, who contributed much to my happiness while they lived, and never caused me a sorrow till they died.

"Besides, there is a deep mystery in the being of these creatures, which proud man never seeks to unravel, or condescends to speculate on. What is their relation to the human race? Why are these spiritual germs embodied in those forms and made subject to man, that hard and cruel master! who assumes to be their superior, because he is endowed with some higher faculties, the most of which he grossly misuses. How beautiful are their characters when studied? how wonderful their intelligence when cultivated? how willing they are to serve us when kindly treated? But man, by his cruelty, ignorance, laziness, and want of judgment, spoils their temper, blunts their intelligence, deteriorates their nature, and then punishes them for being what he himself has made them. Well might Chalmers exclaim, '*All nature groans beneath the cruelty of man.*' Why are these creatures, sinless, as far as we see, placed here as the subjects of this barbarous, unthinking tyrant? That has always appeared to me a solemn question.'

After this little digression, Mrs. M. continued as follows:—

"I had been travelling on the continent and was staying at Brussels on my way home. The bedroom I occupied was within another, in which slept my faithful maid, Rachel, and one of my children. I had been in bed sometime, and had not been to sleep, when I heard Rachel's voice, saying something which I did not distinctly hear, and before I could ask what it was, she uttered a cry that immediately brought me to her bedside. I found her in a state of violent agitation, and as soon as she was composed enough to speak, she told me that she had not been long in bed when she heard a voice call her, which she supposed to be mine, and immediately afterwards, in the glass which was opposite the foot of the bed, she saw a figure in white, enter and proceed to the other end of the room.

"She concluded it was me in my nightdress, and that I had only mentioned her name to ascertain if she was awake, fearing to disturb the child, who was restless, she lay still, and did not answer. The figure went back through the door, but presently returned again, and seemed to be looking about for something, whereupon she half sat up in bed; when it approached, and laid its hand heavily on her knee, there was something painful in the pressure, and she exclaimed, 'Oh, don't do that ma'am!' but she had scarcely uttered the words when she discerned the features, and saw it was her sister. The phantom looked sadly at her, and then retreating to the opposite corner, disappeared. This circumstance, in spite of my arguments and suggestions that it was a dream, made a very painful impression on her; she felt sure some misfortune had happened, and so it proved; her sister had died on that night, leaving a family of young children, about whom, in her last moments, she was very anxious."

"Cases of that sort are very numerous," said Lady A., "I know of two which I can give upon perfectly good authority. A friend of mine was sitting a few years since in the drawing room at her country seat; there was a door at each end, leading to other rooms, both of which were open. A slight rustle caused her to raise her eyes from her work, when she saw her nephew enter at one door, walk straight through, and out at the other. The young man was at college, and she had no reason to expect him then, but concluding some unforeseen business had brought him, and that he was in search of her, she called—'Arthur, here I am,' and pursued him into the adjoining room, and then into the hall.

"Receiving no answer, and not being able to find him in any direction, she rang for the servants, and inquired where he was; but they did not know; they had seen nothing of him. She insisted he had arrived, and he was sought for all over the house and grounds in vain.

The thing remained perfectly incomprehensible, till the post brought a letter, announcing that the young man had been drowned on that day.

"Another instance, equally well established, is that of Dr. C, of Dublin. He resided with his family some few miles from the city, I believe, at or near Howth, and when he returned in the evening after visiting his patients, he frequently, to save time, took a short cut across some sands, which in certain states of the tide were not always safe. Mrs. C. had often entreated him to relinquish this practice and take the more circuitous way; but he thought he was too well acquainted with the place to run any danger. One evening that they were expecting him, as usual, to dinner, his brother, who was standing at the window, saw him arrive; he rode a white horse, and was therefore a conspicuous object.

"When the dinner hour came, as he had not appeared in the drawing room, his brother and Mrs. C, to whom the latter had mentioned having seen him, desired the servants to seek him in his dressing room, and ask if he was ready. He was not in his room, nor was he anywhere to be found; neither had any of the servants seen him, nor was his horse in the stable. Mr. C, however, confident of his arrival, suggested that he might be gone to visit some sick person in the neighbourhood; so, they waited. But in vain; news presently arrived that horse and man had been drowned that evening in crossing the sands."

There was scarcely anyone present unacquainted with examples of this kind of appearance amongst their family or friends, but Captain L. related to us a case still more curious and unaccountable that had happened to himself in India when he was in the Himalaya.

"I was just finishing my breakfast one morning," said he, "when my servant entered and announced a visitor. It was Captain P. B. of ours, who came to invite me to a game of billiards: Our billiard-room was situated about a mile beyond my quarter, and Captain B., who lived at the other extremity, had to pass my residence to go to it.

"'Are you going up there now?' I said.

"'Yes,' said he; 'will you come?'

"'Why, I can't come directly,' I answered; 'for I have a letter to write first; but if you'll go on, I'll join you presently.'

"He left me, and as soon as I had written my letter, I started for the billiard-room. When I entered it. Captain P. B. was not there, nor indeed, anybody but the marker—which was not surprising, as it was earlier than we usually went there.

21

"'Where's Captain B?' I said.

"'Don't know, sir; he has not been here yet.'

"'Not been here?'

"'No, sir, not today.'

"Thinking, that as I was not ready, he had filled up the interval by going somewhere else, I began knocking about the balls; every now and then looking out of the window, expecting to see him approach; but when this had lasted upwards of two hours, I began to be rather impatient, and was just thinking of going away, when I saw him approaching with his wife in an open carriage from an opposite direction.

"'A pretty fellow you are, to keep me kicking my heels here waiting for you,' said I, as he entered the room.

"'Keep you waiting!' he said; 'I have not kept you waiting.'

"'Why, I've been here these two hours and more.'

"'How was I to know that; I did not know you were coming up here.'

"'Why, I told you I'd come as soon as I had finished my letter.'

"'My dear fellow, what are you talking about?' exclaimed my friend, in evident surprise; 'when did you tell me so? I don't recollect making any appointment to meet you today.'

"'What! not this morning, as you were passing my quarter?' said I, amazed in my turn. 'Didn't you ask me to come and play a game at billiards; and didn't I tell you I'd come as soon as I had finished my letter? and I did.'

"P. B. looked at me as if he thought I'd suddenly become insane; but as I suppose my countenance did not confirm that impression, he said, 'Here's some mistake; when do you suppose I made this appointment with you?'

"'Suppose!' I answered, rather indignant; 'what do you mean by *suppose*? Didn't you come into my quarter about three hours ago, just as I was finishing breakfast, and ask me to come up here and play a game at billiards with you?'

"'No; it must have been somebody else. Who gave you the message?'

"'Message! there was no message,' I answered, quite bewildered, 'You came in yourself—you know you did. What's the use of trying to hoax one?'

"'I don't know whether you are trying to hoax me! replied P. B.; 'but upon my soul I have not been in your quarter today; nor have I seen you at all, till I entered this room. Moreover, I went with my wife at an early hour to breakfast with Captain D., and we are now returning thence; and I told the coachman to set me down here as he passed.'

"This was most confounding; and as we were both equally positive in what we asserted, we left the billiard-room together, and proceeded to take the testimony of my servant. On being asked who he had introduced when I was finishing breakfast, he unhesitatingly answered, Captain B. His account, in short, coincided entirely with mine.

"'Now then,' said Captain B, 'as you have your witness, you must hear mine,' and we went on to his quarter, where I received the most satisfactory and unimpeachable evidence, that what he said was correct. He had left home with Mrs. B. at six o'clock, and gone by appointment to breakfast with Captain D., who lived quite in a different direction to my quarter; and Captain D. afterwards testified to his never having left his house till he stepped into the carriage with his wife.

"This event created a great sensation at the time; and people endeavoured by every means to explain it away, but nobody ever could. Captain B. did not like it at all; and his wife and family were very much alarmed, but nothing ensued, and I believe he is alive and well at this moment."

We next turned to Madame Von B., who said she knew so many cases of spiritual appearances, and occurrences of that nature, that she was father perplexed by the abundance of her recollections. Amongst these she selected the following on account of its singularity:—

"We resided a great deal on the continent before I was married, and my mother had a favourite maid, called Françoise, who lived with her many years—a most trustworthy, excellent creature, in whom she had the greatest confidence; insomuch, that when I married, being very young and very inexperienced, as she was obliged to separate from me herself, she transferred Françoise to my service, considering her better able to take care of me than anybody else;

"I was living in Paris then, where Françoise, who was a native of Metz, had some relations settled in business, whom she often used to visit. She was generally very chatty when she returned from these people; for I knew all her affairs, and through her, all their affairs; and I took an interest in whatever concerned her or hers.

"One Sunday evening, after she had been spending the afternoon, with this family, observing that she was unusually silent, I said to her, while she was undressing me, 'Well, Françoise, haven't you anything to tell me? How are your friends? Has Madame Pelletier got rid of her *grippe?*'

"Françoise started as if I had awakened her out of a reverie, and said, '*Oh! oui, Madame; oui, merci; elle se porte bien aujourd'hui.*' (Oh! Yes Madam; Yes, thank you; she is doing well today.)

"'And Monsieur Pelletier and the children, are they well?'

"'*Oui, Madame, merci; ils se portent bien.*' (Yes, Madam, thank you; they are doing well.)

"These curt answers were so unlike those she generally gave me, that I was sure her mind was pre-occupied, and that something had happened since we parted in the morning; so, I turned round to look her in the face, saying '*Mais, qu'avez vous donc, Françoise? Qu'est ce qu'il y a?*' (But so what possesses you, Françoise? What's the matter?)

"Then I saw what I had not observed before, that she was very pale, and that her cheeks had a glazed look, which showed that she had been crying.

"'*Mais, ma bonne Françoise,*' I said; '*vous avez quelque chose—est il arrivé quelque malheur à Metz?*' (But, my good Françoise, you have something—has there been any misfortune in Metz?)

"'*C'est cela, Madame,*' (That's it, Madam) answered Françoise, who had a brother there whom she had not seen for several years, but to whom she still continued affectionately attached. His name was Benoît, and he was in a good service as *garde forestier* to a nobleman who possessed very extensive estates, *près de chez nous,* as Françoise said. He had a wife and children; and some time before the period I am referring to, Françoise had told me, with great satisfaction, that in order to make him more comfortable, the Prince de M—— had given Benoît the privilege of gathering up all the dead wood in the forest to sell for firewood, which, as the estate was very large, rendered his situation extremely profitable. When she said '*c'est cela, Madame,*' Françoise, who had just encased me in my dressing gown, sunk into a chair, and having declared that she was *bête, très bête,* (stupid, very stupid) she gave way to a hearty good cry, after which, being somewhat relieved, she told me the following strange story:—

"'You remember,' she said, 'that the prince was so good as to give Benoît all the dead wood of the forest—and a great thing it was for him and his family, as you will think, when I tell you it was worth upwards of two thousand *francs* a-year to him. In short, he was growing rich, and perhaps he was getting to think too much of his money and too little of the *bon Dieu*—at all events, this privilege which the prince gave him to make him comfortable, and which made him a great man amongst the foresters, has been the cause of a dreadful calamity.'

"'How?' said I.

"'We never heard anything of what had happened,' said she, till yesterday, when Monsieur Pelletier received a letter from Benoît's wife, and another from a cousin of ours, relating what I am going to tell you, and, saying that both he and his family had wished to keep it secret; but that was no longer possible.'

"'Well, and what has happened ?'

"'*La chose la plus incroyable! Eh bien, Madame*, (the most incredible thing! Well, Madam); it appears that one day last autumn, Benoît went out in the forest to gather the deadwood. He had his cart with him, and as he gathered it he bound it into faggots and threw it in the cart. He had extended his search this day to a remote part of the forest and found himself in a spot he did not remember to have visited before; indeed, it was evident to him that he had not, or he could not have escaped seeing an old wooden cross which was lying on the ground; and had apparently fallen into that recumbent position from old age.

"It was such a cross as is usually set up where a life has been lost, whether by murder or suicide; or sometimes when poor wanderers are frozen to death or lost' in the deep winter snows. He looked about for the grave but saw no indication of one; and he tried to remember if any catastrophe had happened there in his time but could recall none. He took up the cross and examined it. He saw that the wood was decayed, and it bore such marks of antiquity, that he had no doubt the person whose grave it had marked had died before he was born— it looked as if it might be a hundred years old.

"'*Eh bien*,' said Françoise, wiping her eyes, into which the tears kept starting, 'of course you will think that Benoît, or anybody in the world who had the fear of God before his eyes, as he could not find the grave to replace it as it should be, would have laid it reverently down where he had found it, saying a prayer for the soul of the deceased; but, alas! the demon of avarice tempted him, and he had not the heart to forego that poor cross, but bound it up into a faggot with the rest of the dead wood he found there, and threw it into his cart!"

"'Well, Françoise,' said I, 'you know I am not a Catholic, but I respect the custom of erecting these crosses, and I do think your brother was very wrong; I suppose he has lost the prince's favour by such impious greediness.'

"'*Pire que ça!* worse than that,' she replied. 'It appears that while he was committing this wicked action, he felt an extraordinary chill come over him, which made him think that, though it had been a mild day, the evening must have suddenly turned very cold, and hastily throwing the faggot into his cart, he directed his steps homeward. But walk as he would, he still felt this chill down his back, so that he turned his head to look where the wind blew from, when he saw, with some dismay, a mysterious-looking figure following close upon his footsteps. It moved noiselessly on and was covered with a sort of black mantle that prevented his discerning the features.

"Not liking its appearance, he jumped into the cart and drove home as fast as he could, without looking behind him; and when he got into his own farmyard he felt quite relieved, particularly, as when he alighted he saw no more of this unpleasant-looking stranger. So, he began unloading his cart, taking out the faggots, one by one, and throwing them upon the ground; but when he threw down the one that contained the cross, he received a blow upon his face, so sharp that made him stagger and involuntarily shout aloud.

"His wife and children were close by, but there was no one else to be seen, and they would have disbelieved him and fancied he had accidentally hit himself with the faggot, but that they saw the distinct mark on his cheek of a blow given with an open hand. However, he went into supper perplexed and uncomfortable; but when he went to bed this fearful phantom stood by his side, silent and terrible, visible to him, but invisible to others. In short, *Madame*, this awful figure haunted him till, in spite of his shame, he resolved to consult our cousin Jerome about it.'

"But Jerome laughed, and said it was all fancy and superstition. 'You got frightened at having brought away this poor devil's cross, and then you fancy he's haunting you,' said he.

"'But Benoît declared that he had thought nothing about the cross, except that it would make firewood, and that he had no more believed in ghosts than Jerome; 'but now,' said he, 'something must be done. I can get no sleep and am losing my health; if you can't help me, I must go to the priest and consult him.'

"'Why don't you take back the cross and put it where you found it?' said Jerome.

"'Because I am afraid to touch it and dare not go to that part of the forest.'

"'So, Jerome who did not believe a word about the ghost, offered to go with him and replace the cross. Benoît gladly accepted, more especially, as he said he saw the apparition standing even then beside him, apparently, listening to the conversation. Jerome laughed at the idea; however, Benoît lifted the cross reverently into the cart and away they went into the forest When they reached the spot, Benoît pointed out the tree under which he had found it; and as he was shaking and trembling, Jerome took up the cross and laid it on the ground, but as he did so he received a violent blow from an invisible hand, and at the same moment saw Benoît fall to the ground. He thought he had been struck too, but it afterwards appeared that he had fainted from having seen the phantom with its upraised hand striking his cousin.

"'However, they left the cross and came away; but there was an end to Jerome's laughter, and he was afraid the apparition would now haunt him. Nothing of the sort happened; but poor Benoît's health has been so shaken by this frightful occurrence that he cannot get the better of it; his friends have advised change of scene, and he is coming to Paris next week.'

"This was the story Françoise told me, and in a few days, I heard he had arrived and was staying with Monsieur Pelletier; but the shock had been too great for his nerves, and he died shortly after. They assured me that previous to that fatal expedition into the forest, he had been a hale, hearty man, totally exempt from superstitious fancies of any sort; and in short, wholly devoted to advancing his worldly prosperity and getting money,"

Third Evening

"I don't know that I could tell you anything interesting in the way of Ghost Stories; I have never attended to them, though I have heard a great many," said Colonel C.; "but I can tell you an extraordinary circumstance which may, perhaps, be considered of a spiritual nature, and which I can myself vouch for the truth of.

"My father, when I was young, resided in the South of England—I shall not give the name of the place, nor of the people immediately concerned, if these stories are to be published; because, for anything I know, some persons may survive to whom the publication might give pain; I lived there with him and my mother and sisters. Our house was on the road between two large towns, situated about eight miles distant from each other; and though we had a little ground and a short avenue in front, we were not more than half a quarter of a mile from the highway. When all was still, we could distinctly hear the carts and carriages as they passed, and even distinguish by the sound of the wheels what kind of vehicle it was.

"There was a carrier that plied, between these two towns, whom I will call Healy, and as everything we used we had from B., he was generally at our house three or four times a week; in short, he did our marketings, in a great degree; my mother giving him an order, as he passed, for what he was to bring back; and many a time Healy has smuggled a novel from the circulating library for my sisters, or done little commissions for me that I could not so well manage for myself. All this made him a popular character with us, for he was very obliging; but for all that, he did not bear the best of characters.

"It was his interest to be well with us, and the gentry in general, who were his customers; and he understood that too well to incur our ill-will; but by his equals and inferiors he was looked upon with a less favourable eye. They had nothing very positive to allege against him;

but they thought him a hard, griping, greedy man, who was honest in his dealings with us because the slightest suspicion would have ruined his trade, but who would take an advantage when he thought no possible damage to himself could accrue from it. He was about forty years of age; tall, with a long face, prominent nose, and dark complexion; his shoulders were round, but his frame was wiry, and he was reputed very strong.

"One evening, between thirty and forty years ago, towards the beginning of winter, we were expecting Healy—my mother was solicitous about some provisions she had ordered for an approaching dinner-party; and I was very anxious for the arrival of a cricket-bat that I wanted for use the day after the next. Of course, long before the time he usually arrived, I was looking out for him, and fancying him late; I said, 'I wondered Healy was not come!' Upon which my father looked at his watch and found that it wanted full half-an-hour of his time, which was nine o'clock; sometimes, indeed, later, but never earlier. It was then exactly half-past eight; and before my father had returned his watch into his pocket, one of my sisters exclaimed, 'Here he is!' and we heard the wheels coming up the avenue—we should have heard him before, but two of my sisters were practising a duet, which was to be produced at the approaching festivity, and drowned the sound.

"Thereupon, I and my mother left the room, and went towards the back door, where Healy had just alighted, and was bringing sundry packages into the kitchen.

"'Have you got my bat, Healy?' said I.

"'No, sir,' he replied; 'there wasn't one in the whole town the size you wanted; but I'll bring you one from S. as I pass tomorrow. I know they've got 'em there. I believe that's all. Ma'am?' he added, addressing my mother.

"She said she believed it was, and was going to pay him his week's account, which she had asked for, but he hurried out, saying, 'Another time, if you please. Ma'am; I'm rather late tonight;' and he was in his cart and away before I had time to give him some directions in regard to the bat.

"'What a hurry he's in!' I said; 'and it wants almost twenty minutes to nine now.'

"'I suppose he has a great many places to stop at,' said my mother; 'if he don't get all his parcels delivered before people are gone to bed, he gets into trouble sometimes. He's a very punctual fellow certainly.'

"We returned to the drawing-room and resumed our occupations; and about half-an-hour afterwards—happening to be all silent at the moment, we heard a pair of light wheels and a brisk trotting horse passing in the road.

"'That's farmer Gould's mare, I'm sure,' said I. 'What a famous trotter she is!'

"'Yes,' said my father; 'I wish he'd part with her. I made him an offer the other day. I should like her for my buggy.'

"'And what did he say? Won't he sell her?'

"'He said nothing—he only laughed, 'and shook his fat sides.'

"'Money is no object to him,' said my mother, 'he won't part with her unless he gets another he likes better.'

"We breakfasted at nine o'clock, and I was getting up, and about half dressed, when one of my sisters burst into my room, crying, 'La! Fred., such a shocking thing has happened! poor Farmer Gould was found dead in the road this morning; they think his horse ran away, for it's not to be found; and the chaise was upset and lying on its side. How lucky, papa did not get the mare!'

"'Who says so?' said I.

"'The postman;' she answered, 'he saw some labourers standing round something in the road; and when he came up to them, he found it was the chaise, and poor farmer Gould quite dead beside it.'

"When I got downstairs I found the whole house occupied with the subject of this sad accident, all lamenting the good man, who was a general favourite, and agreeing that, for so heavy a person, a two-wheeled carriage was very dangerous, as a fall was almost sure to be fatal.

"My father said when he had finished his letters and papers he would walk up to the farm and see if he could be of any use to poor Mrs. Gould; I, with the curiosity of fifteen, begged to go with him; and my mother improved the occasion by giving the governor a serious lecture about his love for high-trotting horses and buggies.

"I expected Healy with my bat about eleven o'clock, as he had nothing else to bring, I knew he wouldn't come up the avenue, but leave it at a cottage near our gate; and wishing to learn if he'd heard any particulars about the accident, I walked down to meet him when the hour approached. Presently, I saw him coming, sitting in front of his cart.

"'Well, Healy,' I said, 'isn't this a shocking thing about poor farmer Gould? You've heard he was found dead in the road this morning?'

"'Yes, Sir, the mare ran away, and pitched him out upon his head; I can't say as ever I liked her myself; but I've got your bat. Master Frederick; a nice un too; I wouldn't come away this morning till I'd got it.'

"I thanked him, and he drove on, as if he had no time to lose in gossip, while I was untying the string of my parcel.

"By the time my father and I reached Gould's farm, the doctor had arrived from B., and we heard he was examining the body in the parlour, where it had been laid by the labourers who found it. The chaise, too, was standing near the door, just as it had been wheeled up, and the mare, they told us, had been found in a neighbouring field, with the harness hanging about her, and unhurt, except on the forehead, where she appeared to have had a violent blow. The farm men, standing about, said, that she had no doubt taken her head, and ran foul of something, and so pitched out Mr. Gould, and overturned the chaise; which seemed likely enough.

"My father said, he should like to see Mr. Wills, the surgeon; so, we stood about outside till he came. When he did, he looked very grave, as, indeed, befitted the occasion; but in answer to my father's inquiries, he said, that he could give no decided opinion of the cause of death till he had investigated the case further; and then he proceeded to examine the chaise, and next the horse. He then walked with us down to the spot where the thing had happened, and narrowly surveyed the ground; but he was very uncommunicative, which, as we knew him well, rather surprised us. He hurried away, saying, that he must prepare for the inquest on the following day.

"My father went to the inquest; and I should have liked to go, too, but I was engaged to play a match at cricket with a few of my young neighbours. However, I was home first, for the inquest lasted a long time, and took a very unexpected turn.

"It appeared that Mr. Wills, who was by marriage a connexion of Gould's wife, had suspected on the first examination of the body that the farmer had not come fairly by his end. It so happened that Gould had dined with him the last day he was at B., and had mentioned to him that he had 'at last got that seventy pounds that he was afraid he should never see;' alluding to some money that had been long owing to him; and as he spoke, he drew from his pocket a bundle of notes, some of which appeared to be of the Bank of England, and some of country banks. As soon, therefore, as Wills had arrived at certain conclusions, he inquired of Mrs. Gould if she had found his money safe.

"In her grief and surprise, it had not occurred to her to search—

and indeed she was not aware of his having any sum of importance about him. They proceeded immediately to examine his pockets, but no notes were there; a few shillings, a silver watch, and some unconsidered trifles, were all that was found about him. Mr. Wills made inquiries at the banker's and others, at B., and by the time the inquest sat he was prepared to say, that there was every reason to think that Mr. Gould had had this money in his waistcoat pocket, where he had seen him deposit it, at the time he left to return home.

"This presented quite a new view of the case to the coroner, who had come there without the slightest suspicion of anything beyond an accident. The labourers were examined as to the attitude in which they had discovered the body, which, they all agreed, was lying on its face; and indeed there were some stains from the dirt of the road, which testified to this being the case; yet, according to Mr. Wills, death had been occasioned by a terrible blow on the back of the head which had fractured the skull; and which, in his opinion, was inflicted by a heavy bludgeon. The man's hair was very thick behind; but on dividing it a wound was visible, from which a small quantity of blood had oozed and dried up.

"After a long investigation, the inquest was adjourned for a few days in order that further evidence might be collected. We were all much excited about this affair; it formed the staple of conversation at our dinner party, and various were the conjectures formed as to who was the criminal, if criminal there were; for some thought it possible that Gould had fallen on his back in the first instance, and then got upon his legs, and fallen a second time on his face; but Mr. Wills was confident the death wound was not the result of a fall; and besides, where was the money? Then all agreed, that if he had been robbed, it was by no ordinary thief; it must have been by someone who knew the sum he had in his pocket, and who did not care for the loose silver and the watch.

"'No doubt,' said my father, 'they will find out if anybody was present when the money was paid to him, or he may have told somebody of it, as he told Wills.'

"We had so many things provided for the party, that for two or three days we wanted nothing of Healy and did not see him; but the servants having mentioned that they wanted soap for the next week's washing, my mother sent a note to the cottage, where he always stopped to enquire for orders, desiring him to bring some on his return, and also a barrel of beer for the use of the kitchen .

"When I heard the cart coming up the avenue, I went to the back door, to have a little gossip.

"'Well Healy,' said I, as he rolled in the barrel of beer; 'have you heard any news?'

"'No sir.' said he.

"'Nothing about farmer Gould?' I asked.

"'No sir, nothing. Shall I put the beer in the cellar?' he enquired.

"This question being answered, I said, 'Did you meet anybody on the road that night?'

"'Lord, sir, I meet loads of people as I never take any notice of. I've enough to do to mind my own business.'

"'You couldn't have been far off when he was attacked—for you know Mr. Wills says he's been killed by a blow on the back of the head, don't you?'

"'Well, sir, I've heard so; but how should he know? He wasn't there, I suppose. Anything else wanted, sir?'

"'I believe not, Healy,' I said; and he got into his cart and drove away while I went back to the drawing-room.

"'What does Healy say?' asked my father. 'Has he heard anything new about this affair?'

"'No, he says he hasn't, but he said very little and seemed rather sulky, I thought.'

"'By the bye, he couldn't have been far off when the thing happened; for he had only been gone half-an-hour when we recognised the step of poor Gould's mare I recollect, and she'd soon overtake him.'

"'So, I told him; and I asked him if he had met anybody on the road that night, but he said he'd plenty to do to mind his own business.'

"My father who was reading the paper at the time, looked up at me over his spectacles; and then fell into a reverie that lasted some minutes, but he said nothing; my mother observed that she thought Healy ought to be summoned as a witness; and my father rejoined, that no doubt he'd be examined.

"On the following day the inquest was resumed; my father went early and had some private conversation with Mr. Wills and I waited outside amongst the assembled crowd, listening to their speculations and conjectures. Presently, the coroner arrived, and I went in with him and heard the whole of the evidence. That of Mr. Wills, and the labourers who found the body was the same as before. Then, as my father had conjectured, Healy was called; his face was familiar to everybody in the room, and there was not one I should think who was not struck with the singularly sulky, dogged expression his features had assumed. There was no manifest reason for it, for he was only summoned like other witnesses, and no breath of suspicion had been cast upon him; at least, as far as we had heard. But he evidently came in a spirit of resistance and wound up for self-defence.

"He declared that he had not overtaken Mr. Gould on the night in question and did not know he was on the road; nor did he hear anything of what had happened till the next morning. He believed he had met some tramps on the road that night—two men and a woman—but he had not particularly noticed them, and he did not recollect meeting anybody else. He had first heard of the accident at a shop where he had gone to buy a bat for Master C. When he said this, he looked up at me and our eyes met. I have often thought of that look since.

"The next witness was Mr. F., who had paid Gould the seventy pounds in notes; and then a Mr. H. B., a solicitor, came forward and volunteered the following evidence, which, he said, he should have given before, but that he had left home on the afternoon preceding this unfortunate business, and had only returned yesterday. He was acquainted with Gould; and had met him at the door of the bank at B——, as he himself was on his way to the coach that was starting for E——. Gould spoke to him and said he had just got that seventy pounds; and when he said so, he clapped his hand on his pocket, implying it was there. He said, 'I came to pay it in here, but I see they're shut, and it does not signify; I shall have to pay away a good deal of it next week;' this was all that passed, as I told him I must be off for I should lose the coach.

'Upon this, he was asked if anybody else had been present when Gould made this communication. He answered, that people had been passing to and fro, but he could not say whether they heard it. There was one person who he thought might, though he could not affirm that he did; and that was Healy, the carrier, who was standing at the door of the tanner's shop, which is next to the bank, and examining some cricket bats that he had in his hand. Gould had spoken loud as was his wont.

"I saw Mr. Wills and my father exchange looks when this evidence was given, and then for the first time the question occurred to me, could Healy be the murderer? I could hardly entertain the suspicion—it is so difficult to believe such a thing of a person one is having constant intercourse with. Healy was recalled and asked if he remembered seeing Mr. Gould and the lawyer together on that day. He declared he did not.

"The harness was afterwards produced; and it appeared that the traces had been cut, which was a strong confirmation of the worst suspicions.

"The inquest was once more adjourned; and Healy plied his trade as usual for the next two days, though everybody had a strange feeling towards him; and he retained his dogged, sulky look; on the third night we missed him. We had expected a parcel from B——, but he did not come; and the next day we heard he had been arrested on suspicion of being the murderer of Mr. Gould. A gentleman's servant, who had been out without leave to some festivity at B——, and had come home and got in at the pantry window without being discovered, at last came forward, and said, that as he was going to the rendezvous, he had seen a cart, which he believed to be Healy's, though it was very dark, drawn right across the road; the horse was out of the shafts and tied to a gate, for he nearly ran against him; he did not see any person with the cart, but the driver might be behind it.

"It was just where there are some large trees overhanging the road, which made it darker than in other parts; and a person driving would not see the obstruction till he was on it. He himself, thinking it was Healy, slipped quietly by, for he did not want to be recognised, as the carrier often came to his master's, and might have betrayed him. He met a one-horse carriage about a couple of miles further on; the horse was trotting pretty fast. He thought it was Mr. Gould, but he could not positively say, as the night was so dark.

"The spot described was precisely where Mr. Gould's body was found; and the man added, that it struck him when he met the gig, that if the cart had not moved out of the way, there would be an accident, and he should have warned the driver to look out, if he had not been upon a lark himself.

"You may imagine the sensation created by this allegation in the neighbourhood, where the carrier was so well known. Till the spring assizes at E——, where he was to be tried, it furnished the staple of conversation, and every fresh bit of evidence, for or against him, was eagerly repeated and canvassed. My father was summoned as a witness to the hour at which Healy had been at our house that night, and also to the recognising the foot of Mr. Gould's mare. The evidence was entirely circumstantial, as nobody had witnessed the murder, though murder there certainly had been; nor was there anybody else to whom suspicion could attach. As for the tramps Healy said he had met, no trace of them could be found, nor did anyone appear to have seen such a party.

"When all the evidence had been heard, my father said he felt considerable doubt what the verdict would be, and he really believed the jury were greatly perplexed; but when Healy stood up, and in the most solemn manner said, 'I am innocent, my Lord! I call God to witness, I am innocent! May this right arm wither if I murdered the man!' So great an impression was made on the court, that, added to the prisoner's previous good character, everybody saw he would be acquitted.

"He was; Healy went forth a free man, and we were all too glad to believe in his innocence, to dispute the justice of the verdict; but lo! the hand of the Lord was on him. He had called upon God to bear witness to his words; and he did. In three days from that time, Richard Healy's stalwart right arm was withered! The muscles shrunk; the skin dried up; and it looked like the limb of a mummy!"

"Though a voice from Heaven testified against him, he could not be arraigned again for the same crime, and he remained at liberty. He attempted for a short time to carry on his business, but people ceased to employ him; and his feeble arm could no longer lift the boxes and hampers with which his cart was wont to be loaded. He went about, avoided by everyone but his own immediate connexions. I often met him, but he never looked me in the face; indeed, he rarely, if ever, raised his eyes; his round shoulders grew rounder, till he came to stoop like an old man. He seemed to move under a heavy burthen that weighed him to the earth.

"After an interval, however, he bought some property; and in his old age—for he survived his trial several years—he was in prosperous circumstances. But everybody said, 'Where did he get the money?'

"We were all deeply interested in this singular story; and in reference to the withered arm, Colonel C. said, that he should certainly not have believed it had he not seen it himself.

"I think, said I, that it was not so difficult to account for the phenomenon as at first appears. Had he been innocent, the solemn adjuration he uttered in court would have been justifiable in the eyes of God and man and would have occasioned him no concern afterwards; but he was guilty; he had called upon God to bear witness to a lie, and, doubtless, the consciousness of this sacrilegious appeal filled him with horror and alarm. He would tremble lest his prayer should be heard and the curse fall upon him. These terrors would direct all his thoughts to his arm and produce the very thing he feared; for Sir Henry Holland asserts that the mind is capable of acting upon the body to such a degree, as sometimes to create disease in a particular part on which the attention is too intently fixed."

Fourth Evening

"The circumstance I am going to mention," said Sir Charles L., "will appear very insignificant after these interesting narratives, but as it happened very lately, you'll perhaps think it worth hearing.

"I was living a few months ago in an hotel, the owner of which died while I was there. He had an apoplectic seizure and expired shortly afterwards. A week before this happened, at a time he was supposed to be in perfect health, an acquaintance of the family called, and without giving any reason, requested his daughter not to attend a ball she was engaged to go to. The young lady did not take her advice; but the visitor confided to another person that she had a particular reason for her request, which reason was as follows:—

"The night before she called, she and her husband had retired to bed in a somewhat anxious state of mind respecting a near relative of theirs, who was very ill, and whom they had been visiting. The husband, however, soon fell asleep, but the wife lay thinking of the sick person, and the consequences that would ensue if she died, when her reflections were interrupted by seeing a bright spot of light suddenly appear upon the wall—that is, upon the wainscot of her room. She looked about to see whence it proceeded; there was no light burning, nor could any be reflected from the window; as she looked it increased in size, till, at last, it was as large as the frame of a picture; then there began to appear in the frame a form, gradually developed, till there was a perfect head and face, hair and all, distinctly visible.

"Whilst this development was proceeding, she lay, as it were, transfixed; she wanted to wake her husband, but she could neither speak nor move; at length she seemed to burst the bonds, and cried to him to look, but as she spoke, the vision faded, and by the time he was sufficiently aroused there was nothing to be seen.

"Both he and she interpreted this occurrence into a bad omen for their sick relative, and augured very ill of her case; but the next morning, as she was standing in her shop, she saw the hotel keeper pass to market, and he nodded to her, whereupon she turned to her husband, and exclaimed—'That's the face I saw last night! Sure, nothing can be going to happen to him!'

"I heard these circumstances from my servant; and the unexpected seizure and death occurred within a few days.'

"When I was at Weimar, about two years ago," said Mademoiselle G., "an accident occurred that occupied the attention of the whole place, and which seems to belong to the same class of phenomena as the story just related. The palace, called the *Château*, in Weimar, is at one end of the park, and at the other end is another *château*, called the Belvedere; both are ducal residences, and an avenue runs from the one palace to the other. Opposite this avenue is the Russian chapel or Greek church—the present dowager duchess being a sister of the Emperor Nicholas—and in front of this chapel a sentinel is always posted.

"'The Grand Duke, Charles Frederick, father of the present sovereign, was, at the period I allude to, residing at the Belvedere not well in health, but by no means alarmingly ill, for had that been the case he would have been brought into Weimar, where etiquette requires that the sovereign should make his first and last appearance in this world—there he must be born, and there die, if possible.

"One night the sentinel, who was standing at the entrance of the Russian chapel, was surprised to see, in the far distance, a long procession winding its way down the avenue from the Belvedere. As there was no stir in the town, for the night was far advanced, and as he had not heard of any solemnity in preparation, the man stared at it in mute wonder, but his amazement was redoubled when it approached near enough for him to distinguish the individual objects to perceive that it was a State funeral, accompanied by the royal mourners, and all the pomp usual at these ceremonies; the velvet pall bore the initials and arms of the duke, and following the bier was his favourite and well known horse, led by one of his attendants. Slowly and mournfully the procession moved on till it reached the chapel; the doors opened to admit the *cortège*; it passed in; and as the doors closed on this mysterious vision the soldier fell to the ground, where he was found in a state of insensibility when the guard was relieved.

"Of course, nobody believed his story; he was placed under arrest, severely punished, and had a nervous fever that brought him to the brink of the grave.

"I was there when this happened," said Mademoiselle G., "and it was the talk of the town; almost everybody laughed at him; but five days afterwards the duke fell suddenly ill, and was found to be in so dangerous a state, that the physicians forbade his being removed into the town. He finally died at the Belvedere, and was buried in the Russian chapel, exactly in the manner portrayed by the shadowy forms seen by the sentinel, and there buried."

We all agreed that these rehearsals, if we may so call them, are amongst the most perplexing of these very perplexing phenomena; a very curious case of this description will be found in one of the letters inserted in the appendix.

"My sister-in-law, Lady S." said Lady R., "Told me, the other day, that during her late residence in St. Petersburg, she was intimately acquainted with a Prussian lady of high rank, to whom the following strange events occurred, an account of which she herself gave to my sister. This Prussian lady was sitting one morning in her *boudoir*, when she heard a rustling sound in the ante-room, which was divided by a *portière* from the *boudoir*. The sound continuing, she rose and drew aside the curtain to ascertain the cause, when, to her surprise, she saw a very pale man, in a *chasseur's* uniform, standing in the middle of the room. She was about to speak to him, and inquire what he was doing there, when he retreated towards the window and vanished.

"Greatly alarmed, she sought her husband, and related what had occurred; but he laughed at her and desired her not to expose herself to ridicule by talking of it. Some days afterwards, whilst in the *boudoir*, she heard the same rustling noise near her, and on looking up, she saw the figure of the *chasseur* suspended in the air between the ceiling and the floor, with his legs dangling in the air. A scream brought her husband, who was in the adjoining room, and he saw the figure as well as herself. Nevertheless, the fear of ridicule kept them silent; but some time afterwards, when they had a party, one of the company exclaimed, 'Good Heavens! This, I remember, is the very room that unfortunate *chasseur's* hung himself in!' And then they learned that the house had been previously occupied by the Danish minister, and that a *chasseur* in his service had, from some cause or other, committed suicide."

"I don't know whether dreams are admissible," said Miss M.; "but the sort of occurrences just related appear to me to be little removed from waking dreams. I know two cases of extraordinary dreaming, the authenticity of which I can answer for, if you would like to hear them."

We accepted gladly, and the lady began as follows:—

"My father was intimate with Mr. S.—whose name, perhaps, is known to you as the particular friend of Mr. Spencer Percival. This gentleman, Mr. S., when he was a young man, had one night a remarkable dream, that he could not in any way account for—the circumstances having no relation to any previous event, train of thought, or conversation whatever.

"He found himself, in his dream, on horseback, in a very extensive forest; he was alone, evening was drawing on, and he sought some place where he could pass the night. After riding a little farther, he espied an inn; he rode up to it and alighted, asking if they could give him lodging for the night, and stabling for his horse. They said 'yes,' and conducted him to an upper chamber. He ordered some refreshments, when it occurred to him that he should like to see how his horse was faring; and he descended, in order to find his way to the stables; in doing so, he got a glimpse of some very ill-looking men in a side chamber, who seemed in close conference; moreover, he thought he saw weapons lying on the table, and there were other circumstances which I do not precisely remember, the effect of which was to create alarm, and lead him to suspect he had fallen into a *repaire de voleurs*.

"He saw his horse rubbed down and fed, and then re-ascended to take his refreshment; betraying no suspicion of evil, but secretly resolved on flight. After his supper, he went down again, stood at the door, and pretended to stroll about. When he saw an opportunity, he went round to the stable, saddled his horse, and cautiously rode away. But he had not gone far, when he heard the tramp of horses' feet behind him, and from the pace they came, he felt sure he was pursued. He urged his horse forward, but the animal was not fresh—he had done his day's work already, and the pursuers were gaining on him, when he saw he was approaching a spot where two roads met. Which of the two should he follow? He had nothing to guide him in his choice, and his life probably depended on his decision! Suddenly, a voice whispered in his ear, 'Take the right!' He did so, and shortly reached a house where he obtained shelter and protection.

"When he awoke, the circumstances of his dream were so vividly impressed on his mind, that he could hardly believe the thing had not actually happened. He related it to his friends; and, for some days, thought a good deal of it; but he was just entering into active life, and the impression soon faded before the varied interests that absorbed him; and the strange dream was entirely forgotten.

"Many years afterwards, when he had reached middle age, he was travelling in Germany, and in the course of an excursion he was making to see the country, he had occasion to cross a part of the Schwarzwald—the Black Forest. He was on horseback and alone; he reached an inn, the aspect of which he fancied was familiar to him. Here he thought he might conveniently pass the night; so, he alighted, ordered his supper, and then went to see his horse fed. On further acquaintance with the place, he did not like the look of it, and he saw suspicious-looking men hanging about. He resolved to seek another resting-place; and leaving some money on the table to pay for what he had had, he went downstairs, and after lounging about a little, strolled to the stable, saddled his horse, and rode off as quietly as he could. But he was missed and pursued, he heard the tramp of the horses as they gained upon him. At this critical moment, he saw he was approaching a place where the roads divided; his life depended on which of the two he should take; suddenly, and strange to say, though he had misty recollections of the scene, now for the first time, the dream of his youth clearly and vividly recurred to him. He remembered the voice that whispered, 'Take the right!' He obeyed the hint, and his pursuers soon gave up the chase. He found a *château* about half-a-mile from the turning; the owner of which hospitably received him. His host said there had been for some time unpleasant suspicions with regard to the inn in question; and that, if he had taken the left-hand road, he would have been quite at their mercy."

This very curious dream reminded us of that of Dr. W., which I have related in the *Night Side of Nature*, (and which Leonaur has repeated in full below); who in the same manner was saved from the attack of an infuriated bull, in his dream, having been shown where to fly for safety; but the case is less remarkable than that of Mr. S., as the dream occurred only the night before the danger presented itself.

★★★★★★

A few years ago. Dr. W——, now residing at Glasgow, dreamed that he received a summons to attend a patient at a place some miles from where he was living; that he started on horseback; and that, as he was crossing a moor, he saw a bull making furiously at him, whose horns he only escaped by taking refuge on a spot inaccessible to the animal, where he waited a long time, till some people, observing his situation, came to his assistance and released him. While at breakfast on the following morning, the summons came; and, smiling at the odd coincidence he started on horseback. He was quite ignorant of the road he had to go; but by-and-by he arrived at the moor, which he recognised, and presently the bull appeared, coming full tilt toward him. But his dream had shown him the place of refuge, for which he instantly made; and there he spent three or four hours, besieged by the animal, till the country people set him free. Dr. W—— declares that, but for the dream, he should not have known in what direction to run for safety.

******

"The other dream I alluded to," said Miss M., "is less curious on that account. Some friends of mine, who reside in the country, had an old nurse who had lived in the family many years, and for whom they had a great regard. When her services ceased to be required, she was settled in a cottage on the estate, where she lived very comfortably, with her only daughter. The daughter, however, married a man who kept a turnpike some miles distant; and one morning, just as the family were leaving home on some expedition, the old woman arrived in considerable agitation, saying that she had had a frightful dream about her daughter, and that she was going off immediately to the place where she lived. The ladies endeavoured to dissuade her from walking all that way, merely on account of a dream. But she said she could not rest and must go. They even promised that if she would wait till the following day they would drive her there in the carriage, in which there was now no room; if there had been they would have taken her, as their road lay not far from the spot.

"With this offer they left her and went their way; but her anxiety would not permit her to wait; and shortly afterwards she set off and walked all the distance to the turnpike. The moment she arrived she saw reason to rejoice in her determination; she found her daughter alone, her husband having been called away on business; and, said the young woman, I am dreadfully alarmed, for there is a quantity of money in the house. The farmers are accustomed to bring the money for their rent here twice a year, as it saves them several miles, and the agent always comes to fetch it on the same day. But a letter to my husband has just arrived from the agent to say, he can't come till tomorrow. Knowing his hand, I opened it; and I am terrified, for the custom of leaving the money here is no secret; and if it should get wind that it has not been fetched away, heaven knows what may happen.

"The old woman then told her daughter that she had dreamed on

43

the preceding night that some thieves had broken into the turnpike house and robbed and murdered the inhabitants.

"But what were these two helpless women to do, mutually confirmed in their apprehensions as they naturally were? It was already late in the day; there was no help near at hand, and besides they did not dare to separate in search of any. They watched anxiously for a traveller, resolved to confide in the first respectable one that passed, and beg him to send assistance. But none came that they thought it safe to trust. Night approached; and it being a little frequented road, except on market days, every moment their hope of help declined. So, they did the best they could in this extremity; they shut and barricaded the lower part of the house, stopping up the door and windows with every piece of furniture they had, and locked themselves up, with the money, in an upper chamber, put out the light, and with a chink of the window open, they set themselves down to listen for the marauders whom they confidently expected to arrive.

"Nor were they disappointed; about eleven o'clock their anxious ears distinguished the sound of approaching footsteps. Presently, they heard voices and the door was attempted; the men said they had lost their way, and on receiving no answer they attempted to force an entrance. Then, the poor women knowing their poor defences would soon yield to violence, began to scream lustily from the window above; and luckily not in vain.

"It happened, that the family, who had gone on some expedition of pleasure in the morning, was just then returning; their road lay within a quarter of a mile of the turnpike; and in the silence of the night, the women's shrill voice reached their ears. They immediately desired the coachman to turn his horses' heads in the direction the cries came from, and before the thieves had effected an entrance into the little fortification, they were scared by the sound of approaching wheels and took to flight."

"A dream of a very singular nature occurred to a young friend of mine," said Mr. S. "She was about fifteen at the time, and a schoolfellow who was going to be married had promised her that she should be one of the bridesmaids. The intended wedding was near at hand; insomuch that the dresses and everything was prepared—in short, the fixing of the day was only delayed by some small matter of business that was not completed. My young friend, to whom the whole thing was an exciting novelty, while impatiently waiting for the affair to come off, dreamt, one night, that a person in a very unusual costume, presented himself at her bedside and informed her that he was Brutus; and that he would reveal to her anything that she particularly desired to know; whereupon she begged him to tell when Miss L. would be married. Brutus answered '*Paulo post Graecas Kalendas.*' When she awoke in the morning, she perfectly remembered the words; but not having the most distant idea of their meaning she ran to her brother to enquire if he could explain them. He told her that they were equivalent to *never*. The prophecy was fulfilled; obstacles entirely unforeseen arose, and the couple were never united."

"Some years ago," said Dr. Forster, "two young friends of mine were staying at Naples, when one of them told the other that he had on the preceding night, seen in his sleep, the face of a beautiful woman; but the features were disfigured by a horrible expression—and that it was, somehow, impressed on his mind that he was in danger, and that he must be on his guard against her. The conviction was so strong as to create considerable uneasiness, and he never went out without scrutinising every female face he saw; but some weeks passed without any fulfilment of his dream or vision.

"And gradually the impression faded. However, he was one day on the Chiaja, surrounded by several people, who like himself, were observing a gang of convicts going to the Castle of St. Elmo; when something occasioned him suddenly to turn his head, and there, close behind him, he recognised the beautiful face of his dream. By an instinctive impulse, he sprang aside, and at the same moment felt himself wounded in the back. The woman was seized and did not attempt to deny the act but alleged that she had mistaken the young Englishman for another person who had done her an irreparable injury, expressing great regret at also at having failed in the revenge she sought. He told me that the dream saved his life; for that, had he not sprung aside, the wound would in all probability have been mortal."

Fifth Evening

"I have but one experience to relate," said Miss D., the next speaker. "When I was a child, I and my elder sister slept in two beds, placed close beside each other. We were in the country, and one night my father, going to the door, perceived an unusual light in the sky, and learnt on inquiry that there was a great fire a mile or two off. He said he'd go to see it, and the night being fine, my mother accompanied him, having first seen us safe in bed. She locked the chamber door, and took the key, thinking that everybody would be out looking at the fire, and we might take the opportunity of playing tricks, for we were quite young at the time—not more than six or seven years old.

"After they were gone, we lay chattering, as children do, about our own little concerns, when our voices were suddenly arrested by terror. At the foot of my bed I perceived a figure, apparently kneeling, for I saw only the head—but that I saw distinctly—it looked dark and sad, and the eyes were intently fixed on me. I crept into my sister's bed, and neither of us dared to look up again till my mother returned and came to see if we were asleep. We had not closed our eyes, and we told her what we had seen, agreeing perfectly in our account of it. The room was searched, but nothing unusual found. The incident made a lasting impression on my sister and myself, and we both remember the face as if we had seen it but yesterday."

One of the ladies present mentioned a very similar circumstance occurring to herself, but as she was alone at the time, she had always endeavoured to believe it an illusion.

"The first part of the story I am going to relate to you," said Dr. S., "was told me by an eminent man in my own profession, who had every opportunity of testing the truth of it; the latter part I give you on my own word.

"Some years ago, there was a house in the suburbs of Dublin that had remained a long time unoccupied, in consequence, it was said, of its evil reputation—the report was, that it was haunted. People who had taken it got rid of it as soon as they could, and those who lived in the neighbourhood affirmed that they saw lights moving about the interior, and, sometimes, a lady in white standing at the window with a child in her arms, when they knew there was no living creature, except rats and mice, within the walls. The wise and learned laughed at these rumours; but still the house remained empty and was getting into a very dilapidated state.

"The former owner of the house was dead. He was a miser or a misanthrope, or both; at all events, for several years he had lived in it utterly alone, and scarcely ever seen by anybody. It was rumoured that for a short time a young female had been occasionally observed by the neighbours, but she disappeared as suddenly as she had appeared, and nobody knew whence she came, nor wither she was gone. His life was a mystery, and whether merely on this account, or whether there were better grounds for it, there had certainly existed a prejudice against him. However, as I said, he had been dead some years, and the relative to whom the property had fallen on his decease was naturally very anxious to let the house, and offered it to any occupant at an extremely low rent.

"At length, a gentleman who wanted to establish a manufactory, seeing that it would answer his purpose—for the premises were extensive, and there was some garden ground behind—took it, and erected buildings on this waste ground for his workmen to inhabit. Between the new part and the old there was a long vestibule, or covered passage, by which they might pass from one to the other without exposing themselves to the weather. A large door, which was open by day and closed at night, divided this passage in two, and on one side there was a small room or office, where a clerk sat and kept the books and memoranda, of various sorts, incident to a considerable business.

"However, the thing was scarcely set going and established before it reached the ears of the master that the workmen objected to pass the night on the premises; the reason alleged being that they were disturbed and alarmed by various sounds, especially footsteps, and the banging of the heavy door in the vestibule which divided the sleeping places from the workrooms. At first, the objection being thought absurd, was not attended to; next, it was supposed to be a trick of some of the workmen to frighten the others; but when it became serious, and they began to act upon it, and steady, respectable men declared they heard these things, the master, still persuaded it was some practical jokers amongst them mystifying the more simple, took measures, first, to ascertain if such sounds as they described were audible; and next, to discover who made them. For this purpose, he sat up himself, and his clerks sat up, and exactly as had been described, at one o'clock this clatter and banging of doors commenced—that is, there was the sound; for the doors remained immovable, and though they heard footsteps they could see nobody.

"'Still,' said the manufacturer, who was not willing to be made the victim of this mischievous conspiracy, 'we must discover who it is; and we shall, when they are more off their guard,' and for this purpose it was arranged that a relation of his own, a young man in whose discretion and courage he had great confidence should sleep in the office.

"Accordingly, a bed was prepared there; and he arranged himself for that night or as many future nights as it might be necessary; determined not to relinquish the investigation till he had unravelled the mystery.

"At dawn of day, the next morning, there was a violent knocking at the outer door; an early passenger had found this young man in the street, with nothing on but his night dress, and in a state of delirium. He was taken home and Dr. W, was sent for. The result was a brain fever; but when he recovered, he said that he had gone to bed and to sleep, that he was wakened by a loud noise, and that just as he was about to rise to ascertain the cause, his door opened, and the apparition of a female dressed in white entered and approached his bedside. He remembered no more, but being seized with horror, supposed he had got out of the window into the street, where he was found.

"This was, certainly, very extraordinary and very serious; still the persuasion that it was some mystification prevailed; and Dr. W.'s offer to pass a night in the office himself, was gladly accepted. He had informed me of the young man's illness and the cause of it; and when I heard of his intention, I requested leave to bear him company.

"The noise had not been interrupted by the catastrophe that had occurred, and nobody had slept in the office during the young man's confinement. The bed had been removed, but we declined having it replaced, for we wished our intention to remain a secret; besides, we preferred watching through the night. It was not till the workmen had all retired that we took up our position, accompanied by a sharp little terrier of mine, and each armed with a pistol. We took care to go over the house, to make sure that nobody was concealed in it; and we examined every door and window to ascertain that it was secure. We had provided ourselves with refreshments also, to sustain our courage; and we entered upon our vigil with great hopes of detecting the imposition.

"Dr. W. is a most enlightened and agreeable companion, and we soon fell into a lively discussion that carried us away so entirely, that, I believe, we had both ceased to think of the object of our watch, when we were recalled to it by the clock in the vestibule striking one; and the loud bang that immediately followed, accompanied by the barking of our little dog, who had been aroused from a tranquil sleep by the uproar. W. and I seized our pistols, and rushed into the passage, followed by the terrier. We saw nothing to account for the noise; but we distinctly heard receding footsteps, which we hastened to pursue, at the same time urging on the dog; but instead of running forward, he slunk behind, with his tail between his legs, and kept at our heels the whole way.

"On we went, distinctly hearing the footsteps preceding us along the vestibule, down some steps, and, finally, down some stairs that led to an unused cellar—in one corner of which lay a heap of rubbish. Here the sound ceased. We removed the rubbish, and under it lay some bones, which we recognised at once as parts of a human skeleton. On further examination, we ascertained that they were the remains of a female and a new-born infant.

"They were buried, and the men were no more disturbed with these mysterious noises. Who the woman was, was never ascertained; nor was any further light thrown upon these strange circumstances."

Some remarks on the terror displayed by animals, on these occasions, elicited a curious story from Mrs. L. "They not only seem to see sometimes," she said, "what we do not; but occasionally to be gifted with a singular foreknowledge.

"Many years ago," she continued, "I and my husband went to pay a visit in the north. I am very fond of animals, and my attention was soon attracted by a dog that was not particularly handsome but seemed gifted with extraordinary intelligence.

"'I see,' said my hostess, 'you are struck with that dog. Well, he is the most mysterious creature; he not only opens and shuts the door, and rings the bell, and does all sorts of wonderful things, but I am sure he understands every word we say, and that he knows as well what I am saying now as you do. Moreover, we got him in a very unaccountable manner.

"'One night, not long ago, we had been out to dinner; and on returning at a pretty late hour, we found the gentleman stretched out comfortably on the dining-room rug. "Where in the world did this dog come from?" I said to the servants. They couldn't tell; they declared the doors had been long shut, and that they had never set eyes on him till that minute.'

"'Well,' I said, 'don't turn him out; he'll no doubt be claimed by someone in the neighbourhood—for he had quite the manners and air of a dog accustomed to good society; and I liked his large, expressive eyes. He made himself quite at home; and now we have discovered what a strangely intelligent creature he is, I hope no one will claim him, for I should be very sorry to part with him. But,' added she, 'poor Mrs. X. can't endure him.' Mrs. X., I must mention, was a widow lady, also on a visit there, with an only son.

"'Why?' said I.

"'It is rather singular, certainly,' said she; but whenever young X. is in the room, the dog never takes his eyes off his face—you see he has peculiar eyes—they're full of meaning; and out of doors he does the same.'

"'Perhaps the dog has taken a fancy to him?' I suggested.

"'It does not seem to be that; no, I think he likes me and Mrs. C. and my children a great deal better. I can't tell what it is; but if you watch, you'll see it.'

"I did, and it was really remarkable, and evidently annoyed Mrs. X. very much. The young man affected to laugh at it, but I don't think he liked it altogether.

"Suddenly, one evening, Mrs. X.—whose visit was to have extended to some weeks longer, announced that she should take her departure in a few days. I suspected this move was occasioned by her desire to get away from the dog, and so did my hostess—and we both thought it absurd.

"Mr. L. being obliged to return to London, we took our leave the morning after this announcement was made; but we had scarcely arrived there, when a letter from my friend followed, informing me that young Mr, X. had been unfortunately drowned in the fishpond, and that the dog had never been seen since the accident, though they had made inquiries and sought for him in every direction. Whence he came, or whither he went, they were never able to discover.

"But," said Mrs. L., "as this is not a ghost story, I will tell you another anecdote that belongs more legitimately to the subjects you are treating of. Once, when we were travelling in the North, Mr. L. fell ill of a fever at Paisley. This detained us there, and the minister called on us. When Mr, L. recovered, we returned his visit; and, in the course of conversation, some of the old customs of the Scotch fell under discussion; amongst others the *cutty stool*, which we had heard still subsisted.

"'Why don't you abolish it?' said Mr. L. 'It would be much better to amend people by other influences than exposure.'

"'Well, sir,' said the good man, 'that was my opinion also; and I had determined to do it. Before taking the step, however, I thought it advisable to publish my reasons; and I was one day sitting at the table writing on the subject, when I looked up, and beheld my father, who was minister here before me, and died in this manse, sitting on the opposite side of the table.'

"'Don't do any such thing, David,' said he; 'morality is loose enough; don't make it looser.'"

Sixth Evening

"The most interesting circumstance of the ghostly kind that I know, as really authentic," said Madame S., "is what happened to the late Lord C, when he was a young man—it is an old story, and you must have beard of the *Radiant Boy*; but as I had it from a member of the family, perhaps you will accept it as my contribution.

"Captain S., who was afterwards Lord C, when he was a young man, happened to be quartered in Ireland. He was fond of sport; and one day the pursuit of game carried him so far that he lost his way. The weather, too, had become very rough, and in this strait he presented himself at the door of a gentleman's house, and sending in his card, requested shelter for the night. The hospitality of the Irish country gentry is proverbial; the master of the house received him warmly, said he feared he could not make him so comfortable as he could have wished, his house being full of visitors already—added to which, some strangers, driven by the inclemency of the night, had sought shelter before him, but that such accommodation as he could give he was heartily welcome to; whereupon he called his butler, and committing his guest to his good offices, told him he must put him up somewhere, and do the best he could for him. There was no lady, the gentleman being a widower.

"Captain S. found the house crammed, and a very jolly party it was. His host invited him to stay and promised him good shooting if he would prolong his visit a few days; and, in fine, he thought himself extremely fortunate to have fallen into such pleasant quarters.

"At length, after an agreeable evening, they all retired to bed, and the butler conducted him to a large room, almost divested of furniture, but with a blazing peat fire in the grate, and a shake down on the floor, composed of cloaks and other heterogenous materials.

"Nevertheless, to the tired limbs of Captain S., who had had a hard day's shooting, it looked very inviting; but before he lay down, he thought it advisable to take off some of the fire, which was blazing up the chimney, in what he thought, an alarming manner. Having done this, he stretched himself upon the couch, and soon fell asleep.

"He believed he had slept about a couple of hours when he awoke suddenly and was startled by such a vivid light in the room, that he thought it was on fire, but on turning to look at the grate he saw the fire was out, though it was from the chimney the light proceeded. He sat up in bed, trying to discover what it was, when he perceived, gradually disclosing itself, the form of a beautiful naked boy, surrounded by a dazzling radiance. The boy looked at him earnestly, and then the vision faded, and all was dark. Captain S., so far from supposing what he had seen to be of a spiritual nature, had no doubt that the host, or the visitors, had been amusing themselves at his expense, and trying to frighten him.

"Accordingly, he felt indignant at the liberty; and on the following morning, when he appeared at breakfast, he took care to evince his displeasure by the reserve of his demeanour, and by announcing his intention to depart immediately. The host expostulated, reminding him of his promise to stay and shoot. Captain S. coldly excused himself and, at length, the gentleman seeing something was wrong, took him aside, and pressed for an explanation; whereupon Captain S., without entering into particulars, said that he had been made the victim of a sort of practical joking that he thought quite unwarrantable with a stranger.

"The gentleman considered this not impossible amongst a parcel of thoughtless young men and appealed to them to make an apology; but one and all, on honour, denied the impeachment. Suddenly, a thought seemed to strike him; he clapped his hand to his forehead, uttered an exclamation, and rang the bell.

"'Hamilton,' said he to the butler, 'where did Captain S. sleep last night?'

"'Well, Sir,' replied the man, in an apologetic tone, 'you know every place was full—the gentlemen were lying on the floor, three or four in a room—so I gave him the *Boy's Room*; but I lit a blazing fire to keep him from coming out.'

"'You were very wrong,' said the host, 'you know I have positively forbidden you to put anyone there and have taken the furniture out of the room to ensure its not being occupied.' Then retiring with Captain S., he informed him very gravely of the nature of the phenomenon he had seen; and, at length, being pressed for further information, he confessed that there existed a tradition in his family, that whoever the *Radiant Boy* appeared to will rise to the summit of power; and when he had reached the climax, will die a violent death, and I must say, he added, that the records that have been kept of his appearance go to confirm this persuasion.

"I need not remind you," said Madam S., "what a remarkable confirmation was afforded by the life and death of Lord C."

"I had never heard these particulars before; but I had heard the story of Lord C.'s *Radiant Boy* alluded to, *ápropos* of the case of the Rev. Mr. A., who saw a very similar apparition some years ago at C. Castle. I have related this case in the *Night Side of Nature*. (Mr. A's story given by Leonaur below), I received the particulars from a relation of Mr. A.'s, who was himself surviving at the time I published it.'

★★★★★★

"The best way of giving you these particulars, will be by subjoining an extract from my journal, entered at the time the event occurred.

"*Sept. 8,* 1803.—Among other guests invited to C—— castle, came the Rev. Henry A——, of Redburgh, and rector of Greystoke, with Mrs. A——, his wife, who was a Miss S——,

of Ulverstone. According to previous arrangements, they were to have remained with us for some days; but their visit was cut short in a very unexpected manner. On the morning after their arrival, we were all assembled at breakfast, when a chaise and four dashed up to the door in such haste that it knocked down part of the fence of my flower-garden. Our curiosity was, of course, awakened to know who could be arriving at so early an hour; when, happening to turn my eyes toward Mr. A——, I observed that he appeared extremely agitated. 'It is our carriage!' said he; 'I am very sorry, but we must absolutely leave you this morning.'

"We naturally felt and expressed considerable surprise, as well as regret at this unexpected departure; representing that we had invited Colonel and Mrs. S——, some friends whom Mr. A—— particularly desired to meet, to dine with us on that day. Our expostulations, however, were vain; the breakfast was no sooner over than they departed, leaving us in consternation to conjecture what could possibly have occasioned so sudden an alteration in their arrangements. I really felt quite uneasy lest anything should have given them offence; and we reviewed all the occurrences of the preceding. evening in order to discover, if offence there was, whence it had arisen. But our pains were vain; and after talking a great deal about it. for some days, other circumstances banished it from our minds.

"It was not till we some time afterward visited the part of the country in which Mr. A—— resides, that we learned the real cause of his sudden departure from C——. The relation of the fact, as it here follows, is in his own words:—

"'Soon after we went to bed, we fell asleep: it might have been between one and two in the morning when I awoke. I observed that the fire was totally extinguished; but although that was the case, and we had no light, I saw a glimmer in the centre of the room, which suddenly increased to a bright flame. I looked out, apprehending that something had caught fire, when, to my amazement, I beheld a beautiful boy, clothed in white, with bright locks, resembling gold, standing by my bedside, in which position he remained some minutes, fixing his eyes upon me with a mild and benevolent expression. He then glided gently away toward the side of the chimney, where it is obvious there is no possible egress, and entirely disappeared. I found myself again in total darkness, and all remained quiet until the usual hour of rising. I declare this to be a true account of what I saw at C—— castle, upon my word as a clergyman.'"

★★★★★★

"It is curious," observed Mrs. E., "how many houses in the north of England where I have been lately residing have something of this sort attached to them. Some friends of mine not long ago heard of a very pretty place to let and finding the rent unusually moderate they took it. They were delighted with their new residence; and often wondered that the proprietor, with whom they were slightly acquainted, did not either live there himself, or insist on more money for it.

"After they had been there some time, his brother, that is, the brother of the proprietor, who did not live very far off, called one morning to see them; and asked them how they liked the place. They expressed their extreme satisfaction; adding, 'We wonder your brother does not live here himself.'

"'There are reasons why it does not suit our family,' he answered.

"When he was going away, my friends proposed to walk through the grounds with him; they had to cross a little brook not far from the

55

house; and as they did so, a hare sprang past them and they all stopped and turned round to look at her, by which means they had a full view of the house.

"'Good Heavens!' exclaimed the visitor, 'there she is!'

"'Where?' enquired my friend, thinking he alluded to the hare.

"'Is any of your family ill?' asked the stranger.

"'No, they answered;' and following the direction of his eyes, they observed at one of the upper windows of the house, a female figure in white, and enveloped in what looked like grave clothes.

"The visitor appearing much agitated, my friend rushed back and ran up to the floor where the female had appeared; and not only was there no one there, but he found that the window was that of a vestibule and much too high from the ground for anyone to reach.

"On returning to their visitor, he said 'one of us will die before this year has expired; it is an unfailing omen in our family, and caused us so much distress, that that is the real reason why we do not live here. But it concerns nobody but ourselves; you will never be troubled by her visitations.' The destiny fell on the seer himself this time; he was dead before the year had expired.

"There is another house in the same part of the county, where some time ago a young friend of mine, one of three sisters, went on a visit for a short time. The first night, after she got into bed, she was startled by the most terrific screams she ever heard, which appeared close to her door. She jumped up and opened it, but there was nobody there. The next day she mentioned the circumstance, but the old lady she was visiting, said her ears must have deceived her, and turned the conversation; but she heard it again several times, and was quite sure there was no mistake. When she went home she told her sisters, who laughed at her; but each of them went to visit subsequently at the same house and heard precisely the same thing; but as it was evidently an unpleasant subject to their hostess, they could get no information on the subject."

"A near relation of mine," said Lord N., "is living in a place at present, where there is very much the same annoyance, and three families successively, had left the house in consequence of it. The building is large, part of it very old, and it is surrounded by a fine park; nevertheless, it has been found difficult to get a tenant—or, at least, to keep one. My relation was warned of the inconvenience before he took it. It is said that a lady was murdered there by her husband; at all events, there is one room—one of the best in the house, shut up, and never allowed to be opened. Whoever sleeps in the room under this, is liable to be disturbed by extraordinary noises—footsteps and moving of furniture, &c.; but the most strange thing is, that every now and then a dreadful piercing scream is heard through the house, that brings any strangers who happen to be there, out of their rooms, in terror, to enquire what has occurred. The family who resided there before, met the apparition of a lady occasionally, and left the place in consequence. My relations have never seen anything; but everybody who stays there any time hears the screams.

"Another relation of mine, a very religious person, and as she belongs to the free church of Scotland, most opposed to the belief in ghosts, went some time since to pay a visit at an old place belonging to our family. On the morning after her arrival, she announced at breakfast that she was going away. She gave no reason, but went, to the consternation of her host. With much difficulty, he has since extracted from her, that in the night an apparition appeared at the foot of her bed—a man dressed in an old-fashioned brown suit.

"He spoke to her, and some conversation passed—the subject of which she declares she will never disclose; she says it was not a good spirit, and nothing would induce her to visit the place again. This house has always been said to be haunted, but this is the only instance I know of the family themselves seeing anything of the sort; but no better evidence could be adduced of such a phenomenon than that of the lady in question. Nobody ever doubted her word, and a more confirmed disbeliever in ghosts never existed.

"A rather curious thing happened to myself lately," continued Lord N. "I went to visit some friends at the Lakes. As they had no vacant rooms, I engaged apartments near them for myself and servant. The house was small, quite modern, and as unghostly as possible. I always dined with my friends, and went to my lodgings about twelve o'clock, and I had been there five or six nights without anything unusual occurring. On the fourth or fifth evening, I had returned home rather earlier than usual, and instead of going to bed, I sat down to write a letter.

"While so engaged, I heard what I thought was a boy cracking a whip close to the drawing-room door. I paid no attention to it at first, though rather wondering at the hour chosen for the amusement. However, as it continued unintermittingly, and grew louder, I got up and opened the door, with the intention of desiring the child to go away. There was no one there.

"It then occurred to me that my ears must have deceived me, and that the sound might have proceeded from some explosive substance in my bed-room fire. The room was on the same floor, and the door shut; but when I opened it, I found the fire almost out— certainly not in a state to produce the noises I had heard. I went forward to stir it, and while doing so, the whip was cracked over my shoulder. I turned round quickly, but could see nothing, and I returned to the drawing-room, and had just seated myself again, when I was amazed to see the table rise about a foot perpendicularly into the air, and at the same moment, both the candles that were on it went out, without being upset or even moved. There was a fire, so that I was not quite in the dark, and I re-lighted them; after which the whip began cracking again vigorously and cracked on till I went to bed and afterwards. I stayed in these apartments a fortnight or three weeks longer; and once, again, I heard the whip, but much fainter and for a shorter time; and one night there were distinct rappings on the mantelpiece, and afterwards on the dressing-table.

"I could make no discovery in regard to these phenomena; and I leave it to the company to decide whether they were of a spiritual nature or not. The only other thing of the sort that ever happened to me was this:—I was travelling on the Continent, and not being very well, was lying in bed, when I suddenly saw the door open, and two of my brothers walk through the room, dressed in deep mourning. I rang the bell furiously, and the people came, but could in no way explain what had happened. I shortly received letters, announcing that another brother had died at that time.

"I will mention another instance that occurred in our family a few years since. During my grandfather's last illness, all the family were assembled at K. Castle, except my brother John, with whom he was not on good terms. While we were living there, waiting to see what turn the illness would take, John died very unexpectedly, but we resolved not to mention the circumstance to Lord A., as it might affect him injuriously; it was therefore kept a profound secret.

"One day, some little time afterwards. Lord A. had been asleep in his armchair, and on waking, he suddenly exclaimed, 'I shall see John on Thursday!' This was on a Monday, and he died on the Thursday following."

"A relation of mine," said Mrs. L., "had a friend with whom a great intimacy had subsisted for many years, but a subject of difference arose that embittered her feelings towards this lady to such a degree, that she felt reconciliation impossible. They continued to live in the same town, but all intercourse was at an end.

"One morning, lately, she was lying awake in her bed, when the door opened, and this lady came in; approaching the bed side, she spoke in a friendly manner, and entered into explanations with regard to the misunderstanding. My relation was not frightened during this interview; but when it was over, and she was gone, she suspected the nature of the visit. When her maid came to her room, she enquired if there had been any news of Miss ———. The servant answered, none; but presently afterwards, a person called to mention the lady's death, which had taken place that morning."

"For my part," said Sir A. C, "I am acquainted with a circumstance that has settled entirely any doubts I might have entertained on the subject of ghosts. Not many miles from my place in S—shire, there is a seat belonging to some connexions of my own. At the time I am about to refer to, an old lady was in possession, and it so happened, that a matter of business rose regarding the heirs of the property, which made it necessary to refer to the title deeds. To the surprise and dismay of the family they could not be found. A vigorous search was instituted. in vain; and the circumstance so preyed on my old relation's mind that she at length committed suicide, under the impression that someone else would lay claim to the estate.

"After her death people complained that they could not live there—the place they said was haunted by this old lady, who, with her grey hair dishevelled, and dressed exactly as she used to be in her life time, they described as walking about the house, looking into drawers and cupboards, and incessantly searching for her deeds. We, of course, did not believe in the story, and were not even altogether convinced when the house, after being let to several strangers in succession, who all gave it up on the same plea, seemed destined to remain without an inhabitant.

"It had stood empty two or three years, though offered at a very low rent, when a lady and gentleman from the West Indies came into the neighbourhood to visit some acquaintance, and being in want of a residence, and hearing this was to be had on very reasonable terms, they proposed to take it. Their friends told them of the objection made by preceding tenants, but they laughed with scorn at the idea of losing so good a house on account of a ghost; so, they closed the bargain, took possession of the place, and sent for their family to join them.

"The children, the youngest of whom was between three and four, and the eldest about ten, were, as a temporary arrangement, placed on the first night of their arrival to sleep in one room; but the next morning, when their mother went at a very early hour to see how they were, to her surprise, she found them all wide awake. They were looking pale and weary and began with one voice to complain that they had been kept awake all night by such a disagreeable old lady, who would keep coming into the room, and looking for something in the drawers. 'I told her I wished she'd go away,' said the eldest, 'and then she did go; but she came back; and we don't like her. Who is she, mamma? Is she to live with us?'

"They then, on being questioned, described her appearance, which exactly coincided with the account given by the former tenants. I can vouch for the truth of these circumstances; and since these children had, certainly, never heard a word on the subject of the apparition, and had, indeed, no idea that it was one, 'I think the evidence,' said Sir A. C, 'is quite unexceptionable.'

"I should say so, too, if it referred to any other question," said Mr. E., a barrister, who happened to be present when the story was related; "but on the subject of ghosts I cannot think any evidence sufficient."

"A state of mind by no means uncommon," I said, "and which it is, of course, in vain to contend with. I can only wonder and admire the confidence that can venture to prejudge so interesting and important a subject of inquiry."

Seventh Evening

"My story will be a very short one," said Mrs. M.; "for I must tell you that though, like everybody else, I have heard a great many ghost stories, and have met people who assured me they had seen such things, I cannot, for my own part, bring myself to believe in them; but a circumstance occurred when I was abroad, that you may perhaps consider of a ghostly nature, though I cannot.

"I was travelling through Germany, with no one but my maid—it was before the time of railways, and on my road from Leipsic to Dresden, I stopped at an inn that appeared to have been long ago part of an aristocratic residence—a castle in short; for there was a stone wall and battlements, and a tower at one side; while the other was a prosaic-looking, square building that had evidently been added in modern times. The inn stood at one end of a small village, in which some of the houses looked so antique that they might, I thought, be coeval with the castle itself. There were a good many travellers, but the host said he could accommodate me; and when I asked to see my room, he led me up to the towers, and showed me a tolerably comfortable one. There were only two apartments on each floor; so, I asked him if I could have the other for my maid, and he said yes, if no other traveller arrived. None came, and she slept there.

"I supped at the *table d'hôte*, and retired to bed early, as I had an excursion to make on the following day; and I was sufficiently tired with my journey to fall asleep directly.

"I don't know how long I had slept—but I think some hours, when I awoke quite suddenly, almost with a start, and beheld near the foot of the bed, the most hideous, dreadful-looking old woman, in an antique dress, that imagination can conceive. She seemed to be approaching me—not as if walking, but gliding, with her left arm and hand extended towards me.

"'Merciful God deliver me!' I exclaimed under my first impulse of amazement; and as I said the words she disappeared,"

"Then, though you don't believe in ghosts, you thought it was one when you saw it, said I.

"I don't know what I thought—I admit I was a good deal frightened, and it was a long time before I fell asleep again.

"In the morning," continued Mrs, M., "my maid knocked, and I told her to come in; but the door was locked, and I had to get out of bed to admit her—I thought I might have forgotten to fasten it. As soon as I was up, I examined every part of the room, but I could find nothing to account for this intrusion. There was neither trap or moving panel, or door that I could see, except the one I had locked. However, I made up my mind not to speak of the circumstance, for I fancied I must have been deceived in supposing myself awake, and that it was only a dream; more particularly as there was no light in my room, and I could not comprehend how I could have seen this woman.

"I went out early and was away the greater part of the day. When I returned I found more travellers had arrived, and that they had given the room next mine to a German lady and her daughter, who were at the *table d'hôte*. I therefore had a bed made up in my room for my maid; and before I lay down, I searched thoroughly, that I might be sure nobody was concealed there.

"In the middle of the night—I suppose about the same time I had been disturbed on the preceding one—I and my maid were awakened by a piercing scream; and I heard the voice of the German girl in the adjoining room, exclaiming, '*Ach! meine mutter! meine mutter!*' (Oh! my mother! my mother!)

"For some time afterwards, I heard them talking, and then I fell asleep—wondering, I confess, whether they had had a visit from the frightful old woman. They left me in no doubt the next morning. They came down to breakfast greatly excited—told everybody the cause—described the old woman exactly as I had seen her, and departed from the house incontinently, declaring they would not stay there another hour."

"What did the host say to it?" we asked.

"Nothing; he said we must have dreamed it—and I suppose we did."

"Your story," said I, "reminds me of a very, interesting letter which I received soon after the publication of *The Night side of Nature*. It was from a clergyman who gave his name, and said he was chaplain to a nobleman. He related that in a house he inhabited, or had inhabited, a lady had one evening gone up stairs, and seen, to her amazement, in a room, the door of which was open, a lady in an antique dress, standing before a chest of drawers, and apparently examining their contents. She stood still, wondering who this stranger could be, when the figure turned her face towards her, and, to her horror, she saw there were no eyes. Other members of the family saw the same apparition also. I believe there were further particulars; but I unfortunately lost this letter, with some others, in the confusion of changing my residence.

"The absence of eyes I take to be emblematical of moral blindness; for in the world of spirits there is no deceiving each other by false seemings; as we are, so we appear."

"Then," said Mrs. W. C, "the apparition—if it was an apparition—that two of my servants saw lately, must be in a very degraded state.

"There is a road, and on one side of it a path, just beyond my garden wall. Not long ago two of my servants were in the dusk of the evening walking up this path, when they saw a large, dark object coming towards them. At first, they thought it was an animal; and when it got close, one of them stretched out her hand to touch it; but she could feel nothing, and it passed on between her and the garden wall, although there was *no space*, the path being only wide enough for two; and on looking back, they saw it walking down the hill behind them. Three men were coming up on the path; and as the thing approached, they jumped off into the road.

"'Good heavens, what is that!' cried the women.

"'I don't know,' replied the men; 'I never saw such a thing as that before.'

"The women came home greatly agitated; and we have since heard there is a tradition that the spot is haunted by the ghost of a man who was killed in a quarry close by."

"I have travelled a great deal," said our next speaker, the Chevalier de La C. G.; and, certainly, I have never been in any country where instances of these spiritual appearances were not adduced on apparently credible authority. I have heard numerous stories of the sort, but the one that most readily occurs to me at present, was told to me not long ago, in Paris, by Count P.—the nephew of the celebrated Count P. whose name occurs in the history of the remarkable incidents connected with the death of the Emperor Paul.

"'Count P., my authority for the following story, was attached to the Russian Embassy; and he told me, one evening, when the conversation turned on the inconveniences of travelling in the East of Europe, that, on one occasion, when in Poland, he found himself about seven o'clock in an autumn evening on a forest road, where there was no possibility of finding a house of public entertainment within many miles. There was a frightful storm; the road, not good at the best, was almost impracticable from the weather, and his horses were completely knocked up.

"On consulting his people what was best to be done, they said, that to go back was as impossible as to go forward; but that by turning a little out of the main road, they should soon reach a castle where possibly shelter might be procured for the night. The count gladly consented, and it was not long before they found themselves at the gate of what appeared a building on a very splendid scale. The courier quickly alighted and rang at the bell, and while waiting for admission, he enquired who the castle belonged to, and was told that it was Count X's.

"It was some time before the bell was answered, but at length an elderly man appeared at a wicket, with a lantern, and peeped out. On perceiving the equipage, he came forward and stepped up to the carriage, holding the light aloft to discover who was inside. Count P. handed him his card and explained his distress.

"'There is no one here, my lord,' replied the man, 'but myself and my family; the castle is not inhabited.'

"'That's bad news,' said the count; 'but nevertheless, you can give me what I am most in need of, and that is, shelter for the night.'

"'Willingly,' said the man, 'if your lordship will put up with such accommodation as we can hastily prepare.'

"'So,' said the count, 'I alighted and walked in; and the old man unbarred the great gates to admit my carriages and people. We found ourselves in an immense *couer*, with the castle *en face*, and stables and offices on each side. As we had a *fourgon* (van) with us, with provender for the cattle and provisions for ourselves, we wanted nothing but beds and a good fire; and as the only one lighted was in the old man's apartments, he first took us there. They consisted of a suite of small rooms in the left wing, that had probably been formerly occupied by the upper servants. They were comfortably furnished, and he and his large family appeared to be very well lodged. Besides the wife, there were three sons, with their wives and children, and two nieces; and in a part of the offices, where I saw a light, I was told there were labourers and women servants, for it was a valuable estate, with a fine forest, and the sons acted as *gardes chasse*.

"'Is there much game in the forest?' I asked.

"'A great deal of all sorts,' they answered.

"'Then I suppose during the season the family live here?'

"'Never,' they replied. 'None of the family ever reside here.'

"'Indeed!' I said;' how is that? It seems a very fine place.'

"'Superb,' answered the wife of the custodian; 'but the castle is haunted.'

"She said this with a simple gravity that made me laugh; upon which they all stared at me with the most edifying amazement.

"'I beg your pardon,' I said; 'but you know, perhaps, in great cities, such as I usually inhabit, there are no ghosts.'

"'Indeed!' said they. 'No ghosts!'

"'At least,' I said, 'I never heard of any; and we don't believe in such things.'

"They looked at each other with surprise but said nothing; not appearing to have any desire to convince me. 'But do you mean to say,' said I, 'that that is the reason the family don't live here, and that the castle is abandoned on that account?'

"'Yes,' they replied, 'that is the reason nobody has resided here for many years.'

"'But how can you live here then?'

"'We are never troubled in this part of the building,' said she. 'We hear noises, but we are used to that.'

"'Well, if there is a ghost, I hope I shall see it,' said I.

"'God forbid!' said the woman, crossing herself. 'But we shall guard against that; your *seigneurie* will sleep not far from this, where you will be quite safe.'

"'Oh! but,' said I, 'I am quite serious, if there is a ghost, I should particularly like to see him, and I should be much obliged to you to put me in the apartments he most frequents.'

"They opposed this proposition earnestly and begged me not to think of it; besides, they said if anything was to happen to my lord, how should they answer for it; but as I insisted, the women went to call the members of the family who were lighting fires and preparing beds in some rooms on the same floor as they occupied themselves. When they came they were as earnest against the indulgence of my wishes as the women had been. Still I insisted.

"'Are you afraid,' I said, 'to go yourselves in the haunted chambers?'

"'No,' they answered. 'We are the custodians of the castle and have

to keep the rooms clean and well aired lest the furniture be spoiled—
my lord talks always of removing it, but it has never been removed
yet—but we would not sleep up there for all the world.'

"'Then it is the upper floors that are haunted?'

"'Yes, especially the long room, no one could pass a night there; the
last that did is in a lunatic asylum now at Warsaw,' said the custodian.

"'What happened to him?'

"'I don't know,' said the man; 'he was never able to tell.'

"'Who was he?' I asked.

"'He was a lawyer. My lord did business with him; and one day he
was speaking of this place and saying that it was a pity he was not at
liberty to pull it down and sell the materials; but he cannot, because
it is family property and goes with the title; and the lawyer said he
wished it was his, and that no ghost should keep him out of it. My
lord said that it was easy for anyone to say that who knew nothing
about it, and that he must suppose the family had not abandoned such
a fine place without good reasons. But the lawyer said it was some
trick, and that it was coiners, or robbers, who had got a footing in the
castle, and contrived to frighten people away that they might keep it
to themselves; so my lord said if he could prove that he should be very
much obliged to him, and more than that, he would give him a great
sum—I don't know how much. So, the lawyer said, he would; and my
lord wrote to me that he was coming to inspect the property, and I
was to let him do anything he liked.

"'Well, he came, and with him his son, a fine young man and a soldier. They asked me all sorts of questions and went over the castle and
examined every part of it. From what they said, I could see that they
thought the ghost was all nonsense, and that I and my family were in
collusion with the robbers or coiners. However, I did not care for that,
my lord knew that the castle had been haunted before I was born.

"'I had prepared rooms on this floor for them—the same I am preparing for your lordship, and they slept there, keeping the keys of the
upper rooms to themselves, so I did not interfere with them. But one
morning, very early, we were awakened by someone knocking at our
bedroom door, and when we opened it, we saw Mr. Thaddeus—that
was the lawyers son—standing there halfdressed and as pale as a ghost;
and he said his father was very ill and he begged us to go to him; to
our surprise he led us upstairs to the haunted chamber, and there we
found the poor gentleman speechless, and we thought they had gone
up there early and that he had had a stroke.

"But it was not so; Mr. Thaddeus said, that after we were all in bed, they had gone up there to pass the night. I know they thought that there was no ghost but us, and that's why they would not let us know their intention. They laid down upon some sofas, wrapped up in their fur cloaks, and resolved to keep awake, and they did so for some time, but at last the young man was overcome by drowsiness, he struggled against it, but could not conquer it, and the last thing he recollects was his father shaking him and saying 'Thaddeus, Thaddeus, for God's sake keep awake!' But he could not, and he knew no more till he woke and saw that day was breaking, and found his father sitting in a corner of the room speechless and looking like a corpse; and there he was when we went up. The young man thought he'd been taken ill or had a stroke, as we supposed at first; but when we found they had passed the night in the haunted chambers, we had no doubt what had happened—he had seen some terrible sight and so lost his senses.'

"He lost his senses, I should say, from terror when his son fell asleep, said I, and he felt himself alone. He could have been a man of no nerve. At all events, what you tell me raises my curiosity. Will you take me upstairs and shew me those rooms?

"'Willingly,' said the man, and fetching a bunch of keys and a light, and calling one of his sons to follow him with another, he led the way up the great staircase to a suite of apartments on the first floor. The rooms were lofty and large, and the man said the furniture was very handsome, but old. Being all covered with canvas cases, I could not judge of it. 'Which is the long room?' I said.

"Upon which he led me into a long narrow room that might rather have been called a gallery. There were sofas along each side, something like a dais at the upper end; and several large pictures hanging on the walls.

"I had with me a bulldog, of a very fine breed, that had been given me in England by Lord F. She had followed me upstairs—indeed, she followed me everywhere—and I watched her narrowly as she went smelling about, but there were no indications of her perceiving anything extraordinary. Beyond this gallery there was only a small octagon room, with a door that led out upon another staircase. When I had examined it all thoroughly, I returned to the long room and told the man, as that was the place especially frequented by the ghost, I should feel much obliged if he would allow me to pass the night there. I could take upon myself to say that Count X., would have no objection.

"'It is not that,' replied the man; 'but the danger to your lordship,' and he conjured me not to insist on such a perilous experiment.

"When he found I was resolved, he gave way, but on condition that I signed a paper, stating that in spite of his representations I had determined to sleep in the long room.

"I confess, the more anxious these people seemed to prevent my sleeping there, the more curious I was; not that I believed in the ghost the least in the world. I thought that the lawyer had been right in his conjecture, but that he had not nerve enough to investigate whatever he saw or heard; and that they had succeeded in frightening him out of his senses. I saw what an excellent place these people had got, and how much it was their interest to maintain the idea that the castle was uninhabitable. Now, I have pretty good nerves—I have been in situations that have tried them severely—and I did not believe that any ghost, if there was such a thing, or any jugglery by which a semblance of one might be contrived, would shake them. As for any real danger, I did not apprehend it; the people knew who I was, and any mischief happening to me would have led to consequences they well understood. So, they lighted fires in both the grates of the gallery, and as they had abundance of dry wood, they soon blazed up. I was determined not to leave the room after I was once in it, lest, if my suspicions were correct, they might have time to make their arrangements; so, I desired my people to bring up my supper, and I ate it there.

"My courier said he had always heard the castle was haunted, but he dare say there was no ghost but the people below, who had a very comfortable berth of it; and he offered to pass the night with me, but I declined any companion and preferred trusting to myself and my dog. My valet, on the contrary, strongly advised me against the enterprise, assuring me that he had lived with a family in France whose *château* was haunted, and had left his place in consequence.

"By the time I had finished my supper it was ten o'clock, and everything was prepared for the night. My bed, though an impromptu, was very comfortable, made of amply stuffed cushions and thick coverlets, placed in front of the fire. I was provided with light and plenty of wood; and I had my regimental cutlass, and a case of excellent pistols, which I carefully primed and loaded in presence of the custodian, saying, you see I am determined to fire at the ghost, so if he cannot stand a bullet, he had better not pay me a visit.

"The old man shook his head calmly but made no answer. Having desired the courier, who said he should not go to bed, to come up stairs immediately if he heard the report of firearms, I dismissed my people and locked the doors, barricading each with a heavy ottoman besides. There was no arras or hangings of any sort behind which a door could be concealed; and I went round the room, the walls of which were panelled with white and gold, knocking every part, but neither the sound, nor Dido, the dog, gave any indications of there being anything unusual. Then I undressed and lay down with my sword and my pistols beside me; and Dido at the foot of my bed, where she always slept.

"I confess I was in a state of pleasing excitement; my curiosity and my love of adventure were roused; and whether it was ghost, or robber, or coiner, I was to have a visit from, the interview was likely to be equally interesting. It was half-past ten when I lay down; my expectations were too vivid to admit of sleep; and after an attempt at a French novel, I was obliged to give it up; I could not fix my attention to it. Besides, my chief care was not to be surprised. I could not help thinking the custodian and his family had some secret way of getting into the room, and I hoped to detect them in the fact; so, I lay with my eyes and ears open in a position that gave me a view of every part of it, till my travelling clock struck twelve, which being pre-eminently the ghostly hour, I thought the critical moment was arrived.

"But no, no sound, no interruption of any sort to the silence and solitude of the night occurred. When half-past twelve, and one struck, I pretty well made up my mind that I should be disappointed in my expectations,, and that the ghost, whoever he was knew better than to encounter Dido and a brace of well charged pistols; but just as I arrived at this conclusion, an unaccountable *frisson* (thrill) came over me, and I saw Dido, who tired with her day's journey, had lain till now quietly curled up asleep, begin to move, and slowly get upon her feet. I thought she was only going to turn, but, instead of lying down, she stood still with her ears erect and her head towards the dais, uttering a low growl.

"'The dais, I should mention, was but the skeleton of a dais, for the draperies were taken off. There was only remaining a canopy covered with crimson velvet, and an arm chair covered with velvet too, but cased in canvas like the rest of the furniture. I had examined this part of the room thoroughly and had moved the chair aside to ascertain that there was nothing under it.

"Well, I sat up in bed and looked steadily in the same direction as the dog, but I could see nothing at first, though it appeared that she did; but as I looked, I began to perceive something like a cloud in the chair, while at the same time a chill which seemed to pervade the very marrow in my bones crept through me, yet the fire was good; and it was not the chill of fear, for I cocked my pistols with perfect self-possession and abstained from giving Dido the signal to advance, because I wished eagerly to see the denouement of the adventure.

"Gradually, this cloud took a form, and assumed the shape of a tall white figure that reached from the ceiling to the floor of the dais, which was raised by two steps. 'At him, Dido! At him!' I said, and away she dashed to the steps, but instantly turned and crept back completely cowed. As her courage was undoubted, I own this astonished me, and I should have fired, but that I was perfectly satisfied that what I saw was not a substantial human form, for I had seen it grow into its present shape and height from the undefined cloud that first appeared in the chair. I laid my hand on the dog who had crept up to my side, and I felt her shaking in her skin.

"I was about to rise myself and approach the figure, though I confess I was a good deal awe struck, when it stepped majestically from the dais, and seemed to be advancing. 'At him!' I said, 'At him. Dido!' and I gave the dog every encouragement to go forward; she made a sorry attempt, but returned when she had got halfway and crouched beside me whining with terror. The figure advanced upon me; the cold became icy; the dog crouched and trembled; and I, as it approached, honestly confess, said Count P., that I hid my head under the bed clothes and did not venture to look up till morning. I know not what it was—as it passed over me I felt a sensation of undefinable horror, that no words can describe—and I can only say that nothing on earth would tempt me to pass another night in that room, and I am sure if Dido could speak, you'd find her of the same opinion.

"I had desired to be called at seven o'clock, and when the custodian, who accompanied my valet, found me safe and in my perfect senses, I must say the poor man appeared greatly relieved; and when I descended the whole family seemed to look upon me as a hero. I thought it only just to them to admit that something had happened in the night that I felt impossible to account for, and that I should not recommend anybody who was not very sure of their nerves to repeat the experiment."

When the *chevalier* had concluded this extraordinary story, I suggested that the apparition of the castle very much resembled that mentioned by the late professor Gregory, in his letters on mesmerism, as having appeared in the Tower of London some years ago, and from the alarm it created, having occasioned the death of a lady, the wife of an officer quartered there, and one of the sentries. Everyone who had read that very interesting publication was struck by the resemblance.

Eighth Evening

"As this was our last evening, I was called upon for a story; but I pleaded that I had told all mine in the *Night Side of Nature* and of personal experience I had very little to tell; but I said I will give you the history of a visit I made several years ago to a haunted house although it resulted in almost nothing.

"After the publication of the *Night Side* I received many valuable communications—I wish I had kept a note of them all, but I never expected to publish again on the same subject. Amongst others, I received a letter from a gentleman called Mc. N., and as it contained several interesting particulars, I requested him to call on me. I remember, in the letter, he told me that a few years previously, he had been on an excursion from home, and that while stopping at an inn, one morning, about five o'clock, the door opened and his father entered; he came to the bedside, looked at him, and then went out again. The young man sprang from his bed, and followed him down stairs, where he lost sight of him. He returned home and found his father had died on that morning.

"He was in a lawyer's office, and, amongst other things, he mentioned to me that there was not very far off a house said to be haunted, of which they had the charge, but that it was impossible to do anything with it. 'We offer it at a mere nominal rent, but no one will stay there.'

"I was often absent from home at this time, but for the next two or three years I sometimes met him and inquired about the house. The report was always the same; till, at length, no one would go into it; it was shut up—the shutters were closed, and the boys of the neighbourhood threw stones at the windows and broke the glass. Yet it was situated in a street where every other house was inhabited, and which had not been built many years.

"It was as much as six or seven years after I had first heard of this house, that I happened to mention the circumstance to some gentlemen of my acquaintance—very eminent men, with honest, inquiring minds; truth seekers, who, if she were in the bottom of a well, would have thought it right to go after her. As they had humility enough to feel that they could not pronounce upon a question that they had never studied or investigated, they expressed a wish to visit the house. Accordingly, I applied to Mr. Mc. N., who had the keys in his office, and he obligingly consented to accompany us. Our expedition was to be kept a profound secret; and it was so, till some time afterwards, when, like most other secrets, it got wind and it spread abroad.

"We started in a carriage, between eleven and twelve o'clock at night, taking with us a young girl who was easily mesmerised, and when in that state a good clairvoyant. She was not told the object of our journey and had no means whatever of learning it. We said we were going to look at a house, and that that was the most convenient time for the gentleman to show it us. We did not drive to the door, but Mr. McN. met us in the next street, where we alighted, lest we should attract observation. We walked to our destination, and Mr. Mc. N. explained to the policeman on duty who he was and where we were going, lest he should suspect mischief. and interrupt us. He then unlocked the door with the aid of the policeman's lantern, for it was a dark winter's night; and on entering, we found ourselves in a narrow passage.

"It was a small house, in no respect different from the others in the street. They seemed all of the same description. A narrow frontage, with one window and the door, on the ground floor; two windows above; two rooms on a floor, three stories in height, and a kitchen, scullery, and cellars underground.

"As soon as the door closed on us, we were in utter darkness, but we had provided ourselves with candles and matches, and when we had lighted them, we entered the back parlour, which Mr. Mc. N. had heard from the different inhabitants was the room in which they had met with most annoyance.

"The clairvoyant was then put to sleep, and asked if she liked the house, and would recommend us to take it. She shuddered and said 'No; that two people had been murdered there, and we should be *troubled.*' We asked in which room; she answered, 'it was before this house was built—that another house stood there then—a very old house.' This was not exactly on the same ground, but the room we were in was on part of it. She said that it was these murdered people who would trouble us. We asked if she could see them, and she answered 'no.'

"We then waited in silence to see if anything occurred; but nothing did, except a metallic sound at the door, which was ajar, like the striking of two pieces of iron. We all heard it but could not say what occasioned it.

"After a little time, someone suggested that we should extinguish the lights. We did so and were then in absolute darkness. There was but one window in the room, and that was coated with dust, and the shutter was shut; besides, as I have said, it was a very dark night, and this room, being at the back, looked into a yard, I believe at all events, not into a street.

"Presently, the clairvoyant started, and exclaimed, 'Look there!' We saw nothing and asked what it was.

"'There!' she said. 'There again! don't you see it?'

"'What?' we asked. 'The lights!' she said. 'There! Now!' These exclamations were made at intervals of two or three seconds.

"We all said we saw nothing whatever.

"'If Mrs. Crowe would take hold of my hand, I think she would see them,' she suggested.

"I did so; and then at intervals of a few seconds, I saw thrown up, apparently from the floor, waves of white light, faint, but perfectly distinct and visible. In order that I might know whether our perceptions of this phenomenon were simultaneous, I desired her, without speaking, to press my hand each time she saw it, which she did; and each time I distinctly saw the wave of white light. I saw it, at these intervals, as long as I held her hand and we were in the dark. Nobody saw it but she and myself; and we did not follow up the experiment by the others taking her hand, which we should have done.

"During this interval, another light suddenly appeared in the middle of the room, away from where we were standing, I saw a bright diamond of light, like an extremely vivid spark— only not the colour of fire; it was white, brilliant, and quiescent, but shed no rays. I did not mention this, because I wished to learn if it was visible to anybody else—but nobody spoke of it; not even the clairvoyant. Whether she saw it or not, I cannot say. When the candles were relighted these lights were no longer visible. I and one of the gentlemen went over the house above and below but saw nothing but the dust and desolation of a long uninhabited dwelling.

74

"When we came away, and Mr. Mc. N. had locked the door, we walked to the carriage. I said, 'then you none of you saw the waves of light.'

"'No,' said they.

"'Well,' said I, 'I certainly did, and I never saw anything like it before. Moreover, I saw another sort of light.'

"'Did you,' said Mr. Mc. N., interrupting me; 'was it a bright spark of light like the oxy-hydrogen light.'

"'Exactly,' said I. 'I could not think what to compare it to; but that was it.'

"I thus was certain that he had seen the same thing as myself; he had not spoken of it from a similar motive; he waited to have his impression confirmed by further testimony.

"You see our results were not great, but the visit was not wholly barren to me. Of course, many wise people will say, I did not see the lights, but that they were the offspring of my excited imagination. But I beg to say that my imagination was by no means excited. If I had been there *alone*, it would have been a different affair; for though I never saw a ghost nor ever fancied I did, I am afraid I should have been very nervous. But I was in exceedingly good company, with two very clever men, besides the lawyer, a lady, and the clairvoyant; so that my nerves were perfectly composed, as I should not object to seeing any ghost in such agreeable society. Moreover, I did not expect any result; because, there is very seldom any on these occasions, as ghosts appear we know not why; but certainly not because people wish to see them. They generally come when least expected and least thought of.

"Mr. McN., on inquiry, learnt that unaccountable lights were amongst the things complained of. What occasioned them and the other phenomena, it had certainly been the proprietor's interest for many years to discover; it had also been the interest of numerous tenants, who having taken the house for a term, found themselves obliged to leave it at a sacrifice. Yet, for all those years, no explanation could be found for the annoyances but that the house was haunted. No tradition seems extant to account for its evil reputation. If what the clairvoyant said was true, the murders must have occurred long ago.

"A gentleman, an inhabitant of the same city, once mentioned to me that a friend of his, many years previously, when quite a young man, had one Sunday evening been walking alone in the fields outside this town; and that he met a young woman, a perfect stranger, who, on some pretence asked him to see her safe home. He did so; she led him to a lone farmhouse, and then inviting him to walk in, shewed him into a room and left him. Whilst waiting for her return, idly looking about, he found hidden under the table, which was covered with a cloth, a dead body. On this discovery, he rushed to the door; it was locked; but the window was not very high from the ground, and by it he escaped; terrified to such a degree, that he not only left the city that very evening, but hastened out of the country, apprehensive that he had been enticed to the house and shut up with the murdered man, for the purpose of throwing the guilt on him; and as justice was not so clear sighted, and much more inexorable than in these days, he feared the circumstantial evidence might go against him. He settled in a foreign country and finally died there.

"Where this locality was, I don't know, except that it was in the environs of the city—environs which have since been covered with buildings; what if the house that we visited should have been erected on the site of that lone farm!

"It may be so; at all events, this story shews how possible it is that some similar event might have occurred on the spot where the haunted house stands."

In conclusion, let me once more recall to my readers that one, whose insight none will dispute, reminds us, in relation to this very subject, that "our philosophy," does not comprehend all wisdom and all truth. Philosophy is a good guide when she opens her eyes, but where she obstinately shuts them to one class of facts because she has previously made up her mind they cannot be genuine, she is a bad one.

Professor A. told me that when he was at Gottingen, as a great favour, and through the interest of an influential professor there, he was allowed to see a book that had belonged to Faust, or Faustus, as we call him. It was a large volume, and the leaves were stiff and hard like wood. They contained his magic rites and formulas, but on the last page was inscribed a solemn injunction to all men, as they loved their own souls, not to follow in his path or practice the teaching that volume contained.

There appears to be a mystery out of the domain—I mean the present domain of science; within the region of the hyper-psychical, regarding our relations, while in this world, with those who have past the gates, a belief in which is, I think, innate in human nature. This belief, in certain periods and places, grows rank and mischievous; at others, it is almost extinguished by reaction, and education; but it never wholly dies; because, everywhere and in all times, circumstances have occurred to keep it alive, amongst individuals, which never reach the public ear. Now, the truth is always worth ascertaining on any subject; even this despised subject of ghosts, and those who have an inherent conviction that they themselves are spirits, temporarily clothed in flesh, feel that they have an especial interest in the question.

We are fully aware that the investigation presents all sorts of difficulties, and that the belief is opposed to all sorts of accepted opinions; but we desire to ascertain the grounds of a persuasion, so nearly concerning ourselves which in all ages and all countries has prevailed in a greater or less degree, and which appears to be sustained by a vast amount of facts, which, however, we admit are not in a condition to be received as anything beyond presumptive evidence. These facts are chiefly valuable, as furnishing cumulative testimony of the 'frequent recurrence of phenomena explicable by no known theory, and therefore as open to the spiritual hypothesis as any other. When a better is offered, supported by something more convincing than pointless ridicule and dogmatic assertion, I for one, shall be ready to entertain it. In the meanwhile, hoping that time may, at length, in some degree, rend the veil that encompasses this department of psychology, we record such experiences as come under our observation and are content to await their interpretation.

Appendix

I have referred in the preceding pages to the loss of several letters, which I should have been glad to insert here.

The following very interesting ones I have fortunately retained. I give them *verbatim*, only suppressing the names of the writers, as requested.

LETTER 1.

Aug. 18, 1854.

Madam,

I have received your kind favour of the 15th, and I really feel that I must now apologise to you, for venturing so quickly to call in question the accuracy of your details. Being unaware, however, of the marvellous coincidence of the *two dreams*, I feel assured you at once appreciated the motives which alone impelled me to write.

Allow me, then, to attempt a narration of the particulars referred to in my last, as having come under my own observation.

Two intimate friends of mine (clergymen of the Church of England) and one of whom is unmarried, have for the last three years occupied a large old-fashioned house in the country. It is a very pretty place—stands within its own grounds—and is quite aloof from any other dwellings. It has long had the reputation in the neighbourhood of being haunted, in consequence, it is said, of a former proprietor having committed suicide there. The story goes thus, he was *laid out* in a chamber which is now called the spare room and is the scene of what I am about to relate.

I may as well tell you that it was only on my last visit, some six weeks since, that I became at all aware of the *character* of the mansion, for my friends felt so annoyed at what has taken place, that they purposely avoided communicating to their visitors what they thought might make them anything but comfortable.

On that occasion there happened to be on a visit to my friend's wife, a lady very nearly related to him. She had the spare room assigned to her as a chamber, and on the very first night of her arrival was so terrified by what took place that she would not again sleep there without company.

She stated that in the middle of the night she was alarmed by the most unearthly groanings and lamentations—the voice seemed close to her bedside. It was afterwards attended by a rustling noise, and she distinctly felt the curtains at the foot of the bed removed. Now, as my knowledge of what was going on could not be disputed, my friends admitted that it was not the *first* time these noises had been heard, nay, that in two instances the apparition of a form in grave-clothes had been seen; the one occurring to a young gentleman of about twenty years of age, who happened to be visiting them, and the other to one of their own servants.

In the former case, it appears that the young man was sitting rather late at night in the study reading—all the family being in bed—when the form emerged, apparently, from the wall dividing the study from the haunted chamber. It remained a short time only and then melted away. So great was the young man's terror that he has never been near the place since. The servant also described a similar appearance, and no one in the house who saw her terror could believe it acted. Independently of all this, no less than four gentlemen, two of them from the University, have experienced all the unearthly groanings and bewailings before mentioned, and in nearly every instance the parties were, like myself, ignorant of the character attributed to the house. But I now come to my own experience.

I was on a visit to my friends about twelve months since, when I met a gentleman who had just left the army for the church. He appeared about 21 years of age, and there was that indescribable *something* in his manner which charmed me immediately. Without any pretence to being set up—so to speak—in piety, there was yet *that* in his sunny countenance and air of cheerfulness, which made you feel that he had been called to a brighter path of usefulness. I certainly very much admired him, and I have since learnt that he is a general favourite. On retiring to rest I found that he was to occupy the next room—not the study side.

From a variety of causes I could not sleep but the imaginative powers were not particularly aroused—my thoughts were of very prosy and worldly things. As near as I could recollect, about an hour after I had been in bed, I heard the most dreadful groans followed by exclamations of the most horrible kind. The voice certainly seemed in the room and was continued for at least two hours, at intervals of about ten minutes. It was that of a man who had committed a deadly sin which could never be pardoned! The agony seemed to me to be intense.

Will you believe it, Madam, in spite of what I thought of my acquaintance of the next chamber, I ascribed it to him. I believed little in the supernatural and concluded it to be some dreadful dream. It is astonishing the thought never struck me that a *continuous* dream of such a character was scarcely possible. It did not, however, and despite of its unearthly character, and the apparent woe of the unfortunate one—the despair, as I said before, of a lost soul—I continued to associate it all with my neighbour next door, until the events which occurred at my last visit entirely upset my conviction, and I became at once assured I had been doing him great injustice.

Like some of the cases in the *Night Side of Nature*, you will perceive here a great difference in the manifestations—to some it was given to *hear*, to others to *see*. Are you still of opinion that this results from what you term comparative freedom of *rapport!* Do you not think there are times when the material may give place to the supernatural? I admit freely the truth of spectral illusions—I have myself experienced one—but knew it to be nothing more. Still, notwithstanding this, and my further belief in a certain connection of mind and matter, I cannot altogether cast from me the persuasion that the Almighty One may *at times* think fit to exercise a power independent of all rule, for the attainment of certain ends to us, perhaps, unknown.

I cannot conclude without telling you that with regard to what I have mentioned above, nothing in the shape of *trick* could possibly have been practised. Trusting I may not have trespassed too much on your patience, I will now remain, Madam, yours very respectfully,

J. H. H.

LETTER 2

Gloucestershire, June 10, 1854.

Madam,

Being not long ago on a visit of some days at the house of a friend, I happened to meet with your work, entitled *The Night side of Nature*.

The title struck my imagination and opening the book I was delighted to find that it treated of subjects which had long engaged my serious thoughts. I was much pleased to see in you such an able and earnest protester against the cold scepticism of the age in reference to truths of the highest order, and those too sustained by a body of evidence which in any other case would be esteemed irresistible.

I must also say that I never met with so great a number of well authenticated facts in any other work as you have given us, whilst the truly catholic spirit of your theological reflections, was to me peculiarly refreshing. I once had a thought of making a similar collection, that design I have however abandoned, the state of my health not admitting of much literary labour. I could relate to you many things as remarkable as any you have described, for the truth of which I can vouch. I will mention one of a most singular nature, and should you be inclined to read anything more from me on these matters, I shall feel a pleasure in the communication. Writing letters, I find to be a relief from a melancholy, induced some two years ago by a variety of heavy afflictions, and this must be my apology for addressing you. But to my narrative:—

Shortly after I entered the ministry, I was introduced to a gentleman of very superior mind who belonged to the same profession, and whom I had never seen equalled for the genius and eloquence which his conversation displayed.

I became at once attached to him, and for some reason or other he evinced a desire to cultivate my friendship. After some months of most agreeable intercourse had elapsed, he was taken seriously ill, and one evening I was hastily summoned to his house. On my entering his chamber he requested that we might be left alone, and he then told me that it was his impression that his disease was mortal—that many supernatural occurrences had marked his life, which he desired might be given to the world when he was gone, and that he wished me to perform this office. Having expressed my willingness to gratify him, he commenced the chapter of extraordinaries.

Here is one event in his remarkable history. Prior to his becoming a minister and when in humble circumstances, he lodged at the house of a tradesman at a certain sea-port town in W—s. He was then in perfect health. One night he retired to rest in peculiarly good spirits, and as his custom was (for it was then summer) he sat near the window and gazed for some time on the beauties of nature. He then amused himself for a while by humming a tune, when presently on looking towards the door, he saw the figure of a man enter—his dress was a blood red night cap, flannel jacket, and breeches. The man approached the bed (his countenance and walk indicating extreme illness), threw himself upon it, gave several groans and apparently expired. My friend was so filled with horror that he lost all power of speech and motion, and remained fixed on his seat till morning, when he told his landlord the occurrence of the night and declared that unless they could find him other apartments he would leave them that very day.

The honest people were disinclined to part with him and agreed to accommodate him on the ground-floor. About *twelve months after this*, he went out on a market day for the purpose of purchasing some provisions, and when he returned, he heard that his old room was taken; but what was his surprise to find in the new lodger the very form, with the very same dress that had so terrified him a year before!

The man was then very ill: he died in a few weeks, and the circumstances were without *any exception* the same as those which my friend had witnessed. This is one of those cases in which it is extremely difficult to ascertain the design of the appearance.

I should much like to know what conjecture you would form, as to the *modus* and end of such a singular incident.

Of the veracity of the narrator it was impossible for me to doubt. As this minister is still *living* I am not at liberty to mention his name.

Pray excuse the freedom of thus addressing you, and believe me to be

Madam, with every sentiment
of respect and esteem,
Yours, very truly,

R. I. O.

Mrs. C. Crowe.

LETTER 3.

Gloucestershire, June 21, 1854.

Madam,

As I find that another communication will not be unacceptable, I proceed to detail a few cases. My first relates to the minister, a part of whose history I have given you, and belongs to the class of prophetic dreams. When he had resolved to study for the ministry and through the influence of friends, had obtained admission to a Dissenting College; as the day affixed for his departure drew near, he was filled with anxiety, from the fact that he had not even money to pay his travelling expenses.

He did not like to borrow, and he had no reason to conclude that anyone suspected the miserable state of his finances. The evening before his expected removal, he laid down to rest with a troubled heart. This was in the very same seaport where the circumstance happened which I have already told you. After some hours of great mental suffering sleep came to his relief, and in his dream there seemed to approach him one of a most pleasing form, who told him that he not only saw that he was in distress, but that he well knew the cause of it, and that if he would walk down on the beach to a certain place which he pointed out as in a picture, he would find under some loose stones enough for his present necessities.

In the morning, accordingly, almost as soon as it was light he hastened to the indicated spot and to his great surprise and delight found a sum amounting to a trifle more than was absolutely necessary for his journey. I would just, in passing, remark that he said that on another occasion, his father who died many years before appeared to him with an angry countenance and assured him that he would suffer much from something he had done in reference to his family, but as this was evidently an unpleasant and even painful topic I did not wish him to enlarge upon it.

The other fact I shall mention, happened to my grandfather who was also a minister. I am well aware that it is of such a nature that the relation of it would in most companies excite a burst of laughter or at least a contemptuous and sceptical smile, but I know I am addressing one who has studied in a very different school of philosophy. It was in the large town of B—m where my grandfather resided for many years, that the event took place. He himself my grandfather, my aunts, and my mother used often to tell it to their friends when the conversation turned on the supernatural. I have probably heard it a hundred times and I am not ashamed to say that on the testimony of such a man as my grandfather I cannot but yield to it my belief.

One morning when *breakfast had just commenced*, my grandfather went from the table, at which my grandmother also was sitting, into the passage, for what purpose I have now forgotten, and there he found (for the front door had been standing open,) a strange looking man in black, with a shuffling gait and a club foot. He declared that he had an instantaneous conviction that this was a supernatural appearance, and that a spirit of evil stood before him.

The man in black exclaimed, moving towards the breakfast room, "I am come to take breakfast with you this morning."

My grandfather convulsively seizing the handle of the door, said, with a stern look, "you are too late sir," to which the other instantly replied, "I am not too late for the remnant," and then rushed into the street.

My grandfather followed, and to his amazement saw this creature at the top of the street, which was of great length, and in a moment or two he vanished. My grandmother heard a loud talking, and when my grandfather returned to the table in considerable agitation, she naturally wished to know what had occurred, but as she was near her confinement he of course concealed the matter from her. The mysterious words of the stranger followed him continually, and he puzzled himself in seeking to explain their meaning. In a few days my grandmother was confined. The child was dead-born and her life for some time hung in jeopardy. He now believed he had arrived at the solution of the difficulty—the infant was the "remnant'" referred to.

I am not the subject of remarkable dreams, I had one, however, lately, and I give it you because it stands connected in my mind with the knowledge of a singular psychical fact which I am confident will greatly interest you, if you have not yet fallen upon it in the course of your reading. About a fortnight ago I thought I saw in my sleep, a young man, who is assistant to our principal surgeon, come into my room, looking exceedingly unwell. He laid himself on the other bed in my chamber, and I thought that he had come there to linger out his last illness, at which I felt not the least surprise or objection.

He seemed to be perfectly resigned, and presently he began to converse with me, and after we had talked for some time, whilst he was replying to something I had said, I distinctly saw his spirit rise up out of his body. He gazed at the corpse with the deepest interest and pleasure. One moment he would stand by the head and survey the face, and the next move to the feet, and then gaze at the entire body. He called me to come and stand by his side and view this lifeless frame, which I did with as much placidity as he seemed himself to possess, and without the slightest idea of their being anything absurd in what I saw.

I could not, however, help saying "O, that I could leave my body and have such a view of it as you have now of yours!" I remember no more. In the morning I had occasion to call on a friend, who has a large library containing many rare books. Not being in the humour for close reading (for I spend many hours at a time there) I took up from a centre table a volume of a lighter kind. It happened to be Mrs.

Child's *Letters from New York*. Turning the leaves over carelessly, my eye lighted on a chapter headed "The spirit surveying its own body!" She there says that she was told by a pious lady, that when once in a swoon, she felt that she left the body and was *standing by it* during the whole time it lasted; that she distinctly heard every word spoken by the doctor and her family, and saw every movement of their countenances, and all that was done with her body. I may observe that I have not heard that anything has occurred to the young man I saw. If I have not already tired your patience you may draw on my memory for something more. A line to that effect will oblige,

> Yours very truly,
>
> R. I. O.

Mrs. Crowe.

LETTER 4

Edinburgh, Aug. 10th.

Madam,

In consequence of a long absence abroad, I never had, till recently, an opportunity of reading your agreeable work, *The Night side of Nature*, which contains a mass of evidence in favour of your theories, to which I take the liberty of adding a few cases from my own experience.

Many years ago I lived in a house in Edinburgh, which belonged to my mother's relatives, and in which my maternal grandfather had died, several years antecedent to my own birth. The room in which I slept was that (but at the time unknown to me) in which my relative had expired. There were two beds in the room—one a large four-poster and the other a sort of couch. The latter was next the door, and both lay between it and the window, which was barred and bolted, and opposite to them was the fireplace, with rather a high mantle-piece. Being summer, the "board" was on the chimney.

It was about eleven o'clock at night; the rest of the family had retired to rest. As there were only about two inches of candle left, I placed the candlestick on the mantlepiece, intending to allow it to burn out, and went to my bed, which was on the couch. I had just lain down, and was looking towards the candle, when, to my extreme horror, I perceived a tall old man in his night dress, standing by the mantlepiece. His sight seemed impaired, for he put forth his hand *and felt for something*, and then moved across the fireplace, in doing which, *he obscured the light on passing it.* My gaze was riveted on him. He then turned towards the large bed on my left and stretching out his hands attempted with a feeble effort to lay himself down, and in doing so I heard him *sigh* distinctly. He disappeared almost at the same moment. He did not appear to have noticed me.

I immediately sprang out of bed and opening the door on my right hand, called out loudly, *but never left the doorway*, as I was resolved that if the figure were that of a living person there should be no means of egress. On the assembling of the family in my room, a search was made; but there was nothing to be seen, and there had been no possibility of a human being having been in the room; the affair was put down to an *illusion*. Yet so strong an impression did it leave on my mind, that a few years since (1851 or 52), when in India, I published in *Saunder's Magazine*, printed at the Delhi Gazette press, an account of this apparition, in a narrative, which I wrote called *Idone, or Incidents in the life of a dreamer*, and which with the exception of this introductory vision, was, in reality, a series of actual dreams of which I had kept a record, and this I endeavoured to weave into a vague story, with the view of illustrating how a person might live *two distinct lives!*

Sometime after the above were published, I read with much interest, *Swedenborg's Theory of the Spiritual World*; and lately when reading your work, I was struck with some peculiar resemblances between my own experience and the cases you cite.

But to return to the family and house in Edinburgh, of my grandfather. Other members of the family have seen unaccountable figures in the same house. An aunt of mine and a cousin, one night, met an old woman on the stairs with a large bunch of keys, and were in the greatest alarm. On another occasion, on going to open a room which had been locked up for some time, in order to prepare it for the reception of my eldest uncle, who had just returned that night from abroad, two members of the family started back and locked the door again, for on entering they had both seen the *mattrass &c. violently heaved up*. On returning with the servants, nothing was visible of an unusual description.

Again, two relatives occupied the same room, and one night, as the fire was burning low, after they had gone to bed (the door being locked) they were alarmed by a sound like wings, over their beds, and by a *dusky form* moving about the room. It walked up to the fireplace and seemed restless. When it had disappeared, they both rose and *unlocked* the door, called for assistance, but, as usual nothing of their visitor was to be seen. A still more remarkable incident occurred in the same house. As two of my aunts were sitting opposite the window, at night, they were startled by the apparition of an absent brother-in-law looking in, and with a pen in his hand. A few days afterwards the intelligence of his death arrived. He had been *signing his will* at the exact time they had seen his apparation. My eldest uncle shortly after his return from abroad went to Musselburgh to visit an old schoolmaster, and as he entered the yard he observed him limping into the school. He tried to overtake him, and on reaching the door he met one of the tutors, who informed him that the Dr. had been confined to his bed for some time with a broken leg.

The same uncle, who was an officer in the army, dreamt that he had obtained his captaincy by the retirement of an officer of the name of Patterson (so far as I remember.) There was no such officer then in the regiment, and he mentioned it as strange that he should have dreamt of a *particular* name. A few *Gazettes* afterwards my uncle obtained his promotion by an officer of *this* name being *brought in from the half-pay to sell out in the same Gazette.*

I have myself heard the most remarkable and unaccountable noises in my grandfather's house. The servants were often in the greatest terror.

I have heard, seemingly, the whole of the furniture, in a particular room, thrown violently about, accompanied with the noise of something rolling on the floor. At other times I have distinctly heard, as it were, a boy's marble falling step by step down the stairs and striking against my door, which was at the foot of them, and yet this was at night, and there were no children in the house. This annoyance, with that of steps heard round my bed, was so common as to cease to make any impression on me.

I may mention that my grandfather was not happy in his family relations, and died in an uneasy frame of mind, on Christmas eve, 1820. Since my family sold his house, I have never heard that its new occupants were disturbed.

I have at different periods of my life had *groups*, as it were, of very remarkable allegorical dreams.

It is somewhat singular that involuntary efforts may be made during sleep, which are I believe beyond the bounds of possibility during waking moments. Indeed, the curious phenomena which you have so ably criticised, are without limit.

Though you do not approve of the concealment of names, I hope you will excuse my asking you to do so in the present instance as many of the parties concerned might be displeased.

      I have the honour to remain,

           Madam,

                Your obedient servant,

                              H. A.

Mrs. Catherine Crowe.

"P.S. I know two remarkable instances of prophetic denunciation or the power of will, under, of course, the control of Providence. In one instance, the death of the party denounced, followed on the week predicted, although at the time he was well. Moreover, the denunciation was never mentioned to him.

"In the other instance, the accomplishment of the denunciation was accomplished to the exact day, and under very remarkable circumstances. I believe this power to be *involuntary*, and more of the nature of inspiration.

The Italian's Story

"How well your friend speaks English!" I remarked one day to an acquaintance when I was abroad, alluding to a gentleman who had just quitted the room. "What is his name?"

"Count Francesco Ferraldi."

"I suppose he has been in England?"

"Oh, yes; he was exiled and taught Italian there. His history is very curious and would interest you, who like wonderful things."

"Can you tell it me?"

"Not correctly, as I never heard it from himself. But I believe he has no objection to tell it—with the exception of the political trans-actions in which he was concerned, and which caused his being sent out of the Austrian dominions; that part of it I believe he thinks it prudent not to allude to. We'll ask him to dinner, if you'll meet him, and perhaps we may persuade him to tell the story."

Accordingly, the meeting took place; we dined *en petit comité*, (in a small committee)—and the count very good-naturedly yielded to our request; "but you must excuse me," he said, "beginning a long way back for my story commences three hundred years ago.

"Our family claims to be of great antiquity, but we were not very wealthy till about the latter half of the 16th century, when Count Jacopo Ferraldi made very considerable additions to the property; not only by getting, but also by saving—he was in fact a miser. Before that period the Ferraldis had been warriors, and we could boast of many distinguished deeds of arms recorded in our annals; but Jacopo, although by the death of his brother, he ultimately inherited, the title and the estates, had begun life as a younger son, and being dissatisfied with his portion, had resolved to increase it by commerce.

"Florence then was a very different city to what it is now; trade flourished, and its merchants had correspondence and large dealings with all the chief cities of Europe. My ancestor invested his little fortune so judiciously, or so fortunately, that he trebled it in his first venture; and as people grow rapidly rich who gain and don't spend, he soon had wealth to his heart's content—but I am wrong in using that term as applied to him—he was never content with his gains but still worked on to add to them, for he grew to love the money for itself, and not for what it might purchase.

"At length, his two elder brothers died, and as they left no issue he succeeded to their inheritance and dwelt in the palace of his ancestors; but instead of circulating his riches he hoarded them; and being too miserly to entertain his friends and neighbours, he lived like an anchorite in his splendid halls, exulting in his possessions but never enjoying them. His great pleasure and chief occupation seems to have been counting his money, which he kept either hidden in strange out-of-the-way places, or in strong iron chests, clamped to the floors and walls.

"But notwithstanding those precautions and that he guarded it like a watchdog, to his great dismay he one day missed a sum of two thousand pounds which he had concealed in an ingeniously contrived receptacle under the floor of his dining-room, the existence of which was only known to the man who made it; at least, so he believed. Small as was this sum in proportion to what he possessed the shock was tremendous; he rushed out of his house like a madman with the intention of dragging the criminal to justice, but when he arrived at the man's shop he found him in bed and at the point of death. His friends and the doctor swore that he had not quitted it for a fortnight; in short, according to their shewing, he was taken ill on his return from working at the count's, the very day he finished the job.

"If this were true, he could not be the thief, as the money was not deposited there till some days afterwards, and although the count had his doubts, it was not easy to disprove what everybody swore, more especially as the man died on the following day and was buried. Baffled and furious, he next fell foul of his two servants—he kept but two, for he only inhabited a small part of the palace. There was not the smallest reason to suspect them, nor to suppose they knew anything of the hiding place, for every precaution had been used to conceal it; moreover, he had found it locked as he himself had locked it after depositing the money, and he was quite sure the key had never been absent from his own person. Nevertheless, he discharged them and took no others.

"The thief, whoever he was, had evinced so much ingenuity, that he trembled to think what such skill might compass with opportunity. So, he resolved to afford none; and henceforth to have his meals sent in from a neighbouring eating-house, and to have a person once a week to sweep and clean his rooms, whom he could keep an eye on while it was doing. As he had no clue to the perpetrators of the robbery, and the man whom he had most reason to suspect was dead, he took no further steps in the business, but kept it quiet lest he should draw too much attention towards his secret hoards; nevertheless, though externally calm, the loss preyed upon his mind and caused him great anguish.

"Shortly after this occurrence, he received a letter from a sister of his who had several years before married an Englishman, saying that her husband was dead, and it being advisable that her dear and only son should enter into commerce, that she was going to send him to Florence, feeling assured that her brother would advise him for the best, and enable him to employ the funds he brought with him advantageously.

"This was not pleasing intelligence; he did not want to promote any body's interest but his own, and he felt that the young man would be a spy on his actions, an intruder in his house, and no doubt an expectant and greedy heir, counting the hours till he died; for this sister and her family were his nearest of kin, and would inherit if he left no will to the contrary. However, his arrival could not be prevented; letters travelled slowly in those days, and ere his could reach England his nephew would have quitted it, so he resolved to give him a cold reception and send him back as soon as he could.

"In the meantime, the young man had started on his journey, full of hope and confidence, and immediately on his arrival hastened to present himself to this rich uncle who was to shew him the path he had himself followed to fortune. It was not for his own sake alone he coveted riches, but his mother and sister were but poorly provided for, and they had collected the whole of their little fortune and risked it upon this venture, hoping, with the aid of their relative, to be amply repaid for the present sacrifice.

"A fine open countenanced lad was Arthur Allen, just twenty years of age; such a face and figure had not beamed upon those old halls for many a day. Well brought up and well instructed too; he spoke Italian as well as English, his mother having accustomed him to it from infancy.

"Though he had heard his uncle was a miser, he had no conception of the amount to which the mania had arisen; and his joyous anticipations were somewhat damped when he found himself so coldly received, and when he looked into those hard grey eyes and contracted features that had never expanded with a genial smile; so fearing the old man might be apprehensive that he had come as an applicant for assistance to set him up in trade, he hastened to inform him of the true state of the case, saying that they had got together two thousand pounds.

"'Of course, my mother,' he said, 'would not have entrusted my inexperience with such a sum; but she desired me to place it in your hands, and to act entirely under your direction.'

"To use the miser's own expression—for we have learnt all these particulars from a memoir left by himself—'When I heard these words the devil entered into me, and I bade the youth bring the money and dine with me on the following day.'

"I daresay you will think the devil had entered into him long before; however, now he recognised his presence, but that did not deter him from following his counsel.

"'Pleased that he had so far thawed his uncle's frigidity, Arthur arrived the next day with his money bags at the appointed hour and was received in an inner chamber; their contents were inspected and counted, and then placed in one of the old man's iron chests. Soon afterwards the tinkle of a bell announced that the waiter from the neighbouring *traiteur's* (caterer's) had brought the dinner, and the host left the room to see that all was ready. Presently he re-entered and led his guest to the table. The repast was not sumptuous, but there was a bottle of old Lacryma Christi which he much recommended and which the youth tasted with great satisfaction. But strange! He had no sooner swallowed the first glass, than his eyes began to stare—there was a gurgle in his throat—a convulsion passed over his face—and his body stiffened.

"'I did not look up,' says the old man in his memoir, 'for I did not like to see the face of the boy that had sat down so hearty to his dinner, so I kept on eating mine—but I heard the gurgle, and I knew what had happened; and presently lest the servant should come to fetch the dinner things, I pushed the table aside and opened the receptacle from which my two thousand pounds had been stolen—curses on the thief! and I laid the body in it, and the wine therewith. I locked it and drove in two strong nails. Then I put back the table—moved away the lad's chair and plate, unlocked the door which was fast, and sat down to finish my dinner. I could not help chuckling as I ate, to think how his had been spoilt.

"'I closed up that apartment, as I thought there might be a smell that would raise observation, and I selected one on the opposite side of the gallery for my dining-room. All went well till the following day. I counted my two thousand pounds again and again, and I kept gloating over the recovery of it—for I felt as if it was my own money, and that I had a right to seize it where I could. I wrote also to my sister, saying, that her son had not arrived; but that when he did, I would do my best to forward his views. My heart was light that day—they say that's a bad sign.

"'Yes, all was so far well; but the next day we were two of us at dinner! And yet I had invited no guest; and the next and the next, and so on always! As I was about to sit down, he entered and took a chair opposite me, an unbidden guest. I ceased dining at home, but it made no difference; he came, dine where I would. This preyed upon me; I tried not to mind, but I could not help it. Argument was vain. I lost my appetite and was reduced nearly to death's door. At last, driven to desperation, I consulted Fra Guiseppe. He had been a fast fellow in his time, and it was said had been too impatient for his father's succession; howbeit, the old man died suddenly; Guiseppe spent the money and then took to religion. I thought he was a proper person to consult, so I told him my case.

"'He recommended repentance and restitution. I tried, but I could not repent, for I had got the money; but I thought, perhaps, if I parted with it to another, I might be released; so I looked about for an advantageous purchase, and hearing that Bartolomeo Malfi was in difficulties, I offered him two thousand pounds, money down, for his land—I knew it was worth three times the sum. We signed the agreement, and then I went home and opened the door of the room where it was; but lo! he sat there upon the chest where the money was fast locked, and I could not get it. I peeped in two or three times, but he was always there; so, I was obliged to expend other moneys in this purchase, which vexed me, albeit the bargain was a good one.

"'Then I consulted friend Guiseppe again, and he said nothing would do but restitution—but that was hard, so I waited; and I said to myself, I'll eat and care not whether he sit there or no. But woe be to him! he chilled the marrow of my bones, and I could not away with him; so, I said one day, "What if I go to England with the money?"

and he bowed his head.

"The old man accordingly took the moneybags from the chest and started for England. His sister and her daughter were still living in the house they had inhabited during the husband's lifetime; in short, it was their own; and being attached to the place they hoped, if the young man succeeded in his undertakings, to be able to keep it. It was a small house with a garden full of flowers, which the ladies cultivated themselves.

"The village church was close at hand, and the churchyard adjoined the garden. The poor ladies had become very uneasy at not hearing of Arthur's arrival; and when the old man presented himself and declared he had never seen anything of him, great was their affliction and dismay; for it was clear that either some misfortune had happened to the boy, or he had appropriated the money and gone off in some other direction. They scarcely admitted the possibility of the last contingency, although it was the one their little world universally adopted, in spite of his being a very well conducted and affectionate youth; but people said it was too great a temptation for his years and blamed his mother for entrusting him with so much money. Whichever it was, the blow fell very heavy on them in all ways, for Arthur was their sole stay and support, and they loved him dearly.

"Since he had set out on this journey, the old man had been relieved from the company of his terrible guest, and was beginning to recover himself a little, but it occasioned him a severe pang when he remembered that this immunity was to be purchased with the sacrifice of two thousand pounds, and he set himself to think how he could jockey the ghost. But while he was deliberating on this subject, an event happened that alarmed him for the immediate safety of the money.

"He had found on the road, that the great weight of a certain chest he brought with him had excited observation whenever his luggage had to be moved; on his arrival two labouring men had been called in to carry it into the house, and he had overheard some remarks that induced him to think they had drawn a right conclusion with regard to its contents. Subsequently, he saw these two men hovering about the house in a suspicious manner, and he was afraid to leave: it or to go to sleep at night, lest he should be robbed.

"So far we learn from Jocopo Ferraldi himself; but there the memoir stops. Tradition says that he was found one morning murdered in his bed and his chest rifled. All the family, that is the mother and

94

daughter and their one servant, were accused of the murder; and notwithstanding their protestation of innocence were declared guilty and executed.

"The memoir I have quoted was found on his dressing table, and he appears to have been writing it when he was surprised by the assassins; for the last words were—'I think I've baulked them, and nobody will understand the—' then comes a large blot and a mark, as if the pen had fallen out of his hand. It seems wonderful that this man, so suspicious and secretive, should thus have entrusted to paper what it was needful he should conceal; but the case is not singular; it has been remarked in similar instances, when some dark mystery is pressing on a human soul, that there exists an irresistible desire to communicate it, notwithstanding the peril of betrayal; and when no other confident can be found, the miserable wretch has often had recourse to paper.

"The family of Arthur Allen being now extinct, a cousin of Jacopo's, who was a penniless soldier, succeeded to the title and estate, and the memoir, with a full account of what had happened, being forwarded to Italy, enquiries were made about the missing two thousand pounds; but it was not forthcoming; and it was at first supposed that the ladies had had some accomplice who had carried it off. Subsequently, however, one of the two men who had borne the money chest into the house, at the period of the old man's arrival, was detected in endeavouring to dispose of some Italian gold coin and a diamond ring, which Jacopo was in the habit of wearing.

"This led to investigation, and he ultimately confessed to the murder committed by himself and his companion, thus exonerating the unfortunate woman. He nevertheless declared that they had not rifled the strong box, as they could not open it, and were disturbed by the barking of a dog before they could search for the keys. The box itself they were afraid to carry away, it being a remarkable one and liable to attract notice; and that therefore their only booty was some loose coin and some jewels that were found on the old man's person. But this was not believed, especially as his accomplice was not to be found, and appeared, on enquiry, to have left that part of the country immediately after the catastrophe.

"There the matter rested for nearly two centuries and a half. Nobody sorrowed for Jacopo Ferraldi, and the fate of the Allens was a matter of indifference to the public, who was glad to see the estate fall into the hands of his successor, who appears to have made a much better use of his riches. The family in the long period that elapsed, had many vicissitudes; but at the period of my birth my father inhabited the same old palace, and we were in tolerably affluent circumstances. I was born there, and I remember as a child the curiosity I used to feel about the room with the secret receptacle under the floor where Jacopo had buried the body of his guest. It had been found there and received Christian burial; but the receptacle still remained, and the room was shut up being said to be haunted. I never saw anything extraordinary, but I can bear witness to the frightful groans and moans that issued from it sometimes at night, when, if I could persuade anybody to accompany me, I used to stand in the gallery and listen with wonder and awe. But I never passed the door alone, nor would any of the servants do so after dark. There had been an attempt made to exclude the sounds by walling up the door; but so far from this succeeding they became twenty time worse, and as the wall was a disfigurement as well as a failure, the unquiet spirit was placated by taking it down again.

"The old man's memoir is always preserved amongst the family papers, and his picture still hangs in the gallery. Many strangers who have heard something of this extraordinary story, have asked to see it. The palace is now inhabited by an Austrian nobleman,—whether the ghost continues to annoy the inmates by his lamentations I do not know.

"I now," said Count Francesco, "come to my personal history. Political reasons a few years since obliged me to quit Italy with my family, I had no resources except a little ready money that I had brought with me, and I had resolved to utilise some musical talent which I had cultivated for my amusement. I had not voice enough to sing in public, but I was capable of giving lessons and was considered, when in Italy, a successful amateur. I will not weary you with the sad details of my early residence in England; you can imagine the difficulties that an unfortunate foreigner must encounter before he can establish a connexion.

"Suffice it to say that my small means where wholly exhausted, and that very often I, and what was worse, my wife and child were in want of bread, and indebted to one of my more prosperous countrymen for the very necessaries of life. I was almost in despair, and I do not know what rash thing I might have done if I had been a single man; but I had my family depending on me, and it was my duty not to sink under my difficulties however great they were.

"One night I had been singing at the house of a nobleman, in St.

James's Square, and had received some flattering compliments from a young man who appeared to be very fond of Italian music, and to understand it. My getting to this party was a stroke of good luck in the first instance, for I was quite unknown to the host, but Signor A. an acquaintance of mine, who had been engaged for the occasion, was taken ill at the last moment, and had sent me with a note of introduction to supply his place.

"I knew, of course, that I should be well paid for my services, but I would have gladly accepted half the sum I expected if I could have had it that night, for our little treasury was wholly exhausted, and we had not sixpence to purchase a breakfast for the following day. When the great hall door shut upon me, and I found myself upon the pavement, with all that luxury and splendour on one side, and I and my desolation on the other, the contrast struck me cruelly, for I too had been rich, and dwelt in illuminated palaces, and had a train of liveried servants at my command, and sweet music had echoed through my halls. I felt desperate and drawing my hat over my eyes I began pacing the square, forming wild plans for the relief or escape from my misery. No doubt I looked frantic; for you know we Italians have such a habit of gesticulating, that I believe my thoughts were accompanied by movements that must have excited notice; but I was too much absorbed to observe anything, till I was roused by a voice saying, 'Signor Ferraldi, still here this damp chilly night! Are you not afraid for your voice—it is worth taking care of.'

"'To what purpose,' I said savagely, 'It will not give me bread!'

"If the interruption had not been so sudden, I should not have made such an answer, but I was surprised into it before I knew who had addressed me. When I looked up I saw it was the young man I had met at Lord L.'s, who had complimented me on my singing. I took off my hat and begged his pardon, and was about to move away, when he took my arm.

"'Excuse me,' he said, 'let us walk together,' and then after a little pause, he added, with an apology, 'I think you are an exile.'

"'I am,' I said.

"'And I think,' he continued, 'I have surprised you out of a secret that you would not voluntarily have told me. I know well the hardships that beset many of your countrymen—as good gentlemen as we are ourselves—when you are obliged to leave your country; and I beg therefore you will not think me impertinent or intrusive, if I beg you to be frank with me and tell me how you are situated!'

"This offer of sympathy was evidently so sincere, and it was so welcome, at such a moment, that I did not hesitate to comply with my new friend's request—I told him everything—adding that in time I hoped to get known, and that then I did not fear being able to make my way; but that meanwhile we were in danger of starving.

"During this conversation we were walking round and round the square, where in fact he lived. Before we parted at his own door, he had persuaded me to accept of a gift, I call it, for he had then no reason to suppose I should ever be able to repay him, but he called it an advance of ten guineas upon some lessons I was to give him; the first instalment of which was to be paid the following day.

"I went home with a comparatively light heart, and the next morning waited on my friendly pupil, whom I found, as I expected, a very promising scholar. He told me with a charming frankness, that he had not much influence in fashionable society, for his family, though rich, was *parvenue*, but he said he had two sisters, as fond of music as himself, who would be shortly in London, and would be delighted to take lessons, as I had just the voice they liked to sing with them.

"This was the first auspicious incident that had occurred to me, nor did the omen fail in its fulfilment. I received great kindness from the family when they came to London. I gave them lessons, sung at their parties, and they took every opportunity of recommending me to their friends.

"When the end of the season approached, however, I felt somewhat anxious about the future—there would be no parties to sing at, and my pupils would all be leaving town; but my new friends, whose name, by the way, was Greathead, had a plan for me in their heads, which they strongly recommended me to follow. They said they had a house in the country with a large neighbourhood—in fact, near a large watering-place; and that if I went there during the summer months, they did not doubt my getting plenty of teaching; adding, 'We are much greater people there than we are here, you see; and our recommendation will go a great way.'

"I followed my friend's advice, and soon after they left London, I joined them at Salton, which was the name of their place. As I had left my wife and children in town, with very little money, I was anxious that they should join me as soon as possible; and therefore, the morning after my arrival, I proceeded to look for a lodging at S., and to take measures to make my object known to the residents and visitors there. My business done, I sent my family directions for their journey, and then returned to Salton to spend a few days, as I had promised my kind patrons.

"The house was modern, in fact it had been built by Mr. Greathead's grandfather, who was the architect of their fortunes; the grounds were extensive, and the windows looked on a fine lawn, a picturesque ruin, a sparkling rivulet, and a charming flower-garden; there could not be a prettier view than that we enjoyed while sitting at breakfast. It was my first experience of the lovely and graceful English homes, and it fully realised all my expectations, both within doors and without. After breakfast Mr. Greathead and his son asked me to accompany them round the grounds, as they were contemplating some alterations.

"'Among other things,' said Mr. G., 'we want to turn this rivulet; but my wife has a particular fancy for that old hedge, which is exactly in the way, and she won't let me root it up.'

"The hedge alluded to enclosed two sides of the flower-garden, but seemed rather out of place, I thought.

"'Why?' said I. 'What is Mrs. Greathead's attachment to the hedge?'

"'Why? it's very old; it formerly bordered the churchyard, for that old ruin you see there, is all that remains of the parish church; and this flower-garden, I fancy, is all the more brilliant for the rich soil of the burial-ground. But what is remarkable is, that the hedge and that side of the garden are full of Italian flowers, and always have been so as long as anybody can remember. Nobody knows how it happens, but they must spring up from some old seeds that have been long in the ground. Look at this cyclamen growing wild in the hedge.'

"The subject of the alterations was renewed at dinner, and Mrs. Greathead, still objecting to the removal of the hedge, her younger son, whose name was Harry, said, 'It is very well for mamma to pretend it is for the sake of the flowers, but I am quite sure that the real reason is that she is afraid of offending the ghost.'

"'What nonsense, Harry,' she said. 'You must not believe him, Mr. Ferraldi.'

"'Well mamma,' said the boy, 'you know you will never be convinced that that was not a ghost you saw.'

"'Never mind what it was,' she said; 'I won't have the hedge removed.' Presently, she added, 'I suppose you would laugh at the idea of anybody believing in a ghost, Mr. Ferraldi.'

"'Quite the contrary,' I answered; 'I believe in them myself, and upon very good grounds, for we have a celebrated ghost in our family.'

"'Well,' she said, 'Mr. Greathead and the boys laugh at me; but when I came to live here, upon the death of Mr. Greathead's grand-father,—for his father never inhabited the place, having died by an accident before the old gentleman,—I had never heard a word of the place being haunted; and, perhaps, I should not have believed it if I had. But, one evening, when the younger children were gone to bed, and Mr. Greathead and George were sitting with some friends in the dining-room, I, and my sister, who was staying with me, strolled into the garden. It was in the month of August, and a bright starlight night. We were talking on a very interesting matter, for my sister had that day, received an offer from the gentleman she afterwards married.

"'I mention that, to show you that we were not thinking of any-thing supernatural, but, on the contrary, that our minds were quite absorbed with the subject we were discussing. I was looking on the ground, as one often does, when listening intently to what another person is saying; my sister was speaking, when she suddenly stopped, and laid her hand on my arm, saying, "Who's that?"

"'I raised my eyes and saw, not many yards from us, an old man, withered and thin, dressed in a curious antique fashion, with a high peaked hat on his head. I could not conceive who he could be, or what he could be doing there, for it was close to the flower-garden; so, we stood still to observe him. I don't know whether you saw the remains of an old tombstone in a corner of the garden? It is said to be that of a former rector of the parish; the date, 1550, is still legible upon it. The old man walked from one side of the hedge to that stone and seemed to be counting his steps. He walked like a person pacing the ground, to measure it; then he stopped, and appeared to be noting the result of his measurement with a pencil and paper he held in his hand; then he did the same thing, the other side of the hedge, pacing up to the tombstone and back.

"'There was a talk, at that time, of removing the hedge, and dig-ging up the old tombstone; and it occurred to me, that my husband might have been speaking to somebody about it, and that this man might be concerned in the business, though, still, his dress and appear-ance puzzled me. It seemed odd, too, that he took no notice of us; and I might have remarked, that we heard no footsteps, though we were quite close enough to do so; but these circumstances did not strike me then. However, I was just going to advance, and ask him what he was doing? when I felt my sister's hand relax the hold she had of my arm, and she sank to the ground; at the same instant I lost sight of the mysterious old man, who suddenly disappeared.

"'My sister had not fainted; but she said her knees had bent under her, and she had slipped down, collapsed by terror. I did not feel very comfortable myself, I assure you; but I lifted her up, and we hastened back to the house and told what we had seen. The gentlemen went out, and, of course, saw nothing, and laughed at us; but shortly afterwards, when Harry was born, I had a nurse from the village, and she asked me one day, if I had ever happened to see "the old gentleman that walks!" I had ceased to think of the circumstance, and inquired what old gentleman she meant? and then she told me that, long ago, a foreign gentleman had been murdered here; that is, in the old house that Mr. Greathead's grandfather pulled down when he built this; and that, ever since, the place has been haunted, and that nobody will pass by the hedge, and the old tombstone after dark; for that is the spot to which the ghost confines himself.'

"'But I should think,' said I, 'that so far from desiring to preserve these objects, you would rather wish them removed, since the ghost would, probably, cease to visit the spot at all.'

"'Quite the contrary,' answered Mrs. G, 'The people of the neighbourhood say, that the former possessor of the place entertained the same idea, and had resolved to remove them; but that then, the old man became very troublesome, and was even seen in the house; the nurse positively assured me, that her mother had told her, old Mr. Greathead had also intended to remove them; but that he quite suddenly counter-ordered the directions he had given, and, though he did not confess to anything of the sort, the people all believed that he had seen the ghost. Certain, it is, that this hedge has always been maintained by the proprietors of the place.'

"The young men laughed and quizzed their mother for indulging in such superstitions; but the lady was quite firm in her opposition, alleging, that independently of all considerations connected with the ghost, she liked the hedge on account of the wild Italian flowers; and she liked the old tombstone on account of its antiquity.

"Consequently, some other plan was devised for Mr. Greathead's alterations, which led the course of the rivulet quite clear of the hedge and the tombstone.

"In a few days, my family arrived, and I established myself at S., for the summer. The speculation answered very well, and through the recommendations of Mr. and Mrs. Greathead, and their personal kindness to myself and my wife, we passed the time very pleasantly. When the period for our returning to London approached, they invited us to spend a fortnight with them before our departure, and, accordingly, the day we gave up our lodgings, we removed to Salton.

"Preparations for turning the rivulet had then commenced; and soon after my arrival, I walked out with Mr. Greathead to see the works. There was a boy, about fourteen, amongst the labourers; and while we were standing close to him, he picked up something, and handed it to Mr. G., saying, 'Is this yours, sir?' which, on examination, proved to be a gold coin of the sixteenth century,—the date on it was 1545. Presently, the boy who was digging, picked up another, and then, several more.

"'This becomes interesting,' said Mr. Greathead, 'I think we are coming upon some buried treasure,' and he whispered to me, that he had better not leave the spot.

"'Accordingly, he did stay, till it was time to dress for dinner; and, feeling interested, I remained also. In the interval, many more coins were found; and when he went in, he dismissed the workmen, and sent a servant to watch the place,—for he saw by their faces, that if he had not happened to be present he would, probably, never have heard of the circumstance. A few more turned up the following day, and then the store seemed exhausted. When the villagers heard of this money being discovered, they all looked upon it as the explanation of the old gentleman haunting that particular spot. No doubt he had buried the money, and it remained to be seen, whether now, that it was found, his spirit would be at rest.

"My two children were with me at Salton on this occasion. They slept in a room on the third floor, and one morning, my wife having told me that the younger of the two seemed unwell, I went upstairs to look at her. It was a cheerful room, with two little white beds in it, and several old prints and samplers, and bits of work such as you see in nurseries, framed and hung against the wall. After I had spoken to the child, and while my wife was talking to the maid, I stood with my hands in my pockets, idly looking at these things. Amongst them was one that arrested my attention, because at first, I could not understand it, nor see why this discoloured parchment, with a few lines and dots on it, should have been framed and glazed. There were some words here and there which I could not decipher; so, I lifted the frame off the nail and carried it to the window.

"Then I saw that the words were Italian, written in a crabbed, old-fashioned hand, and the whole seemed to be a plan, or sketch, rudely drawn, of what I at first thought was a camp—but, on closer examination, I saw was part of a churchyard, with tombstones, from one of which lines were drawn to various dots, and along these lines were numbers, and here and there a word as *right, left, &c.* There were also two lines forming a right angle, which intersected the whole, and after contemplating the thing for some time, it struck me that it was a rude sort of map of the old churchyard and the hedge, which had formed the subject of conversation some days before.

"At breakfast, I mentioned what I had observed to Mr. and Mrs. Greathead, and they said they believed it was; it had been found when the old house was pulled down and was kept on account of its antiquity.

"'Of what period is it?' I asked, 'and how happens it to have been made by an Italian?'

"'The last question I can't answer,' said Mr. Greathead; 'but the date is on it, I believe.'

"'No,' said I, 'I examined it particularly—there is no date.'

"'Oh, there is a date and name, I think—but I never examined it myself;' and to settle the question he desired his son Harry to run up and fetch it, adding, 'you know Italian architects and designers of various kinds, were not rare in this country a few centuries ago.'

"Harry brought the frame, and we were confirmed in our conjectures of what it represented, but we could find no date or name.

"'And yet I think I've heard there was one,' said Mr. Greathead. 'Let us take it out of the frame?'

"This was easily done, and we found the date and the name; the count paused, and then added, 'I dare say you can guess it?'

"'Jacopo Ferraldi?' I said.

"'It was,' he answered; and it immediately occurred to me that he had buried the money supposed to have been stolen on the night he was murdered, and that this was a plan to guide him in finding it again. So, I told Mr. Greathead the story I have now told you and mentioned my reasons for supposing that if I was correct in my surmise, more gold would be found.

"With the old man's map as our guide, we immediately set to work—the whole family vigorously joining in the search; and, as I expected, we found that the tombstone in the garden was the point from which all the lines were drawn, and that the dots indicated where the money lay. It was in different heaps, and appeared to have been enclosed in bags, which had rotted away with time. We found the whole sum mentioned in the memoir, and Mr. Greathead being lord of the manor, was generous enough to make it all over to me, as being the lawful heir, which, however, I certainly was not, for it was the spoil of a murderer and a thief, and it properly belonged to the Allens, But that family had become extinct; at least, so we believed, when the two unfortunate ladies were executed, and I accepted the gift with much gratitude and a quiet conscience. It relieved us from our pressing difficulties and enabled me to wait for better times.

"'And,' said I, 'how of the ghost? was he pleased or otherwise, by the *denouement?*'

"'I cannot say,' replied the count; 'I have not heard of his being seen since; I understand, however, that the villagers, who understand these things better than we do, say, that they should not be surprised if he allowed the hedge and tombstone to be removed now without opposition; but Mr. Greathead, on the contrary, wished to retain them as mementoes of these curious circumstances.'

The Dutch Officer's Story

"Well, I think nothing can be so cowardly as to be afraid to own the truth? said the pretty Madame de B., an Englishwoman, who had married a Dutch officer of distinction.

"Are you really venturing to accuse the general of cowardice," said Madame L.

"Yes," said Madame de B , "I want him to tell Mrs. Crowe a ghost story—a thing that he saw himself—and he pooh, poohs it, though he owned it to me before we were married, and since too, saying that he never could have believed such a thing if he had not seen it himself."

While the wife was making this little *tirade*, the husband looked as if she was accusing him of picking somebody's pocket—*il perdait contenance* (he lost his countenance) quite. "Now, look at him," she said, "don't you see guilt in his face, Mrs. Crowe?"

"Decidedly" I answered; "so experienced a seeker of ghost stories as myself cannot fail to recognise the symptoms. I always find that when the circumstances is mere hearsay, and happened to nobody knows who, people are very ready to tell it; when it has happened to one of their own family, they are considerably less communicative, and will only tell it under protest; but when they are themselves the parties concerned, it is the most difficult thing imaginable to induce them to relate the thing seriously, and with its details; they say they have forgotten it, and don't believe it; and as an evidence of their incredulity, they affect to laugh at the whole affair. If the general will tell me the story, I shall think it quite as decisive a proof of courage as he ever gave in the field."

Betwixt bantering and persuasion, we succeeded in our object, and the general began as follows:—

"You know the Belgian Rebellion (he always called it so) took place in 1830. It broke out at Brussels on the 28th of August, and we immediately advanced with a considerable force to attack that city; but as the Prince of Orange hoped to bring the people to reason, without bloodshed, we encamped at Vilvorde, whilst he catered Mussels alone, to hold a conference with the armed people. I was a Lieutenant-Colonel then, and commanded the 20th Foot, to which regiment I had been lately appointed.

"We had been three or four days in cantonment, when I heard two of the men, who were digging a little drain at the back of my tent, talking of Jokel Falck, a private in my regiment, who was noted for his extraordinary disposition to somnolence, one of them remarked that he would certainly have got into trouble for being asleep on his post the previous night, if it had not been for Mungo. 'I don't know how many times he has saved him,' added he.

"To which the other answered, that Mungo was a very valuable friend, and had saved many a man from punishment.

"This was the first time I had ever heard of Mungo, and I rather wondered who it was they alluded to; but the conversation slipped from my mind and I never thought of asking anybody.

"Shortly after this I was going my rounds, being field-officer of the day, when I saw by the moonlight, the sentry at one of the outposts stretched upon the ground. I was some way off when I first perceived him; and I only knew what the object was from the situation, and because I saw the glitter of his accoutrements; but almost at the same moment that I discovered him, I observed a large black Newfoundland dog trotting towards him. The man rose as the dog approached and had got upon his legs before I reached the spot. This occupied the space of about two minutes—perhaps, not so much.

"'You were asleep on your post,' I said; and turning to the mounted orderly that attended me, I told him to go back and bring a file of the guard to take him prisoner, and to send a sentry to relieve him.

"'Non, mon colonel,' said he, and from the way he spoke I perceived he was intoxicated, 'it's all the fault of that damné Mungo. Il m'a manqué (He missed me.)'

"But I paid no attention to what he said and rode on, concluding Mungo was some slang term of the men for drink.

"Some evenings after this, I was riding back from my brother's quarter—he was in the 15th, and was stationed about a mile from us—when I remarked the same dog I had seen before, trot up to a sentry who, with his legs crossed, was leaning against a wall. The man started and began walking backwards and forwards on his beat. I recognised the dog by a large white streak on his side—all the rest of his coat being black.

"When I came up to the man, I saw it was Jokel Falck, and although I could not have said he was asleep, I strongly suspected that that was the fact.

"'You had better take care of yourself, my man,' said I. 'I have half a mind to have you relieved and make a prisoner of you. I believe I should have found you asleep on your post, if that dog had not roused you.'

"Instead of looking penitent, as was usual on these occasions, I saw a half smile on the man's face, as he saluted me.

"'Whose dog is that?' I asked my servant, as I rode away.

"'*Je ne sais pas mon. Colonel*,' he answered, smiling too.

"On the same evening at mess, I heard one of the subalterns say to the officer who sat next him, 'It's a fact, I assure you, and they call him Mungo.'

"'That's a new name they've got for Schnapps, isn't it?' I said.

"'No, sir; it's the name of a dog,' replied the young man, laughing.

"'A black Newfoundland, with a large white streak on his flank?'

"'Yes, sir, I believe that is the description, replied he, tittering still.

"'I have seen that dog two or three times,' said I. 'I saw him this evening—who does he belong to?'

"'Well, sir, that is a difficult question,' answered the lad; and I heard his companion say, 'To Old Nick, I should think.'

"'Do you mean to say you've really seen Mungo?' said somebody at the table.

"'If Mungo is a large Newfoundland—black, with a white streak on its side—I saw him just now. Who does he belong to?'

"By this time, the whole mess table was in a titter, with the exception of one old captain, a man who had been years in the regiment. He was of very humble extraction and had risen by merit to his present position.

"'I believe Captain T. is better acquainted with Mungo than anybody present,' answered Major R., with a sneer. 'Perhaps he can tell you who he belongs to.'

"The laughter increased, and I saw there was some joke, but not understanding what it meant, I said to Captain G., 'Does the dog belong to Jokel Falck?'

"'No, sir,' he replied, 'the dog belongs to nobody now. He once belonged to an officer called Joseph Aveld.'

107

"'Belonging to this regiment?'

"'Yes, sir.'

"'He is dead, I suppose?'

"'Yes, sir, he is.'

"'And the dog has attached himself to the regiment?'

"'Yes, sir.'

"During this conversation, the suppressed laughter continued, and every eye was fixed on Captain T., who answered me shortly, but with the utmost gravity.

"'In fact,' said the major, contemptuously, 'according to Captain T, Mungo is the ghost of a deceased dog.'

"This announcement was received with shouts of laughter, in which I confess I joined, whilst Captain T. still retained an unmoved gravity.

"'It is easier to laugh at such a thing than to believe it, sir,' said he. '*I* believe it, because I know it.'

"I smiled and turned the conversation.

"If anybody at the table except Captain T. had made such an assertion as this, I should have ridiculed them without mercy; but he was an old man, and from the circumstances I have mentioned regarding his origin, we were careful not to offend him; so no more was said about Mungo, and in the hurry of events that followed. I never thought of it again. We marched on to Brussels the next day; and after that, had enough to do till we went to Antwerp, where we were besieged by the French the following year.

"During the siege, I sometimes heard the name of Mungo again; and, one night, when I was visiting the guards and sentries as grand rounds, I caught a glimpse of him, and I felt sure that the man he was approaching when I observed him, had been asleep; but he was screened by an angle of the bastion, and by the time I turned the corner, he was moving about.

"This brought to my mind all I had heard about the dog; and as the circumstance was curious, in any point of view, I mentioned what I had seen to Captain T. the next day, saying, 'I saw your friend Mungo, last night.'

"'Did you, sir?' said he. 'It's a strange thing! No doubt, the man was asleep!'

"'But do you seriously mean to say, that you believe this to be a visionary dog, and not a dog of flesh and blood?'

"'I do, sir; I have been quizzed enough about it; and, once or twice, have nearly got into a quarrel, because people will persist in laughing at what they know nothing about; but as sure as that is a sword you hold in your hand, so sure is that dog a spectre, or ghost—if such a word is applicable to a four-footed beast!'

"'But, it's impossible!' I said. 'What reason have you for such an extraordinary belief!'

"'Why, you know, sir, man-and-boy, I have been in the regiment all my life. I was born in it. My father was pay-sergeant of No. 3 company, when he died; and I have seen Mungo myself, perhaps twenty times, and known, positively, of others seeing him twice as many more.'

"'Very possibly; but that is no proof, that it is not some dog that has attached himself to the regiment.'

"'But I have seen and heard of the dog for fifty years, sir; and my father before me, had seen and heard of him as long!'

"'Well, certainly, that is extraordinary,—if you are sure of it, and that it's the same dog!'

"'It's a remarkable dog, sir. You won't see another like it with that large white streak on his flank. He won't let one of our sentries be found asleep, if he can help; unless, indeed, the fellow is drunk. He seems to have less care of drunkards, but Mungo has saved many a man from punishment. I was once, not a little indebted to him myself. My sister was married out of the regiment, and we had had a bit of a festivity, and drank rather too freely at the wedding, so that when I mounted guard that night—I wasn't to say, drunk, but my head was a little gone, or so; and I should have been caught nodding; but Mungo, knowing, I suppose, that I was not an habitual drunkard, woke me just in time.'

"'How did he wake you?' I asked.

"'I was roused by a short, sharp bark, that sounded close to my ears. I started up and had just time to catch a glimpse of Mungo before he vanished!'

"'Is that the way he always wakes the men?'

"'So they say; and, as they wake, he disappears.'

"I recollected now, that on each occasion when I had observed the dog, I had, somehow, lost sight of him in an instant; and, my curiosity being awakened, I asked Captain T., if ours were the only men he took charge of, or, whether he showed the same attention to those of other regiments?

"'Only the 20th, sir; the tradition is, that after the Battle of Fontenoy, a large black mastiff was found lying beside a dead officer. Although he had a dreadful wound from a sabre cut on his flank, and was much exhausted from loss of blood, he would not leave the body; and even after we buried it, he could not be enticed from the spot. The men, interested by the fidelity and attachment of the animal, bound up his wounds, and fed and tended him; and he became the dog of the regiment. It is said, that they had taught him to go his rounds before the guards and sentries were visited, and to wake any men that slept. How this may be, I cannot say; but he remained with the regiment till his death and was buried with all the respect they could show him. Since that, he has shown his gratitude in the way I tell you, and of which you have seen some instances.'

"'I suppose the white streak is the mark of the sabre cut. I wonder you never fired at him.'

"'God forbid sir, I should do such a thing,' said Captain T., looking sharp round at me. 'It's said that a man did so once, and that he never had any luck afterwards; that may be a superstition, but I confess I wouldn't take a good deal to do it.'

"'If, as you believe, it's a spectre, it could not be hurt, you know; I imagine ghostly dogs are impervious to bullets.'

"'No doubt, sir; but I shouldn't like to try the experiment. Besides, it would be useless, as I am convinced already.'

"I pondered a good deal upon this conversation with the old captain. I had never for a moment entertained the idea that such a thing was possible. I should have as much expected to meet the minotaur or a flying dragon as a ghost of any sort, especially the ghost of a dog; but the evidence here was certainly startling. I had never observed anything like weakness and credulity about T.; moreover, he was a man of known courage, and very much respected in the regiment. In short, so much had his earnestness on the subject staggered me, that I resolved whenever it was my turn to visit the guards and sentries, that I would carry a pistol with me ready primed and loaded, in order to settle the question.

"If T. was right, there would be an interesting fact established, and no harm done; if, as I could not help suspecting, it was a cunning trick of the men, who had trained this dog to wake them, while they kept up the farce of the spectre, the animal would be well out of the way; since their reliance on him no doubt led them to give way to drowsiness when they would otherwise have struggled against it; indeed, though none of our men had been detected—thanks, perhaps, to Mungo—there had been so much negligence lately in the garrison that the general had issued very severe orders on the subject.

"However, I carried my pistol in vain; I did not happen to fall in with Mungo; and sometime afterwards, on hearing the thing alluded to at the mess-table, I mentioned what I had done, adding, 'Mungo is too knowing, I fancy, to run the risk of getting a bullet in him.'

"'Well,' said Major R., 'I should like to have a shot at him, I confess. If I thought I had any chance of seeing him, I'd certainly try it; but I've never seen him at all.'

"'Your best chance,' said another, 'is when Jokel Falck is on duty. He is such a sleepy scoundrel, that the men say if it was not for Mungo he'd pass half his time in the guard house.'

"'If I could catch him I'd put an ounce of lead into him; that he may rely on.'

"'Into Jokel Falck, sir?' said one of the subs, laughing.

"'No, sir,' replied Major R.; 'into Mungo—and I'll do it, too.'

"'Better not, sir,' said Captain T., gravely; provoking thereby a general titter round the table.

"Shortly after this, as I was one night going to my quarter, I saw a mounted orderly ride in and call out a file of the guard to take a prisoner.

"'What's the matter?' I asked.

"'One of the sentries asleep on his post, sir; I believe it's Jokel Falck.'

"'It will be the last time, whoever it is,' I said; 'for the general is determined to shoot the next man that's caught.'

"'I should have thought Mungo had stood Jokel Falck's friend, so often that he'd never have allowed him to be caught,' said the adjutant 'Mungo has neglected his duty.'

"'No, sir,' said the orderly, gravely. 'Mungo would have waked him, but Major R. shot at him.'

"'And killed him,' I said.

"'The man made no answer but touched his cap and rode away.

"I heard no more of the affair that night; but the next morning, at a very early hour, my servant woke me, saying that Major R. wished to speak to me. I desired he should be admitted, and the moment he entered the room, I saw by his countenance that something serious had occurred; of course, I thought the enemy had gained some unexpected advantage during the night and sat up in bed inquiring eagerly what had happened.

"To my surprise he pulled out his pocket-handkerchief and burst into tears. He had married a native of Antwerp, and his wife was in the city at this time. The first thing that occurred to me was, that she had met with some accident, and I mentioned her name.

"'No, no,' he said; 'my son, my boy, my poor Fritz!'

"'You know that in our service, every officer first enters his regiment as a private soldier, and for a certain space of time does all the duties of that position. The major's son, Fritz, was thus in his noviciate. I concluded he had been killed by a stray shot, and for a minute or two I remained in this persuasion, the major's speech being choked by his sobs. The first words he uttered were—

"'Would to God I had taken Captain T.'s advice.'

"'About what?' I said. 'What has happened to Fritz?'

"'You know,' said he, 'yesterday I was field officer of the day; and when I was going my rounds last night, I happened to ask my orderly, who was assisting to put on my sash, what men we had told off for the guard. Amongst others, he named Jokel Falck, and remembering the conversation the other day at the mess table, I took one of my pistols out of the holster, and, after loading, put it in my pocket. I did not expect to see the dog, for I had never seen him; but as I had no doubt that the story of the spectre was some dodge of the men, I determined if ever I did, to have a shot at him.

"'As I was going through the Place de Meyer, I fell in with the general, who joined me, and we rode on together, talking of the siege. I had forgotten all about the dog, but when we came to the rampart, above the Bastion du Matte, I suddenly saw exactly such an animal as the one described, trotting beneath us. I knew there must be a sentry immediately below where we rode, though I could not see him, and I had no doubt that the animal was making towards him; so, without saying a word, I drew out my pistol and fired, at the same moment jumping off my horse, in order to look over the bastion, and get a sight of the man. Without comprehending what I was about, the general did the same, and there we saw the sentry lying on his face, fast asleep.'

"'And the body of the dog?' said I.

"'Nowhere to be seen," he answered, 'and yet I must have hit him—I fired bang into him. The general says it must have been a delusion, for he was looking exactly in the same direction, and saw no dog at all—but I am certain I saw him, so did the orderly.'

"'But Fritz?' I said.

"'It was Fritz—Fritz was the sentry,' said the major, with a fresh burst of grief. The court-martial sits this morning, and my boy will be shot, unless interest can be made with the general to grant him a pardon.'

"I rose and dressed myself immediately, but with little hope of success. Poor Fritz being the son of an officer, was against him rather than otherwise—it would have been considered an act of favouritism to spare him. He was shot; his poor mother died of a broken heart, and the major left the service immediately after the surrender of the city."

"And have you ever seen Mungo again?" said I.

"No," he replied; "but I have heard of others seeing him."

"And are you convinced that it was a spectre, and not a dog of flesh and blood?"

"I fancy I was then—but, of course, one can't believe—"

"Oh, no;" I rejoined; "Oh, no; never mind facts, if they don't fit into our theories."

The Old French Gentleman's Story

I spent the summer of fifty-six at Dieppe—a charming watering-place for those who can bear an exciting air and are not very particular about what they eat. Dieppe, as travellers see it who are hurrying through to Paris, has a most unpromising aspect, with its muddy basins and third and fourth rate inns on the quays, but if you are not hastening from the packet to the train, which the great proportion of people do; you have only to pass up one of the short streets you will see *en face*, when you issue from the Custom-House, into which you have been introduced on landing, and you will find yourself on an esplanade of considerable extent, with a wide expanse of clear salt water before you, a fine terrace walk along the shore, and several newly erected hotels opposite the sea.

Of course, there is an *etablissement* where the usual amusements are provided; the bathing is excellent, and the company numerous, for Dieppe is the favourite watering place of the fashionable world of Paris. The beauty of the place is greatly increased by a judicious suggestion of the emperor's. I was told that when he and the empress were there in '55, they complained of the absence of flowers on the esplanade; it was objected that none would grow there; however, he recommended them to try hollyhocks, china-asters, and poppies, the latter are the finest I ever saw, and the brilliant and varied masses of colour produce a very good effect. But they do not feed you well here; '*La Viande est longue* à *Dieppe*' (Meat is long in Dieppe) as the *garçon* of the Hotel Royal urged when I objected to the meat which, on application of the knife fell into strips of packthread; the poultry is lean and bad; fish scarce, because it all goes to London or Paris, by contract, and everything dear. Nevertheless, Dieppe is a very nice place and the surrounding country is exceedingly pretty and picturesque.

Some members of the Jockey Club were in the Hotel Royal, living very fast indeed. They all bore very aristocratic names and titles, but not the impress of high blood. How should they? Judging from what I saw, such a course of profligate self-indulgence, unredeemed, even by good breeding, must have effaced the stamp, if it ever was there. They inhabited a pavilion in the *cour*, (court), and the luxurious repasts that we constantly saw served to them gave us an awful idea of the amount of their bill. They played at cards all day—the live long summer day! And only suspended this amusement when the *garçon* appeared with their trays loaded with expensive wines and high-seasoned dishes.

One other amusement they had, which was no less an amusement to us—they had a drag—a regular English four-in-hand. The *cour* of the hotel was divided from the road by iron rails, with a large gate at each extremity for carriages, so that to an English whip, nothing would have been easier than to drive in at one of these gates, and round the sweep, and out at the other; but this the jockey club could never accomplish; when the gentlemen took the reins from the coachman, if they were in, they could not get out; and if they were out, they could not get in; so after a few ambitious attempts and ignominious failures, they submitted to the inglorious expediency of mounting and dismounting outside the gates. The French have certainly a remarkable incapacity for riding or driving, which is strange, as they are active men and have generally light figures. The emperor is almost the only Frenchman I ever saw ride well; but he rides like an English gentleman.

There were many elegantly dressed women, of all nations, at Dieppe, but there was one who particularly attracted my attention, and for whom, when I afterwards heard her story, I felt an extraordinary interest. This was the Countess Adeline de-Givry-Monjerac, at least so I will call her here. When I first saw her, she was going down to bathe, attended by her maid, a grave elderly person, and I was so much struck by her appearance, that I took the first opportunity of enquiring her name. She was tall and very pale, with fine, straight features, and an expression of countenance at once noble and melancholy. Her figure was so good, and her bearing at once so graceful and dignified, that her unusual height did not strike you till you saw her standing beside other women. She was leaning on her maid's arm, and stooped a little, apparently from feebleness. Her attire was a *peignoir* of grey taffetas, lined with blue, and on her head she wore a simple *capote* of the same. Her age, I judged to be about forty.

She lodged in the Hotel Royal, as I did also, but lived entirely in private; and we only saw her there as she went in and out. Later in the season, the Duchesse de B., and other persons, arrived from Paris, with whom she was acquainted, and I often observed her in conversation with them on the promenade; but her countenance never lost its expression of melancholy. However, I should have left Dieppe, ignorant of the singular circumstances I am about to relate, but for an accident.

There was a verandah in the court of the hotel, in which many of us preferred to breakfast, rather than in the salon; and the verandah not being very extensive, and the candidates numerous, there was often a little difficulty in securing a table. One morning, I had just laid my parasol on the only one I saw vacant, when the *garçon* warned me that it was already engaged by *ce monsieur,* indicating an old gentleman, who was standing with his back to me, in conversation with one of a sisterhood called *Soeurs de la Providence,* who was soliciting him to buy some of the lottery tickets she held in her hand; they were for the *Loterie de Bienfaisance,* the proceeds of which are devoted to charitable purposes.

There are innumerable lotteries of this, sort in France, authorised by the government; and they seem to me to be the substitute for our magnificent private charities in England, for very large sums are collected. The tickets only cost a *franc.* I believe the *tirage* (draw)is conducted with perfect fairness; and people thus subscribe *franc* for the poor, with the agreeable, but very remote, chance of being repaid, *même ici bas,* (even here low) a hundred thousand-fold.

The old gentleman turned his head on hearing my conversation with the waiter; and, begging I would not derange myself on his account, desired that I might have the table. Grateful for such an unusual exertion of politeness—for the politeness of the modern French gentleman does not include the smallest modicum of self-sacrifice—I modestly declined, and said, "I would wait." He answered, "by no means." And while we were engaged in this amicable contest, the waiter brought his breakfast, and placed it on the table; seeing which, he proposed, that as he was denied the pleasure of making way for me, I should have my coffee placed on the other side, and we should breakfast together; an offer which I gladly accepted.

He was a pleasant, garrulous, old gentleman. Monsieur de Vennacour was his name, *proprietaire à Paris,* and he told me how he had lost his fortune by the revolutions, and how he lived now in a *petit apartment* in the *Rue des Ecuries d'Anjou,* and belonged to a coterie of old ladies and gentlemen like himself, who had a *petit whisk* every night during the winter. While we were talking, the countess passed us on her way to the bath; and, happening to catch her eye as she crossed the court, he bowed to her; whereupon I asked him if he knew her?

"A little," he said; "but I knew her husband well; and her mother's hotel was next to that my family formerly inhabited. She was a beautiful woman, Madame de Lignerolles."

"Then, she is dead?" said I.

"No;" he replied. "She has retired from the world,—she is in a convent. *C'est une histoire bien triste celle de Madame de Lignerolles et sa fille, et aussi bien etrange!*" (It is a very sad story that of Madame de Lignerolles and her daughter, and also very strange!)

"If it is not a secret, perhaps you will tell it me?" said I; for I saw that my new acquaintance desired nothing better. He was a famous raconteur: and I wish I could tell the story in English as well, and as dramatically, as he told it me in French; however, I'll repeat it as faithfully as I can.

"Madame de Lignerolles *née* Hermione de Givry, was married early to the Marquis de Lignerolles, without any particular *penchant* for or against the union. The marquis was a great deal older than herself, but it was considered a good match, for he was very rich, and his genealogy was unexceptionable. Not more so, however, than the young lady's; for the de Givry's heraldic tree had apparently sprung from an acorn floated to the west by Deucalion himself. At the period of Hermione's marriage her father, mother, and two brothers, older than herself, still lived.

"Her father, the Comte de Givry had been a younger son, and had inherited the fortune on the death of his elder brother who was killed in a duel the day before he was to have been married to a woman he passionately loved. He died by the hand of one of his most intimate friends, with whom he had never had a word of difference before, and the subject of quarrel was a peacock! But it was always remarked by the world, that the eldest scions of the house of Givry were singularly unfortunate; they seldom prospered in their loves, and if they did, they were sure to die before their hopes were realised.

"People in general called it *a destiny*; others whispered that it was a curse; but the family laughed contemptuously if anyone presumed to hint such a thing in their presence and asserted that it was merely *le hazard*; and as the world in these days is very much disposed to believe in *le hazard*, few persons sought to penetrate further into the cause of these misadventures. However, Hermione's elder brother, Etienne, did

117

not escape his *mauvais destin* (bad destiny); the lady he was engaged to marry was seized with the smallpox, and, from being a pretty person, became a very ugly one. During her illness, he had sworn nothing should break his engagement, and accordingly, disfigured as she was, he married her; but he had better, for both their sakes, have left it alone. He was disgusted and she was jealous; they parted within a month after the wedding, and he was soon after killed by a fall from his horse in the Bois de Boulogne, and died, leaving no issue.

"Upon his decease, the second son, Armande, now the heir, was recalled from Prussia, whither he had gone with his regiment, but they were on the eve of a battle, and it was not consistent with his honour to leave till it was over. He was the first officer that fell in the fight, and thus the hopes of the ancient family of Givry became centred in the offspring of Hermione. But, Adeline, the fair object of my admiration, was the sole fruit of the marriage, and great were the lamentations of the old count and countess that the continuation of this noble stock rested on so frail a tenure, for the child was exceedingly delicate; she outgrew her strength, and for some years was supposed to be *poitrinaire* (consumptive.)

"But, either, thanks to the wonderful care that was bestowed upon her, or to an inherent good constitution, she survived this trying period and grew up to marriageable years, rewarding all the solicitude of her family by her charms and amiability. She was not so beautiful as her mother had been—and even was still—but she was quite sufficiently handsome; and there was so much grace in her movements and her manners, and she had such a noble and pure expression of countenance—a true indication of her character—that Adeline de Lignerolle's perfections were universally admitted by the men, and scarcely denied by the women, insomuch, that these attractions, added to her lineage and fortune, caused her to be looked upon as one of the most desirable matches in the kingdom.

"Her father, the old Marquis de Lignerolles-Givry—for he was constrained to adopt the latter name—had died previous to this period; and as her grandfather Monsieur de Givry undertook the affair of her marriage, numerous were the propositions he privately received, and frequent the closetings and consultations on the subject. In these cases, the more people have, the more they require; and as Adeline had better blood, and more money, than most people, the family exigence in these respects was considerable, and the difficulties that lay in the way of procuring a suitable alliance, manifold.

"She had reached the age of seventeen, and this important point was still unsettled, when she and her mother went to visit a relative of Madame de Lignerolles, who was united to a Portuguese nobleman. On her marriage, she had followed her husband to his own country; but he was now on a mission to the French court; and the Paris season being over, they had taken a *château* on the Loire, for the summer months.

"There were other young people in the house, and all sorts of amusements going on, which no one seemed to enjoy, at first, more than Adeline de Givry; but, at the end of a fortnight, a change began to be observable in her spirits and demeanour, which did not escape the observation of her young companions; and by their means awakened the attention of Madame de Saldanha, their hostess; who hinted to her cousin, Madame de Lignerolles, that Adeline was falling in love with the young Count de la Cruz; at least, such was the opinion of her own daughter, Isabella; adding, that if so abnormal a circumstance, as a young lady choosing her own husband *was* to happen, she could not have fixed on a more desirable individual than Rodriguez de la Cruz,—a man unexceptionable in person, mind, and manners; whose genealogy might vie with that of the De Givry's themselves; and whose name was associated with distinguished deeds of arms during the Holy Wars.

"But this indulgent view of the case was not shared by Madame de Lignerolles. She seemed exceedingly surprised and incredulous; but when the other insisted on the probability of such a result, since the two young people had been residing for six weeks under the same roof; and pointed out to the lady that the assiduous attentions paid by De la Cruz to herself were, doubtless, not without an object, suggesting that that object was to gain her interest in his favour, she evinced so much displeasure and indignation, that Madame de Saldanha apologised and gave up the point, saying, she was very likely mistaken, and that it was a mere fancy of Isabella's.

"Nevertheless, these suspicions were perfectly well founded. De la Cruz was waiting for his father's consent to make his proposals in form; and this consent was only delayed till the old gentleman had time to come to Paris and make the needful inquiries regarding fortune and family; about which, he considered himself entitled to be quite as particular as the De Givry's.

"It was remarked that, from this time, Madame de Lignerolles observed her daughter with a jealous eye, and sought every means of keeping her away from the young Portuguese; added to which, as it afterwards appeared, she severely reproved Adeline for what she called the levity of her conduct.

"Moreover, she hastened her departure; and in a few days after the conversation with Madama de Saldanha, took her leave; saying, that her presence was required by her father, in Paris. To Paris, however, she did not immediately go. There was in Brittany an ancient *château* belonging to the family, which, for some reason or other, they very rarely visited; it was supposed, because they possessed others more agreeable. At all events, whatever might be the cause, it was known that the old count had a mortal aversion to this residence, insomuch, that his daughter had never been there since her infancy; when something very unpleasant was reported to have happened to her mother's eldest brother shortly before his death. Thither, however, they now travelled with all speed, accompanied only by two maids and a man.

"Madame de Lignerolle's was a person, in whom the maternal instinct had never been largely developed. She was even, still, at eight-and-thirty, a beautiful woman; and it was generally suspected, that she did not feel at all delighted at having this tall, handsome daughter, to proclaim her age; and, perhaps shortly, make her a grandmother. But, her manner to Adeline—usually, more indifferent than harsh—now assumed a new character; she seemed engrossed with her own thoughts; was cold and constrained; spoke little; and when she did, it was with a gravity truly portentous.

"They were not unexpected at Château Noir—for such was the ominous name of the old castle, which frowned upon them in the gloom of a dusky November evening; but instead of the liveried servants, by whom they were accustomed to be greeted, an elderly housekeeper, a concierge, and a few rustic menials, appeared to be its only inhabitants. However, they had done their best to make ready for this visit; fires were lighted, and dinner was prepared and served, accompanied by plenty of apologies for its not being better.

"The evening passed in silence; they were tired and went early to bed. The next two days, Mdme. de Lignerolles kept her room, and Adeline strolled about the neglected grounds, occupied with her own thoughts of the future, not without wondering a little at her mother's mysterious behaviour. On the third day, she was summoned to the presence of Mdme. de Lignerolles, who received and bade her be seated, with the same significant solemnity, and then proceeded to inform her that she had a most painful secret to communicate—a, secret that had long pressed upon her conscience, but which she could never find resolution to disclose; that lately, however, her confessor had so strongly urged her to perform this act of duty, that, with the greatest reluctance, she had resolved to obey his injunctions—her doing so having become more imperative from the fact of Adeline's having arrived at marriageable years, as in the event of any alliance presenting itself, honour would constrain her to speak. The dreadful secret was, that Adeline was not her child; that the nurse who had had the charge of her infancy, confessed on her deathbed, that she had substituted her own infant for the countess's, that the latter had subsequently died, but that she could not leave the world in peace without avowing her crime.

"'I did not believe her,' said Mdme. de Lignerolles, 'but she reminded me that my child had a mole under the left breast, which you, Adeline, have not. This cruel change was effected during our absence from France. Shortly after my confinement, I was ordered to spend the winter in Italy, and the child was left to the care of my father and mother, who by that time had nearly lost her eyesight. To this circumstance, and the little notice men usually take of infants, the woman trusted to escape detection.

"'Of course, I could not discern the difference between the child I had left and the one I found. I had no suspicion; and whatever alterations I remarked, I attributed to the lapse of time—though I must own that maternal instinct offered a strong confirmation of the nurse's confession. While I believed you my own offspring, I had none of those tender yearnings which I have heard other women speak of, and I often reproached myself for the want of them. However, I endeavoured to do my duty by you, and no pains or expense were spared on your education, which was already nearly completed.

"'When I became acquainted with this dreadful secret, of which, when the nurse died, I was the sole possessor. But, aware of the intense grief such a disclosure would occasion my husband, who was then in excessively bad health, I determined during his lifetime to preserve silence. After his death, I ought to have exerted courage to speak; but my mother adored you—it would have killed her. She is now gone, and there is only your grandfather left. I well know the suffering it will cause him, and, believe me, I feel for you—but my duty is plain. You will be amply provided for,' but ere the sentence could be finished, Adeline, who had sat like a statue, listening to this harangue, with wondering eyes and open lips, suddenly rose and rushed out of the room. That she was not Mdme. de Lignerolles daughter caused her little grief, nor was she of an age very highly to appreciate the position and splendours she was losing; but she thought of her grandfather, whom she really loved; she thought of De la Cruz, and her heart filled with anguish.

"She was not pursued to her retreat; the whole day she kept to her chamber, and Mdme. de Lignerolles kept to hers. On the following morning, a note was handed to her from Mdme. de L., announcing that she was starting for Paris to communicate this distressing intelligence to M. de Givry; and desiring Adeline to remain where she was, under the care of Mdme. Vertot, the housekeeper, till she received further directions; assuring her, at the same time, that everything should be done for her happiness and welfare, and, in due time, a suitable *parti* (departure) be provided for her."

Just as Monsieur de Venacour reached this point of his story, Madame de Montjerac returned from bathing, and if I looked at her with interest before, it may be well imagined how much more she inspired now.

"How extraordinary!" I said, as my eyes rested on her noble countenance and majestic figure, "that that distinguished-looking woman is really the daughter of a good-for-nothing servant; and yet I should have said, if ever there was a person who bore the unmistakeable impress of aristocracy, it is she."

He nodded his head, and significantly lifting his fore-finger to the side of his nose, said "*Ecoutez!*" and forthwith proceeded with his narration as follows.

"On Madam de Lignerolle's arrival in Paris, she sent for her father, threw herself at his feet, and with tears and lamentations, disclosed this dreadful secret, which, she said, had been making the misery of her life for the last two years; but whatever distress it occasioned her, it was quite evident that that of Monsieur de Givry was much more severe. He was wounded on all sides; his pride, his love of lineage, his personal affection for Adeline, and his horror of the notoriety such an extraordinary event must naturally acquire. So powerful were the two last sentiments, that for a moment he even entertained the idea of accepting Adeline as the heiress of Givry and concealing the whole affair from her and everybody else; but to this proposition his daughter objected that the poor girl was already in possession of the truth, and that it was impossible to make her a party to such a deception.

"Then," said Monsieur de Givry, "she must die! There is no other expedient."

"'*Mais, non, mon père*' cried Hermione, starting from her seat, evidently taken quite aback by this unexpected proposition.

"De Givry waved his hand with a melancholy smile; '*Enfant!*' he said. 'Do you think I intend to become an assassin? God forbid!' And then he explained that he did not mean a real but a fictitious death, for which purpose she must be removed to a foreign country, under the pretence of the re-appearance of pulmonary symptoms; that a husband must be found for her who would bind himself to leave France for ever, and to keep this secret, under pain of forfeiting the very handsome allowance he proposed to make them; for the safe conduct of which part of the business, it would be necessary to confide their unhappy circumstances to the family physician and lawyer. In the meantime, as these arrangements could not be made in a day, it was decided that Adeline should remain where she was till all was ready for their completion.

"'I shall take her out of the country myself,' he said, 'and you must accompany us. Every consideration must be shown her; she is the victim, and not the criminal.'

"In the course of this conversation, as may be imagined. Monsieur de Givry more than once lamented the extinction of his race; his daughter, however, on that point, offered him some consolation, by suggesting that she was still a young woman, and that for her father's sake, although she had never intended to marry again, she would consent to do so provided she could meet with an unobjectionable *parti*.

"Shortly after this melancholy disclosure, De la Cruz arrived with his father in Paris; where they were so well received by Madame de Lignerolles, that the old gentleman, fascinated by her beauty and manners, expressed his surprise that his son had not fallen in love with the mother, instead of the daughter. However, at his son's desire, he made formal propositions for the young lady's hand; which, to the surprise of the young man. Monsieur de Givry said, was already promised; adding, however, that his granddaughter's state of health would, probably, retard the union; the physicians having discovered that the seeds of consumption were beginning to develop themselves in her constitution, and, consequently, recommended her removal to a warmer climate.

"In the meanwhile, the poor young girl was pining alone in the dreary, old *château*, with no companion but her own maid,—receiving no intelligence, and ignorant of her future fate. All she knew was, that she never could be the wife of Rodriguez de la Cruz. She supposed, that when he made his proposals, he would be informed of the circumstances above related, and that she should never hear more of him. But, in this, she was mistaken. About three weeks after her mother had left her, a letter from him arrived, saying, that he had succeeded in discovering were she was, and that he had lost no time in writing to inform her of the ill fortune that had attended his proposals; adding, that if her sentiments continued unchanged, he would come to Château Noir, accompanied by his own chaplain, who would unite them; after which, he had no doubt, it would be easy to obtain her grandfather's forgiveness; he, probably, having only refused his consent because he was trammelled by a prior engagement.

"But this letter was addressed to Mademoiselle de Lignerolles; and it was evident, from the whole tenor of it, that the writer knew nothing of the change in her fortunes. Honour forbad her to take advantage of this ignorance; but the struggle threw her into agonies of grief. She passed a miserable day and retired early to bed; where she might indulge her tears, and avoid the curious eyes of her maid, who was greatly perplexed at these unusual proceedings. Sleep was far from her eyes, and her mind was busy, framing the answer she had to write on the following day to De la Cruz, when she heard a knock at her chamber door. 'Come in,' she said; not doubting that it was her maid, or Madame Vertot.

"Immediately, she heard the handle turned, and she saw in a mirror that was opposite, the door open, and a miserable, haggard-looking woman enter. She was attired in rags, and she led by the hand two naked children. They approached the foot of the bed, and the woman held out a letter, as if she wished Adeline to take it, which she made an effort to do; but a sudden horror seized her, and she uttered a scream which roused her maid who slept in the adjoining apartment. She was found insensible; but the usual applications restored her; and, without telling what had happened, she requested the servant to pass the rest of the night in her room.

"The next day, she felt very poorly in consequence of this horrid vision; but she wrote to De la Cruz such a letter, as she felt her altered circumstances demanded. She could not bring herself to avow that she was the daughter of Robertine Collet; but sent him, simply, a cold, haughty refusal, which precluded all possibility of any further advances. The next day, she changed her room, and she saw no more of the frightful apparition.

"She had done her duty to De la Cruz, but she was miserable;

and when, shortly afterwards, her grandfather arrived, accompanied by Dr. Pecher, the family physician, they found her exceedingly ill, and confined to her bed. This Dr. Pecher was a clever and worthy man; and having been necessarily made the confidant of the painful secret, it had been privately arranged between him and Monsieur de Givry, that he should marry the girl; and that they should, thereupon, quit the country,—Monsieur de G. making ample provision for their future maintenance.

"But the main thing needful, was to restore her to health; and in the course of his attendance on her, he learnt from her maid how she had been first attacked; and then elicited from herself, the cause of her alarm. Of course, he looked upon the vision as an illusion; in short, the premonitory symptoms of her illness,—and mentioned it in that light, to Monsieur de Givry. But to his surprise, Monsieur de G. took a different view of the matter; and hastening to Adeline's room, he made her repeat to him the exact description of what she had seen; after which, he started immediately for Paris, without explaining the motive of this sudden departure,

"On his arrival, he presented himself before his daughter, and taxed her with having deceived him; what her motive could be he was unable to imagine; he supposed it to be pecuniary, and that she did not wish to part with the large portion to be paid to Adeline on her marriage; but he believed that the traditionary apparition of his family would not have appeared to anyone who was not a member of it; and that therefore the girl, who had accurately described the appearance of these figures, of which the young people were always kept in entire ignorance, must be actually his granddaughter.

"Madame de Lignerolles persisted in her story, and all she could be brought to own was, that it was possible, the woman, Collett, had deceived her. Strong in his own opinion. Monsieur de Givry returned to Château Noir, Dr. Pecher having recommended the young lady's removal; and after writing his daughter a very urgent and serious letter, he started on a tour of a few weeks, with Adeline, for the recovery of her health.

"No answer reached him for some time, but at the end of a month, he received one, acknowledging the cruel deception she had practiced, alleging as her excuse, an ardent passion for Rodriguez de la Cruz; and the wish to detach him from Adeline, and marry him herself. But she had failed, and he was on the point of marriage with a lady selected for him by his father. The letter concluded by the announcement, that she was about to retire to a convent where she should, in due time, take the veil.

"Monsieur de Givry assumed this to be a mere ebullition of shame and disappointment; but she kept her word. Mademoiselle de Lignerolles, some years later, married the Baron de Montjerac, from whom, said Monsieur de Venacour, I heard the story. By him she had two sons; but the constant apprehension that in the eldest will be fulfilled the *mauvais destin* entailed on the heirs of Givry, preys, it is said, on her mind and health, and is the cause of the expression of melancholy for which her fine countenance is so remarkable.

"Some centuries earlier, when power was irresponsible. Count Armand de Givry, a cruel and oppressive lord of the soil, who then inhabited Château Noir, had put to death one of his serfs, and turned his wife and two children out of doors in inclement weather, forbidding any of his tenants to shelter or assist them. The children were without clothes, and the three poor creatures perished from cold and starvation, but leaving behind them a terrible retribution, in the form of a curse pronounced by the wretched woman's lips in her dying agonies, which, strange to say, seems to have been pretty literally fulfilled.

"When they were nearly at the last extremity, some good Christian had had the courage to write a pathetic letter for her, which, however, it was necessary she should deliver herself, as no one else durst do it. She watched her opportunity; concealed herself in the park and waylaid the count as he returned one day from shooting. But instead of taking the letter, he set his dogs upon her, who would have torn her to pieces, but for the courageous interference of one of his followers.

"The curse ran, that never should the heir of Givry prosper till one of them took the letter; and that the last scion of the house should *Renier le croix et se vouer à l'Enfer*. (Renounce the cross and devote oneself to Hell.)

"Since that, it was said that, no eldest son or daughter of the house of Givry had lived and prospered, whilst the letter, in some way or other had been offered to every one of them; but as the cadets of the family lived and married and prospered like other people, they did not choose to believe in the story; at least, whatever their secret thoughts on the subject may have been, they publicly threw ridicule on the tradition, whenever it was alluded to; but Monsieur de Givry had sufficient faith in it to believe, that if Adeline had been the daughter of Robertine Collet, she would never have been visited by the ghost of Madeleine Dogue and her children."

The Swiss Lady's Story

"It was not I," said Madame de Geirsteche; "it was my mother who saw the apparition you have heard of; but I can tell you all the particulars of the story if you have patience to listen to it."

"You would be conferring a great favour," I said; "from what I have heard of the circumstance, I am already much interested."

We were in the steamboat that plies between Vevay and Geneva when this conversation occurred, and as there could not be a more convenient opportunity of hearing the narration, we retired from the crowd of travellers that thronged the deck, and Madame de G. began as follows.

"My husband's father, the elder Monsieur Geirsteche, was acquainted with two young men named Zwengler. He was at school and at college with them, and their intimacy continued after their education was finished. When one was fourteen and the other ten, they had the misfortune to lose both their parents by an accident. They were crossing the Alps, when by the fall of an avalanche their carriage was overturned down a precipice, and they and their servants perished.

"The Zwenglers were people of good family but small fortune; and as they had always lived fully up to what they had, their property, when it came to be divided between their four children, for they had two daughters besides the sons I have named, afforded but an inadequate portion to each; but this misfortune was mitigated by their rich relations—a wealthy uncle adopted the boys, and an equally wealthy aunt took the girls. This was but just, for they had both been enriched by what ought to have been the inheritance of the other sister, the mother of these children, who, having married Monsieur Zwengler contrary to the wishes of her parents, was cut off with a shilling. This uncle and aunt had never married, for their father objected to every match that was proposed, as not sufficiently advantageous; whilst the brother and sister, taking warning by the fate of Madame Zwengler, preferred living single to the risk of incurring the same penalty. The daughters having good fortunes married early, and I believe did well enough; it is on the history of the sons that my story turns.

"As I mentioned, they were at the same school with my husband's father when the catastrophe happened to their parents, and he remembered afterwards the different manner in which the news had affected them; Alfred's grief was apparently stormy and violent; that of the other was less demonstrative, but more genuine. Alfred, in short, was secretly elated at the independence he expected would be the consequence of this sudden bereavement; and he lost no time in assuming over Louis the importance and authority of an elder brother. Louis was an enthusiastic, warm-hearted, and imaginative child, too young to appreciate his loss in a worldly point of view, but mourning his parents—especially his mother—sincerely.

"Alfred's hopes of independence were considerably abated, when he found himself under the guardianship of Mr. Altorf, his uncle, a proud, pompous, tenacious, arbitrary man; on the other hand, he was somewhat consoled by the expectation of becoming the heir to his large fortune, the magnitude of which he had frequently heard descanted on by his parents. He soon discovered, too, that as the heir expectant he had acquired an importance that he had never enjoyed before; and in order to make sure of these advantages, he neglected no means of recommending himself to the old gentleman, insomuch, that Mr. Altorf, being very fond of the study of chemistry, Alfred affected great delight in the same pursuit, sacrificing his own inclinations to shut himself up in his uncle's laboratory, with crucibles and chemicals that he often wished might be consumed in the furnace they employed.

"Louis, the while, pursued his studies, thoughtless of the future as young people usually are; but as he advanced in age, he began to exhibit symptoms of a failing constitution, and as the law for which his uncle designed him required more study than was compatible with health, he was allowed to follow his inclination and become a soldier. With this view, he was sent to Paris, and committed to the surveillance of a friend of his uncle there, who was in the French service.

"No profession being proposed for Alfred, he lived on with his uncle, confirmed in the belief that though his brother, if he survived, would be remembered in the old man's will, he himself should inherit the bulk of the property. It was a weary life to him, shut up half the day in the laboratory, that he detested, in constant association with an uncongenial companion. Moreover, up to the period of his being of age, he was kept almost entirely without money, and was excluded from all the pleasures suitable to his years.

"When he attained his majority, he became possessed of the small patrimony that devolved on him as the eldest son of his father and was enabled to make himself some amends for the privations he had previously submitted to. Not that he threw off his uncle's authority or became openly less submissive and conformable; but secretly he contrived to procure himself many relaxations and enjoyments, from which he had before been shut out; and in the attaining and purchasing these pleasures he freely squandered all the proceeds of his inheritance, reckoning securely on the future being well provided for.

"His uncle inhabited a villa outside of Geneva, on the road to Ferney, and seldom came into the town, except when he visited his banker. His chemicals and other articles, Alfred usually purchased, and he had made acquaintance with several young men, whose society and amusements he availed himself of these opportunities to enjoy. One frosty day in December, he was strolling arm in arm with some of these youths, when, on turning a corner, he unexpectedly saw sailing down the street before them, the massive figure of his uncle, attired in his best chocolate suit, his hair powdered, and a long pigtail hanging down his back. The air of conscious importance and pomposity with which he strode along, amused these gay companions, and they were diverting themselves at the old gentleman's expense, when his foot slipped on a slide, and he fell down.

"This was irresistible; and they all burst into a simultaneous shout of laughter. A passer-by immediately assisted him to rise; and as he did so, he turned round to see from whence the merriment proceeded— perhaps he had recognised his nephew's voice—at all events, Alfred felt sure he *saw*, if he did not *hear*, and thought it prudent to apologise for his ill-timed hilarity, which he sought to excuse by alleging that he had not at first been aware who it was that had fallen. Mr. Altorf looked stern; but as he said nothing, and never alluded to the subject again, Alfred congratulated himself at having got off so well, and endeavoured to efface any unpleasant impression that might remain by extra attentions and compliances.

"Everything went on as usual till the following year, when one morning the old gentleman was found dead in his bed, and the medical men pronounced that he had expired in a fit of apoplexy.

"When the will—which was dated several years back—came to be read, it was found that after two trifling legacies, and five thousand pounds to Louis, the whole estate was bequeathed to Alfred, whose breast dilated with joy, as the words fell upon his ear, although it was no more than he was prepared for; but the first flush of triumph had not subsided, when the lawyer arrested the incipient congratulations of the company, by saying, 'Here is a codicil, I see, dated the fourteenth of December, last year.'

"The company resumed their seats, and a cold chill crept through Alfred s veins, as the reader proceeded as follows:—

I hereby revoke the bequest hereabove made to my nephew Alfred Zwengler, and I give and bequeath the whole of my estates, real and personal, to my nephew, Louis Zwengler. To my nephew, Alfred Zwengler, I give and bequeath my bust, which stands on the hall table. It is accounted a good likeness, and when I am gone, it will serve to keep him merry. May he have many a hearty laugh at it—on the wrong side of his mouth.

"The auditors looked confounded on hearing this extraordinary paragraph, but Alfred understood it too well.

"It is unnecessary to dwell upon his feelings; a quarter of an hour ago he was one of the richest men of his canton—now there were not many poorer in all Switzerland than Alfred Zwengler. He had awakened from his long dream of wealth and importance, and habits of expense, to poverty and utter insignificance; while Louis, whom he had always despised—Louis, over whom he had domineered, and assumed the airs of an elder brother and a great man, had leapt into his shoes at one bound, and left him grovelling in the mud. How he hated him.

"But he might die; what letters they had had from Paris reported him very sickly; he might be killed in battle, for Europe was full of wars in those days; but he might do neither; and at all events, in the meantime what was Alfred to do? A thousand wild and desperate schemes passed through his brain for bettering his situation, but none seemed practicable. The sole remnant of the property he had inherited from his father, that still remained in his possession, was a house in Geneva, called l'Hotel Dupont, that he had mortgaged to nearly its full value, intending at his uncle's death, to pay the money and redeem it. It had been let, but was now empty and under repair, and the creditors talked of selling it to pay themselves.

"But Alfred induced them to wait, by giving out that as soon as his brother understood his situation, he would advance the necessary sum to relieve him. Perhaps he really entertained this expectation, but he had no precise right to do so, for he had never given Louis a crown piece, though the latter had suffered much more from his uncle's parsimony than he had, having inherited nothing whatever from his parents. However, Alfred wrote to Louis, dating his letter from that house, dilating on his difficulties, and the hardness of his fate, and hinting that, had he come into possession of his uncle's fortune, as he had every right to expect he should, how he should have felt it his duty to act towards an only brother.

"He received no answer to this appeal; and, at first, he drew very unfavourable conclusions from his brother's silence; but, as time went on, and Louis neither appeared to take possession of his inheritance, nor wrote to account for his absence, hope began once more to dawn in the horizon; the brighter, that no letters whatever arrived from him; even the lawyers who had applied for instructions, received no answer. The last letter his uncle had had from him, had mentioned the probability of his joining the Republican forces in the south, if his health permitted him to do so. Altogether, there certainly were grounds for anxiety or hope, as it might be; I need not say which it was on this occasion.

"Rumours of bloody battles, too, prevailed, in which many had fallen. Even the creditors were content to wait, not being inclined to push to extremity a debtor, who might be on the verge of prosperity, for it was not likely that Louis would make a will; and it was even possible that he might have died before his uncle. In either case, Alfred was the undoubted heir; and, accordingly, he began once more to taste some of the sweets of fortune;—hats were doffed, hands were held out to him, and one or two sanguine spirits went so far as to offer loans of small sums and temporary accommodation.

"At length, affairs being in this state of uncertainty, the lawyers thought it necessary to investigate the matter, and endeavour to ascertain what was become of the heir. Measures were accordingly taken, which evidently kept Alfred in a violent state of agitation; but the result, apparently, made him amends for all he had suffered. It was proved that Louis, with his military friend, had joined the Republican forces in the south, but was supposed to have perished in an encounter with the Chouans; nobody could swear to having seen him dead; but, as the Republicans had been surprised and fallen into an ambush, they had been obliged to retreat, leaving their dead upon the field.

"This being the case, the property was given up to Alfred; a portion being sequestered, in order that it might accumulate for a certain number of years, for the purpose of refunding: the original heir, should he—contrary to all expectation—reappear. If not, at the expiration of that term, the sequestrated portion would be released.

"Alfred Zwengler was now at the summit of his wishes; and one might have thought, would have felt the more intense satisfaction, in the possession of his wealth, from the narrow escape he had had of losing it; but this did not seem to be the case. He had, formerly, been very fond of society, though he had few opportunities of entering into it; but when he had, nobody enjoyed it more. Now, he did not shun mankind; on the contrary, he sought their company; but he was moody, silent, and apparently unhappy. People said, that he lived in constant fear of his brother's turning up again and reclaiming his inheritance. It might be so; nobody knew the cause of the change in him, for he was uncommunicative, even to his nearest acquaintance.

"One thing, that gave colour to this supposition was, that he evidently disliked to hear Louis named; and whenever he was alluded to, he invariably asserted that he did not believe he was dead, and that he expected every day to see him come back. After saying this, it was observed that, he would turn deathly pale,—rising from his chair, and walking about the room in manifest agitation.

"Preferring the town to the country, Mr. Zwengler had declared his intention of residing in his own house, which had lately been repaired under his special directions, and fitted up with all the appliances of comfort and elegance; but he was scarcely settled there before he took a sudden and uncountable dislike to it and offered it for sale. As it was an excellent property, Mr. Geirsteche, my husband's father bought it; and Mr. Zwengler purchased another house and removed his furniture thither.

"Mr. Geirsteche had no intention of living in the house; he bought it as an investment; for being situated in one of the best streets of the city, it was sure to let well; and accordingly, it was not long before he found an eligible tenant in Mr. Bautte, an eminent watchmaker of Geneva, who furnished it handsomely. He was very rich, and wanted it for his family, who expressed themselves delighted with their new residence. Nevertheless, they had not been in it three months before they expressed a desire to live in the environs of the city rather than in it. As Mr. Bautte had taken a long lease of the house, he put up a ticket announcing that it was to be let.

"A gentleman from Lucerne, named Maurice, who had just married his sister's governess, and wished therefore to reside at a distance from his family, took it for three years, with the option of keeping it on for whatever term he pleased at the end of that period. He gave directions for the furnishing, and when it was ready, they came to Geneva and took up their abode in their new house. At the end of a year, they applied to Mr. Bautte for permission to sub-let the house. There was no such provision in the agreement, and Mr. Bautte at first, we were told, objected, but consented after an interview with Mr. Maurice. But these frequent removals had begun to draw observation, and it began to be rumoured that there was something objectionable about the Hotel du Pont.

The common people whispered that it was haunted; some said it was infested with rats; others that it was ill drained; in short, it got a bad reputation, and nobody was willing to take it. Mr. Maurice and his wife, who were gone to Paris for a few months, and had not yet removed their furniture, being informed of this, advertised it to be let furnished. So many strangers come to Geneva, that there is no want of tenants for good furnished houses, and it was soon engaged by a French family from Dijon. They took it for a year, but at the end of that time they left it for a residence much inferior in every respect, and yet more expensive; the rent Mr. Maurice asked being very moderate.

"I don't know who were the next tenants, but family after family took the house, for it was a very attractive one, but nobody lived in it long. When Mr. Maurice's three years had expired, Mr. Bautte bought his furniture, and continued to let the house furnished. He would have been glad to sell his lease, which was for thirty years, but nobody was inclined to buy it.

"I now," said Madame de G. "come to that part of the story that concerns my mother. I have frequently heard the story from her own lips, and nothing made her so angry as to see people listen to it with incredulity. My grandfather, Mr. Colman, was, as you are aware, much given to the pursuit of literature, and as that is one that seldom brings wealth, his means were somewhat restricted, although he had a small independence of his own. He had three daughters and two sons, and when his family had outgrown their childhood, and my mother, who was the eldest, had attained the age of seventeen, they came to Geneva for the sake of giving the young people, some advantages of education that he could not afford them in England; besides there was a good deal of literary society to be had here then, and the place was cheaper than it is now.

"Having no acquaintance, they applied on their arrival to an agent, who offered them several houses and L'Hotel du Pont amongst the number. At first, they were about to decline it as a residence beyond their means; but when the rent was named, they took it immediately. It was so far the best house they had seen, and the cheapest, that when the agreement was signed, they expressed their surprise to the agent, at what appeared the unreasonable demands of the other proprietors.

"'Why, this house is particularly situated, sir,' said the agent. 'The gentleman who furnished it was obliged to leave Geneva almost immediately after he had settled himself here; and he being absent, and caring more for a good tenant than a high rent, we don't stand out for a price as people must do when they look to make money by a house.'

"Mr. Colman congratulated himself on his good luck in finding such a liberal proprietor, and in a few days he and his family were comfortably established in the Hotel du Pont. The only difficulty they had found was in procuring servants. They had one English maid with them, and, at last, they succeeded in getting two girls as cook and housemaid. The latter was a German, who had been brought there by a family who had gone on to Italy; and the former was a French-woman, who had married a gentleman's valet, and had followed him from Paris to Geneva.

"As soon as everything was arranged, they resumed their usual habits—one of which was, that for an hour or two before they went to bed the father read aloud to them, in a room they called the library— it was, in fact, his writing-room—whilst the ladies worked. A few evenings after they had recommenced this practice, a discussion arose between Mr. Colman and his eldest daughter, Mary, as to the precise meaning of a French word, and the dictionary had to be appealed to to decide the question. Mary said it was in her bedchamber and left the room to fetch it. The library was on the ground-floor, and the staircase was a broad, handsome one as far as the first flight; it had been made by Alfred Zwengler when the house was repaired, and there was a wide landing at the top, the whole being lighted sufficiently for ordinary purposes by a lamp that hung in the hall.

"The stairs were very easy of ascent, and my mother—I mean Mary—for she was afterwards my mother, who was a lively, active girl, was springing up two steps at a time, when, to her amazement, she saw a gentleman in uniform standing on the landing above. She stopped suddenly, but as he did not appear to notice her, she continued to ascend, concluding it was some stranger, who had got into the house by mistake, for he did not look a thief; but when she reached the landing he was gone. She stood at first bewildered. There were four doors opening into bedrooms, but they were all shut; and after thinking a moment, she concluded it was the shadow of some cloaks and hats, and sticks, that were hanging in the hall, that had deceived her.

"She did not pause to consider how this could be but turned into her own room; felt for the book, which she remembered to have left on her bed and ran downstairs again to her father; so occupied with the disputed question, that for the moment she forgot what had happened, and as her father resumed his reading immediately, she did not mention it. When they were going to bed, and they were lighting their candles in the hall, she said, 'you can't think what a start I had, this evening, when I went for the dictionary. It must have been the shadow of those cloaks and things, but I could have declared I saw an officer in uniform standing at the top of the stairs. I even saw his epaulette and the colour of his clothes.'

"'*La!* Mary,' said one of the younger ones, 'weren't you frightened?'

"'Frightened! no, why should I be frightened at a shadow?'

"'Or a handsome young officer either,' said one of the boys.

"She playfully gave him a tap on the head, and they all went to bed, thinking no more of the matter.

"The kitchen was at the back of the house, on the same floor as the library, and a few evenings after this occurrence, one of the girls being in the store-room, heard sounds of distress proceeding thence; and on opening the kitchen-door, to inquire what was the matter, she saw Jemima, the English girl, in hysterics, and the other two standing over her, sprinkling her face with water. They said that she had left the kitchen to fetch some worsted to mend her master's stockings, but that before she could have got upstairs, she had rushed back again, thrown herself into a chair, and '*gone off*' as they expressed it. On hearing the noise, Mr. and Mrs. Colman joined them, but, for a long time, they could extract nothing from her—but that she had seen *something*.

"My grandfather asked if it was a rat, or a robber! but she only shook her head; and it was not till they had all left the kitchen and sent her a glass of wine, that she was sufficiently collected to tell them that, as she got to the foot of the stairs, she saw an officer in uniform, going up before her. He had his cap in his hand, and his sword at his side; and supposing he was some friend of her master's, she was going to follow him up; but when he reached the landing, to her surprise and horror, he disappeared through the wall.

"When the family heard this, combining it with what had happened to Mary—though the circumstance had never been mentioned in the hearing of the servants; nor, indeed, even alluded to a second time—they began to ask themselves whether it was possible any such person could get into the house? and they examined every part of it with care, but found nothing that threw a light on the mystery. After this, Jemima was afraid to go upstairs alone at night, and Gretchen shared her fears; but the Frenchwoman laughed at them both and said she should like to see a ghost that would frighten her.

"One night, however, about nine o'clock, when the family were in the library, they suddenly heard a great noise upon the stairs, as if something had fallen from the top to the bottom, and when they all rushed out to see what was the matter, they found the cook lying across the lower step in a state of insensibility, and the coalscuttle upset beside her, with its contents scattered around. They carried her into the library, and when she revived, she insisted on immediately leaving the house; she would not sleep in it another night on any account whatever, and away she went. Gretchen and Jemima said, they were sure she had seen the ghost, but was too proud to own it, after turning their fears into ridicule; and the family began to be very much perplexed.

"My grandfather had a truly philosophical mind and did not think it a proof of wisdom to hold decided opinions on subjects that he had not investigated. He had never believed in spiritual appearances, but he had never thought seriously on the subject at all and did not feel himself qualified to assert that such things were impossible. Certainly, it was a singular coincidence, that Jemima's description of the apparition exactly coincided with what my mother had seen; and though the Frenchwoman had confessed to nothing, yet it was at the same hour and the same place that she had taken fright. He tried, whether—by placing the cloaks and the lamp in certain relative positions—he could produce any reflection that might deceive the eye; but there was not the most remote approximation to such a thing; in short, he perceived that that explanation of the appearance was altogether inadmissible.

"'Well,' he said, 'if anybody sees this figure again, I beg they will call me!'

"They were not a nervous family, I suppose; my mother was quite the reverse, I know. I never saw anybody with more courage; at all events, they do not seem to have been alarmed, though both the boys afterwards saw the same figure on the same spot and ran to call their father; but when Mr. Colman came it was gone. However, they declared they had seen it cross the landing; and that it had seemed to them, to walk through the wall, just as Jemima had described.

"Some weeks after this, towards the same hour, as Mr. Colman was about to commence reading aloud, he discovered that he had left his spectacles in the pocket of his coat, when he dressed for dinner; and my mother, who was always alert and active, left the room to fetch them. Presently, she re-entered the room,—pale, and somewhat agitated, but perfectly collected; and said, that when she had ascended the stairs about halfway, she heard a slight rustle above, which caused her to raise her eyes; when she saw, distinctly, the same figure she had seen before. 'I was not frightened!' she said, 'and I stopped with one foot on the next stair, and looked at it steadily, that I might be sure I was not under a delusion. The face was pale, and it looked at me with such a sad expression, that I thought if it was really a ghost, it might wish to say something; so, I asked it.'

"'Asked it!' they all exclaimed. 'What did you say?'

"'I said, if you have anything to communicate, I conjure you—speak!'

"'And did it?'

"'No,' answered Mary, 'but it made a sign—'

"'Good Heavens!' said Mrs. Colman, 'do you know what you're saying?'

"'Perfectly,' said Mary, calmly. 'With one hand it pointed to the wall—just where Jemima and the boys saw it go in—and with the other it made a movement, as if it was going to strike the wall with something heavy.'

"'Perhaps there's some money buried there,' said one of the boys.

"Mr. Colman, who had hitherto been a silent but amazed listener to his daughter's narration, asked her what the gesture appeared to signify.

"'It was as if it wanted the wall to be pulled down—at least, I thought so. I wish I had asked if that was what it wished, but I had not presence of mind; if I see it again, I will.'

"'But we could not pull down the wall, you know, my dear,' said Mrs. Colman.

"'I suppose we might, if we engaged to build it up again,' suggested one of the party.

"'But if we told anybody, we should not get the money,' said the boys.

"'Hush!' said Mary, 'Don't speak in that way; think what a solemn thing it is. I shall never forget his face—never, to the day of my death; and it looked at me so gratefully when I spoke to it, and then it disappeared into the wall.'

"Of course, this extraordinary occurrence formed the subject of conversation for the rest of the evening, and Mr. Colman narrowly questioned his daughter with regard to the particulars; but her story was always consistent, and as he had a very high opinion of Mary's courage and sense, the circumstance made so much impression on him, that he set about making enquiries as to the owner and antecedents of the house. It was difficult to obtain much information—for saying a house is haunted, is an injury to the landlord, and sometimes brings people into trouble—but he ascertained that it had had several tenants, that nobody had staid in it long, and that one of the persons who had inhabited it for a short time, was Mr. Bautte himself, whereupon he resolved to pay him a visit.

Mr. Bautte, as I have mentioned, was a watchmaker; and though very rich, still attended to his trade, so that it was easy to obtain an interview with him. Mr. Colman called at his place of business, which was not a shop, but a room on the first floor of a private house. He asked about the engraving of a seal that he had to his watchchain; and then, having ascertained which was Mr.. B., he told him he was his tenant. Mr. B. bowed and said, 'I hope you like the house, sir.'

"My grandfather said that, perhaps, he might not have observed it but for what had happened, but that he fancied this was said with a sort of misgiving, as if he was conscious that there was something objectionable about the house.

"'Why,' said my grandfather, drawing him rather aside, 'I like the house very much; but there's one great inconvenience about it—we can't get any servants to stay with us. One has left us already, and the others have given us warning, and nobody seems willing to come in their places. I understand you lived in the house yourself a short time; may I ask if you found any similar difficulty?'

"'Well, sir,' said Mr. Bautte, trying to look unconcerned, 'you are aware how ignorant and foolish such people are—I fancy from the construction of the house that the sounds from the next door penetrate the walls.'

"'We hear no sounds,' said Mr. Colman. 'I have heard no complaints of any. Did any of your family ever say they saw anything extraordinary there?'

"'Well, sir, since you put the question so directly, I can't deny that the female part of my family did assert something of the sort; but women have generally a tendency to superstition, and are easily terrified.'

"'Very true,' said Mr. Colman, 'but I should take it as a great favour if you would tell me what they said they saw—I have no idea of leaving the house; you need not be afraid of that; and of course I shall not mention this conversation to any one—what did they say they saw?'

"Mr. Bautte thus exhorted, {confessed that his family, and everybody who had lived in the house, asserted that they had seen the apparition of a young man in uniform, who always appeared on the stairs or the landing; adding, that he himself had never seen it, although he had put himself in the way of it repeatedly, and he firmly believed it was some extraordinary delusion or optical deception, though it was impossible to account for its affecting so many persons in the same way.

"My grandfather then told him what had occurred in his family; especially to his eldest daughter, in whose testimony, he assured Mr. Bautte, he placed the greatest reliance; and he ventured to propose an examination of the spot, where the figure was said invariably to disappear. At first, Mr. Bautte laughed at the idea; for—besides his scepticism, which made him unwilling to take any proceeding that countenanced what he considered an absurd superstition—he urged, that the staircase and landing in question, were of very recent erection, being one of Mr. Zwengler's improvements when he repaired the house. However, after a short argument, wherein my grandfather represented that nobody but the parties concerned need know the real reason for what they did, that the expense would be small, and the possible result beneficial to the property, Mr. Bautte consented, provided Mr. Geierstecke made no objection; he being still the owner of the house.

"Mr. G., who, you know, was my husband's father, was aware that the Hotel du Pont had frequently changed its tenants but was quite ignorant of the cause. He had no immediate interest in the matter, as Mr. Bautte held a thirty-years lease, and had naturally assumed that these frequent changes were purely accidental. Everybody, who became acquainted with the house, had a strong motive for keeping the secret; for—besides the ridicule and penalty they might have incurred—they all wanted to get it off their hands.

"It's true, that amongst the servants and common people of the neighbourhood, there were strange whispers going about; the source of which it would not have been easy to trace. A glazier said he knew a man, who had heard another declare, that he was acquainted with a bricklayer, who had helped to build the staircase; who used to say, he did not wonder that nobody could live in the Hotel du Pont; and that it was his opinion that nobody ever would be able to live in it; and a woman who kept a shop opposite, had been heard to say, that she saw somebody go into that house that never came out again; but whenever she alluded to this subject, her husband always reproved her, and told her she did not know what she was talking about.

"This gossip had, however, never reached Mr. Geierstecks, and he was exceedingly surprised when Mr. Bautte communicated Mr. Colman's proposal, and the reason of it. He immediately called upon my grandfather, who recited the circumstances to him, and introduced my mother; from whose lips he wished to hear the account of her two rencontres with the ghost; and also, a particular description of its appearance.

"At the commencement of his visit, he was inclined to be jocular on the subject; but after he had seen my mother, and heard her describe the dress of the apparition, which was that of an officer in the Republican Army of France, he seemed a good deal struck, and became serious. He said, he did not believe in ghosts; though he had heard people affirm, that they had seen such things; he always supposed them to be under a delusion; but that my mother's testimony was so clear, and from the account of her family she was so unlikely a person to be deceived, that he felt bound to give his assent to the proposed investigation; only stipulating for entire secrecy, and that he might fix the day for it himself. 'I'll speak to a builder,' said he; 'Mr. Bautte, of course, will wish to be present; and, perhaps, I may bring a friend with me.'

"As I mentioned before, he had been early acquainted with the Zwengler's; and betwixt him and Alfred the intimacy still continued, although the latter was by no means the pleasant companion he had been formerly. Mr. Geierstecke concluding that his uncle's will, and the sudden vicissitudes of fortune he had experienced, had affected his spirits, pitied him; and had often endeavoured to argue him out of his depression, but with little effect.

"I have heard him say, that after he left my grandfather's house on that day, he went to Mr. Zwengler's with the intention of telling him

140

the circumstances I have related, and also of giving him notice of the impending investigation; but when he had got to the door, and his hand was upon the bell, he shrunk from the interview. Not, he said, that he admitted a suspicion; on the contrary, he repelled it; but he could not overcome an uneasy feeling at the striking resemblance between Louis Zwengler and the ghost (if ghost there was), as described by my mother.

"He feared that, if his words did not betray this feeling, his countenance would, and he could not face Alfred in this state of mind; so, he turned from the door and went home. Still he felt he could not allow this thing to be done without warning his friend of their intention, and he sat down to write him a letter; but it was a difficult thing to communicate,—at least, he somehow found it so. He could have mentioned it jocularly; but that, under all the circumstances, he could not do so; and he had torn up two or three unsuccessful efforts, when the door opened, and the servant announced Mr. Zwengler himself.

"My father-in-law told me that he felt his knees tremble, and his cheek turn pale, when he rose to receive his visitor, who seemingly rather more cheerful than usual, said he had called to ask him why he did not come in today, when he was at his door. 'I was at the window,' said he, 'and was quite disappointed to see you turn away.'

"This was too good an opportunity to be lost, and Mr. Geierstecke answered, that it was quite true, and that he had actually had his hand upon the bell, when he thought it was useless troubling him with such nonsense.

"'What nonsense?' asked Zwengler.

"'It's about that house I bought of you,' said Mr. Geierstecke. 'People say they can't live in it;' adding, while he affected to laugh; 'They say there's a ghost in it, and they want to pull down the staircase to look for him.'

"'How absurd,' said Mr. Zwengler; 'and are you going to do it?' but the voice sounded as if there was something in his throat.

"'We are,' replied Mr. G. 'Mr. Bautte has never been able to keep a tenant, and I can't refuse, for it appears they all assert the same thing. Even Mr. Bautte's family would not live in it—they say they see—'

"'Ha! ha!' laughed Zwengler, rising suddenly, and pushing back his chair in a hurried manner, 'but I must leave you—I've an appointment; I merely called as I passed the door, to ask why you'd not come in. Bless me! I'm late,' he added, as he looked at his watch; and he hurried out of the room, crying 'Goodnight,' as he disappeared.

"Mr. Geierstecke used to say that he believed that he (Mr. G. himself) continued standing on the same spot, like a statue, for nearly half an hour after the door closed on his visitor.

"I had scarcely had time to rise from my chair,' he said, 'before he was gone, and I felt; paralysed. I did not know what to do. I wished I had never bought the house, and I lay awake all night, thinking of horrors, and then trying to persuade myself that perhaps there was no cause for my apprehensions after all.'

"'I saw nothing more of Zwengler, though I frequently passed his house purposely; and, at length, the day arrived which I had—not without design—fixed at the interval of a week from my first visit to Mr. Colman. We all assembled at the appointed time, with a respectable workman whom I was in the habit of employing, to whom we accounted for our proceeding, by alleging that there was a bad smell sometimes, which we thought might proceed from a dead rat.'

"'I never felt more nervous and agitated in my life, than while the man was demolishing the wall, and we were waiting the denouement; while Mary, the heroine, stood pale and earnest, with her eyes eagerly fixed on the spot.'

"'We had better have a light, sir,' said the mason presently, 'There is something here—'

"One of the boys went for a light, while silent and breathless they waited its arrival.

"When it came it disclosed a fearful sight. There lay, huddled up, as if thrust in in haste, the bones of a perfect skeleton, and what appeared to be burnt remnants of clothes. Before they touched anything, Mr. Bautte sent for the police, and these sad relics were removed by their officers. There was no means of discovering how life had been taken, but the medical men said that some strong chemical preparation had been used to consume the flesh and clothes and prevent any bad odour.

"Everybody knew the Zwenglers and their history; and on this discovery, the *prefèt* sent for my mother, and took her deposition as to the appearance of the figure she had seen. He also examined Jemima and the Frenchwoman who had left our service; and the testimony of all parties coinciding, he issued an order to arrest Alfred. But when they went to his house he was not there. The servants said he had been absent nearly a week; that he left, saying he was going on business to Dôle, and his stay was uncertain. He had taken no baggage with him but a carpet bag. A messenger was despatched to Dôle, but nothing was known of him there; and the enquiries that were instituted at the Messageries and Voituriers threw no light on his mode of conveyance, if, indeed, he had left Geneva.

"Various people, who had lived in the house, now confessed to have been troubled with the same apparition; and several amongst the neighbours of the lower ranks avowed that they had strong suspicions that Alfred Zwengler did not come fairly by his fortune, alleging different reasons for their opinion; one of which was singular—it was, that a little deaf and dumb girl, who lived near him, described to her mother, that when he passed their door, she always saw him as enveloped in a black cloud.

"Howbeit, Alfred Zwengler never appeared more; and it was generally thought that terrified by the impending disclosure he had thrown himself either into the lake or the river, to escape it. He left no will, and the fortune went to his sisters; But this strange circumstance resulted in my mother's marriage to Monsieur de Beaugarde the *prefect*, who was so captivated by her courage, that he made her an offer immediately; and the acquaintance with Mr. Geierstecke, thus commenced, led to my marriage with his son."

In answer to my enquiry, of how it was supposed the murder was committed, Madame de G. said, the conjecture was, that Louis had made his escape from the Chouans, and returned unexpectedly—a neighbour even testified to having seen him enter the house one night at the time it was under repair—and that his brother by a sudden and dreadful impulse, had struck him down unawares. One of the masons who had been employed in building the staircase, but who was killed by a fall shortly before the discovery, had been heard to hint that before he died he must unburden his mind of a secret that weighed heavily on his conscience. 'Not that the guilt lies on my soul, he used to say, but perhaps it's a sin to hold my tongue.'

However, he had no time to speak; but one came from the grave to tell the tale and bear awful witness against the unhappy Alfred Zwengler.

The Sheep-Farmer's Story

The following singular story was related to me in a dialect which, though I understood, from having lived much in the country where it was spoken, I cannot attempt to imitate, not being "to the manner born;" neither, if I could, would it be agreeable, or very comprehensible, to my readers in general. I shall, therefore, tell it in plain English; and hope it will interest others as much as it did me.

Sandy Shiels, the narrator, was a sheep-farmer in the Lammermuirs. He lived in a lone house, in a wild and desolate country, with his wife and children, his farm-servants, and his dogs, and seldom saw a stranger enter his door, from week's end to week's end; but on certain occasions, more or less frequent, Sandy attended the fairs and markets about the country; and at the cattle shows, sometimes, appeared in Edinburgh itself. He was a shrewd and a simple man—for the two characteristics are by no means incompatible—hard-handed and hard-featured, but not unkindly; a serious churchman, a great reader of his Bible, and a keen observer of Nature and Nature's language, as men who are born and bred amongst mountains generally are.

His wife was a plain, hardworking woman, by whom he had two children, yet young; but he had an elder son by a former marriage, called Ihan Dhu; a Highland appellation not common in the Lammermuirs; but his mother was a Highland woman, and had given it to him. Ihan Dhu means Black John; and it suited him well; for, instead of the brawny figure and sandy hue which so generally prevails in the south, he had inherited the slight figure, the dark complexion, and black hair and eyes of his mother,, who was a specimen of the genuine Highland type; which, contrary to the belief commonly entertained in England, is (Lord Jeffrey informed me), *a little dark man.*

The two farm-servants were called Donald and Bob. The former a heavy, stolid lout, who had just intellect enough to do what he was told; the latter, a smart, lively, good-natured lad, who was fond of reading, when he could get a book; and wide awake about everything that his very limited sphere brought him in contact with. The only other member of the family was a girl, called Annie Goil, an orphan niece of Mrs. Shields; who, in conjunction with her aunt, did all the work of the house and dairy. The whole household lived and ate, and sat together, and with them the two sheep dogs, Coully and Jock. In the summer, it was pleasant enough; but in the winter, when the snow fell and the sheep were on the hills, they had often a hard time of it.

Annie Goil was a pretty lass; and, naturally enough, there being no other at hand, the three young men, Ihan, Donald, and Rob, were all candidates for her favour. Nevertheless, they lived tolerably well together; the rivalry, apparently, not running very high. Ihan was, of course, much the best match; and he might, perhaps, feel pretty confident that whenever he chose seriously to put in his claim, it could not be resisted. Rob, possibly, comforted and consoled himself with the sundry little marks of preference she bestowed on him, which might be genuine, or might be designed to *agacer* (annoy) Ihan. As for Donald, he was of so slow and undemonstrative a nature, that though she and the other two often jeered him and pretended to think he was the one destined to carry off the prize, he exhibited neither anger nor jealousy; if he felt either, he kept them to himself.

Nevertheless, a sharp word, or sour look, would occasionally pass between them; that is, between Ihan and Rob; for any dissatisfaction on the part of Donald was only expressed by increased stolidity and silence; and so persuaded was the old man that their feelings towards each other were not very genial; to say the least, that he had been heard to say to his wife, that Annie Goil was a good girl; but, perhaps, it would have been better, if she had never come amongst them.

Still they rubbed on "middling well," as Sandy said, and certainly far better than might have been expected under such circumstances.

The winter preceding the circumstances I am about to relate, had been a very severe one, and Sandy Shiels, who had exposed himself too much to the weather, was laid up with an attack of rheumatism. As he was a very active man, still not much past middle life, who when in health diligently looked after his business himself; his loss during this confinement was much felt; and the others had enough to do to make up for his absence.

On the 27th of February, the snow was on the ground, and the wind blew wildly over the Lammermuir hills; the sheep sought shelter and munched their turnips sadly in the nooks and hollows. Donald was abroad, with the dogs looking after them, and seeing that no stray lamb perished in the cold; while Ihan and Rob were off to Gifford. Ihan to do business there for his father; for there was a three days fair, or market, which Sandy, when in health, never failed to attend, both as a buyer and seller; and Rob to fetch some medicine for the patient, and other matters wanted at the farm.

Rob set out at dawn of day, for it was a long walk of ten miles through the snow, and the sooner he could return the better, as the things he was to bring were wanted. Ihan rode a rough little Shetland pony; he did not start till midday and was not expected back till the evening after the next. On the first day he had to go on as far as Haddington, which is four miles beyond Gifford, where he was to consult a lawyer about a disputed point in his father's lease. He was to sleep there at the house of a friend, and to be back to the Gifford market early the next morning.

Annie Goil stood at the door covertly watching Ihan as he mounted his pony, well equipped for his cold ride, his neck enveloped in a red comforter, knitted for him by Annie herself. She leant against the door-post looking about her with an air of indifference; while Ihan seemed wholly occupied in tightening his girths and seeing that his stirrups were of the right length. Neither spoke; still he lingered over his gear, and still she stood leaning against the post, when suddenly Mrs. Shiels called from above, "Is Ihan gone? Stop him?" and hurrying downstairs appeared at the door.

"Ihan," she said, "I forgot to tell Rob to bring sixpennyworth of camphorated spirits for your father; if he has not left Gifford before you get there, tell him to get it."

"He will have left, I should think," answered Ihan.

"Perhaps not," said Mrs. Shiels, "but if he has you must bring it, though I want it tonight."

"Very well," said Ihan as he rode away, and Mrs. Shiels and Annie re-entered the house.

The hours passed drearily at the farm, with the sick man groaning in his pain, and the two lonely women dividing their time betwixt his chamber and their household cares. As the day advanced Annie went frequently to the door and looked up the glen; and Mrs. Shiels, glancing at the Dutch timepiece that stood in the kitchen, observed that she wondered Rob had not come back. Annie responding that the snow was deep, and it must be very heavy walking, again went to the door and looked up the glen; but there was nobody in sight. The hours dragged on, and as it grew later, large flakes began to fall and obscure what little light remained. Sandy grew impatient and accused Rob of idling and lingering at the fair; Mrs. Shiels wondered; and Annie having done her work, took up her station at the door with her gown-skirt over her head; there she stood listening for the sound of a step, for it was too dark to see, and at last, she heard a heavy foot approaching, but it was Donald returning from the hills, followed by Jock.

"You haven't seen anything of Rob, have you?" said Annie.

"How should I see Rob! He's gone to Gifford ar'n't he?"

"You might have been on that side of the hill?"

"Ar'nt he come back with the stuff?"

"No; he might have been here three hours since. I can't think what's become of him."

"Stopped at the Fair, maybe; there's dancing the night at the Lion."

"Nonsense!" said Annie, pouting her lips at him, and turning away to prepare their evening meal.

Donald shook himself and stamped his feet to get rid of the snow, and then entered the kitchen. Mrs. Shiels hearing a foot, came down, hoping to find Rob; and was very much disappointed when she saw it was Donald.

"What can that boy be doing, all this time?" she said.

"Perhaps he met Ihan and went back for the camphor;" suggested Annie.

"He'd never think of such a thing! Ihan would not let him; that is, if he had got any way on," said Mrs. Shiels.

"There's dancing the night at the Lion," reiterated Donald.

"Why, the boy would never think of staying for that!" exclaimed Mrs. Shiels; indignant at the mere notion of such a disorderly proceeding.

"To be sure, he wouldn't," said Annie; "Donald knows that well enough;" and her lip curled as she spoke!

Annie was evidently disturbed at Rob's prolonged absence, and angry with Donald's insidious attempts to put an ill construction on it. But still Rob did not come.

Annie went on preparing the supper, which consisted of porridge; and when she had poured it into the bowls, she made two messes for the dogs.

147

"Where's Coullie?" she said looking rounds

"Arn't he here?" inquired Donald.

"No.—Don't you see he's not?"

"Well, I thought he came in with me," said Donald; and going to the door he began whistling the familiar whistle that calls home the dogs. Jock leaving his bowl of porridge, that Annie had set down, went to the door too.

Presently they both returned; Donald sat down to his supper, saying, he supposed the dog would come presently; and Jock applied himself to his.

As the night drew on, the wonders and conjectures increased, and the family grew more and more fidgety and perplexed at Rob's absence. Donald went to bed as he had to be up betimes in the morning; Mrs. Shields did the same, because she slept in her sick husband's room; Annie lingered as long as she could; then she made up a good fire, set a saucepan of porridge on the hob, left a bowl and a spoon, and salt on the table, and went to bed too. When she was undressed and had extinguished her candle, she opened the lattice window of her chamber and put out her head. The snow still fell, and it was very dark; after listening for some minutes, she shut the window, and softly opening her chamber door, she crept downstairs again to the kitchen. There she unhooked a lantern from the wall, put a lighted candle in it, and returning to her room, she hung it on the latch of the window before she got into bed.

She thought she should not sleep, but after a little while she did, and soundly too, till next morning. When she opened her eyes at dawn of day, the candle was burnt out, but the sight of the lantern in so unusual a place, reminded her immediately why she had placed it there, and she wondered whether Rob had come home in the night, and been let in by Donald. When she came down, Donald was already outside the house cleaning his shoes and feeding the pigs. She called to him, "Is Rob come?"

"I don't know," he answered. Of course, then, he was not. It was most extraordinary.

"Is Coullie come in?" she asked,

"I ha'nt seen him," he said.

He was very silent; swallowed his mess of porridge in haste, and then set off to the hills with Jock, When Mrs. Shiels came down, the same questions were reiterated; and when she found Rob was not come, she was very angry, and expressed her conviction that he had staid for the dance at the Lion. Even Annie no longer defended him, for where else could he be all night?" A pretty rating he will get when he comes back thought she; and she could not deny that he well deserved it.

She expected him early, and every now and then she went to the door as on the preceding day; but hour after hour passed, and he did not come. All sorts of conjectures were formed as to the cause of the delay, but Mrs. Shiels and her husband admitted but one solution, of the difficulty—"the boy's head had got clean turned, and he was gone to the bad althegither."

At night, Donald came home to the great surprise of all, without Coullie; he said he had seen nothing of the dog. Now Coullie was devoted to Rob—in short, he was the only person the animal cared for—and it occurred to Annie that he had somehow come upon Rob's footsteps, and tracked him to Gifford, and she expected whenever they did come, to see them both arrive together.

But that night passed and the next day, and then, towards evening, Annie, who had been to the door, announced that she heard the pony's foot; here was at hand one who doubtless would be able to solve the mystery about the absentee. It was the first question addressed to him—"Where's Rob?"

"How should I know?"

"Haven't you seen him?"

"Seen him, no; I've not seen him since the day before yesterday. Why? what's the matter?"

"He's never come back from Gifford, Where was he when you saw him?"

"I never saw him at all, except in the morning before he set off."

"You did not meet him on the road, nor in the village?"

"No; I saw nothing of him after he left this."

"Did you hear if he had been there?"

"I never asked; I bought the camphor—here it is. How's father?"

At night, Donald came home, still without Coullie; and as the dog had never strayed before, it was natural to conclude that he had gone after Rob, wherever the latter might be. The irritation of Mr. and Mrs. Shiels increased hourly, so did Annie's wonder and perplexity. The two young men, Ihan and Donald, were differently affected; Ihan seemed rather pleased, and he covertly taunted Annie with this desertion of her favourite; Donald was only more silent and stolid than he had been before.

But the next day, and the next passed, and so on through the winter, and neither the man nor the dog were seen or heard of. It was ascertained by enquiry that he had been at Gifford, and made his purchases, and it was supposed, had left it early, but *that* no one knew. Certainly, he was not at the ball at the Lion. Somebody had seen him in company with a young man from Edinburgh, in a tax cart, but nobody knew who he was; and, finally, Mr. and Mrs. Shiels declared their conviction that, tempted by fine promises—being an ambitious lad—he had gone off to Edinburgh with this acquaintance, to better his fortune; and Ihan appeared to adopt their opinion. Annie had considerable difficulty in doing so; but, at length, even she ceased to defend him, since there was no other way of accounting for his absence.

Before the winter was over, Donald had left. He had come home one night, with his hands dreadfully mangled by a pole-cat, which he said he had found devouring a rabbit under a bush and had rashly attempted to lay hold of. Hereupon, he went away to the infirmary in Edinburgh, to be under Dr. S.; and Sandy Shiels engaged a man to fill his situation, and also bought a dog in place of Coullie, whose loss he much regretted, well-broken sheep dogs being very valuable

Sometime had elapsed—the fine weather had set in; and with it, the farmer had got rid of his rheumatism, and resumed his former habits of active occupation; when one day, as he was crossing the hill between his own farm and a place called 'The Hopes,' he observed a dog trotting along, that struck him as being very like Coullie. He gave a whistle, and the animal stopped and looked round, and on calling him by his name, he came up and fondled his master, appearing very glad to see him, and finally accompanying him where he was going.

'The Hopes' was a gentleman's house, about three miles from Shiels' farm, and when he reached the gate, he was surprised to hear the keeper at the lodge say, patting the dog familiarly, "Well, Willie, so you've come back again?" Whereupon Sandy asked him if he knew him.

"Oh, yes, I know him," he said; "he's a great favourite of the ladies here. They found him on the hill nearly starved, some time ago, and he followed them home, and has lived here, off and on, ever since."

"That's very odd," said Sandy, "for the dog's mine. I brought him up from a pup, and we broke him ourselves—that is, a lad did, that lived with me then, called Rob. But, one day last winter, the lad disappeared, and the dog too, and I've never seen either of them since, till just now I saw the dog on the hill."

"Well," said the keeper, "I think it was early in March the ladies brought him home here. He often goes away; but he comes back again, and the ladies take him along with them when they walk out."

Sandy could not conceive why the dog had deserted his home, or why he had remained starving on the hill, when he knew very well where his food awaited him. The keeper agreed in its being very extraordinary, since he must have known his way over every part of the moor for miles round; and suggested that he might have gone after the young man who had disappeared, and been on his way back, when the ladies met him; but, even if that were so, why had he not returned home since, especially as he was frequently absent for hours, and sometimes all night?

When Sandy Shiels had concluded his business, and was about to depart, he whistled the dog, who followed him willingly enough; but as he approached his own house, Coullie shrunk behind, and seemed inclined to turn tail, and run away; however, he came on in obedience to his master's call, and was joyfully received by the family in general, who listened with interest to the account of his adventures, as far as they were known; all agreeing that his absence must, in some way, be connected with that of Rob. It was observed that one of his first movements was to examine the premises after his own fashion, sniffing about, first below, and afterwards above stairs in the attic in which Rob and Donald formerly slept. What was the result of these investigations we cannot tell; but when they were concluded, he stretched himself before the kitchen fire, and went to sleep.

The following days, Sandy took him on the hill when he went to look at the sheep, and he did his duty as formerly; but on the third or fourth evening he was missed and was absent all night. He returned in the morning, and was gently chided for this irregularity—the family concluding he had been to visit his friends at 'The Hopes' however, a few evenings after, when they were sitting at supper, with the doors closed, and the dogs lying quietly dozing on the hearth, Coullie suddenly started up, and began to show signs of uneasiness; while, almost at the same moment, something like a low whistle reached their ears, which seemed to proceed from the air, rather than the earth.

They had heard no sound of footsteps, but Ihan rose from the table and opened the door; whereupon Coullie seized the opportunity to dart out, and Ihan returned, saying he could see nobody, but that Coullie was off at the rate of ten miles an hour. Everybody wondered where he was gone; and at last it was concluded that some person from 'The Hopes' had been passing near the house, and that the dog had recognised the whistle, and followed him. The truant was found at the door in the morning, and chided as before, but that did not prevent his repeating the offence, till their wonder was greatly increased by the following circumstance:—

Sandy Shiels always read prayers to his family on the Sunday evenings; and one nighty while he was thus engaged, and the dogs were lying apparently asleep, Coullie suddenly uttered two or three low whines. Annie raised her head from her book to bid him be silent, and observing that he was sitting up, looking eagerly towards the door, which was open, she turned her eyes in that direction, and saw to her astonishment, a man standing in the dusk of the passage. As all the inmates of the house were present, and the outer door was shut, so that no stranger could have come in, she uttered an exclamation of surprise which interrupted the reader, and caused everybody to turn their heads; but with the sound of her voice the figure had disappeared, and the others saw nothing, Coullie ran to the door, and became uneasy, while Sandy asked what was the matter.

"I saw a man in the passage," said Annie, looking very pale and agitated.

"A man," said Ihan, rising; "I saw no man;" and going into the passage, he opened the outer door to look round; whereupon, Coullie seized the opportunity, and rushed out.

"There's nobody that I see," said Ihan; "but the dog's off again."

"I'm sure I saw somebody," said Annie.

"Go and look upstairs," said Mrs. Shiels; Ihan went and returned, saying there was nobody in the house but themselves, and Annie must have been mistaken.

But Annie shook her head, and beginning to cry, asserted that she had not been mistaken, and that she believed the man she saw was Rob, adding, that she always thought that the whistle they sometimes heard, and which agitated Coullie so much, was Rob's whistle.

At this suggestion, Ihan fired and showed symptoms of great irritation; and if Sandy had not been present, high words would have arisen betwixt him and Annie. As it was his countenance was clouded all the rest of the evening.

This event made a great impression on the young girl; she thought of it day and night, and she watched with increasing interest Coullie's inexplicable proceedings, which still continued. Sometimes of an evening they would hear footsteps, whereon the dog would betray great uneasiness till they opened the door, and he could dart off on his mysterious errand. Once or twice they confined him and would not let him go; but the animal seemed so much distressed and whined so piteously, that they ceased to oppose his inclinations. Although when they heard these footsteps they searched the premises in all directions, nobody was ever to be found. Annie wished them to endeavour to find out where Coullie went; but nobody seemed to have sufficient curiosity to take any trouble about the matter, though they all admitted the singularity of the circumstances.

No doubt, it was difficult, inasmuch as he always started on these expeditions at night, while he ran off so rapidly that it would have been impossible to overtake him or keep him in sight. This state of things continued till the month of October, which became very cold; and one morning, towards the end of it, Annie, when she went to the door, found there had been a fall of snow in the night. Coullie, who had gone off the evening before, was there waiting to be let in, and she observed the track of his feet on the ground. It immediately occurred to her that here was an opportunity of discovering what she wished so much to know.

She had nobody to consult, for her aunt and uncle were not come down; and being a stout country girl, she threw her shawl over her head, and calling the dog to follow her, she set off uphill and down dale, guided by the marks of Coullie's footsteps which remained perfectly distinct for about four miles in the direction of Gifford, when they turned off to the left, and stopped at the edge of an old quarry. The dog, who had trotted cheerily beside her, now began to descend into the hollow, stopping and looking up every now and then, whining as if inviting her to follow; but after several attempts she found the descent too steep. When at the bottom, Coullie disappeared for a minute or two under the embankment, and she heard him still whining; but finding she could make no further investigations without assistance, she called the dog who joined her directly, and they returned home to find Mrs. Shiels in a dreadful state of mind at Annie's unaccountable and unprecedented absence.

However, when she communicated the cause of it, and the discovery she had made, Sandy was sufficiently aroused to say that he would send someone down to examine the quarry. He did so, and the result was that they found the remains of poor Rob under circumstances that led to the conclusion that he had somehow gone out of his way and fallen into the pit; for on medical examination, it appeared that

153

both his legs were broken. As the quarry was abandoned and in a lonely spot, a person might very possibly die there under such circumstances without being able to make his distress known.

Poor Rob's remains were committed to the earth; Coullie left off his erratic habits and became an ordinary, but intelligent, sheep dog; and the family at Shiel's farm, after due comment, on the singular events that had led to the discovery of his body, which could only be accounted for by admitting a spiritual agency (a view of the case which Ihan always repelled with scorn) turned their thoughts into other channels, with the exception of Annie, who had a strong persuasion that Rob had not come fairly by his end; and oftentimes she would say to Coullie when alone with the dog, "Ah, Coullie, if you had a tongue that could speak, I think you could tell a tale!"

And Coullie looked at her with his large wise eyes full of affection; for she petted and cherished him for Rob's sake, and always gave him the largest mess at supper time.

Sometimes, too, Annie had strange thoughts about Ihan; he had become more dark, and silent, and sulky, since Rob's death; was it because he was jealous of the interest she had exhibited, or was it from any other cause? Did he meet Rob that day on his way to Gifford? What could Rob be doing so much out of the road as the Quarry? These thoughts naturally made her more and more cold to Ihan, whilst her reserve aggravated his ill-temper and dissatisfaction.

And Annie was not the only person to whom these questions suggested themselves. People would gossip amongst themselves secretly; it got abroad that there had been a good deal of jealousy amongst the young men, and it was whispered that the first Mrs. Shiels had aptly named her son when she called him Ihan Dhu—Black John. At length, these reports reached Sandy Shiels and his son; the latter appeared sullenly indifferent, but they made the old man very unhappy; and every night when he prayed aloud with the family before retiring to rest, he besought God, saying, "Oh Lord if it be thy pleasure, may them that are innocent be justified!"

At term time, when, in Scotland, servants frequently, especially farm servants, change their situations, the man whom Shiels had engaged in Donald's place left; and having heard that Donald, who had been in service at Dunse, was leaving also, Sandy wrote and proposed to him to return; the proposal was accepted, and they were expecting him, when a cart was heard to stop at the door, out of which they looked to see him alight; but the visitor proved to be an old Highland woman who introduced herself as Rob's grandmother—his father and mother having emigrated. She said she had heard the account of her boy's death, and the attachment displayed by the dog, and that she had come all the way to see the animal and had brought the money to purchase him; if his master did not object. She had travelled from Argyleshire to Haddington by coach; and at the latter place she had hired a cart and a lad to drive her to her destination. She added that she and her old man "were no that puir but that they could afford to buy the dog that had been so faithful to their ain boy."

Sandy Shiels and his family made her welcome; invited her to stay and take a day or two's, repose after her journey, and granted her request with regard to Coullie. Annie was very much interested in the old woman; and the latter was deeply impressed with the circumstances the young girl related to her; enquiring minutely into every particular of places and persons connected with the boy's death. She said it was "wonderfu';" adding, that she had "seen" Rob's funeral,—meaning by the second sight—"but not the manner of his death; but she had no doubt God would shew it her before she died."

On the third day she departed; and Sandy Shiels, who had business at Gifford, drove her and Annie, who wished to accompany her, in his cart. They started in time to meet the coach, Coullie making the fourth passenger; and in due time reached the village and drove up to the door of the Lion, where three or four men were sitting on the bench outside smoking and drinking beer; but the moment the cart stopped—almost before it had stopped—Coullie bounded out of it and with indescribable fury attacked one of the men. His master called him, but he was deaf to his voice; and so violent was his rage that it was not without the assistance of the others that he could draw him off. Even then, whilst holding him back with an iron grasp, the dog growled and shewed his teeth, and with flashing eyes, struggled to renew the onslaught.

"Wha's that?" asked the old woman, who had witnessed the scene with surprise.

"That's our Donald, that I told you of—he that lived with us in poor Rob's time," said Annie "What a very extraordinary thing of Coullie to do! I never saw him in such a way before. Besides, he couldn't have forgotten Donald!"

"Forget him!" exclaimed the old woman; "Na, na; Coullie no forgets. Mind ye lass; tak tent o' that man—there's bluid upon him!"

Donald in the meantime, had retreated into the house in search of some water to wash his hand that Coullie had bitten. When he came out the old woman and the dog had departed.

But the lookers on were not uninterested observers of what had past. A new idea struck them; the tide of opinion was rather turned in Ihan's favour. However, this was but the undercurrent of gossip. Donald went home with Sandy Shiels and Annie, who whatever they might have thought, said nothing; but after this, in the nightly prayer, Sandy not only besought God that the innocent might be justified; but also, that the guilty might be brought to repentance; and sometimes he would go further, dilating on the duties enjoined by a *true* repentance; such as reparation, where reparation could be made; and, at all events, where it could not, taking the burthen of our guilt on our own shoulders, even though it weigh us down to death, rather than let the guiltless man suffer, though it were only the breath of slander.

One morning, about three weeks after the departure of the old Highland woman, when they opened the door they found Coullie waiting to be let in. However, kindly treated by his new owners, he had found his way back; a letter arrived from them shortly afterwards, saying, they had missed him, and that they did not doubt that he would reach his former home, "and, may, be yet give testimony agen the wicked."

Annie kept the contents of this epistle to herself, but it did not escape her eye that Donald seemed cowed by Coullie's enmity, which the animal never failed to exhibit as much as he durst. Moreover, as time passed, Donald lost his appetite and the healthy hue of his complexion; in short it was evident he was far from happy in his situation; and she thought that Sandy's significant and awful prayers were eating into his soul and wearing him away.

Farm servants are usually hired for six months; and at last Donald gave warning that he should leave next term—he did not think the place agreed with him; so, it seemed indeed; but that was the year 1832; and ere term time arrived, the cholera came, and seized upon Donald as one of its first victims in those parts.

Before he died, he made his confession in presence of the doctor, to the effect, that he was jealous of Rob, because in the morning he and Ihan had overheard a conversation between him and Annie, and she had promised him a lock of her hair. That he met him as he was returning from Gifford, induced him to go out of his road towards the quarry, by saying one of the sheep had fallen in, and when Rob was off his guard, he pushed him over; but not without a desperate struggle, Rob being very active and strong.

He was dreadfully frightened and ran from the place not knowing what would happen, and for some time he hourly expected Rob to come home. But at length finding he did not, he ventured to approach the spot; but Coullie was there and he flew at him and bit him so severely that he resolved to leave the country and go to the Infirmary. He had heard of Rob's remains, being found and buried, while he was living at Dunse; and thinking there would be no more enquiry about the matter, he accepted the farmer's offer to come back, because he wanted to see Annie.

And so, he died, justifying the innocent, according to the old man's prayers; but Ihan did not long survive. Sandy said he feared he had taken to whiskey drinking from disappointment and vexation, and the cholera found him also an easy prey.

My Friend's Story

"I don't know how often you have promised to tell me a remarkable thing in the ghostly line, that happened to yourself," said I, the other day to my friend; "but something has always come in the way; now I shall be very much obliged to you for the particulars, if you have no objection to my printing the story."

"None," she said, "but as regards names of persons and places; the circumstances are so singular that I think they deserve to be recorded. That part of the affair which happened to myself I vouch for; and I can only say that I have most entire confidence in the truth of the rest, and that all the enquiries I made, tended to confirm the story.

"I remember your asking me once, why I so seldom visited our place in S—, and I told you it was because it was so dreadfully *triste* that I could not inhabit it. You will perhaps suppose that what I am going to relate happened there, but it did not, for the house has not even the recommendation of being haunted—that would at least give it an interest—but I am sorry to say the sole interest it possesses is, that it happens to be ours. Dull as it is, however, we lived there shortly after I was married, for some time. I had no children then, which made it all the duller, particularly when my husband was called away; and on one of these occasions, some acquaintance I had, who were living at a place called the Belfry, about two miles distant, invited me to visit them for a few days.

"The Belfry is a common place square house, just such as the doctor or lawyer would inhabit in a provincial town; a little white swing gate, a round grass plot, with a few straggling dahlias, a gravel road leading to the small portico, and a terrible loud bell to ring when you want to be admitted. So much for the exterior. The interior is not at all more suggestive to the fancy. On the ground floor, there is the usual parlour on one side, and drawing-room on the other, with a long passage leading to the offices at the back; upstairs, a sort of corridor, with dingy bedrooms opening into it. Decidedly not lively, but perfectly prosaic, it was by no means calculated to inspire ghostly terrors; and, indeed, I must confess the supernatural, as it is called, was a subject that, at that time, had never engaged my attention. I mention all this to show you that what happened was not 'the offspring of my excited imagination,' as the learned always tell you these things are. Moreover, I was young; and, to the best of my belief, in very good health.

"The room they gave me was the best. It was plainly but comfortably furnished, with a large four-post bed, and it looked into the churchyard; but this is not an uncommon prospect in country towns, and I thought nothing about it. Now that we understand these things better, I should think it not ghostly, but unhealthy.

"The first two or three nights I slept there, nothing particular occurred; but on the fourth or fifth night, soon after I had fallen asleep, I was awoke by a noise which appeared very near me, and on listening attentively, I heard a rustling sound, and footsteps on the floor. I forgot for the moment that I had locked my door, and concluding it was the housekeeper, who sometimes looked in when I was going to bed, to ask if I was comfortable, I said, 'Is that you Mrs. H?' But there was no answer, upon which I sat up and looked around; and seeing nobody, though I heard the sound still, I jumped out of bed.

"Then I observed, for if was a bright moonlight night, that there was a large tree in the churchyard, which grew very close to the window, and I concluded that a breeze had arisen, and caused the branches to touch the glass; so, I got into bed again quite satisfied, and settled myself to sleep. But scarcely had I closed my eyes, when the footsteps began again, much too distinct this time to be mistaken for anything else; and whilst I was listening in amazement, I heard a heavy, heavy sigh. I had raised myself on my elbow, in order to have my ears freer to listen, and presently I saw the curtains at the foot of the bed, which were closed, slowly and gently opened. I saw no figure, but they were held apart, apparently by the two hands of someone standing there. I bounded out of bed, and rushed out of the room into the corridor, screaming for help.

"All who heard me, got up and came out of their rooms, to enquire what had happened; but I had not courage to tell the truth, I was afraid of giving offence, or incurring ridicule, and I said I had been awakened by a noise in my room, and I was afraid somebody was concealed there. They went in with me and searched; of course, nobody was found; and one suggested that it was a mouse, another that it was a dream, and so forth. But then, and still more the next morning, I fancied, from their manner, they were better acquainted with my midnight visitor than they chose to say. However, I changed my room, and soon after quitted the Belfry, which I have never slept at since, so there concludes the story, so far as I am concerned; but there is a sequel to the tale.

"I must tell you that I never mentioned these circumstances, because I knew I should only be laughed at; besides I thought it might annoy my hosts, as they had an idea of going abroad for some time, and it might have interfered with their letting the house.

"Now to my sequel.

"Two or three years after this occurrence, I fell desperately ill; first I was confined of an infant which did not survive; and then I was attacked with typhus fever, which raged in the neighbourhood. I was at death's door for eleven weeks, and not expected to recover; but you see, I did, *nonobstant messrs, les medicins* (notwithstanding messrs, the medicine); but I was so long regaining my strength, that I was recommended to try the effects of a sea voyage. Even then, I could not sit up, and was lifted about like a baby; and as a fine lady's maid would have been of no use on board the yacht, a sailor's daughter from the coast was engaged to attend me; a strong, healthy young woman, to whom my weight was a feather. She tended me most faithfully, and I found her simple, truthful, and straightforward; insomuch, that I had thoughts of engaging her in my service permanently. With this view, and also because it helped to pass the time, I questioned her about her family, and the manner of life of her class, in the out of the way part of the country from which she came.

"'I suppose, Mary, you've never been away from home before?'

"'Oh, yes, Ma'am; I was in service as housemaid for a short time at the Belfry, not far from your place, Ma'am; but I soon left that, and I have never been out again.'

"'But why did you leave? Didn't you like the place?'

"'No, Ma'am.'

"'But why? Perhaps you'd too much to do?'

"'No, Ma'am, it wasn't a hard place; but unpleasant things happened, and so I left.'

"'What sort of unpleasant things?' said I, my own adventure there suddenly recurring to my memory.

"She hesitated, and said, that perhaps it would alarm me; she had

160

also made a sort of promise to her master and mistress not to talk about it, and she never had mentioned what happened except to her parents, in order to account for leaving so suddenly. I assured her that I should not be alarmed, and overcame her scruples, and then she told me what follows.

"It appeared that she was engaged as housemaid at the Belfry about two years before my visit there. Shortly after her arrival, her mistress being taken very unwell, her master went to sleep at the other side of the house, whilst Mary made her bed in the dressing-room, in order to be near at hand if the invalid required any assistance in the night. She had directions to keep some refreshment ready in case it was wanted, and towards two o'clock in the morning, her mistress saying she should like a little broth, Mary rose, and half dressed, proceeded downstairs with a candle in her hand, to fetch some which she had left simmering on the kitchen fire.

"As she descended the last flight of stairs, she was a good deal startled at seeing a bright light issuing from the kitchen—the door of which was open—much brighter than could possibly proceed from the fire, for the whole passage was illuminated by it. Her first and very natural idea was that there were thieves in the house; and she was about to rush upstairs again to her master's room, when it occurred to her that one of the servants might be sitting up for some object of her own, and she stopped to listen, but there was not the least sound—all was silent. It then occurred to her that possibly something might have caught fire; so half-frightened, she advanced on tiptoe and peeped in, when, to her surprise, she saw a lady dressed in white, sitting by the fire, into which she was sadly and thoughtfully gazing. Her hands were clasped upon her knees, and two large greyhounds—beautiful dogs, said Mary—sat at her feet, both looking up fondly in her face. Her dress seemed to be of cambric or dimity, and from Mary's description, was that worn by ladies in the seventeenth century.

"The kitchen was as bright as if illuminated by twenty candles, but this did not strike her she said, till afterwards; so quite reassured by the appearance of a lady instead of a band of robbers, it did not occur to her to question who she was or how she came there; and saying, 'I beg your pardon ma'am', she entered the kitchen, dropped a curtsey, and was going towards the fire, but as she advanced the vision retreated, till, at last, lady, chair, and dogs, glided through the closed window; and then the figure appeared standing erect in the garden, with its face close to the panes, and the eyes looking sorrowfully and earnestly on poor Mary.

"'And what did you do then, Mary?' said I.

"'Oh, ma'am, then I *fared* to feel very queer, and I fell upon the floor with a scream.'

"Her master heard the cry and came down to see what was the matter. When she told him what she had seen, he endeavoured to persuade her it was all fancy; but Mary said she knew better than that; however, she promised not to talk of it, as it might frighten her sick mistress.

"Subsequently, she met the same melancholy apparition pacing the corridor into which the room that I had slept in opened; and not liking these rencontres she gave warning and left the place.

"She knew nothing more, for her home was at some distance from the Belfry, which she had not since revisited: but when I had recovered my health and returned to that part of the country, I found, on enquiry, that this apparition was believed to haunt not only the house, but the neighbourhood; and I conversed with several people who affirmed they had seen her, generally alone, but sometimes accompanied by the two dogs.

"One woman said she had no fear, and that she had determined if she met the ghost, to try and touch her, in order to ascertain if it was positively an apparition; she did meet her in the dusk of the evening on the path that runs by the high road between the Belfry and G——. and put out her arm to take hold of her dress. She felt no substance, but she described the sensation as if she had plunged her hand into cold water.

"Another person saw her go through the hedge, and he observed, that he could see the hedge through the figure as she glided into the field.

"It is whispered that this unfortunate lady was an ancestress of the original proprietor of the place, who married a man she adored, contrary to the advice of her friends; and too late she discovered that he had taken her only for her money, which was needed to repair his ruined fortunes; he, the while being deeply enamoured of her younger sister, whose portion was too small for his purpose.

"The sister came to live with the newly married couple; and suspecting nothing, the bride was some time wholly unable to account for her husband's mysterious conduct and total alienation. At length she awakened to the dreadful reality, but unable to overcome her passion, she continued to live under his roof, suffering all the tortures of jealousy and disappointed love. She shunned the world; and the worlds who soon learnt the state of affairs, shunned her husband's society; so, she dragged on her dreary existence with no companionship but that of two remarkable fine greyhounds, which her husband had given her before marriage. Riding or walking, she was always accompanied by these animals—they and their affection were all she could call her own on earth.

"She died young; not without some suspicions that her end was hastened—at least, passively, by neglect, if not by more active means.

"When she was gone, the husband and the sister married; but the tradition runs, that the union was anything but blest. It is said that on the wedding night, immediately after her attendant had left her, screams were heard proceeding from the bridal chamber; and that on going upstairs, the bride was found in hysterics, and the groom pale, and apparently horror-stricken. After a little while, they desired to be left alone, but in the morning, it was evident that no heads had pressed the pillows. They had past the night without going to bed, and the next day they left their home—she never to return. She is supposed to have gone out of her mind, and to have died abroad in that state, carefully tended by him to the last. After her decease, he returned once to the Belfry, a prematurely aged, melancholy man; and after staying a few days, and destroying several letters and papers, to do which appeared the object of his visit, he went away, and was seen no more in that county."

Alas, for poor human nature! How we are cursed in the realisation of our own wishes! How we struggle and sin to attain what we are never to enjoy!

Night Side of Nature Fact or Fiction?

1

The following details were written down at the time the events occurred, and they were communicated by Councillor Hahn to Dr. Kerner in the year 1828:—

"After the campaign of the Prussians against the French, in the year 1806, the reigning prince of Hohenlohe gave orders to Councillor Hahn, who was in his service, to proceed to Slawensick, and there to wait his return. His serene highness advanced from Leignitz toward his principality, and Hahn also commenced his journey toward Upper Silesia on the 19th November. At the same period, Charles Kern, of Kuntzlau, who had fallen into the hands of the French, being released on parole, and arriving at Leignitz in an infirm condition, he was allowed to spend some time with Hahn, while awaiting his exchange.

"Hahn and Kern had been friends in their youth, and their destinies having brought them both at this time into the Prussian states, they were lodged together in the same apartment of the castle, which was one on the first floor, forming an angle at the back of the building, one side looking toward the north and the other to the east. On the right of the door of this room was a glass door, which led into a chamber divided from those which followed by a wainscot partition. The door in this wainscot, which communicated to those adjoining rooms, was entirely closed up, because in them all sorts of household utensils were kept. Neither in this chamber, nor in the sitting-room which preceded it, was there any opening whatever which could furnish the means of communication from without; nor was there anybody in the castle besides the two friends, except the prince's two coachmen and Hahn's servant.

"The whole party were fearless people; and as for Hahn and Kern, they believed in nothing less than ghosts or witches, nor had any previous experience induced them to turn their thoughts in that direction. Hahn, during his collegiate life, had been much given to philosophy—had listened to Fichte, and earnestly studied the writings of Kant. The result of his reflections was a pure materialism; and he looked upon created man, not as an aim, but merely as a means to a yet undeveloped end. These opinions he has since changed, like many others who think very differently in their fortieth year to what they did in their twentieth. The particulars here given are necessary in order to obtain credence for the following extraordinary narrative; and to establish the fact that the phenomena were not merely accepted by ignorant superstition, but coolly and courageously investigated by enlightened minds.

"During the first days of their residence in the castle, the two friends, living together in solitude, amused their long evenings with the works of Schiller, of whom they were both great admirers; and Hahn usually read aloud. Three days had thus passed quietly away, when, as they were sitting at the table, which stood in the middle of the room, about nine o'clock in the evening, their reading was interrupted by a small shower of lime which fell around them. They looked at the ceiling, concluding it must have come thence but could perceive no abraded parts; and while they were yet seeking to ascertain whence the lime had proceeded, there suddenly fell several larger pieces, which were quite cold, and appeared as if they had belonged to the external wall. At length, concluding the lime must have fallen from some part of the wall, giving up further inquiry, they went to bed, and slept quietly till morning, when, on awaking, they were somewhat surprised at the quantity which strewed the floor, more especially as they could still discover no part of the walls or ceiling from which it could have fallen. But they thought no more of the matter till evening, when, instead of the lime falling as before, it was thrown, and several pieces struck Hahn.

"At the same time they heard heavy blows, sometimes below, and sometimes over their heads, like the sound of distant guns; still, attributing these sounds to natural causes, they went to bed as usual, but the uproar prevented their sleeping, and each accused the other of occasioning it by kicking with his feet against the foot-board of his bed, till, finding that the noise continued when they both got out and stood together in the middle of the room, they were satisfied that this was not the case. On the following evening, a third noise was added, which resembled the faint and distant beating of a drum. Upon this, they requested the governess of the castle to send them the key of the apartments above and below, which was brought them by her son; and while he and Kern went to make their investigations, Hahn remained in their own room. Above, they found an empty room; below, a kitchen. They knocked, but the noise they made was very different to that which Hahn continued all the while to hear around him.

"When they returned, Hahn said, jestingly, 'The place is haunted!' On this night, when they went to bed, with a light burning, they heard what seemed like a person walking about the room with slippers on, and a stick, with which he struck the floor as he moved step by step. Hahn continued to jest, and Kern to laugh, at the oddness of these circumstances, for some time, when they both, as usual, fell asleep, neither in the slightest degree disturbed by these events, nor inclined to attribute them to any supernatural cause. But on the following evening the affair became more inexplicable: various articles in the room were thrown about; knives, forks, brushes, caps, slippers, padlocks, funnel, snuffers, soap—everything, in short, that was moveable; while lights darted from the corners, and everything was in confusion; at the same time, the lime fell and the blows continued.

"Upon this, the two friends called up the servants, Knittel, the castle watch, and whoever else was at hand, to be witnesses of these mysterious operations. In the morning all was quiet, and generally continued so till after midnight. One evening, Kern going into the chamber to fetch something, and hearing an uproar that almost drove him backward to the door, Hahn caught up the light, and both rushed into the room, where they found a large piece of wood lying close to the wainscot. But supposing this to be the cause of the noise, who had set it in motion? For Kern was sure the door was shut, even while the noise was making; neither had there been any wood in the room. Frequently, before their eyes, the knives and snuffers rose from the table, and fell, after some minutes, to the ground; and Hahn's large shears were once lifted in this manner between him and one of the prince's cooks, and falling to the ground, stuck into the floor.

"As some nights, however, passed quite quietly, Hahn was determined not to leave the rooms; but when, for three weeks, the disturbance was so constant that they could get no rest, they resolved on removing their beds into the large room above, in hopes of once more enjoying a little quiet sleep. Their hopes were vain—the thumping continued as before; and not only so, but articles flew about the room which they were quite sure they had left below. 'They may fling as they will,' cried Hahn, 'sleep I must;' while Kern began to undress, pondering on these matters as he walked up and down the room. Suddenly Hahn saw him stand, as if transfixed, before the looking-glass on which he had accidentally cast his eyes. He had so stood for some time, when he was seized with a violent trembling, and turned from the mirror with his face as white as death. Hahn, fancying the cold of an uninhabited room had seized him, hastened to throw a cloak over him, when Kern, who was naturally very courageous, recovered himself, and related, though with trembling lips, that as he had accidentally looked in the glass, he had seen a white female figure looking out of it; she was in front of his own image, which he distinctly saw behind her.

"At first, he could not believe his eyes; he thought it must be fancy, and for that reason he had stood so long; but when he saw that the eyes of the figure moved, and looked into his, a shudder had seized him, and he had turned away. Hahn, upon this, advanced with firm steps to the front of the mirror and called upon the apparition to show itself to him; but he saw nothing, although he remained a quarter of an hour before the glass, and frequently repeated his exhortation. Kern then related that the features of the apparition were very old, but not gloomy or morose; the expression was that of indifference; but the face was very pale, and the head was wrapped in a cloth which left only the features visible.

"By this time, it was four o'clock in the morning; sleep was banished from their eyes, and they resolved to return to the lower room and have their beds brought back again: but the people who were sent to fetch them returned, declaring they could not open the door, although it did not appear to be fastened. They were sent back again; but a second and a third time they returned with the same answer. Then Hahn went himself and opened it with the greatest ease. The four servants, however, solemnly declared that all their united strength could make no impression on it.

"In this way a month had elapsed: the strange events at the castle had got spread abroad; and among others who desired to convince themselves of the facts were two Bavarian officers of dragoons, namely, Captain Cornet and Lieutenant Magerle, of the regiment of Minuci. Magerle offering to remain in the room alone, the others left him; but scarcely had they passed into the next apartment, when they heard Magerle storming like a man in a passion and cutting away at the tables and chairs with his sabre, whereupon the captain thought it advisable to return, in order to rescue the furniture from his rage. They found the door shut, but he opened it on their summons, and related, in great excitement, that as soon as they had quitted the room, some cursed thing had begun to fling lime and other matters at him, and, having examined every part of the room without being able to discover the agent of the mischief, he had fallen into a rage and cut madly about him.

"The party now passed the rest of the evening together in the room, and the two Bavarians closely watched Hahn and Kern in order to satisfy themselves that the mystery was no trick of theirs. All at once, as they were quietly sitting at the table, the snuffers rose into the air and fell again to the ground behind Magerle, and a leaden ball flew at Hahn and hit him upon the breast, and presently afterward they heard a noise at the glass-door, as if somebody had struck his fist through it, together with a sound of falling glass. On investigation they found the door entire, but a broken drinking-glass on the floor. By this time the Bavarians were convinced, and they retired from the room to seek repose in one more peaceful.

"Among other things, the following, which occurred to Hahn, is remarkable. One evening about eight o'clock, being about to shave himself, the implements for the purpose, which were lying on a pyramidal stand in a corner of the room, flew at him, one after the other—the soap-box, the razor, the brush, and the soap—and fell at his feet, although he was standing several paces from the pyramid. He and Kern, who was sitting at the table, laughed, for they were now so accustomed to these events that they only made them subjects of diversion. In the meantime, Hahn poured some water, which had been standing on the stove, in a basin, observing, as he dipped his finger into it, that it was of a nice heat for shaving. He seated himself before the table and strapped his razor, but when he attempted to prepare the lather, the water was clean vanished out of the basin. Another time, Hahn was awakened by goblins throwing at him a squeezed-up piece of sheet-lead in which tobacco had been wrapped, and when he stooped to pick it up, the self-same piece was flung at him again. When this was repeated a third time, Hahn flung a heavy stick at his invisible assailant.

"Dorfel, the book-keeper, was frequently a witness to these strange events. He once laid his cap on the table by the stove; when, being about to depart, he sought for it, it had vanished. Four or five times he examined the table in vain; presently afterward he saw it lying exactly where he had placed it when he came in. On the same table, Knittel having once placed his cap and drawn himself a seat, suddenly, although there was nobody near the table, he saw the cap flying through the room to his feet, where it fell.

"Hahn now determined to find out the secret himself, and for this purpose seated himself, with two lights before him, in a position where he could see the whole of the room and all the doors and windows it contained;—but the same things occurred, even when Kern was out, the servants in the stables, and nobody in the room but himself; and the snuffers were as usual flung about, although the closest observation could not detect by whom.

"The forest-master, Radzensky, spent a night in the room, but, although the two friends slept, he could get no rest. He was bombarded without intermission, and in the morning his bed was found full of all manner of household articles.

"One morning, in spite of all the drumming and flinging, Hahn was determined to sleep; but a heavy blow on the wall close to his bed soon awoke him from his slumbers. A second time he went to sleep and was awaked by a sensation as if some person had dipped his finger in water and was sprinkling his face with it. He pretended to sleep again, while he watched Kern and Knittel, who were sitting at the table; the sensation of sprinkling returned, but he could find no water on his face.

"About this time, Hahn had occasion to make a journey as far as Breslau; and when he returned he heard the strangest story of all. In order not to be alone in this mysterious chamber, Kern had engaged Hahn's servant, a man of about forty years of age, and of entire singleness of character, to stay with him. One night as Kern lay in his bed, and this man was standing near the glass-door in conversation with him, to his utter amazement he beheld a jug of beer, which stood on a table in the room at some distance from him, slowly lifted to a height of about three feet, and the contents poured into a glass that was standing there also, until the latter was half full. The jug was then gently replaced, and the glass lifted and emptied as by someone drinking; while John, the servant, exclaimed in terrified surprise, 'Lord Jesus! it swallows!' The glass was quietly replaced, and not a drop of beer was to be found on the floor. Hahn was about to require an oath of John in confirmation of this fact; but forbore, seeing how ready the man was to take one, and satisfied of the truth of the relation.

"One night, Knetsch, an inspector of the works, passed the night with the two friends, and in spite of the unintermitting flinging they all three went to bed. There were lights in the room, and presently all three saw two napkins, in the middle of the room, rise slowly up to the ceiling, and, having there spread themselves out, flutter down again. The china bowl of a pipe belonging to Kern flew about and was broken. Knives and forks were flung, and at last one of the latter fell on Hahn's head, though fortunately with the handle downward: and having now endured this annoyance for two months, it was unanimously resolved to abandon this mysterious chamber, for this night at all events. John and Kern took up one of the beds and carried it into the opposite room, but they were no sooner gone than a pitcher for holding chalybeate-water flew to the feet of the two who remained behind, although no door was open, and a brass candlestick was flung to the ground. In the opposite room the night passed quietly, although some sounds still issued from the forsaken chamber.

"After this there was a cessation to these strange proceedings, and nothing more remarkable occurred, with the exception of the following circumstance. Some weeks after the abovementioned removal, as Hahn was returning home and crossing the bridge that leads to the castle-gate, he heard the foot of a dog behind him. He looked round and called repeatedly on the name of a greyhound that was much attached to him, thinking it might be her; but, although he still heard the foot, even when he ascended the stairs, as he could see nothing, he concluded it was an illusion. Scarcely, however, had he set his foot within the room, than Kern advanced and took the door out of his hand, at the same time calling the dog by name,—immediately adding, however, that he thought he had seen the dog, but that he had no sooner called her than she disappeared.

"Hahn then inquired if he had really seen the dog. 'Certainly, I did,' replied Kern, 'she was close behind you—half within the door—and that was the reason I took it out of your hand, lest, not observing her, you should have shut it suddenly and crushed her. It was a white dog, and I took it for Flora.' Search was immediately made for the dog, but she was found locked up in the stable and had not been out of it the whole day. It is certainly remarkable—even supposing Hahn to have been deceived with respect to the footsteps—that Kern should have seen a white dog behind him, before he had heard a word on the subject from his friend, especially as there was no such animal in the neighbourhood; besides, it was not yet dark, and Kern was very sharp-sighted.

"Hahn remained in the castle for half a year after this, without experiencing anything extraordinary; and even persons who had possession of the mysterious chambers were not subjected to any annoyance.

"The riddle, however, in spite of all the perquisitions and investigations that were set on foot remained unsolved—no explanation of these strange events could be found; and even supposing any motive could exist, there was nobody in the neighbourhood clever enough to have carried on such a system of persecution, which lasted so long, that the inhabitants of the chamber became almost indifferent to it.

"In conclusion, it is only necessary to add that Councillor Hahn wrote down this account for his own satisfaction, with the strictest regard to truth. His words are:—

"'I have described these events exactly as I heard and saw them: from beginning to end I observed them with the most entire self-possession. I had no fear, nor the slightest tendency to it; yet the whole thing remains to me perfectly inexplicable. Written the 19th of November, 1808.

"'Augustus Hahn, Councillor.'

"Doubtless many natural explanations of these phenomena will be suggested by those who consider themselves above the weakness of crediting stories of this description. Some say that Kern was a dexterous juggler, who contrived to throw dust in the eyes of his friend Hahn; while others affirm that both Hahn and Kern were intoxicated every evening! I did not fail to communicate these objections to Hahn, and here insert his answer:—

"'After the events alluded to, I resided with Kern for a quarter of a year in another part of the castle of Slawensick (which has since been struck by lightning, and burnt), without finding a solution of the mystery, or experiencing a repetition of the annoyance, which discontinued from the moment we quitted those particular apartments. Those persons must suppose me very weak, who can imagine it possible that, with only one companion, I could have been the subject of his sport for two months without detecting him. As for Kern himself, he was, from the first, very anxious to leave the rooms; but as I was unwilling to resign the hope of discovering some natural cause for these phenomena, I persisted in remaining; and the thing that at last induced me to yield to his wishes was the vexation at the loss of his china-pipe, which had been flung against the wall and broken. Besides, jugglery requires a juggler, and I was frequently quite alone when these events occurred. It is equally absurd to accuse us of intoxication.

"'The wine there was too dear for us to drink at all, and we confined ourselves wholly to weak beer. All the circumstances that happened are not set down in the narration; but my recollection of the whole is as vivid as if it had occurred yesterday. We had also many witnesses, some of whom have been mentioned. Councillor Klenk also visited me at a later period, with every desire to investigate the mystery; and when, one morning, he had mounted on a table, for the purpose of doing so, and was knocking at the ceiling with a stick, a powder-horn fell upon him, which he had just before left on the table in another room. At that time Kern had been for some time absent. I neglected no possible means that could have led to a discovery of the secret; and at least as many people have blamed me for my unwillingness to believe in a supernatural cause as the reverse. Fear is not my failing, as all who are acquainted with me know; and, to avoid the possibility of error, I frequently asked others what they saw when I was myself present; and their answers always coincided with what I saw myself. From 1809 to 1811 I lived in Jacobswald, very near the castle where the prince himself was residing. I am aware that some singular circumstances occurred while he was there; but as I did not witness them myself, I cannot speak of them more particularly.

"'I am still as unable as ever to account for those events, and I am content to submit to the hasty remarks of the world, knowing that I have only related the truth, and what many persons now alive witnessed as well as myself.

"'Councillor Hahn.

"'Ingelfinger, August 24, 1828.'" (Translated from the original German C.C.)

The only key to this mystery ever discovered was, that after the destruction of the castle by lightning, when the ruins were removed, there was found the skeleton of a man without a coffin. His skull had been split, and a sword lay by his side!

2

I will here only relate one, of a very remarkable nature, that occurred in the prison of Weinsberg, in the year 1835.

Dr. Kerner, who has published a little volume containing a report of the circumstances, describes the place where the thing happened to be such a one as negatives at once all possibility of trick or imposture. It was in a sort of block-house or fortress—a prison within a prison—with no windows but what looked into a narrow passage, closed with several doors. It was on the second floor; the windows were high up, heavily barred with iron, and immovable without considerable mechanical force. The external prison is surrounded by a high wall, and the gates are kept closed day and night. The prisoners in different apartments are of course never allowed to communicate with each other, and the deputy-governor of the prison and his family, consisting of a wife, niece, and one maid-servant, are described as people of unimpeachable respectability and veracity. As depositions regarding this affair were laid before the magistrates, it is on them I found my narration.

"On the 12th September, 1835, the deputy-governor or keeper of the jail, named Mayer, sent in a report to the magistrates that a woman called Elizabeth Eslinger was every night visited by a ghost, which generally came about eleven o'clock, and which left her no rest, as it said she was destined to release it, and it always invited her to follow it; and as she would not, it pressed heavily on her neck and side till it gave her pain. The persons confined with her pretended also to have seen this apparition.
    "Signed
    "Mayer."

A woman named Rosina Schahl condemned to eight days' confinement for abusive language, deposed, that about eleven o'clock, Eslinger began to breathe hard as if she was suffocating; she said a ghost was with her, seeking his salvation.

    "I did not trouble myself about it but told her to wake me when it came again. Last night I saw a shadowy form, between four and five feet high, standing near the bed; I did not see it move. Eslinger breathed very hard and complained of a pressure on the side. For several days she has neither ate nor drank anything.
    "Signed
    "Schahl."

    "Court Resolves,
    "That Eslinger is to be visited by the prison physician, and a report made as to her mental and bodily health.
    "Signed by the magistrates
    "Eckhardt
    "Theurer
    "Knorr"

174

"Report.

"Having examined the prisoner, Elizabeth Eslinger, confined here since the beginning of September, I found her of sound mind, but possessed with one fixed idea, namely, that she is and has been for a considerable time troubled by an apparition, which leaves her no rest, coming chiefly by night, and requiring her prayers to release it. It visited her before she came to the prison and was the cause of the offence that brought her here. Having now, in compliance with the orders of the supreme court, observed this woman for eleven weeks, I am led to the conclusion that there is no deception in this case, and also that the persecution is not a mere monomaniacal idea of her own, and the testimony not only of her fellow-prisoners, but that of the deputy-governor's family, and even of persons in distant houses, confirms me in this persuasion.

"Eslinger is a widow, aged thirty-eight years, and declares that she never had any sickness whatever, neither is she aware of any at present; but she has always been a ghost-seer, though never till lately had any communication with them; that now, for eleven weeks that she has been in the prison, she is nightly disturbed by an apparition, that had previously visited her in her own house, and which had been once seen also by a girl of fourteen—a statement which this girl confirms. When at home, the apparition did not appear in a defined human form, but as a pillar of cloud, out of which proceeded a hollow voice, signifying to her that she was to release it, by her prayers, from the cellar of a woman in Wimmenthal, named Singhaasin, whither it was banished, or whence it could not free itself. She (Eslinger) says that she did not then venture to speak to it, not knowing whether to address it as *Sie*, *Ihr*, or *Du* (that is, whether she should address it in the second or third person)—which custom among the Germans has rendered a very important point of etiquette. It is to be remembered that this woman was a peasant, without education, who had been brought into trouble by treasure-seeking, a pursuit in which she hoped to be assisted by this spirit. This digging for buried treasure is a strong passion in Germany.

"The ghost now comes in a perfect human shape, and is dressed in a loose robe, with a girdle, and has on its head a four-cornered cap. It has a projecting chin and forehead, fiery, deep-set eyes, a long beard, and high cheek-bones, which look as if they were covered with parchment. A light radiates about and above his head, and in the midst of this light she sees the outlines of the spectre.

"Both she and her fellow-prisoners declare, that this apparition comes several times in a night, but always between the evening and morning bell. He often comes through the closed door or window, but they can then see neither door nor window, nor iron bars; they often hear the closing of the door and can see into the passage when he comes in or out that way, so that if a piece of wood lies there they see it. They hear a shuffling in the passage as he comes and goes. He most frequently enters by the window, and they then hear a peculiar sound there. He comes in quite erect. Although their cell is entirely closed, they feel a cool wind when he is near them. (It is to be observed this is the sensation felt by Reichenbach's patients on the approach of the magnet, see number 18.) All sorts of noises are heard, particularly a crackling. When he is angry, or in great trouble, they perceive a strange mouldering, earthy smell. He often pulls away the coverlet and sits on the edge of the bed. At first the touch of his hand was icy cold, since he became brighter it is warmer; she first saw the brightness of his finger-ends; it afterward spread further. If she stretches out her hand she cannot feel him, but when he touches her she feels it. He sometimes takes her hands and lays them together, to make her pray. His sighs and groans are like a person in despair; they are heard by others as well as Eslinger. While he is making these sounds, she is often praying aloud, or talking to her companions, so they are sure it is not she who makes them. She does not see his mouth move when he speaks. The voice is hollow and gasping. He comes to her for prayers, and he seems to her like one in a mortal sickness, who seeks comfort in the prayers of others. He says he was a catholic priest in Wimmenthal and lived in the year 1414."

(Wimmenthal is still catholic; the woman Eslinger herself is a Lutheran and belongs to Backnang.)

"He says, that among other crimes, a fraud committed conjointly with his father, on his brothers, presses sorely on him; he cannot get quit of it; it obstructs him. He always entreated her to go with him to Wimmenthal, whither he was banished, or consigned, and pray there for him.

"She says she cannot tell whether what he says is true; and does not deny that she thought to find treasures by his aid. She has often told him that the prayers of a sinner, like herself, cannot help him, and that he should seek the Redeemer; but he will not forbear his entreaties. When she says these things, he is sad, and presses nearer to her, and lays his head so close that she is obliged to pray into his mouth. *He seems hungry for prayers.* She has often felt his tears on her cheek and neck; they felt icy cold; but the spot soon after burns, and they have a bluish red mark. (These marks are visible on her skin.)

"One night this apparition brought with him a large dog, which leaped on the beds, and was seen by her fellow-prisoners also, who were much terrified, and screamed. The ghost, however, spoke, and said, 'Fear not; this is my father.' He had since brought the dog with him again, which alarmed them dreadfully, and made them quite ill.

"Both Mayer and the prisoners asserted, that Eslinger was scarcely seen to sleep, either by night or day, for ten weeks. She ate very little, prayed continually, and appeared very much wasted and exhausted. She said she saw the spectre alike, whether her eyes were opened or closed, which showed that it was a magnetic perception, and not *seeing* by her bodily organs. It is remarkable that a cat belonging to the jail, being shut up in this room, was so frightened when the apparition came, that it tried to make its escape by flying against the walls; and finding this impossible, it crept under the coverlet of the bed, in extreme terror. The experiment was made again, with the same result; and after this second time the animal refused all nourishment, wasted away, and died.

"In order to satisfy myself," says Dr. Kerner, "of the truth of these depositions, I went to the prison on the night of the 15th of October and shut myself up without light in Eslinger's cell. About half-past eleven I heard a sound as of some hard body being flung down, but not on the side where the woman was, but the opposite; she immediately began to breathe hard and told me the spectre was there. I laid my hand on her head and adjured it as an evil spirit to depart. I had scarcely spoken the words when there was a strange rattling, crackling noise, all round the walls, which finally seemed to go out through the window; and the woman said that the spectre had departed.

"On the following night it told her that it was grieved at being addressed as an evil spirit, which it was not, but one that deserved pity; and that what it wanted was prayers and redemption.

"On the 18th of October, I went to the cell again, between ten and eleven, taking with me my wife, and the wife of the keeper, Madame Mayer. When the woman's breathing showed me the spectre was there, I laid my hand on her, and adjured it, in gentle terms, not to trouble her further. The same sort of sound as before commenced, but it was softer, and this time continued all along the passage, where there was certainly nobody. We all heard it.

"On the night of the 20th I went again, with Justice Heyd. We both heard sounds when the spectre came, and the woman could not conceive why we did not see it. We could not; but we distinctly felt a cool wind blowing upon us when, according to her account, it was near, although there was no aperture by which air could enter."

On each of these occasions Dr. Kerner seems to have remained about a couple of hours.

Madame Mayer now resolved to pass a night in the cell, for the purpose of observation; and she took her niece, a girl aged nineteen, with her: her report is as follows:—

"It was a rainy night, and, in the prison, pitch dark. My niece slept sometimes; I remained awake all night, and mostly sitting up in bed.

"About midnight I saw a light come in at the window; it was a yellowish light and moved slowly; and though we were closely shut in, I felt a cool wind blowing on me. I said to the woman, 'The ghost is here, is he not?' She said 'Yes,' and continued to pray, as she had been doing before. The cool wind and the light now approached me; my coverlet was quite light, and I could see my hands and arms; and at the same time, I perceived an indescribable odour of putrefaction; my face felt as if ants were running over it. (Most of the prisoners described themselves as feeling the same sensation when the spectre was there.) Then the light moved about and went up and down the room; and on the door of the cell I saw a number of little glimmering stars, such as I had never before seen. Presently, I and my niece heard a voice which I can compare to nothing I ever heard before. It was not like a human voice. The words and sighs sounded as if they were drawn up out of a deep hollow and appeared to ascend from the floor to the roof in a column; while this voice spoke, the woman was praying aloud; so, I was sure it did not proceed from her. No one could produce such a sound. They were strange, superhuman sighs and entreaties for prayers and redemption.

"It is very extraordinary that, whenever the ghost spoke, I always *felt it beforehand*. (Proving that the spirit had been able to establish a rapport with this person. She was in a magnetic relation to him.) We heard a crackling in the room also. I was perfectly awake, and in possession of my senses; and we are ready to make oath to having seen and heard these things."

On the 9th of December, Madame Mayer spent the night again in the cell, with her niece and her maid-servant; and her report is as follows:—

"It was moonlight, and I sat up in bed all night, watching Eslinger. Suddenly I saw a white shadowy form, like a small animal, cross the room. I asked her what it was; and she answered, 'Don't you see it's a lamb? It often comes with the apparition.' We then saw a stool, that was near us, lifted and *set down* again on its legs. She was in bed and praying the whole time. Presently, there was such a noise at the window that I thought all the panes were broken. She told us it was the ghost, and that he was sitting on the stool. We then heard a walking and shuffling up and down, although I could not see him; but presently I felt a cool wind blowing on me, and out of this wind the same hollow voice I had heard before, said, 'In the name of Jesus, look on me!'

"Before this, the moon was gone, and it was quite dark; but when the voice spoke to me, I saw a light around us, though still no form. Then there was a sound of walking toward the opposite window, and I heard the voice say, 'Do you see me now?' And then, for the first time, I saw a shadowy form, stretching up as if to make itself visible to us, but could distinguish no features.

"During the rest of the night, I saw it repeatedly, sometimes sitting on the stool, and at others moving about; and I am perfectly certain that there was no moonlight now, nor any other light from without. How I saw it, I cannot tell; it is a thing not to be described.

"Eslinger prayed the whole time, and the more earnestly she did so, the closer the spectre went to her. It sometimes sat upon her bed.

"About five o'clock, when he came near to me, and I felt the cool air, I said, 'Go to my husband, in his chamber, and leave a sign that you have been there!' He answered distinctly, 'Yes.' Then we heard the door, which was fast locked, open and shut; and we saw the shadow float out (for he floated rather than walked), and we heard the shuffling along the passage.

"In a quarter of an hour we saw him return, entering by the window; and I asked him if he had been with my husband, and what he had done. He answered by a sound like a short, low, hollow laugh. Then he hovered about without any noise, and we heard him speaking to Eslinger, while she still prayed aloud. Still, as before, I always knew when he was going to speak. After six o'clock, we saw him no more. In the morning, my husband mentioned, with great surprise, that his chamber door, which he was sure he had fast bolted and locked, even taking out the key when he went to bed, he had found wide open."

On the 24th, Madame Mayer passed the night there again; but on this occasion she only saw a white shadow coming and going, and standing by the woman, who prayed unceasingly. She also heard the shuffling.

Between prisoners and the persons in authority who went to observe, the number of those who testify to this phenomenon is considerable; and, although the amount of what was perceived varied according to the receptivity of the subject in each case, the evidence of all is perfectly coincident as to the character of the phenomena. Some saw only the light; others distinguished the form in the midst of it; all heard the sound and perceived the mouldering earthy smell.

That the receptivity of the women was greater than that of the men, after what I have elsewhere said, should excite no surprise; the preponderance of the sympathetic system in them being sufficient to account for the difference.

Frederica Follen, from Lowenstein, who was eight weeks in the same cell with Eslinger, was witness to all the phenomena, though she only once arrived at seeing the spectre in its perfect human form, as the latter saw it; but it frequently spoke to her, bidding her amend her life, and remember that it was one who had tasted of death that give her this counsel. This circumstance had a great effect upon her.

When any of them swore, the apparition always evinced much displeasure, grasped them by the throat, and forced them to pray. Frequently, when he came or went, they said it sounded like a flight of pigeons.

Catherine Sinn, from Mayenfels, was confined in an adjoining room for a fortnight. After her release, she was interrogated by the minister of her parish, and deposed that she had known nothing of Eslinger, or the spectre:

"But every night, being quite alone, I heard a rustling and a noise at the window, which looked only into the passage. I felt and heard, though I could not see anybody, that someone was moving about the room; *these sounds* were accompanied by a cool wind, though the place was closely shut up. I heard also a crackling, and a shuffling, and a sound as if gravel were thrown; but could find none in the morning. Once it seemed to me that a hand was laid softly on my forehead. I did not like staying alone, on account of these things, and begged to be put into a room with others; so, I was placed with Eslingen and Follen. The same things continued here, and they told me about the ghost; but not being alone, I was not so frightened. I often heard him speak; it was hollow and slow, not like a human voice; but I could seldom catch the words. When he left the prison, which was generally about five in the morning, he used to say, 'Pray!' and when he did so, he would add, 'God reward you!' I never saw him distinctly till the last morning I was there; then I saw a white shadow standing by Eslinger's bed.

"Signed,   Catherine Sinn.
"Minister Binder, Mayenfels."

It would be tedious, were I to copy the depositions of all the prisoners, the experience of most of them being similar to the above. I will therefore content myself with giving an abstract of the most remarkable particulars.

Besides the crackling, rustling as of paper, walking, shuffling, concussions of the windows and of their beds, &c., &c., they heard sometimes a fearful cry, and not unfrequently the bed-coverings were pulled from them; it appearing to be the object of the spirit to manifest himself thus to those to whom he could not make himself visible; and as I find this pulling off the bedclothes, and heaving up the bed as if someone were under it, repeated in a variety of cases, foreign and English, I conclude the motive to be the same. Several of the women heard him speak.

All these depositions are contained in Dr. Kerner's report to the magistrates; and he concludes by saying, that there can be no doubt of the fact of the woman Elizabeth Eslinger suffering these annoyances, by whatever name people may choose to call them.

Among the most remarkable phenomena, is the real or apparent opening of the door, so that they could see what was in the passage. Eslinger said that the spirit was often surrounded by a light, and his eyes looked fiery; and there sometimes came with him two lambs, which occasionally appeared as stars. He often took hold of Eslinger, and made her sit up, put her hands together, that she might pray; and once he appeared to take a pen and paper from under his gown, and wrote, laying it on her coverlet.

It is extremely curious that, on two occasions, Eslinger saw Dr. Kerner and Justice Heyd enter with the ghost, when they were not there in the body, and both times Heyd was enveloped in a black cloud. The ghost, on being asked, told Eslinger that the cloud indicated that trouble was impending. A few days afterward his child died very unexpectedly, and Dr. Kerner now remembered, that the first time Eslinger said she had seen Heyd in this way, his father had died directly afterward. Kerner attended both patients and was thus associated in the symbol. Follen also saw these two images, and spoke, believing the one to be Dr. Kerner himself.

On other occasions she saw strangers come in with the ghost, whom afterward, when they *really* came in the body, she recognised. This seems to have been a sort of second sight.

Dr. K. says, "I think justly enough, that if Eslinger had been feigning, she never would have ventured on what seemed so improbable."

Some of the women, after the spectre had visibly leaned over them, or had spoken into their ears, were so affected by the odour he diffused that they vomited and could not eat till they had taken an emetic; and those parts of their persons that he touched became painful and swollen, an effect I find produced in numerous other instances.

The following particulars are worth observing, in the evidence of a girl sixteen years of age, called Margaret Laibesberg, who was confined for ten days for plucking some grapes in a vineyard. She says she knew nothing about the spectre, but that she was greatly alarmed the first night at hearing the door burst open and something come shuffling in. Eslinger bade her not fear and said that it would not injure her. The girl, however, being greatly terrified every night, and hiding her head under the bed-clothes, on the fourth Eslinger got out of her own bed, and, coming to her, said: "Do, in the name of God, look at him! He will do you no harm, I assure you."

"Then," says the girl, "I looked out from under the clothes, and I saw two white forms, like two lambs—so beautiful that I could have looked at them for ever. Between them stood a white, shadowy form, as tall as a man, but I was not able to look longer, for my eyes failed me."

The terrors of this girl were so great, that Eslinger had repeatedly occasion to get out of bed and fetch her to lie with herself. When she could be induced to look, she always saw the figure, and he bade her also pray for him. Whenever he touched her, which he did on the forehead and eyes, she felt pain, but says nothing of any subsequent swelling. Both this girl and another, called Neidhardt, who was brought in on the last day of Margaret L————'s imprisonment, testified that on the previous night they had heard Eslinger ask the ghost why he looked so angry; and that they had heard him answer that it was "because she had on the preceding night neglected to pray for him as much as usual," which neglect arose from two gentlemen having passed the night in the cell.

When on the tenth day the girl Margaret L———— was released, she said that there was something so awful to her in this apparition, that she had firmly resolved and vowed to be pious and lead henceforth a virtuous life.

Some of them seem to have felt little alarm; Maria Bar, aged forty-one, said: "I was not afraid, for I have a good conscience." The offences for which these women were confined appear to have been very slight ones, such as quarrelling, &c.

In a room that opened into the same passage, men were shut up for disputing with the police, neglect of regulations, and similar misdemeanours. These persons not only heard the noises as above described, such as the walking, shuffling, opening and shutting the door, &c., &c., but some of them saw the ghost. Christian Bauer deposed that he had never heard anything about the ghost, but that, being disturbed by a knocking and rustling toward three o'clock on the second morning of his incarceration, he looked up and saw a white figure bending over him, and heard a strange hollow voice say: "You must needs have patience!" He said he thought it must be his grandfather, at which Stricker, his companion, laughed. Stricker deposed that he heard a hollow voice say: "You must needs have patience;" and that Bauer told him that there was a white apparition near him, and that he supposed it was his grandfather. Bauer said that he was frightened the first night but got used to it and did not mind.

It is worthy of observation, that when they heard the door of the women's room open, they also heard the voice of Eslinger praying, which seems as if the door not only appeared to open, but actually did so. We have already seen that this spirit could open doors. In the *Seeress of Prevorst*, (by Justinus Kerner and translated from the German by Catherine Crowe), the doors were constantly *audibly* and *visibly* opened, as by an unseen hand, when she saw a spectre enter; and I know to an absolute certainty that the same phenomenon takes place in a house not far from where I am writing; and this, sometimes, when there are two people sleeping in the room—a lady and gentleman. The door having been fast locked when they went to bed, the room thoroughly examined, and every precaution taken—for they are unwilling to believe in the spiritual character of the disturbances that annoy them—they are aroused by a consciousness that it is opening, and they do find it open, on rising to investigate the fact.

One of the most remarkable proofs, either of the force of volition or of the electrical powers of the apparition that haunted Eslinger, or else of his power to imitate sounds, was the real, or apparent, violent shaking of the heavy, iron-barred window, which it is asserted the united efforts of six men could not shake at all when they made the experiment.

The supreme court having satisfied itself that there was no imposture in this case, it was proposed that some men of science should be invited to investigate the strange phenomenon, and endeavour if possible to explain it. Accordingly, not only Dr. Kerner himself and his son, but many others, passed nights in the prison for this purpose. Among these, besides some ministers of the Lutheran church, there was an engraver called Duttenhofer; Wagner, an artist; Kapff, professor of mathematics at Heilbroun; Frass, a barrister; Doctors Seyffer and Sicherer, physicians; Heyd, a magistrate; Baron von Hugel, &c., &c.: but their perquisitions elicited no more than has been already narrated—all heard the noises, most of them saw the lights, and some saw the figure. Duttenhofer and Kapff saw it without a defined outline; it was itself bright but did not illuminate the room. Some of the sounds appeared to them like the discharging of a Leyden jar. There was also a throwing of gravel, and a heavy dropping of water, but neither to be found. Professor Kapff says that he was quite cool and self-possessed, till there was such a violent concussion of the heavy, barred window, that he thought it must have come in; then both he and Duttenhofer felt horror-struck.

As they could not see the light emitted by the spectre when the room was otherwise lighted, they were in the dark; but they took every care to ascertain that Eslinger was in her bed while these things were going on. She prayed aloud the whole time, unless when speaking to them. By the morning, she used to be dreadfully exhausted, from this continual exertion.

It is also mentioned that the straw on which she lay was frequently changed and examined, and every means taken to ascertain that there was nothing whatever in her possession that could enable her to perform any sort of jugglery. Her fellow-prisoners were also invited to tell all they knew or could discover; and a remission of their sentences promised to those who would make known the imposition, if there was one.

Dr. Sicherer, who was accompanied by Mr. Frass, says that, having heard of these phenomena, which he thought the more unaccountable from the circumstances of the woman's age and condition, &c.— she being a healthy, hard-working person, aged thirty-eight, who had never known sickness—he was very desirous of inquiring personally into the affair.

While they were in the court of the prison, waiting for admittance, they heard extraordinary noises, which could not be accounted for, and during the night there was a repetition of those above described—especially the apparent throwing of gravel, or peas, which seemed to fall so near him that he involuntarily covered his face. Then followed the feeling of a cool wind; and then the oppressive odour, for which, he says, he can find no comparison, and which almost took away his breath. He was perfectly satisfied that it was no smell originating in the locality or the state of the prison. Simultaneously with the perception of this odor, he saw a thick, grey cloud, of no defined shape, near Eslinger's bed. When this cloud disappeared, the odour was no longer perceptible. It was a fine moonlight night, and there was light enough in the room to distinguish the beds, &c.

The same phenomena recurred several times during the night: Eslinger was heard, each time the ghost was there, praying and reciting hymns. They also heard her say, "Don't press my hands so hard together!"—"Don't touch me!" &c. The voice of the spirit they did not hear. Toward three or four o'clock, they heard heavy blows, footsteps, opening and shutting of the door, and a concussion of the whole house, that made them think it was going to fall on their heads. About six o'clock, they saw the phantom again; and altogether these phenomena recurred at least ten times in the course of the night.

Dr. Sicherer concludes by saying that he had undertaken the investigation with a mind entirely unprepossessed; and that in the report he made, at the desire of the supreme court, he had recorded his observations as conscientiously as if he had been upon a jury. He adds that he had examined everything; and that neither in the person of the woman, nor in any other of the inmates of the prison, could he find the smallest grounds for suspicion, nor any clew to the mystery, which, in a scientific point of view, appeared to him utterly inexplicable. Dr. Sicherer's report is dated Heilbronn, January 8, 1836.

Mr. Fraas, who accompanied him, confirms the above statement in every particular, with the addition that he several times saw a light, of a varying circumference, moving about the room; and that it was while he saw this, that the woman told him the ghost was there. He also felt an oppression of the breath and a pressure on his forehead each time before the apparition came, especially once, when, although he had carefully abstained from mentioning his sensations, she told him it was standing close at his head. He stretched out his hand, but perceived nothing, except a cool wind and an overpowering smell.

Dr. Seyffer being there one night, with Dr. Kerner, in order to exclude the possibility of light entering through the window, they stopped it up. They, however, saw the phosphorescent light of the spectre, as before. It moved quietly about, and remained a quarter of an hour. The room was otherwise perfectly dark; the sounds accompanying it were like the dropping of water and the discharge of a Leyden jar. They fully ascertained that these phenomena did not proceed from the woman.

I have already given the depositions of Madame Mayer, the wife of the deputy-governor or keeper of the prison, who is spoken of as a highly respectable person. Mayer himself, however, though quite unable to account for all these extraordinary proceedings, found great difficulty in believing that there was anything supernatural in the affair; and he told Eslinger that, if she wished him to be convinced, she must send the ghost to do it!

He says: "The night after I had said this, I went to bed and to sleep, little expecting such a visitor; but, toward midnight, I was awakened by something touching my left elbow. This was followed by a pain; and in the morning, when I looked at the place, I saw several blue spots. I told Eslinger that this was not enough, and that she must tell the ghost to touch my other elbow. This was done on the following night, and, at the same time, I perceived a smell like putrefaction. The blue spots followed." (It will be remembered that Eslinger had blue spots also.)

Mayer continues to say that the spectre made known its presence in his chamber by various sounds, such as were heard in the other part of the house. He never saw the figure distinctly, but his wife did: she always prayed when it was there. He, however, felt the cool wind that they all described.

The ghost told Eslinger that he should continue his visits to the prison after she had quitted it, and he did so. The second night after her release, they felt his approach, especially from the cool wind, and Madame Mayer desired him to testify his presence to her husband. Immediately there were sounds like a wind-instrument, and these were repeated at her desire.

The prisoners also heard and felt the apparition after Eslinger's departure; and Mayer says he is perfectly assured that in this jail, where the inmates were frequently changed, everybody was locked up, and every place thoroughly examined, it was utterly impossible for any trick to be played: besides which, all parties agreed that the sounds were often of a description that could not have been produced by any known means.

But it was not to the prison alone that this apparition confined his visits. To whomsoever Eslinger sent him, he went—testifying his presence by the same signs as above described. He visited the chambers of several of the magistrates, of a teacher named Neuffer, of the referendary burgher, of a citizen named Rummel, and many others. Of these, some only perceived his presence by the noises, the cool air, the smell, or the touch; others saw the light also, and others perceived the figure with more or less distinctness.

A Mr. Dorr, of Heilbronn, seems to have scoffed very much at these rumors, and Dr. Kerner bade Eslinger ask the ghost to convince him, which she did.

Mr. Dorr says: "When I heard these things talked of, I always laughed at them, and was thought very sensible for so doing. Now I shall be laughed at in my turn, no doubt." He then relates that, on the morning of the 30th of December, 1835, he awoke, as usual, about five o'clock, and was thinking of some business he had in hand, when he became conscious that there was something near him, and he felt as if it blew cold upon him. He started up, thinking some animal had got into his room, but could find nothing. Next he heard a noise, like sparks from an electrical machine, and then a report close to his right ear. Had there been anything visible, it was light enough to see it. This report was frequently heard in the prison.

Wherever the apparition once made a visit, he generally continued to go for several successive nights. He also visited Professor Kapff at Heilbronn, and Baron von Hugel at Eschenau, without being desired to do so by Eslinger; and Neuffer, whom he also went to, she knew nothing of.

When he visited Dr. Kerner's chamber, his wife, who had prided herself on her incredulity, and boasted of being born on St. Thomas's day, was entirely converted, for she not only heard him, but saw him distinctly. He visited them for several nights, accompanied by the noises and the light.

One night, while lying awake observing these phenomena, they fancied they heard their horse come out of his stable, which was under their room. In the morning, he was found standing outside, with his halter on; it was not broken, and it was evident that the horse had not got loose by any violence. Moreover, the door of the stable was closed behind him, as it had been at night when he was shut up.

Dr. Kerner's sister, who came from a distance to visit them, had heard very little about this affair, yet she was awakened by a sound that seemed like someone trying to speak into her ear; and, looking up, she saw two stars, like those described by Margaret Laibesberg. She observed that they emitted no rays. She also felt the cool air and perceived the corpse-like odor. This odour accompanied the ghost even when it appeared at Heilbronn.

It is remarkable that some of these persons, both men and women, felt themselves unable to move or call out while the spectre was there, and that they were relieved the moment he went away. They appeared to be magnetized; but this feeling was by no means universal. Many were perfectly composed and self-possessed the whole time and made their observations to each other. All agreed that the speaking of the apparition seemed like that of a person making efforts to speak. Now, as we are to presume that he did not speak by means of organs, as we do, but that he imitated the sounds of words as he imitated other sounds, by some means with which we are unacquainted—for since the noises were heard by everybody within hearing, we must suppose that they actually existed—we, who know the extreme difficulty of imitating human speech, may conceive how this imitation should be very defective.

Dutthenhofer and others remarked that there was no echo from the sounds, as well as that the phosphorescence shed no light around; and though the spectre could touch *them*, or produce the sensation that he did, they could not feel *him*: but, as in all similar cases, could thrust their hands through what appeared to be his body. The sensation of his falling tears, and the marks they left, seem most unaccountable; and yet, in the records of a ghost that haunted the countess of Eberstein, in 1685, we find the same thing asserted. This account was made public by the authority of the consistorial court, and with the consent of the family.

At length, on the 11th of February, the ghost took his departure from Eslinger; at least, after that day he was no more seen or heard by her or anybody else. He had always entreated her to go to Wimmenthal, where he had formerly lived, to pray for him; and, after she was released from the jail, by the advice of her friends, she did it. Some of them accompanied her, and they saw the apparition near her while she was kneeling in the open air, though not all with equal distinctness. A very respectable woman, called Wörner—a stranger to Eslinger, whom she says she never saw or spoke to till that day—offered to make oath that she had accompanied her to Wimmenthal, and that, with the other friends, she had stood about thirty paces off, quite silent and still, while the woman knelt and prayed; and that she had seen the apparition of a man, accompanied by two smaller spectres, hovering near her. "When the prayer was ended, he went close to her, and there was a light like a falling star; then I saw something like a white cloud, that seemed to float away: and after that, we saw no more."

Eslinger had been very unwilling to undertake this expedition: she took leave of her children before she started, and evidently expected mischief would befall her; and now, on approaching her, they found her lying cold and insensible. When they had revived her, she told them that, on bidding her farewell, before he ascended—which he did, accompanied by two bright infantine forms—the ghost had asked her to give him her hand; and that, after wrapping it in her handkerchief, she had complied. "A small flame had arisen from the handkerchief when he touched it; and we found the marks of his fingers like burns, but without any smell." This, however, was not the cause of her fainting; but she had been terrified by a troop of frightful animals that she saw rush past her, when the spirit floated away.

From this time, nobody, either in the prison or out of it, was troubled with this apparition.

3

But perhaps one of the most remarkable cases of haunting in modern times, is that of Willington, near Newcastle, in my account of which, however, I find myself anticipated by Mr. Howitt; and as he has had the advantage of visiting the place, which I have not, I shall take the liberty of borrowing his description of it, prefacing the account with the following letter from Mr. Proctor, the owner of the house, who it will be seen vouches for the general authenticity of the narrative. The letter was written in answer to one from me, requesting some more precise information than I had been able to obtain:—

"Josh. Proctor hopes C. Crowe will excuse her note having remained two weeks unanswered, during which time J. P. has been from home, or particularly engaged. Feeling averse to add to the publicity the circumstances occurring in his house, at Willington, have already obtained, J. P. would rather not furnish additional particulars; but if C. C. is not in possession of the number of 'Howitt's Journal,' which contains a variety of details on the subject, he will be glad to forward her one. He would, at the same time, assure C. Crowe of the strict accuracy of that portion of W. Howitt's narrative which is extracted from *Richardson's Table Book*. W. Howitt's statements, derived from his recollection of verbal communications with branches of J. Proctor's family, are likewise essentially correct, though, as might be expected in some degree, erroneous circumstantially.

"J. P. takes leave to express his conviction that the unbelief of the educated classes in apparitions of the deceased and kindred phenomena is not grounded on a fair philosophic examination of the facts, which have induced the popular belief of all ages and countries; and that it will be found by succeeding ages to have been nothing better than unreasoning and unreasonable prejudice.

"Willington, near Newcastle-on-Tyne,

7th mo. 22, 1847."

"Visits to Remarkable Places.

"by William Howitt.

"The Haunted House at Willington, near Newcastle-on-Tyne.

"We have of late years settled it as an established fact that ghosts and haunted houses were the empty creation of ignorant times. We have comfortably persuaded ourselves that such fancies only hovered in the twilight of superstition, and that in these enlightened days they had vanished for ever. How often has it been triumphantly referred to, as a proof that all such things were the offspring of ignorance, that nothing of the kind is heard of now? What shall we say, then, to the following facts? Here we have ghosts and a haunted house still. We have them in the face of our vaunted noonday light—in the midst of a busy and a populous neighbourhood—in the neighbourhood of a large and most intelligent town—and in a family neither ignorant nor in any other respect superstitious. For years have these ghosts and hauntings disturbed the quiet of a highly respectable family, and continue to haunt and disturb, spite of the incredulity of the wise, the investigations of the curious, and the anxious vigilance of the suffering family itself.

"Between the railway running from Newcastle-on-Tyne to North Shields, and the River Tyne, there lie in a hollow some few cottages, a parsonage, a mill, and a miller's house: these constitute the hamlet of Willington. Just above these the railway is carried across the valley on lofty arches, and from it you look down on the mill and cottages, lying at a considerable depth below. The mill is a large steam flour-mill, like a factory, and the miller's house stands near it, but not adjoining it. None of the cottages which lie between these premises and the railway, either, are in contact with them. The house stands on a sort of little promontory, round which runs the channel of a water-course, which appears to fill and empty with the tides. On one side of the mill and house, slopes away upward a field to a considerable distance, where it is terminated by other enclosures; on the other stands a considerable extent of ballast-hill—i. e., one of the numerous hills on the banks of the Tyne made by the deposit of ballast from the vessels trading thither. At a distance, the top of the mill seems about level with the country around it. The place lies about half-way between Newcastle and North Shields.

"This mill is, I believe, the property of, and is worked by, Messrs. Unthank and Procter. Mr. Joseph Procter resides on the spot in the house just by the mill, as already stated. He is a member of the society of friends—a gentleman in the very prime of life—and his wife, an intelligent lady, is of a family of friends in Carlisle. They have several young children. This very respectable and well-informed family, belonging to a sect which of all others is most accustomed to control, to regulate, and to put down even the imagination—the last people in the world, as it would appear, in fact, to be affected by any mere imaginary terrors or impressions—have for years been persecuted by the most extraordinary noises and apparitions.

"The house is not an old house, as will appear; it was built about the year 1800. It has no particularly spectral look about it. Seeing it in passing, or within, ignorant of its real character, one should by no means say that it was a place likely to have the reputation of being haunted. Yet looking down from the railway, and seeing it and the mill lying in a deep hole, one might imagine various strange noises likely to be heard in such a place in the night, from vessels on the river—from winds sweeping and howling down the gulley in which it stands—from engines in the neighbourhood connected with coal-mines, one of which, I could not tell where, was making at the time I was there a wild sighing noise, as I stood on the hill above. There is not any passage, however, known of under the house, by which subterranean noises could be heard; nor are they merely noises that are heard,—distinct apparitions are declared to be seen.

"Spite of the unwillingness of Mr. Procter, that these mysterious circumstances should become quite public, and averse as he is to make known himself these strange visitations, they were of such a nature that they soon became rumoured over the whole neighbourhood. Numbers of people hurried to the place to inquire into the truth of them, and at length a remarkable occurrence brought them into print. What this occurrence was, the pamphlet which appeared, and which was afterward reprinted in 'The Local Historian's Table-Book,' published by Mr. M. A. Richardson, of Newcastle, and which I here copy, will explain. It will be seen that the writer of this article has the fullest faith in the reality of what he relates, as, indeed, vast numbers of the best informed inhabitants of the neighbourhood have.

"Authentic Account of a Visit to the Haunted House at Willington.

"Were we to draw an inference from the number of cases of reported visitations from the invisible world that have been made public of late, we might be led to imagine that the days of supernatural agency were about to recommence, and that ghosts and hobgoblins were about to resume their sway over the fears of mankind. Did we, however, indulge in such an apprehension, a glance at the current tone of the literature and philosophy of the day, when treating of these subjects, would show a measure of unbelief regarding them as scornful and uncompromising as the veriest atheist or materialist could desire. Notwithstanding the prevalence of this feeling among the educated classes, there is a curiosity and interest manifested in every occurrence of this nature, that indicate a lurking faith at bottom, which an affected scepticism fails entirely to conceal.

"We feel, therefore, that we need not apologise to our readers for introducing the following particulars of a *visit* to a house in this immediate neighbourhood, which had become notorious for some years previous, as being 'haunted;' and several of the reputed deeds, or misdeeds, of its supernatural visitant had been published far and wide by rumour's thousand tongues. We deem it as worthy to be chronicled as the doings of its contemporary *genii* at Windsor, Dublin, Liverpool, Carlisle, and Sunderland, and which have all likewise hitherto failed, after public investigation, to receive a solution consistent with a rejection of spiritual agency.

"We have visited the house in question, which is well known to many of our readers, as being near a large steam corn-mill, in full view of Willington viaduct, on the Newcastle and Shields railway; and it may not be irrelevant to mention that it is quite detached from the mill, or any other premises, and has no cellaring under it. The proprietor of the house, who lives in it, declines to make public the particulars of the disturbance to which he has been subjected, and it must be understood that the account of the visit we are about to lay before our readers is derived from a friend to whom Dr. Drury presented a copy of his correspondence on the subject, with power to make such use of it as he thought proper.

"We learned that the house had been reputed, at least one room in it, to have been haunted forty years ago, and had afterward been undisturbed for a long period, during some years of which quietude the present occupant lived in it unmolested. We are also informed that about the time that the premises were building, *viz*., in 1800 or 1801, there were reports of some deed of darkness having been committed by someone employed about them. We should extend this account beyond the limits we have set to ourselves, did we now enter upon a full account of the strange things which have been seen and heard about the place by several of the neighbours, as well as those which are reported to have been seen, heard, and felt, by the inmates, whose servants have been changed, on that account, many times. We proceed, therefore, to give the following letters which have been passed between individuals of undoubted veracity, leaving the reader to draw his own conclusions on the subject."

"(Copy, No. 1.)
"17th June, 1840.
"To Mr. Procter:
"Sir: Having heard from indisputable authority, *viz*., that of my excellent friend, Mr. Davison, of Low Willington, farmer, that you and your family are disturbed by most unaccountable noises at night, I beg leave to tell you that I have read attentively Wesley's account of such things, but with, I must confess, no great belief; but an account of this report coming from one of your sect, which I admire for candour and simplicity, my curiosity is excited to a high pitch, which I would fain satisfy. My desire is to remain alone in the house all night with no companion but my own watch-dog, in which, as far as courage and fidelity are concerned, I place much more reliance than upon any three young gentlemen I know of. And it is also my hope that, if I have a fair trial, I shall be able to unravel this mystery. Mr. Davison

will give you every satisfaction if you take the trouble to inquire of him concerning me.

"I am, sir, yours most respectfully,

"Edward Drury.

"At C. C. Embleton's, Surgeon,

"No. 10 Church street, Sunderland."

"(Copy, No. 2.)

"Joseph Procter's respects to Edward Drury, whose note he received a few days ago, expressing a wish to pass a night in his house at Willington. As the family is going from home on the 23rd instant, and one of Unthank and Procter's men will sleep in the house, if Edward Drury feel inclined to come on or after the 24th, to spend a night in it, he is at liberty so to do, with or without his faithful dog, which, by-the-by, can be of no possible use, except as company. At the same time, Joseph Procter thinks it best to inform him that particular disturbances are far from frequent at present, being only occasional, and quite uncertain, and therefore the satisfaction of Edward Drury's curiosity must be considered as problematical. The best chance will be afforded by sitting up alone in the third story, till it be fairly daylight, say two or three a. m.

"Willington, 6th mo. 21st, 1840."

"Joseph Procter will leave word with T. Maun, foreman, to admit Edward Drury.

"Mr. Procter left home with his family on the 23rd of June, and got an old servant, who was then out of place in consequence of ill-health, to take charge of the house during their absence. Mr. Procter returned alone, on account of business, on the 3rd of July, on the evening of which day Mr. Drury and his companion also unexpectedly arrived. After the house had been locked up, every corner of it was minutely examined. The room out of which the apparition issued is too shallow to contain any person. Mr. Drury and his friend had lights by them and were satisfied that there was no one in the house besides Mr. Procter, the servant, and themselves."

"(Copy, No. 3.)

"Monday Morning, July 6th, 1840.

"To Mr. Procter:

"Dear Sir: I am sorry I was not at home to receive you yesterday, when you kindly called to inquire for me. I am happy to state, that I am really surprised that I have been so little affected as I am, after that horrid and most awful affair. The only bad effect that I feel is a heavy dullness in one of my ears, the right one. I call it heavy dullness because I not only do not hear distinctly but feel in it a constant noise. This I never was affected with before; but I doubt not it will go off. I am persuaded that no one went to your house at any time more *disbelieving in respect to seeing anything peculiar*, and now no one can be more satisfied than myself. I will, in the course of a few days, send you a full detail of all I saw and heard.

"Mr. Spence and two other gentlemen came down to my house in the afternoon to hear my detail; but, sir, could I account for these noises from natural causes, yet so firmly am I persuaded of the horrid apparition, that I would affirm that what I saw with my eyes was a punishment to me for my scoffing and unbelief; that I am assured that, as far as the horror is concerned, they are happy that believe and have not seen. Let me trouble you, sir, to give me the address of your sister, from Cumberland, who was alarmed, and also of your brother. I would feel a satisfaction in having a line from them; and, above all things, it will be a great cause of joy to me, if you never allow your young family to be in that horrid house again. Hoping you will write a few lines at your leisure,

"I remain, dear sir, yours very truly,

"Edward Drury."

"(Copy, No. 4.)

"Willington, 7th mo. 9, 1840.

"Respected Friend, E. Drury: Having been at Sunderland, I did not receive thine of the 6th till yesterday morning. I am glad to hear thou art getting well over the effects of thy unlooked-for visitation. I hold in respect thy bold and manly assertion of the truth, in the face of that ridicule and ignorant conceit with which that which is called the supernatural, in the present day, is usually assailed.

"I shall be glad to receive thy detail, in which it will be needful to be very particular in showing that thou couldst not be asleep or attacked by nightmare, or mistake a reflection of the candle, as some sagaciously suppose.

"I remain, respectfully, thy friend,

"Josh. Procter.

"P. S.—I have about thirty witnesses to various things which cannot be satisfactorily accounted for on any other principle than that of spiritual agency."

"(Copy, No. 5.)

"Sunderland, July 13, 1840.

"Dear Sir: I hereby, according to promise in my last letter, forward you a true account of what I heard and saw at your house, in which I was led to pass the night from various rumours circulated by most respectable parties—particularly from an account by my esteemed friend Mr. Davison, whose name I mentioned to you in a former letter. Having received your sanction to visit your mysterious dwelling, I went on the 3d of July, accompanied by a friend of mine, T. Hudson. This was not according to promise, nor in accordance with my first intent, as I wrote to you I would come alone; but I felt gratified at your kindness in not alluding to the liberty I had taken, as it ultimately proved for the best. I must here mention that, not expecting you at home, I had in my pocket a brace of pistols, determining in my mind to let one of them drop before the miller, as if by accident, for fear he should presume to play tricks upon me; but, after my interview with you, I felt there was no occasion for weapons, and did not load them, after you had allowed us to inspect as minutely as we pleased every portion of the house. I sat down on the third story landing, fully expecting to account for any noises that I might hear, in a philosophical manner.

"This was about eleven o'clock p. m. About ten minutes to twelve, we both heard a noise, as if a number of people were pattering with their bare feet upon the floor; and yet so singular was the noise, that I could not minutely determine whence it proceeded. A few minutes afterward we heard a noise, as if someone was knocking with his knuckles among our feet; this was followed by a hollow cough from the very room from which the apparition proceeded. The only noise after this, was as if a person was rustling against the wall in coming up stairs. At a quarter to one, I told my friend that, feeling a little cold, I would like to go to bed, as we might hear the noise equally well there; he replied that he would not go to bed till daylight. I took up a note which I had accidentally dropped, and began to read it, after which I took out my watch to ascertain the time and found that it wanted ten minutes to one.

"In taking my eyes from the watch, they became riveted upon a closet-door, which I distinctly saw open, and saw also the figure of a female attired in greyish garments, with the head inclining downward, and one hand pressed upon the chest as if in pain, and the other, *viz*., the right hand, extended toward the floor, with the index finger pointing downward. It advanced with an apparently cautious step across the floor toward me; immediately as it approached my friend, who was slumbering, its right hand was extended toward him: I then rushed at it, giving, as Mr. Procter states, a most awful yell; but, instead of grasping it, I fell upon my friend, and I recollected nothing distinctly for nearly three hours afterward. I have since learned that I was carried down stairs in an agony of fear and terror.

"I hereby certify that the above account is strictly true and correct in every respect.

"Edward Drury.

"North Shields."

"The following more recent case of an apparition seen in the window of the same house from the outside, by four credible witnesses, who had the opportunity of scrutinizing it for more than ten minutes, is given on most unquestionable authority. One of these witnesses is a young lady, a near connection of the family, who, for obvious reasons, did not sleep in the house; another, a respectable man, who has been many years employed in, and is foreman of, the manufactory; his daughter, aged about seventeen; and his wife, who first saw the object and called out the others to view it. The appearance presented was that of a bareheaded man, in a flowing robe like a surplice, who glided backward and forward about three feet from the floor, or level with the bottom of the second story window, seeming to enter the wall on each side, and thus present a side view in passing. It then stood still in the window, and a part of the body came through both the blind, which was close down, and the window, as its luminous body intercepted the view of the framework of the window.

"It was semi-transparent, and as bright as a star, diffusing a radiance all around. As it grew more dim, it assumed a blue tinge, and gradually faded away from the head downward. The foreman passed twice close to the house under the window, and also went to inform the family, but found the house locked up. There was no moonlight, nor a ray of light visible anywhere about, and no person near. Had any magic lantern been used, it could not possibly have escaped detection; and it is obvious nothing of that kind could have been employed on the inside, as in that case the light could only have been thrown upon the blind, and not so as to intercept the view both of the blind and of the window from without. The owner of the house slept in that room and must have entered it shortly after this figure had disappeared.

"It may well be supposed what a sensation the report of the visit of Mr. Drury and its result must have created. It flew far and wide, and when it appeared in print, still wider; and, what was not a little singular, Mr. Procter received, in consequence, a great number of letters from individuals of different ranks and circumstances, including many of much property, informing him that their residences were, and had been for years, subject to annoyances of precisely a similar character.

"So, the ghosts and the hauntings are not gone, after all! We have turned our backs on them, and, in the pride of our philosophy, have refused to believe in them; but they have persisted in remaining, notwithstanding!

"These singular circumstances being at various times related by parties acquainted with the family at Willington, I was curious, on a tour northward some time ago, to pay this haunted house a visit, and to solicit a night's lodging there. Unfortunately, the family was absent, on a visit to Mrs. Procter's relatives in Carlisle, so that my principal purpose was defeated; but I found the foreman and his wife, mentioned in the foregoing narrative, living just by. They spoke of the facts above detailed with the simple earnestness of people who had no doubts whatever on the subject. The noises and apparitions in and about this house seemed just like any other facts connected with it—as matters too palpable and positive to be questioned, any more than that the house actually stood, and the mill ground. They mentioned to me the circumstance of the young lady, as above stated, who took up her lodging in their house, because she would no longer encounter the annoyances of the haunted house—and what trouble it had occasioned the family in procuring and retaining servants.

"The wife accompanied me into the house, which I found in charge of a recently-married servant and her husband, during the absence of the family. This young woman—who had, previous to her marriage, lived sometime in the house—had never seen anything, and therefore had no fear. I was shown over the house, and especially into the room on the third story, the main haunt of the unwelcome visitors, and where Dr. Drury had received such an alarm. This room, as stated, was and had been for some time abandoned as a bedroom, from its bad character, and was occupied as a lumber-room.

"At Carlisle, I again missed Mr. Procter: he had returned to Willington, so that I lost the opportunity of hearing from him or Mrs. Procter any account of these singular matters. I saw, however, various members of his wife's family, most intelligent people, of the highest character for sound and practical sense, and they were unanimous in their confirmation of the particulars I had heard, and which are here related.

"One of Mrs. Procter's brothers—a gentleman in middle life, and of a peculiarly sensible, sedate, and candid disposition, a person apparently most unlikely to be imposed on by fictitious alarms or tricks— assured me that he had himself, on a visit there, been disturbed by the strangest noises; that he had resolved, before going, that if any such noises occurred, he would speak, and demand of the invisible actor who he was, and why he came thither: but the occasion came, and he found himself unable to fulfil his intention. As he lay in bed one night, he heard a heavy step ascend the stairs toward his room, and someone striking, as it were, with a thick stick on the banisters, as he went along. It came to his door, and he essayed to call, but his voice died in his throat. He then sprang from his bed, and, opening the door, found no one there—but now heard the same heavy steps deliberately descending, though invisible, the steps before his face, and accompanying the descent with the same loud blows on the banisters.

"My informant now proceeded to the room door of Mr. Procter, who he found had also heard the sounds, and who now also arose, and with a light they made a speedy descent below, and a thorough search there, but without discovering anything that could account for the occurrence.

"The two young ladies, who, on a visit there, had also been annoyed by this invisible agent, gave me this account of it: The first night, as they were sleeping in the same bed, they felt the bed lifted up beneath them. Of course, they were much alarmed. They feared lest someone had concealed himself there for the purpose of robbery. They gave an alarm, search was made, but nothing was found. On another night, their bed was violently shaken, and the curtains suddenly hoisted up all round to the very tester, as if pulled by cords, and as rapidly let down again, several times! Search again produced no evidence of the cause. The next, they had the curtains totally removed from the bed, resolving to sleep without them, as they felt as though evil eyes were lurking behind them. The consequences of this, however, were still more striking and terrific.

"The following night, as they happened to awake, and the chamber was light enough (for it was summer) to see everything in it, they both saw a female figure, of a misty substance, and bluish grey hue, come out of the wall at the bed's head, and through the head-board, in a horizontal position, and lean over them. They saw it most distinctly—they saw it as a female figure come out of, and again pass into, the wall. Their terror became intense, and one of the sisters from that night refused to sleep any more in the house but took refuge in the house of the foreman during her stay; the other shifting her quarters to another part of the house. It was the young lady who slept at the foreman's who saw, as above related, the singular apparition of the luminous figure in the window, along with the foreman and his wife.

"It would be too long to relate all the forms in which this nocturnal disturbance is said by the family to present itself. When a figure appears, it is sometimes that of a man, as already described, which is often very luminous, and passes through the walls as though they were nothing. This male figure is well known to the neighbours by the name of "Old Jeffrey!" At other times, it is the figure of a lady, also in grey costume, and as described by Mr. Drury. She is sometimes seen sitting wrapped in a sort of mantle, with her head depressed, and her hands crossed on her lap. The most terrible fact is, that she is without eyes.

"To hear such sober and superior people gravely relate to you such things, gives you a very odd feeling. They say that the noise made is often like that of a paviour with his rammer thumping on the floor. At other times it is coming down stairs, making a similar loud sound. At others it coughs, sighs, and groans, like a person in distress; and, again, there is the sound of a number of little feet pattering on the floor of the upper chamber, where the apparition has more particularly exhibited itself, and which, for that reason, is solely used as a lumber-room. Here these little footsteps may be often heard as if careering a child's carriage about, which in bad weather is kept up there.

"Sometimes, again, it makes the most horrible laughs. Nor does it always confine itself to the night. On one occasion, a young lady, as she assured me herself, opened the door in answer to a knock, the housemaid being absent, and a lady in fawn-coloured silk entered, and proceeded upstairs. As the young lady, of course, supposed it a neighbour come to make a morning call on Mrs. Procter, she followed her up to the drawing-room, where, however, to her astonishment, she did not find her, nor was anything more seen of her.

"Such are a few of the 'questionable shapes' in which this troublesome guest comes. As may be expected, terror of it is felt by the neighbouring cottagers, though it seems to confine its malicious disturbance almost solely to the occupants of this one house. There is a well, however, near to which no one ventures after it is dark, because it has been seen near it.

"It is useless to attempt to give any opinion respecting the real causes of these strange sounds and sights. How far they may be real or imaginary, how far they may be explicable by natural causes or not—the only thing which we have here to record is, the very singular fact of a most respectable and intelligent family having for many years been continually annoyed by them, as well as their visitors. They express themselves as most anxious to obtain any clew to the true cause, as may be seen by Mr. Procter's ready acquiescence in the experiment of Mr. Drury. So great a trouble is it to them, that they have contemplated the necessity of quitting the house altogether, though it would create great inconvenience as regarded business.

"And it only remains to be added that we have not heard very recently whether these visitations are still continued, though we have a letter of Mr. Procter's to a friend of ours, dated September, 1844, in which he says: 'Disturbances have for a length of time been only very unfrequent, which is a comfort, as the elder children are getting old enough (about nine or ten years) to be more injuriously affected by anything of the sort.'

"Over these facts let the philosophers ponder, and if any of them be powerful enough to exorcise 'Old Jeffrey,' or the bluish-grey and misty lady, we are sure that Mr. Joseph Procter will hold himself deeply indebted to them. We have lately heard that Mr. Procter has discovered an old book, which makes it appear that the very same 'hauntings' took place in an old house, on the very same spot, at least two hundred years ago."

To the above information, furnished by Mr. Howitt, I have to subjoin that the family of Mr. Procter are now quitting the house, which he intends to divide into small tenements for the work-people. A friend of mine who lately visited Willington, and who went over the house with Mr. Procter, assures me that the annoyances still continue, though less frequent than formerly.

Mr. Procter informed her that the female figure generally appeared in a shroud, and that it had been seen in that guise by one of the family only a few days before. A wish being expressed by a gentleman visiting Mr. Procter that some natural explanation of these perplexing circumstances might be discovered, the latter declared his entire conviction, founded on an experience of fifteen years, that no such elucidation was possible.

4

The circumstances of the so-called Stockwell ghost, which I extract from a report published at the time, are as follows:—

The pamphlet was entitled: "An authentic, candid, and Circumstantial Narrative of the astonishing Transactions at Stockwell, in the County of Surrey, on Monday and Tuesday, the 6th and 7th days of January, 1772; containing a Series of the most surprising and unaccountable Events that ever happened, which continued, from first to last, upward of twenty hours, and at different places: published with the consent and approbation of the family and other parties concerned, to authenticate which the original copy is signed by them.

"Before we enter upon a description of the most extraordinary transactions that perhaps ever happened, we shall begin with an account of the parties who were principally concerned, and, in justice to them, give their characters, by which means the impartial world may see what credit is due to the following narrative:—

"The events, indeed, are of so strange and singular a nature, that we cannot be at all surprised the public should be doubtful of the truth of them, more especially as there have been too many impositions of this sort; but, let us consider, here are no sinister ends to be answered, no contributions to be wished for, nor would be accepted, as the parties are in reputable situations and good circumstances, particularly Mrs. Golding, who is a lady of an independent fortune: Richard Fowler and his wife might be looked upon as an exception to this assertion; but, as their loss was trivial, they must be left out of the question, except so far as they appear corroborating evidences. Mr. Pain's maid lost nothing.

"How or by what means these transactions were brought about, has never transpired: we have only to rest our confidence on the veracity of the parties, whose descriptions have been most strictly attended to, without the least deviation: nothing here offered is either exaggerated or diminished—the whole stated in the clearest manner, just as they occurred: as such only we lay them before the candid and impartial public.

"Mrs. Golding, an elderly lady at Stockwell, in Surrey, at whose house the transactions began, was born in the same parish (Lambeth), has lived in it ever since, and has always been well known and respected as a gentlewoman of unblemished honour and character. Mrs. Pain, a niece of Mrs. Golding, has been married several years to Mr.

Pain, a farmer, at Brixton causeway, a little above Mr. Angel's—has several children, and is well known and respected in the parish. Mary Martin, Mr. Pain's servant, an elderly woman, has lived two years with them and four years with Mrs. Golding, where she came from. Richard Fowler lives almost opposite to Mr. Pain, at the Brick pound—an honest, industrious, and sober man. And Sarah Fowler, wife to the above, is an industrious and sober woman.

"These are the subscribing evidences that we must rest the truth of the facts upon; yet there are numbers of other persons who were eye-witnesses of many of the transactions during the time they happened, all of whom must acknowledge the truth of them.

"Another person who bore a principal part in these scenes was Ann Robinson, Mrs. Golding's maid, a young woman about twenty years old, who had lived with her but one week and three days. So much for the *historiæ personæ*, and now for the narrative.

"On Monday, January the 6th, 1772, about ten o'clock in the forenoon, as Mrs. Golding was in her parlour, she heard the china and glasses in the back kitchen tumble down and break; her maid came to her and told her the stone plates were falling from the shelf; Mrs. Golding went into the kitchen and saw them broke. Presently after, a row of plates from the next shelf fell down likewise, while she was there, and nobody near them; this astonished her much, and while she was thinking about it, other things in different places began to tumble about, some of them breaking, attended with violent noises all over the house; a clock tumbled down and the case broke; a lantern that hung on the staircase was thrown down and the glass broken to pieces; an earthen pan of salted beef broke to pieces and the beef fell about: all this increased her surprise and brought several persons about her, among whom was Mr. Rowlidge, a carpenter, who gave it as his opinion that the foundation was giving way and that the house was tumbling down, occasioned by the too great weight of an additional room erected above: so ready are we to discover natural causes for everything! But no such thing happened, as the reader will find; for whatever was the cause, that cause ceased almost as soon as Mrs. Golding and her maid left any place and followed them wherever they went. Mrs. Golding ran into Mr. Gresham's house, a gentleman living next door to her, where she fainted.

"In the interim, Mr. Rowlidge and other persons were removing Mrs. Golding's effects from her house, for fear of the consequences he had prognosticated. At this time all was quiet; Mrs. Golding's maid, remaining in the house, was gone up stairs, and when called upon several times to come down, for fear of the dangerous situation she was thought to be in, she answered very coolly, and after some time came down as deliberately, without any seeming fearful apprehensions.

"Mrs. Pain was sent for from Brixton Causeway, and desired to come directly, as her aunt was supposed to be dead: this was the message to her. When Mrs. Pain came, Mrs. Golding was come to herself, but very faint.

"Among the persons who were present was Mr. Gardner, a surgeon, of Clapham, whom Mrs. Pain desired to bleed her aunt, which he did. Mrs. Pain asked him if the blood should be thrown away: he desired it might not, as he would examine it when cold. These minute particulars would not be taken notice of, but as a chain to what follows. For the next circumstance is of a more astonishing nature than anything that had preceded it: the blood that was just congealed, sprang out of the basin upon the floor, and presently after the basin broke to pieces! This china basin was the only thing broke belonging to Mr. Gresham; a bottle of rum that stood by it broke at the same time.

"Among the things that were removed to Mr. Gresham's, was a tray full of china, a japan bread-basket, some mahogany waiters, with some bottles of liquors, jars of pickles, &c., and a pier-glass, which was taken down by Mr. Saville (a neighbour of Mrs. Golding's); he gave it to one Robert Hames, who laid it on the grass-plat at Mrs. Gresham's: but, before he could put it out of his hands, some parts of the frame on each side flew off! It rained at that time; Mrs. Golding desired it might be brought into the parlour, where it was put under a sideboard, and a dressing-glass along with it. It had not been there long, before the glasses and china which stood on the sideboard began to tumble about and fall down, and broke both the glasses to pieces. Mr. Saville and others being asked to drink a glass of wine or rum, both the bottles broke in pieces before they were uncorked!

"Mrs. Golding's surprise and fear increasing, she did not know what to do, or where to go. Wherever she and her maid were, these strange, destructive circumstances followed her, and how to help or free herself from them was not in her power or any other person's present. Her mind was one confused chaos, lost to herself and everything about her—drove from her own home, and afraid there would be no other to receive her. At last she left Mr. Gresham's and went to Mr. Mayling's, a gentleman at the next door; here she stayed about three quarters of an hour, during which time nothing happened. Her maid stayed at Mr. Gresham's to put up what few things remained unbroken of her mistress's, in a back apartment, when a jar of pickles that stood upon a table turned upside down; then a jar of raspberry jam broke to pieces; next two mahogany waiters and a quadrille-box likewise broke in pieces.

"Mrs. Pain, not choosing her aunt should stay too long at Mr. Mayling's, for fear of being troublesome, persuaded her to go to her house at Rush Common, near Brixton Causeway, where she would endeavour to make her as happy as she could, hoping by this time all was over, as nothing had happened at that gentleman's house while she was there. This was about two o'clock in the afternoon.

"Mr. and Miss Gresham were at Mr. Pain's house when Mrs. Pain, Mrs. Golding, and her maid, went there. It being about dinner-time, they all dined together; in the interim, Mrs. Golding's servant was sent to her house to see how things remained. When she returned, she told them nothing had happened since they left it. Sometime after, Mr. Gresham and miss went home, everything remaining quiet at Mr. Pain's; but about eight o'clock in the evening a fresh scene began. The first thing that happened was, a whole row of pewter dishes, except one, fell from off a shelf to the middle of the floor, rolled about a little while, then settled; and, what is almost beyond belief, as soon as they were quiet, turned upside down! They were then put on the dresser and went through the same a second time. Next fell a whole row of pewter plates from off the second shelf over the dresser to the ground, and, being taken up and put on the dresser one in another, they were thrown down again.

"The next thing was, two eggs that were upon one of the pewter shelves, one of them flew off, crossed the kitchen, struck a cat on the head, and then broke in pieces.

"Next, Mary Martin, Mrs. Pain's servant, went to stir the kitchen fire; she got to the right-hand side of it, being a large chimney, as is usual in farmhouses. A pestle and mortar that stood nearer the left-hand end of the chimney-shelf, jumped about six feet on the floor! Then went candlesticks and other brasses, scarcely anything remaining in its place. After this, the glasses and china were put down on the floor for fear of undergoing the same fate: they presently began to dance and tumble about, and then broke to pieces. A teapot that was among them flew to Mrs. Golding's maid's foot and struck it.

"A glass tumbler that was put on the floor jumped about two feet and then broke. Another that stood by it jumped about at the same time, but did not break till some hours after, when it jumped again, and then broke. A china bowl that stood in the parlour jumped from the floor to behind a table that stood there. This was most astonishing, as the distance from where it stood was between seven and eight feet but was not broke. It was put back by Richard Fowler to its place, where it remained some time, and then flew to pieces.

"The next thing that followed was a mustard-pot, that jumped out of a closet and was broke. A single cup that stood upon the table (almost the only thing remaining) jumped up, flew across the kitchen, ringing like a bell, and then was dashed to pieces against the dresser. A candlestick that stood on the chimney-shelf flew across the kitchen to the parlor-door, at about fifteen feet distance. A teakettle under the dresser was thrown out about two feet; another kettle, that stood at one end of the range, was thrown against the iron that is fixed to prevent children from falling into the fire. A tumbler with rum-and-water in it, that stood upon a waiter upon a table in the parlor, jumped about ten feet, and was broke. The table then fell down, and along with it a silver tankard belonging to Mrs. Golding—the waiter in which stood the tumbler, and a candlestick. A case-bottle then flew to pieces.

"The next circumstance was, a ham that hung in one side of the kitchen-chimney raised itself from the hook and fell down to the ground. Some time after, another ham, that hung on the other side of the chimney, likewise underwent the same fate. Then a flitch of bacon, which hung up in the same chimney, fell down.

"All the family were eye-witnesses to these circumstances, as well as other persons, some of whom were so alarmed and shocked, that they could not bear to stay, and were happy in getting away, though the unhappy family were left in the midst of their distresses. Most of the genteel families around were continually sending to inquire after them, and whether all was over or not. Is it not surprising that some among them had not the inclination and resolution to try to unravel this most intricate affair, at a time when it would have been in their power to have done so? There certainly was sufficient time for so doing, as the whole, from first to last, continued upward of twenty hours.

"At all the times of action, Mrs. Golding's servant was walking backward and forward, in either the kitchen or parlour, or wherever some of the family happened to be. Nor could they get her to sit down five minutes together, except at one time for about half an hour toward the morning, when the family were at prayers in the parlor; then all was quiet: but in the midst of the greatest confusion, she was as much composed as at any other time, and with uncommon cool-ness of temper advised her mistress not to be alarmed or uneasy, as she said these things could not be helped. Thus, she argued, as if they were common occurrences, which must happen in every family!

"This advice surprised and startled her mistress almost as much as the circumstances that occasioned it. For how can we suppose that a girl of about twenty years old (an age when female timidity is too of-ten assisted by superstition) could remain in the midst of such calami-tous circumstances (except they proceed from causes best known to herself), and not be struck with the same terror as every other person was who was present? These reflections led Mr. Pain (and, at the end of the transactions, likewise Mrs. Golding) to think that she was not altogether so unconcerned as she appeared to be; but, hitherto, the whole remains mysterious and unrivalled.

"About ten o'clock at night, they sent over the way to Richard Fowler, to desire he would come and stay with them. He came and continued till one in the morning and was so terrified that he could remain no longer.

"As Mrs. Golding could not be persuaded to go to bed, Mrs. Pain at that time (one o'clock) made an excuse to go upstairs to her young-est child, under pretence of getting it to sleep, but she really acknowl-edges it was through fear, as she declares she could not sit up to see such strange things going on, as everything, one after another, was broke, till there was not above two or three cups and saucers remain-ing out of a considerable quantity of china, &c, which was destroyed to the amount of some pounds.

"About five o'clock on Tuesday morning, Mrs. Golding went up to her niece, and desired her to get up, as the noises and destruction were so great, she could continue in the house no longer. At this time all the tables, chairs, drawers, &c., were tumbling about. When Mrs. Pain came down, it was amazing beyond all description. Their only security then was to quit the house, for fear of the same catastrophe as had been expected the morning before at Mrs. Golding's. In con-sequence of this resolution, Mrs. Golding and her maid went over the way to Richard Fowler's. When Mrs. Golding's maid had seen her safe to Richard Fowler's, she came back to Mrs. Pain, to help her to dress the children in the barn, where she had carried them for fear of the house falling. At this time all was quiet. They then went to Fowler's, and then began the same scene as had happened at the other places. It must be remarked, all was quiet here as well as elsewhere, till the maid returned.

"When they got to Mr. Fowler's, he began to light a fire in his back room. When done, he put the candle and candlestick upon a table in the fore-room. This apartment Mrs. Golding and her maid had passed through. Another candlestick, with a tin lamp in it, that stood by it, were both dashed together, and fell to the ground. A lantern, with which Mrs. Golding was lighted across the road, sprang from a hook to the ground, and a quantity of oil spilled on the floor. The last thing was, the basket of coals tumbled over, the coals rolling about the room. The maid then desired Richard Fowler not to let her mistress remain there, as she said wherever she was the same things would follow. In consequence of this advice, and fearing greater losses to himself, he desired she would quit his house; but first begged her to consider within herself, for her own and the public's sake, whether or not she had been guilty of some atrocious crime, for which Providence was determined to pursue her on this side of the grave: for he could not help thinking she was the object that was to be made an example to posterity, by the all-seeing eye of Providence, for crimes which but too often none but that Providence can penetrate, and by such means as these bring to light.

"Thus, was the poor gentlewoman's measure of affliction complete, not only to have undergone all which has been related, but to have added to it the character of a bad and wicked woman, when till this time she was esteemed as a most deserving person. In candour to Fowler, he could not be blamed. What could he do? what would any man have done that was so circumstanced? Mrs. Golding soon satisfied him: she told him she would not stay in his house or any other person's, as her conscience was quite clear, and she could as well wait the will of Providence in her own house as in any other place whatever; upon which she and her maid went home. Mr. Pain went with them. After they had got to Mrs. Golding's the last time, the same transactions once more began upon the remains that were left.

"A nine-gallon cask of beer, that was in the cellar, the door being open, and no person near it, turned upside down. A pail of water, that stood on the floor, boiled like a pot! A box of candles fell from a shelf in the kitchen to the floor; they rolled out, but none were broke: and a round mahogany table overset in the parlour.

"Mr. Pain then desired Mrs. Golding to send her maid for his wife to come to them. When she was gone, all was quiet. Upon her return she was immediately discharged, and no disturbances have happened since. This was between six and seven o'clock on Tuesday morning.

"At Mrs. Golding's were broke the quantity of three pailfuls of glass, china, &c. At Mrs. Pain's they filled two pails.

"Thus, ends the narrative—a true, circumstantial, and faithful account of which we have laid before the public; and have endeavoured as much as possible, throughout the whole, to state only facts, without presuming to obtrude any opinion on them. If we have in part hinted anything that may appear unfavourable to the girl, it is not from a determination to charge her with the cause, right or wrong, but only from a strict adherence to truth, most sincerely wishing this extraordinary affair may be unravelled.

"The above narrative is absolutely and strictly true, in witness whereof we have set our hands this eleventh day of January, 1772:—

"Mary Golding
"John Pain,
"Mary Pain,
"Richard Fowler,
"Sarah Fowler,
"Mary Martin."

"The original copy of this narrative, signed as above, with the parties' own hands, was put into the hands of Mr. Marks, bookseller, in St. Martin's Lane, to satisfy persons who choose to inspect the same."

5

The following interesting letter, written by a member of a very distinguished English family, will furnish its own explanation:—

"As you express a wish to know what degree of credit is to be attached to a garbled tale which has been sent forth, after a lapse of between thirty and forty years, as an 'accredited ghost-story,' I will state the facts as they were recalled to my mind last year by a daughter of Sir William A. C———, who sent the book to me, requesting me to tell her if there was any foundation for the story, which she could scarcely believe, since she had never heard my mother allude to it. I read the narrative with surprise, it being evidently not furnished by any of the family, nor indeed by anyone who was with us at the time! yet, though full of mistakes in names, &c., &c., some particulars come so near the truth as to puzzle me. The facts are as follows:—

"Sir James, my mother, with myself and my brother Charles, went abroad toward the end of the year 1786. After trying several different places, we determined to settle at Lille, where we found the masters particularly good, and where we had also letters of introduction to several of the best French families. There Sir James left us, and, after passing a few days in an uncomfortable lodging, we engaged a nice, large family house, which we liked very much, and which we obtained at a very low rent, even for that part of the world.

"About three weeks after we were established in our new residence, I walked one day with my mother to the bankers, for the purpose of delivering our letter of credit from Sir Robert Herries, and drawing some money, which, being paid in heavy five-*franc* pieces, we found we could not carry, and therefore requested the banker to send, saying, 'We live in the Place du Lion D'or.'

"Whereupon he looked surprised and observed that he knew of no house there fit for us, 'except, indeed,' he added, 'the one that has been long uninhabited, on account of the *revenant* that walks about it.' He said this quite seriously, and in a natural tone of voice, in spite of which we laughed, and were quite entertained at the idea of a ghost; but at the same time, we begged him not to mention the thing to our servants, lest they should take any fancies into their heads; and my mother and I resolved to say nothing about the matter to anyone.

"'I suppose it is the ghost,' said my mother, laughing, 'that wakes us so often by walking over our heads.' We had, in fact, been awakened several nights by a heavy foot, which we supposed to be that of one of the men-servants, of whom we had three English and four French; of women-servants we had five English, and all the rest were French. The English ones, men and women, every one of them, returned ultimately to England with us.

"A night or two afterward, being again awakened by the step, my mother asked Creswell, 'Who slept in the room above us?'

"'No one, my lady,' she replied—'it is a large, empty garret.'

"About a week or ten days after this, Creswell came to my mother, one morning, and told her that all the French servants talked of going away, because there was a *revenant* in the house; adding that there seemed to be a strange story attached to the place, which was said, together with some other property, to have belonged to a young man, whose guardian, who was also his uncle, had treated him cruelly and confined him in an iron cage; and as he had subsequently disappeared, it was conjectured he had been murdered. This uncle, after inheriting the property, had suddenly quitted the house and sold it to the father of the man of whom we had hired it. Since that period, though it had been several times let, nobody had ever stayed in it above a week or two, and for a considerable time past it had had no tenant at all.

"'And do you really believe all this nonsense, Creswell?' said my mother.

"'Well, I don't know, my lady,' answered she; 'but there's the iron cage in the garret over your bedroom, where you may see it, if you please.'

"Of course, we rose to go; and as just at that moment an old officer, with his *Croix de St. Louis*, called on us, we invited him to accompany us and we ascended together. We found, as Creswell had said, a large empty garret with bare brick walls; and in the further corner of it stood an iron cage, such as wild beasts are kept in, only higher; it was about four feet square, and eight in height, and there was an iron ring in the wall at the back, to which was attached an old rusty chain with a collar fixed to the end of it. I confess it made my blood creep when I thought of the possibility of any human being having inhabited it! And our old friend expressed as much horror as ourselves, assuring us that it must certainly have been constructed for some such dreadful purpose.

"As, however, we were no believers in ghosts, we all agreed that the noises must proceed from somebody who had an interest in keeping the house empty; and since it was very disagreeable to imagine that there were secret means of entering it at night, we resolved, as soon as possible, to look out for another residence, and in the meantime to say nothing about the matter to anybody. About ten days after this determination, my mother, observing one morning that Creswell, when she came to dress her, looked exceedingly pale and ill, inquired if anything was the matter with her.

"'Indeed, my lady,' she answered, 'we have been frightened to death, and neither I nor Mrs. Marsh can sleep again in the room we are now in.'

"'Well,' returned my mother, 'you shall both come and sleep in the little spare room next us; but what has alarmed you?'

"'Someone, my lady, went through our room in the night; we both saw the figure, but we covered our heads with the bedclothes, and lay in a dreadful fright till morning.'

"On hearing this, I could not help laughing, upon which Creswell burst into tears; and seeing how nervous she was, we comforted her by saying we had heard of a good house, and that we should very soon abandon our present habitation.

"A few nights afterward, my mother requested me and Charles to go to her bedroom and fetch her frame, that she might prepare her work for the next day. It was after supper, and we were ascending the stairs by the light of a lamp which was always kept burning, when we saw going up before us a tall, thin figure, with hair flowing down his back, and wearing a loose powdering gown. We both at once concluded it was my sister Hannah, and called out: 'It won't do, Hannah—you cannot frighten us!' Upon which the figure turned into a recess in the wall; but, as there was nobody there when we passed, we concluded that Hannah had contrived, somehow or other, to slip away and make her escape by the back stairs.

"On telling this to my mother, she said: 'It is very odd, for Hannah went to bed with a headache before you came in from your walk;' and sure enough, on going to her room, there we found her fast asleep; and Alice, who was at work there, assured us that she had been so for more than an hour. On mentioning this circumstance to Creswell, she turned quite pale and exclaimed that that was precisely the figure she and Marsh had seen in their bedroom.

"About this time, my brother Harry came to spend a few days with us, and we gave him a room up another pair of stairs, at the opposite end of the house. A morning or two after his arrival, when he came down to breakfast, he asked my mother angrily whether she thought he went to bed drunk and could not put out his own candle, that she sent those French rascals to watch him. My mother assured him that she never thought of doing such a thing; but he persisted in the accusation, adding: 'Last night I jumped up and opened the door, and, by the light of the moon through the skylight, I saw the fellow in his loose gown at the bottom of the stairs. If I had not been in my shirt, I would have gone after him and made him remember coming to watch me.'

"We were now preparing to quit the house, having secured another, belonging to a gentleman who was going to spend some time in Italy; but, a few days before our removal, it happened that Mr. and Mrs. Atkyns, some English friends of ours, called, to whom we mentioned these circumstances, observing how extremely unpleasant it was to live in a house that somebody found means of getting into, though how they contrived it we could not discover, nor what their motive could be except it was to frighten us; adding, that nobody could sleep in the room Marsh and Creswell had been obliged to give up. Upon this Mrs. Atkyns laughed heartily, and said she should like, of all things, to sleep there, if my mother would allow her, adding, that with her little terrier she should not be afraid of any ghost that ever appeared. As my mother had, of course, no objection to this fancy of hers, she requested Mrs. Atkyns to ride home with the groom, in order that the latter might bring her night-things before the gates of the town would be shut, as they were then residing a little way in the country. Mr. Atkyns smiled and said she was very bold; but he made no difficulties, and sent the things,—and his wife retired with her dog to her room when we retired to ours, apparently without the least apprehension.

"When she came down in the morning, we were immediately struck at seeing her look very ill; and on inquiring if she too had been frightened, she said she had been awakened in the night by something moving in her room, and that, by the light of the night-lamp, she saw most distinctly a figure, and that the dog, which was spirited and flew at everything, never stirred, although she had endeavoured to make him. We saw clearly that she had been very much alarmed; and when Mr. Atkyns came, and endeavoured to dissipate the feeling by persuading her that she might have dreamed it, she got quite angry. We could not help thinking that she had actually seen something; and my mother said, after she was gone, that though she could not bring herself to believe it was really a ghost, still she earnestly hoped that she might get out of the house without seeing this figure, which frightened people so much.

"We were now within three days of the one fixed for our removal. I had been taking a long ride, and, being tired, had fallen asleep the moment I lay down; but, in the middle of the night, I was suddenly awakened—I cannot tell by what, for the steps over our heads we had become so used to that it no longer disturbed us. Well, I awoke. I had been lying with my face toward my mother, who was asleep beside me, and, as one usually does on awaking, I turned to the other side, where, the weather being warm, the curtain of the bed was undrawn, as it was, also, at the foot; and I saw standing by a chest of drawers, which were betwixt me and the window, a thin, tall figure, in a loose powdering gown, one arm resting on the drawers, and the face turned toward me.

"I saw it quite distinctly by the night-light, which burned clearly. It was a long, thin, pale, young face, with, oh, such a melancholy expression as can never be effaced from my memory! I was, certainly, very much frightened; but my great horror was, lest my mother should awake and see the figure. I turned my head gently toward her and heard her breathing high in a sound sleep. Just then the clock on the stairs struck four. I dare say it was nearly an hour before I ventured to look again, and when I did take courage to turn my eyes toward the drawers, there was nothing; yet I had not heard the slightest sound, though I had been listening with the greatest intensity.

"As you may suppose, I never closed my eyes again; and glad I was when Creswell knocked at the door, as she did every morning, for we always locked it, and it was my business to get out of bed and let her in; but on this occasion, instead of doing so, I called out, 'Come in; the door is not fastened;' upon which she answered that it was, and I was obliged to get out of bed and admit her as usual.

"When I told my mother what had happened, she was very grateful to me for not waking her and commended me much for my resolution; but as she was always my first object, that was not to be wondered at. She however resolved not to risk another night in the house; and we got out of it that very day, after instituting, with the aid of the servants, a thorough search, with a view to ascertain if there was any possible means of getting into the rooms except by the usual modes of ingress; but our search was vain—none could be discovered.

"I think, from the errors in the names, &c., that the publisher of the *Accredited Ghost-Stories* must have obtained his account from the inhabitants of Lille."

Considering the number of people that were in the house, the fearlessness of the family, and their disinclination to believe in what is called *the supernatural*, together with the great interest the owner of this large and handsome residence must have had in discovering the trick, if there had been one, I think it is difficult to find any other explanation of this strange story, than that the sad and disappointed spirit of this poor, injured, and probably murdered boy, had never been disengaged from its earthly relations, to which regret for its frustrated hopes and violated rights still held it attached.

6

At Bishopwearmouth, near Sunderland, in the year 1840; and as the particulars of this case have been published and attested by two physicians and two surgeons, not to mention the evidence of numerous other persons, I think we are bound to accept the facts, whatever interpretation we may choose to put upon them.

The patient, named Mary Jobson, was between twelve and thirteen years of age; her parents, respectable people in humble life, and herself an attendant on a Sunday-school. She became ill in November, 1839, and was soon afterward seized with terrific fits, which continued, at intervals, for eleven weeks. It was during this period that the family first observed a strange knocking, which they could not account for. It was sometimes in one place, and sometimes in another; and even about the bed, when the girl lay in a quiet sleep, with her hands folded outside the clothes.

They next heard a strange voice, which told them circumstances they did not know, but which they afterward found to be correct. Then there was a noise like the clashing of arms, and such a rumbling that the tenant below thought the house was coming down; footsteps where nobody was to be seen, water falling on the floor, no one knew whence, locked doors opened, and above all, sounds of ineffably sweet music. The doctors and the father were suspicious, and every precaution was taken, but no solution of the mystery could be found.

This spirit, however, was a good one, and it preached to them, and gave them a great deal of good advice. Many persons went to witness this strange phenomenon, and some were desired to go by the voice, when in their own homes. Thus Elizabeth Gauntlett, while attending to some domestic affairs at home, was startled by hearing a voice say, "Be thou faithful, and thou shalt see the works of thy God, and shalt hear with thine ears!"

She cried out, "My God! what can this be!" and presently she saw a large white cloud near her.

On the same evening the voice said to her, "Mary Jobson, one of your scholars is sick; go and see her, and it will be good for you." This person did not know where the child lived, but having inquired the address, she went: and at the door she heard the same voice bid her go up.

On entering the room, she heard another voice, soft and beautiful, which bade her be faithful, and said, "I am the Virgin Mary." This voice promised her a sign at home; and accordingly, that night, while reading the Bible, she heard it say, "Jemima, be not afraid; it is I: if you keep my commandments it shall be well with you." When she repeated her visit the same things occurred, and she heard the most exquisite music.

The same sort of phenomena were witnessed by everybody who went—the immoral were rebuked, the good encouraged. Some were bidden instantly to depart and were forced to go. The voices of several deceased persons of the family were also heard and made revelations.

Once the voice said, "Look up, and you shall see the sun and moon on the ceiling!" and immediately there appeared a beautiful representation of these planets in lively colours, *viz.*, green, yellow, and orange. Moreover, these figures were permanent; but the father, who was a long time sceptical, insisted on whitewashing them over; however, they still remained visible.

Among other things, the voice said, that though the child appeared to suffer, she did not; that she did not know where her body was; and that her own spirit had left it, and another had entered; and that her body was made a speaking trumpet. The voice told the family and visitors many things of their distant friends, which proved true.

The girl twice saw a divine form standing by her bedside who spoke to her, and Joseph Ragg, one of the persons who had been invited by the voice to go, saw a beautiful and heavenly figure come to his bedside about eleven o'clock at night, on the 17th of January. It was in male attire, surrounded by a radiance; it came a second time on the same night. On each occasion it opened his curtains and looked at him benignantly, remaining about a quarter of an hour. When it went away, the curtains fell back into their former position. One day, while in the sick child's room, Margaret Watson saw a lamb, which passed through the door and entered a place where the father, John Jobson, was; but he did not see it.

One of the most remarkable features in this case is the beautiful music which was heard by all parties, as well as the family, including the unbelieving father; and indeed, it seems to have been, in a great degree, this that converted him at last. This music was heard repeatedly during a space of sixteen weeks: sometimes it was like an organ, but more beautiful; at others there was singing of holy songs, in parts, and the words distinctly heard. The sudden appearance of water in the room too was most unaccountable; for they felt it, and it was really water. When the voice desired that water should be sprinkled, it immediately appeared as if sprinkled. At another time, a sign being promised to the sceptical father, water would suddenly appear on the floor; this happened "not once, but twenty times."

During the whole course of this affair, the voices told them that there was a miracle to be wrought on this child; and accordingly on the 22nd of June, when she was as ill as ever and they were only praying for her death, at five o'clock the voice ordered that her clothes should be laid out, and that everybody should leave the room except the infant, which was two years and a half old. They obeyed; and having been outside the door a quarter of an hour, the voice cried,

"Come in!" and when they entered, they saw the girl completely dressed and quite well, sitting in a chair with the infant on her knee, and she had not had an hour's illness from that time till the report was published, which was on the 30th of January, 1841.

Now, it is very easy to laugh at all this, and assert that these things never happened, because they are absurd and impossible; but while honest, well-meaning, and intelligent people, who were on the spot, assert that they did, I confess I find myself constrained to believe them, however much I find in the case which is discrepant with my notions. It was not an affair of a day or an hour—there was ample time for observation—for the phenomena continued from the 9th of February to the 22nd of June; and the determined unbelief of the father regarding the possibility of spiritual appearances, insomuch that he ultimately expressed great regret for the harshness he had used, is a tolerable security against imposition. Moreover, they pertinaciously refused to receive any money or assistance whatever and were more likely to suffer in public opinion than otherwise by the avowal of these circumstances.

Dr. Clanny, who publishes the report with the attestations of the witnesses, is a physician of many years' experience, and is also, I believe, the inventor of the improved Davy lamp; and he declares his entire conviction of the facts, assuring his readers that "many persons holding high rank in the established church, ministers of other denominations, as well as many lay-members of society, highly respected for learning and piety, are equally satisfied." When he first saw the child lying on her back, apparently insensible, her eyes suffused with florid blood, he felt assured that she had a disease of the brain; and he was not in the least disposed to believe in the mysterious part of the affair, till subsequent investigation compelled him to do so: and that his belief is of a very decided character we may feel assured, when he is content to submit to all the obloquy he must incur by avowing it.

He adds that, since the girl has been quite well, both her family and that of Joseph Ragg have frequently heard the same heavenly music as they did during her illness; and Mr. Torbock, a surgeon, who expresses himself satisfied of the truth of the above particulars, also mentions another case, in which he, as well as a dying person he was attending, heard divine music just before the dissolution.

7

Yet, so late as the year 1835, a suit was brought before the sheriff of Edinburgh, in which Captain Molesworth was defendant, and the landlord of the house he inhabited (which was at Trinity, about a couple of miles from Edinburgh) was plaintiff, founded upon circumstances not so varied, certainly, but quite as inexplicable. The suit lasted two years, and I have been favored with the particulars of the case by Mr. M———— L————, the advocate employed by the plaintiff, who spent many hours in examining the numerous witnesses, several of whom were officers of the army, and gentlemen of undoubted honor and capacity for observation.

Captain Molesworth took the house of a Mr. Webster, who resided in the adjoining one, in May or June, 1835; and when he had been in it about two months, he began to complain of sundry extraordinary noises, which, finding it impossible to account for, he took it into his head (strangely enough) were made by Mr. Webster. The latter naturally represented that it was not probable he should desire to damage the reputation of his own house, and drive his tenant out of it, and retorted the accusation. Still, as these noises and knockings continued, Captain Molesworth not only lifted the boards in the room most infected, but actually made holes in the wall which divided his residence from Mr. Webster's, for the purpose of detecting the delinquent—of course without success. Do what they would, the thing went on just the same: footsteps of invisible feet, knockings, and scratchings, and rustlings, first on one side, and then on the other, were heard daily and nightly. Sometimes this unseen agent seemed to be knocking to a certain tune, and if a question were addressed to it which could be answered numerically—as, "How many people are there in this room?" for example—it would answer by so many knocks. The beds, too, were occasionally heaved up, as if somebody were underneath, and where the knockings were, the wall trembled visibly, but, search as they would, no one could be found.

Captain Molesworth had had two daughters, one of whom, named Matilda, had lately died; the other, a girl between twelve and thirteen, called Jane, was sickly, and generally kept her bed; and, as it was observed that, wherever she was, these noises most frequently prevailed, Mr. Webster, who did not like the *mala fama* that was attaching itself to his house, declared that she made them, while the people in the neighborhood believed that it was the ghost of Matilda, warning her sister that she was soon to follow.

Sheriff's officers, masons, justices of peace, and the officers of the regiment quartered at Leith, who were friends of Captain Molesworth, all came to his aid, in hopes of detecting or frightening away his tormentor, but in vain. Sometimes it was said to be a trick of somebody outside the house, and then they formed a cordon round it; and next, as the poor sick girl was suspected, they tied her up in a bag—but it was all to no purpose.

At length, ill and wearied out by the annoyances and the anxieties attending the affair, Captain Molesworth quitted the house, and Mr. Webster brought an action against him for the damages committed by lifting the boards, breaking the walls, and firing at the wainscoat, as well as for the injury done to his house by saying it was haunted, which prevented other tenants taking it.

The poor young lady died, hastened out of the world, it is said, by the severe measures used while she was under suspicion; and the persons that have since inhabited the house have experienced no repetition of the annoyance.

8

One occurred very lately in the neighborhood of London, as I learned from the following newspaper paragraph. I subsequently heard that the little girl had been sent away; but whether the phenomena then ceased, or whether she carried the disturbance with her, I have not been able to ascertain, nor does it appear certain that she had anything to do with it:—

"A Mischievous and Mysterious Ghost.—(From a correspondent.)—The whole of the neighborhood of Black Lion-lane, Bayswater, is ringing with the extraordinary occurrences that have recently happened in the house of a Mr. Williams, in the Moscow-road, and which bear a strong resemblance to the celebrated Stockwell ghost affair in 1772. The house is inhabited by Mr. and Mrs. Williams, a grown-up son and daughter, and a little girl between ten and eleven years of age. On the first day, the family, who are remarkable for their piety, were startled all at once by a mysterious movement among the things in the sitting-rooms and kitchen, and other parts of the house.

At one time, without any visible agency, one of the jugs came off the hook over the dresser, and was broken; then followed another, and next day another. A china teapot, with the tea just made in it, and placed on the mantel-piece, whisked off on to the floor, and was smashed. A pewter one, which had been substituted immediately after, did the same, and, when put on the table, was seen to hop about as if bewitched, and was actually held down while the tea was made for

Mr. Williams's breakfast, before leaving for his place of business. When for a time all had been quiet, off came from its place on the wall, a picture in a heavy gilt frame, and fell to the floor without being broken.

All was now amazement and terror, for the old people are very superstitious, and ascribing it to a supernatural agency, the other pictures were removed, and stowed away on the floor. But the spirit of locomotion was not to be arrested. Jugs and plates continued at intervals to quit their posts, and skip off their hooks and shelves into the middle of the room, as though they were inspired by the magic flute, and at supper, when the little girl's mug was filled with beer, the mug slided off the table on to the floor. Three times it was replaced, and three times it moved off again. It would be tedious to relate the fantastic tricks which have been played by household articles of every kind.

An Egyptian vase jumped off the table suddenly, when no soul was near, and was smashed to pieces. The teakettle popped off the fire into the grate as Mr. Williams had filled the teapot, which fell off the chimney-piece. Candlesticks, after a dance on the table, flew off, and ornaments from the shelves, and bonnets and cap-boxes flung about in the oddest manner. A looking-glass hopped off a dressing-table, followed by combs and brushes and several bottles, and a great pincushion has been remarkably conspicuous for its incessant jigs from one part to another. The little girl, who is a Spaniard, and under the care of Mr. and Mrs. Williams, is supposed by their friends to be the cause of it all, however extraordinary it may seem in one of her age, but up to the present time it continues a mystery, and the *modus operandi* is invisible."—*Morning Post.*

To imagine that these extraordinary effects were produced by the voluntary agency of the child, furnishes one of those remarkable instances of the credulity of the skeptical, to which I have referred. But when we read a true statement of the effects involuntarily exhibited by Angelique Cottin, we begin to see that it is just possible the other strange phenomena may be provided by a similar agency.

The French Academy of Sciences had determined, as they had formerly done by Mesmerism, that the thing should not be true. Monsieur Arago was nonsuited; but although it is extremely possible that either the phenomenon had run its course and arrived at a natural termination, or that the removal of the girl to Paris had extinguished it, there appears no doubt that it had previously existed.

Angelique Cottin was a native of La Perriere, aged fourteen, when, on the 15th of January, 1846, at eight o'clock in the evening, while weaving silk-gloves at an oaken frame, in company with other girls, the frame began to jerk, and they could not by any efforts keep it steady. It seemed as if it were alive, and becoming alarmed, they called in the neighbors, who would not believe them; but desired them to sit down and go on with their work. Being timid, they went one by one, and the frame remained still till Angelique approached, when it recommenced its movements, while she was also attracted by the frame: thinking she was bewitched or possessed, her parents took her to the presbytery that the spirit might be exorcised. The curate, however, being a sensible man, refused to do it, but set himself, on the contrary, to observe the phenomenon, and being perfectly satisfied of the fact, he bade them take her to a physician.

Meanwhile, the intensity of the influence, whatever it was, augmented; not only articles made of oak, but all sorts of things were acted upon by it and reacted upon her, while persons who were near her, even without contact, frequently felt electric shocks. The effects, which were diminished when she was on a carpet or a waxed cloth, were most remarkable when she was on the bare earth. They sometimes entirely ceased for two or three days, and then recommenced. Metals were not affected.

Anything touched by her apron or dress would fly off, although a person held it; and Monsieur Hebert, while seated on a heavy tub or trough, was raised up with it. In short, the only place she could repose on, was a stone covered with cork; they also kept her still by isolating her. When she was fatigued the effects diminished. A needle suspended horizontally, oscillated rapidly with the motion of her arm, without contact, or remained fixed, while deviating from the magnetic direction. Great numbers of enlightened medical and scientific men witnessed these phenomena, and investigated them with every precaution to prevent imposition. She was often hurt by the violent involuntary movements she was thrown into, and was evidently afflicted by chorea.

Unfortunately, her parents, poor and ignorant, insisted much against the advice of the doctors, on exhibiting her for money; and under these circumstances, she was brought to Paris; and nothing is more probable than that after the phenomena had really ceased, the girl may have been induced to simulate what had originally been genuine. The thing avowedly ceased altogether on the 10th of April, and there has been no return of it.

9

To these instances I will add an account of the ghost seen in C—— castle, copied from the handwriting of C—— M—— H—— in a book of manuscript extracts, dated C—— castle, December 22, 1824, and furnished to me by a friend of the family:—

"In order to introduce my readers to the haunted room, I will mention that it forms part of the old house, with windows looking into the court, which in early times was deemed a necessary security against an enemy. It adjoins a tower built by the Romans for defence; for C—— was properly more a border tower than a castle of any consideration. There is a winding staircase in this tower, and the walls are from eight to ten feet thick.

"When the times became more peaceable, our ancestors enlarged the arrow-slit windows, and added to that part of the building which looks toward the River Eden; the view of which, with its beautiful banks, we now enjoy. But many additions and alterations have been made since that.

"To return to the room in question, I must observe that it is by no means remote or solitary, being surrounded on all sides by chambers that are constantly inhabited. It is accessible by a passage cut through a wall, eight feet in thickness, and its dimensions are twenty-one by eighteen. One side of the wainscoting is covered with tapestry; the remainder is decorated with old family-pictures, and some ancient pieces of embroidery, probably the handiwork of nuns. Over a press, which has doors of Venetian glass, is an ancient oaken figure, with a battle-axe in his hand, which was one of those formerly placed on the walls of the city of Carlisle, to represent guards.

"There used to be, also, an old-fashioned bed and some dark furniture in this room; but, so many were the complaints of those who slept there, that I was induced to replace some of these articles of furniture by more modern ones, in the hope of removing a certain air of gloom, which I thought might have given rise to the unaccountable reports of apparitions and extraordinary noises which were constantly reaching us. But I regret to say I did not succeed in banishing the nocturnal visitor, which still continues to disturb our friends.

"I shall pass over numerous instances, and select one as being especially remarkable, from the circumstance of the apparition having been seen by a clergyman well known and highly respected in this county, who, not six weeks ago, repeated the circumstances to a company of twenty persons, among whom were some who had previously been entire disbelievers in such appearances.

"The best way of giving you these particulars, will be by subjoining an extract from my journal, entered at the time the event occurred.

"*Sept. 8, 1803.*—Among other guests invited to C——— castle, came the Rev. Henry A———, of Redburgh, and rector of Greystoke, with Mrs. A———, his wife, who was a Miss S———, of Ulverstone. According to previous arrangements, they were to have remained with us for some days; but their visit was cut short in a very unexpected manner. On the morning after their arrival, we were all assembled at breakfast, when a chaise and four dashed up to the door in such haste that it knocked down part of the fence of my flower-garden. Our curiosity was, of course, awakened to know who could be arriving at so early an hour; when, happening to turn my eyes toward Mr. A———, I observed that he appeared extremely agitated. 'It is our carriage!' said he; 'I am very sorry, but we must absolutely leave you this morning.'

"We naturally felt and expressed considerable surprise, as well as regret at this unexpected departure; representing that we had invited Colonel and Mrs. S———, some friends whom Mr. A——— particularly desired to meet, to dine with us on that day. Our expostulations, however, were vain; the breakfast was no sooner over than they departed, leaving us in consternation to conjecture what could possibly have occasioned so sudden an alteration in their arrangements. I really felt quite uneasy lest anything should have given them offence; and we reviewed all the occurrences of the preceding evening in order to discover, if offence there was, whence it had arisen. But our pains were vain; and after talking a great deal about it for some days, other circumstances banished it from our minds.

"It was not till we some time afterward visited the part of the country in which Mr. A——— resides, that we learned the real cause of his sudden departure from C———. The relation of the fact, as it here follows, is in his own words:—

"Soon after we went to bed, we fell asleep: it might have been between one and two in the morning when I awoke. I observed that the fire was totally extinguished; but although that was the case, and we had no light, I saw a glimmer in the centre of the room, which suddenly increased to a bright flame. I looked out, apprehending that something had caught fire, when, to my amazement, I beheld a beautiful boy, clothed in white, with bright locks, resembling gold, standing by my bedside, in which position he remained some minutes, fixing his eyes upon me with a mild and benevolent expression. He then glided gently away toward the side of the chimney, where it is obvious there is no possible egress, and entirely disappeared. I found myself again in total darkness, and all remained quiet until the usual hour of rising. I declare this to be a true account of what I saw at C———— castle, upon my word as a clergyman."

I am acquainted with some of the family, and with several of the friends of Mr. A————, who is still alive, though now an old man, and I can most positively assert that his own conviction, with regard to the nature of this appearance, has remained ever unshaken. The circumstance made a lasting impression upon his mind, and he never willingly speaks of it; but when he does, it is always with the greatest seriousness, and he never shrinks from avowing his belief, that what he saw admits of no other interpretation than the one he then put upon it.

Now, let us see whether in this department of the phenomenon of ghost-seeing, namely, the lights that frequently accompany the apparitions, there is anything so worthy of ridicule as Grose and other such commentators seem to think.

10

About six years ago, Mr. C————, a gentleman engaged in business in London, heard of a good country-house in the neighbourhood of the metropolis, which was to be had at a low rent. It was rather an old-fashioned place and was surrounded by a garden and pleasure-ground; and having taken a lease of it for seven years, furnished as it was, his family removed thither, and he joined them once or twice a week, as his business permitted.

They had been some considerable time in the house without the occurrence of anything remarkable, when one evening, toward dusk, Mrs. C————, on going into what was called the oak bed-room, saw a female figure near one of the windows. It was apparently a young woman with dark hair hanging over her shoulders, a silk petticoat, and a short, white robe, and she appeared to be looking eagerly through the window, as if expecting somebody. Mrs. C———— clapped her hand upon her eyes, "as thinking she had seen something she ought not to have seen," and when she looked again the figure had disappeared.

Shortly after this, a young girl who filled the situation of under nursery-maid, came to her in great agitation, saying that she had had a terrible fright, from seeing a very ugly old woman looking in upon her as she passed the window in the lobby. The girl was trembling violently, and almost crying, so that Mrs. C——— entertained no doubts of the reality of her alarm. She, however, thought it advisable to laugh her out of her fear, and went with her to the window, which looked into a closed court, but there was no one there, neither had any of the other servants seen such a person. Soon after this, the family began to find themselves disturbed with strange, and frequently very loud, noises during the night. Among the rest, there was something like the beating of a crow-bar upon the pump in the abovementioned court; but, search as they would, they could discover no cause for the sound.

One day, when Mr. C——— had brought a friend from London to stay the night with him, Mrs. C——— thought proper to go up to the oak bedroom, where the stranger was to sleep, for the purpose of inspecting the arrangements for his comfort, when, to her great surprise, some one seemed to follow her up to the fireplace, though, on turning round, there was nobody to be seen. She said nothing about it, however, and returned below, where her husband and the stranger were sitting. Presently, one of the servants (not the one mentioned above) tapped at the door and requested to speak with her, and Mrs. C——— going out, she told her, in great agitation, that in going up stairs to the visitor's room, a footstep had followed her all the way to the fireplace, although she could see nobody. Mrs. C——— said something soothing, and that matter passed, she, herself, being a good deal puzzled, but still unwilling to admit the idea that there was anything extra-natural in these occurrences.

Repeatedly, after this, these footsteps were heard in different parts of the house, when nobody was to be seen; and often, while she was lying in bed, she heard them distinctly approach her door, when, being a very courageous woman, she would start out with a loaded pistol in her hand, but there was never anyone to be seen. At length it was impossible to conceal from herself and her servants that these occurrences were of an extraordinary nature, and the latter, as may be supposed, felt very uncomfortable. Among other unpleasant things, while sitting all together in the kitchen, they used to see the latch lifted and the door open, though no one came in that they could see; and when Mr. C——— himself watched for these events, although they took place, and he was quite on the alert, he altogether failed in detecting any visible agent.

One night, the same servant who had heard the footsteps following her to the bed-room fireplace, happening to be asleep in Mrs.

C——'s chamber, she became much disturbed, and was heard to murmur, "Wake me! wake me!" as if in great mental anguish. Being aroused, she told her mistress a dream she had had, which seemed to throw some light upon these mysteries. She thought she was in the oak bedroom, and at one end of it she saw a young female in an old-fashioned dress, with long dark hair, while in another part of the room was a very ugly old woman, also in old-fashioned attire. The latter addressing the former said, "What have you done with the child, Emily? What have you done with the child?" To which the younger figure answered, "Oh, I did not kill it. He was preserved, and grew up, and joined the —— regiment, and went to India."

Then addressing the sleeper, the young lady continued, "I have never spoken to mortal before; but I will tell you all. My name is Miss Black; and this old woman is Nurse Black. Black is not her name, but we call her so because she has been so long in the family." Here the old woman interrupted the speaker by coming up and laying her hand on the dreaming girl's shoulder, while she said something; but she could not remember what, for, feeling excruciating pain from the touch, she had been so far aroused as to be sensible she was asleep, and to beg to be wholly awakened.

As the old woman seemed to resemble the figure that one of the other servants had seen looking into the window, and the young one resembled that she had herself seen in the oak chamber, Mrs. C—— naturally concluded that there was something extraordinary about this dream, and she consequently took an early opportunity of inquiring in the neighbourhood what was known as to the names or circumstances of the former inhabitants of this house; and, after much investigation, she learned that, about seventy or eighty years before, it had been in the possession of a Mrs. Ravenhall, who had a niece, named Miss Black, living with her. This niece Mrs. C—— supposed might be the younger of the two persons who was seen. Subsequently, she saw her again in the same room, wringing her hands, and looking with a mournful significance to one corner. They had the boards taken up on that spot, but nothing was found.

One of the most curious incidents, connected with this story, remains to be told. After occupying the house three years, they were preparing to quit it—not on account of its being haunted, but for other reasons—when on awaking one morning, a short time before their departure, Mrs. C—— saw, standing at the foot of her bed, a dark-complexioned man, in a working dress, a fustian jacket, and red comforter round his neck—who, however, suddenly disappeared. Mr. C——— was lying beside her at the time, but asleep. This was the last apparition seen. But the strange thing is, that a few days after this, it being necessary to order in a small quantity of coals to serve till their removal, Mr. C——— undertook to perform the commission on his way to London.

Accordingly, the next day, she mentioned to him that the coals had arrived; which he said was very fortunate, since he had entirely forgotten to order them. Wondering whence they had come, Mrs. C——— hereupon inquired of the servants, who none of them knew anything about the matter; but on interrogating a person in the village, by whom they had frequently been provided with this article, he answered that they had been ordered by a dark man, in a fustian jacket and red comfort, who had called for the purpose.

After this last event, Mr. and Mrs. C——— quitted the house; but I have heard that its subsequent tenants encountered some similar annoyances, although I have no means of ascertaining the particulars.

11

The following very curious relation I have received from the gentleman to whom the circumstance occurred, who is a professional man residing in London:—

"I was brought up by a grandfather and four aunts, all ghost-seers and believers in supernatural appearances. The former had been a sailor and was one of the crew that sailed round the world with Lord Anson. I remember, when I was about eight years old, that I was awakened by the screams of one of these ladies, with whom I was sleeping, which summoned all the family about her to inquire the cause of the disturbance. She said that she had 'seen Nancy by the side of the bed, and that she was slipping into it.' We had scarcely got downstairs in the morning, before intelligence arrived that that lady had died, precisely at the moment my aunt said she saw her. Nancy was her brother's wife. Another of my aunts, who was married and had a large family, foretold my grandfather's death, at a time that we had no reason to apprehend it. He, also, had appeared at her bedside; he was then alive and well, but he died a fortnight afterward. But it would be tedious were I to enumerate half the instances I could recall of a similar description; and I will therefore proceed to the relation of what happened to myself.

"I was, some few years since, invited to pass a day and night at the house of a friend in Hertfordshire, with whom I was intimately acquainted. His name was B——, and he had formerly been in business as a saddler, in Oxford street, where he realised a handsome fortune, and had now retired to enjoy his *otium cum dignitate*, in the rural and beautiful village of Sarratt.

"It was a gloomy Sunday, in the month of November, when I mounted my horse for the journey, and there was so much appearance of rain, that I should certainly have selected some other mode of conveyance, had I not been desirous of leaving the animal in Mr. E——'s straw-yard for the winter. Before I got as far as St. John's wood, the threatening clouds broke, and by the time I reached Watford I was completely soaked. However, I proceeded, and arrived at Sarratt before my friend and his wife had returned from church. The moment they did so, they furnished me with dry clothes, and I was informed that we were to dine at the house of Mr. D——, a very agreeable neighbour.

"I felt some little hesitation about presenting myself in such a costume, for I was decked out in a full suit of Mr. B——'s, who was a stout man, of six feet in height, while I am rather of the diminutive order; but my objections were overruled; we went, and my appearance added not a little to the hilarity of the party. At ten o'clock we separated, and I returned with Mr. and Mrs. B—— to their house, where I was shortly afterward conducted to a very comfortable bed-room.

"Fatigued with my day's ride, I was soon in bed, and soon asleep, but I do not think I could have slept long before I was awakened by the violent barking of dogs. I found that the noise had disturbed others as well as myself, for I heard Mr. B——, who was lodged in the adjoining room, open his window and call to them to be quiet. They were obedient to his voice, and as soon as quietness ensued I dropped asleep again; but I was again awakened by an extraordinary pressure upon my feet; *that I was perfectly awake, I declare*; the light that stood in the chimney-corner shone strongly across the foot of the bed, and I saw the figure of a well-dressed man in the act of stooping, and supporting himself in so doing by the bed-clothes. He had on a blue coat, with bright gilt buttons, but I saw no head; the curtains at the foot of the bed, which were partly looped back, just hung so as to conceal that part of his person.

"At first I thought it was my host, and as I had dropped my clothes, as is my habit, on the floor at the foot of the bed, I supposed he was come to look after them, which rather surprised me: but, just as I had raised myself upright in bed, and was about to inquire into the occasion of his visit, the figure passed on. I then recollected that I had locked the door; and, becoming somewhat puzzled, I jumped out of bed; but I could see nobody; and on examining the room I found no means of ingress but the door through which I had entered, and one other; both of which were locked on the inside. Amazed and puzzled I got into bed again, and sat some time ruminating on the extraordinary circumstance, when it occurred to me that I had not looked under the bed; so I got out again, fully expecting to find my visitor, whoever he was, there; but I was disappointed. So, after looking at my watch, and ascertaining that it was ten minutes past two, I stepped into bed again, hoping now to get some rest.

"But, alas! sleep was banished for that night; and after turning from side to side, and making vain endeavours at forgetfulness, I gave up the point, and lay till the clocks struck seven, perplexing my brain with the question of who my midnight visitor could be, and also how he had got in and how he had got out of my room. About eight o'clock I met my host and his wife at the breakfast-table, when, in answer to their hospitable inquiries of how I had passed the night, I mentioned, first, that I had been awaked by the barking of some dogs, and that I had heard Mr. B——— open his window and call to them. He answered that two strange dogs had got into the yard and had disturbed the others. I then mentioned my midnight visitor, expecting that they would either explain the circumstance, or else laugh at me and declare I must have dreamed it.

"But, to my surprise, my story was listened to with grave attention, and they related to me the tradition with which this spectre, for such I found they deemed it to be, was supposed to be connected. This was to the effect, that many years ago a gentleman so attired had been murdered there, under some frightful circumstances, and that his head had been cut off. On perceiving that I was very unwilling to accept this explanation of the mystery, for, in spite of my family peculiarity, I had always been an entire disbeliever in supernatural appearances, they begged me to prolong my visit for a day or two, when they would introduce me to the rector of the parish, who could furnish me with such evidence with regard to circumstances of a similar nature, as would leave no doubt on my mind as to the possibility of their occurrence. But I had made an engagement to dine at Watford, on my way back, and I confess, moreover, that after what I had heard I did not feel disposed to encounter the chance of another visit from the mysterious stranger; so, I declined the proffered hospitality, and took my leave.

"Some time after this, I happened to be dining at C——— street, in company with some ladies resident in the same county, when, chancing to allude to my visit to Sarratt, I added, that I had met with a very extraordinary adventure there, which I had never been able to account for, when one of these ladies immediately said that she hoped I had not had a visit from the headless gentleman, in a blue coat and gilt buttons, who was said to have been seen by many people in that house.

"Such is the conclusion of this marvellous tale as regards myself; and I can only assure you that I have related facts as they occurred, and that I had never heard a word about this apparition in my life, till Mr. B——— related to me the tradition above alluded to. Still, as I am no believer, in supernatural appearances, I am constrained to suppose that the whole affair was the product of my imagination.

"I must add, that Mr. B——— mentioned some strange circumstances connected with another house in the county, inhabited by a Mr. M———, which were corroborated by the ladies above alluded to. Both parties agreed that, from the unaccountable noises, &c., &c., which were heard there, that gentleman had the greatest difficulty in persuading any servants to remain with him.

"A——— W——— M———.

"C——— street, 5th September, 1846."

12

"About the month of August," says Captain E———, "my attention was requested by the schoolmaster-sergeant, a man of considerable worth, and highly esteemed by the whole corps, to an event which had occurred in the garrison hospital. Having heard his recital, which, from the serious earnestness with which he made it, challenged attention, I resolved to investigate the matter; and, having communicated the circumstances to a friend, we both repaired to the hospital for the purpose of inquiry.

"There were two patients to be examined—both men of good character, and neither of them suffering from any disorder affecting the brain; the one was under treatment for consumptive symptoms, and the other for an ulcerated leg: and they were both in the prime of life.

"Having received a confirmation of the schoolmaster's statement from the hospital-sergeant, also a very respectable and trustworthy man, I sent for the patient principally concerned, and desired him to state what he had seen and heard, warning him, at the same time, that it was my intention to take down his deposition, and that it behooved him to be very careful, as possibly serious steps might be taken for the purpose of discovering whether an imposition had been practised in the wards of the hospital—a crime for which, he was well aware, a very severe penalty would be inflicted. He then proceeded to relate the circumstances, which I took down in the presence of Mr. B——— and the hospital-sergeant, as follows:—

"'It was last Tuesday night, somewhere between eleven and twelve, when all of us were in bed, and all lights out except the rush-light that was allowed for the man with the fever, when I was awoke by feeling a weight upon my feet, and at the same moment, as I was drawing up my legs, Private W———, who lies in the cot opposite mine, called out, "I say, Q———, there's somebody sitting upon your legs!"—and as I looked to the bottom of my bed, I saw someone get up from it, and then come round and stand over me, in the passage between my cot and the next. I felt somewhat alarmed, for the last few nights the ward had been disturbed by sounds as of a heavy foot walking up and down; and as nobody could be seen, it was beginning to be supposed among us that it was haunted, and fancying this that came up to my bed's head might be the ghost, I called out, "Who are you, and what do you want?"

"'The figure then, leaning with one hand on the wall, over my head, and stooping down, said, in my ear, "I am Mrs. M———;" and I could then distinguish that she was dressed in a flannel gown, edged with black riband, exactly similar to a set of grave-clothes in which I had assisted to clothe her corpse, when her death took place a year previously.

"'The voice, however, was not like Mrs. M———'s, nor like anybody else's, yet it was very distinct, and seemed somehow to sing through my head. I could see nothing of a face beyond a darkish color about the head, and it appeared to me that I could see through her body against the window-glasses.

"'Although I felt very uncomfortable, I asked her what she wanted. She replied, "I am Mrs. M———, and I wish you to write to him that was my husband, and tell him. . . . ."

"'I am not, sir,' said Corporal Q———, 'at liberty to mention to anybody what she told me, except to her husband. He is at the *dépôt* in Ireland, and I have written and told him. She made me promise not to tell anyone else. After I had promised secrecy, she told me something of a matter that convinced me I was talking to a spirit, for it related to what only I and Mrs. M——— knew, and no one living could know anything whatever of the matter; and if I was now speaking my last words on earth, I say solemnly that it was Mrs. M———'s spirit that spoke to me then, and no one else. After promising that if I complied with her request, she would not trouble me or the ward again, she went from my bed toward the fireplace, and with her hands she kept feeling about the wall over the mantel-piece. After a while, she came toward me again; and while my eyes were upon her, she somehow disappeared from my sight altogether, and I was left alone.

"'It was then that I felt faint-like, and a cold sweat broke out over me; but I did not faint, and after a time I got better, and gradually I went off to sleep.

"'The men in the ward said, next day, that Mrs. M——— had come to speak to me about purgatory, because she had been a Roman catholic, and we had often had arguments on religion: but what she told me had no reference to such subjects, but to a matter only she and I knew of.'

"After closely cross-questioning Corporal Q———, and endeavouring without success to reason him out of his belief in the ghostly character of his visitor, I read over to him what I had written, and then, dismissing him, sent for the other patient.

"After cautioning him, as I had done the first, I proceeded to take down his statement, which was made with every appearance of good faith and sincerity:—

"'I was lying awake,' said he, 'last Tuesday night, when I saw someone sitting on Corporal Q———'s bed. There was so little light in the ward, that I could not make out who it was, and the figure looked so strange that I got alarmed and felt quite sick. I called out to Corporal Q——— that there was somebody sitting upon his bed, and then the figure got up; and as I did not know but it might be coming to me, I got so much alarmed, that being but weakly' (this was the consumptive man), 'I fell back, and I believe I fainted away. When I got round again, I saw the figure standing and apparently talking to the corporal, placing one hand against the wall and stooping down. I could not, however, hear any voice; and being still much alarmed, I put my head under the clothes for a considerable time. When I looked up again I could only see Corporal Q———, sitting up in bed alone, and he said he had seen a ghost; and I told him I had also seen it. After a time, he got up and gave me a drink of water, for I was very faint. Some of the other patients being disturbed by our talking, they bade us be quiet, and after some time I got to sleep. The ward has not been disturbed since.'

"The man was then cross-questioned; but his testimony remaining quite unshaken, he was dismissed, and the hospital-sergeant was interrogated with regard to the possibility of a trick having been practised. He asserted, however, that this was impossible; and, certainly, from my own knowledge of the hospital regulations, and the habits of the patients, I should say that a practical joke of this nature was too serious a thing to have been attempted by anybody, especially as there were patients in the ward very ill at the time, and one very near his end. The punishment would have been extremely severe, and discovery almost certain, since everybody would have been adverse to the delinquent.

"The investigation that ensued was a very brief one, it being found that there was nothing more to be elicited; and the affair terminated with the supposition that the two men had been dreaming. Nevertheless, six months afterward, on being interrogated, their evidence and their conviction were as clear as at first, and they declared themselves ready at any time to repeat their statement upon oath."

13

Dr. Kerner relates the following singular story, which he declares himself to have received from the most satisfactory authority. Agnes B———, being at the time eighteen years of age, was living as servant in a small inn at Undenheim, her native place. The host and hostess were quiet old people, who generally went to bed about eight o'clock, while she and the boy, the only other servant, were expected to sit up till ten, when they had to shut up the house and retire to bed also. One evening, as the host was sitting on a bench before the door, there came a beggar, requesting a night's lodging. The host, however, refused, and bade him seek what he wanted in the village; whereon the man went away.

At the usual hour the old people went to bed; and the two servants, having closed the shutters, and indulged in a little gossip with the watchman, were about to follow their example, when the beggar came round the corner of the neighbouring street, and earnestly entreated them to give him a lodging for the night, since he could find nobody that would take him in. At first the young people refused, saying they dared not, without their master's leave; but at length the entreaties of the man prevailed, and they consented to let him sleep in the barn, on condition that, when they called him in the morning, he would immediately depart. At three o'clock they rose, and when the boy entered the barn, to his dismay, he found that the old man had expired in the night. They were now much perplexed with the apprehension of their master's displeasure; so, after some consultation, they agreed that the lad should convey the body out of the barn and lay it in a dry ditch that was near at hand, where it would be found by the laborers, and excite no question, as they would naturally conclude he had laid himself down there to die.

This was done, the man was discovered and buried, and they thought themselves well rid of the whole affair; but, on the following night, the girl was awakened by the beggar, whom she saw standing at her bedside. He looked at her, and then quitted the room by the door.

"Glad was I," she says, "when the day broke; but I was scarcely out of my room when the boy came to me, trembling and pale, and, before I could say a word to him of what I had seen, he told me that the beggar had been to his room in the night, had looked at him, and then gone away. He said he was dressed as when we had seen him alive, only he looked blacker, which I also had observed."

Still afraid of incurring blame, they told nobody, although the apparition returned to them every night; and although they found removing to the other bed-chambers did not relieve them from his visits. But the effects of this persecution became so visible on both, that much curiosity was awakened in the village with respect to the cause of the alteration observed in them; and at length the boy's mother went to the minister, requesting him to interrogate her son, and endeavour to discover what was preying on his mind. To him the boy disclosed their secret; and this minister, who was a protestant, having listened with attention to the story, advised him, when next he went to Mayence, to market, to call on Father Joseph, of the Franciscan convent, and relate the circumstance to him.

This advice was followed; and Father Joseph, assuring the lad that the ghost could do him no harm, recommended him to ask him, in the name of God, what he desired. The boy did so; whereupon the apparition answered, "Ye are children of mercy, but I am a child of evil; in the barn, under the straw, you will find my money. Take it; it is yours."

In the morning, the boy found the money accordingly, in an old stocking hid under the straw; but having a natural horror of it, they took it to their minister, who advised them to divide it into three parts, giving one to the Franciscan convent at Mayence, another to the reformed church in the village, and the other third to that to which they themselves belonged, which was of the Lutheran persuasion. This they did and were no more troubled with the beggar. With respect to the minister who gave them this good advice, I can only say, all honour be to him! I wish there were many more such!

The circumstance occurred in the year 1750 and is related by the daughter of Agnes B———, who declared that she had frequently heard it from her mother.

The circumstance of this apparition looking darker than the man had done when alive, is significant of his condition, and confirms what I have said above, namely, that the moral state of the disembodied soul can no longer be concealed as it was in the flesh, but that as he is, he must necessarily appear.

14

The proceedings of the ghost in the following case will doubtless be equally displeasing to the critics. The account is extracted verbatim from a work published by the Bannatyne Club, and is entitled, *Authentic Account of the Appearance of a Ghost in Queen Ann's County, Maryland, United States of North America, proved in the following remarkable trial, from attested notes taken in court at the time by one of the counsel.*

It appears that Thomas Harris had made some alteration in the disposal of his property, immediately previous to his death; and that the family disputed the will and raised up difficulties likely to be injurious to his children.

"William Brigs said, that he was forty-three years of age; that Thomas Harris died in September, in the year 1790. In the March following he was riding near the place where Thomas Harris was buried, on a horse formerly belonging to Thomas Harris. After crossing a small branch, his horse began to walk on very fast. It was between the hours of eight and nine o'clock in the morning. He was alone: it was a clear day. He entered a lane adjoining to the field where Thomas Harris was buried. His horse suddenly wheeled in a panel of the fence, looked over the fence into the field where Thomas Harris was buried, and neighed very loud. Witness then saw Thomas Harris coming toward him, in the same apparel he had last seen him in in his lifetime; he had on a sky-blue coat. Just before he came to the fence, he varied to the right and vanished; his horse immediately took the road. Thomas Harris came within two panels of the fence to him; he did not see his features, nor speak to him. He was acquainted with

Thomas Harris when a boy, and there had always been a great intimacy between them. He thinks the horse knew Thomas Harris, because of his neighing, pricking up his ears, and looking over the fence.

"About the first of June following, he was ploughing in his own field, about three miles from where Thomas Harris was buried. About dusk Thomas Harris came alongside of him and walked with him about two hundred yards. He was dressed as when first seen. He made a halt about two steps from him. J. Bailey who was ploughing along with him, came driving up, and he lost sight of the ghost. He was much alarmed: not a word was spoken. The young man Bailey did not see him; he did not tell Bailey of it. There was no motion of any particular part: he vanished. It preyed upon his mind so as to affect his health. He was with Thomas Harris when he died but had no particular conversation with him. Sometime after, he was lying in bed, about eleven and twelve o'clock at night, when he heard Thomas Harris groan; it was like the groan he gave a few minutes before he expired: Mrs. Brigs, his wife, heard the groan. She got up and searched the house: he did not, because he knew the groan to be from Thomas Harris.

"Sometime after, when in bed, and a great fire-light in the room, he saw a shadow on the wall, and at the same time he felt a great weight upon him. Sometime after, when in bed and asleep, he felt a stroke between his eyes, which blackened them both: his wife was in bed with him, and two young men were in the room. The blow awaked him, and all in the room were asleep; is certain no one in the room struck him: the blow swelled his nose.

"About the middle of August, he was alone, coming from Hickey Collins's, after dark, about one hour in the night, when Thomas Harris appeared, dressed as he had seen him when going down to the meeting-house branch, three miles and a half from the graveyard of Thomas Harris. It was starlight. He extended his arms over his shoulders. Does not know how long he remained in this situation. He was much alarmed. Thomas Harris disappeared. Nothing was said. He felt no weight on his shoulders. He went back to Collins's and got a young man to go with him. After he got home he mentioned it to the young man. He had, before this, told James Harris he had seen his brother's ghost.

"In October, about twilight in the morning, he saw Thomas Harris about one hundred yards from the house of the witness; his head was leaned to one side; same apparel as before; his face was toward him;

236

he walked fast and disappeared: there was nothing between them to obstruct the view; he was about fifty yards from him, and alone; he had no conception why Thomas Harris appeared to him. On the same day, about eight o'clock in the morning, he was handing up blades to John Bailey, who was stacking them; he saw Thomas Harris come along the garden fence, dressed as before; he vanished, and always to the east; was within fifteen feet of him; Bailey did not see him. An hour and a half afterward, in the same place, he again appeared, coming as before; came up to the fence; leaned on it within ten feet of the witness, who called to Bailey to look there (pointing toward Thomas Harris).

"Bailey asked what was there. Don't you see Harris? Does not recollect what Bailey said. Witness advanced toward Harris. One or the other spoke as witness got over the fence on the same panel that Thomas Harris was leaning on. They walked off together about five hundred yards; a conversation took place as they walked; he has not the conversation on his memory. He could not understand Thomas Harris his voice was so low. He asked Thomas Harris a question, and he forbid him. Witness then asked, 'Why not go to your brother, instead of me?' Thomas Harris said, 'Ask me no questions.' Witness told him his will was doubted. Thomas Harris told him to ask his brother if he did not remember the conversation which passed between them on the east side of the wheat-stacks, the day he was taken with his death-sickness; that he then declared that he wished all his property kept together by James Harris, until his children arrived at age, then the whole should be sold and divided among his children; and, should it be immediately sold, as expressed in his will, that the property would be most wanting to his children while minors, therefore he had changed his will, and said that witness should see him again.

"He then told witness to turn and disappeared. He did not speak to him with the same voice as in his lifetime. He was not daunted while with Thomas Harris, but much afterward. Witness then went to James Harris and told him that he had seen his brother three times that day. Related the conversation he had with him. Asked James Harris if he remembered the conversation between him and his brother, at the wheat-stack; he said he did; then told him what had passed. Said he would fulfil his brother's will. He was satisfied that witness had seen his brother, for that no other person knew the conversation. On the same evening, returning home about an hour before sunset, Thomas Harris appeared to him, and came alongside of him. Witness told him that his brother said he would fulfil his will. No more conversation on this subject. He disappeared. He had further conversation with Thomas Harris, but not on this subject. He was always dressed in the same manner. He had never related to any person the last conversation, and never would.

"Bailey, who was sworn in the cause, declared that as he and Brigs were stacking blades, as related by Brigs, he called to witness and said, 'Look there! Do you not see Thomas Harris?' Witness said, 'No.' Brigs got over the fence, and walked some distance—appeared by his action to be in deep conversation with some person. Witness saw no one.

"The counsel was extremely anxious to hear from Mr. Brigs the whole of the conversation of the ghost, and on his cross-examination took every means, without effect, to obtain it. They represented to him, as a religious man, he was bound to disclose the whole truth. He appeared agitated when applied to, declaring nothing short of life should make him reveal the whole conversation, and, claiming the protection of the court, that he had declared all he knew relative to the case.

"The court overruled the question of the counsel. Hon. James Tilgman, judge.

"His excellency Robert Wright, late governor of Maryland, and the Hon. Joseph H. Nicholson, afterward judge of one of the courts in Maryland, were the counsel for the plaintiff.

"John Scott and Richard T. Earl, Esqs., were counsel for the defendant."

15

Some ninety years ago, there flourished in Glasgow a club of young men, which, from the extreme profligacy of its members, and the licentiousness of their orgies, was commonly called the "Hell-Club!" Besides their nightly or weekly meetings, they held one grand annual saturnalia, in which each tried to excel the other in drunkenness and blasphemy; and on these occasions there was no star among them whose lurid light was more conspicuous than that of young Mr. Archibald B———, who, endowed with brilliant talents and a handsome person, had held out great promise in his boyhood, and raised hopes, which had been completely frustrated by his subsequent reckless dissipations.

One morning, after returning from this annual festival, Mr. Archibald B——— having retired to bed, dreamed the following dream:—

He fancied that he himself was mounted on a favourite black horse, that he always rode, and that he was proceeding toward his own house—then a country-seat embowered by trees, and situated upon a hill, now entirely built over, and forming part of the city—when a stranger, whom the darkness of night prevented his distinctly discerning, suddenly seized his horse's rein, saying, "You must go with me!"

"And who are you?" exclaimed the young man, with a volley of oaths, while he struggled to free himself.

"That you will see by-and-by!" returned the other, in a tone that excited unaccountable terror in the youth, who, plunging his spurs into his horse, attempted to fly. But in vain: however fast the animal flew, the stranger was still beside him, till at length, in his desperate efforts to escape, the rider was thrown; but instead of being dashed to the earth, as he expected, he found himself falling—falling—falling still, as if sinking into the bowels of the earth.

At length, a period being put to this mysterious descent, he found breath to inquire of his companion, who was still beside him, whither they were going: "Where am I? where are you taking me?" he exclaimed.

"To hell!" replied the stranger, and immediately interminable echoes repeated the fearful sound, "To hell!—to hell!—to hell!"

At length a light appeared, which soon increased to a blaze; but, instead of the cries, and groans, and lamentings, which the terrified traveller expected, nothing met his ear but sounds of music, mirth, and jollity; and he found himself at the entrance of a superb building, far exceeding any he had seen constructed by human hands. Within, too, what a scene! No amusement, employment, or pursuit of man on earth, but was here being carried on with a vehemence that excited his unutterable amazement. "There the young and lovely still swam through the mazes of the giddy dance! There the panting steed still bore his brutal rider through the excitements of the goaded race! There, over the midnight bowl, the intemperate still drawled out the wanton song or maudlin blasphemy! The gambler plied for ever his endless game, and the slaves of Mammon toiled through eternity their bitter task; while all the magnificence of earth paled before that which now met his view!"

He soon perceived that he was among old acquaintances, whom he knew to be dead, and each he observed was pursuing the object, whatever it was, that had formerly engrossed him; when, finding himself relieved of the presence of his unwelcome conductor, he ventured to address his former friend Mrs. D————, whom he saw sitting, as had been her wont on earth, absorbed at loo, requesting her to rest from the game, and introduce him to the pleasures of the place, which appeared to him to be very unlike what he had expected, and, indeed, an extremely agreeable one. But, with a cry of agony, she answered that there was no rest in hell; that they must ever toil on at those very pleasures: and innumerable voices echoed through the interminable vaults, "There is no rest in hell!"—while, throwing open their vests, each disclosed in his bosom an ever-burning flame! These, they said, were the pleasures of hell: their choice on earth was now their inevitable doom! In the midst of the horror this scene inspired, his conductor returned, and at his earnest entreaty, restored him again to earth; but, as he quitted him, he said, "Remember!—in a year and a day we meet again!"

At this crisis of his dream, the sleeper awoke, feverish and ill; and, whether from the effect of his dream, or of his preceding orgies, he was so unwell as to be obliged to keep his bed for several days, during which period he had time for many serious reflections, which terminated in a resolution to abandon the club and his licentious companions altogether.

He was no sooner well, however, than they flocked around him, bent on recovering so valuable a member of their society; and having wrung from him a confession of the cause of his defection, which, as may be supposed, appeared to them eminently ridiculous, they soon contrived to make him ashamed of his good resolutions. He joined them again, resumed his former course of life, and when the annual saturnalia came round, he found himself with his glass in his hand at the table—when the president, rising to make the accustomed speech, began with saying, "Gentlemen, this being leap-year, it is a year and a day since our last anniversary," &c., &c.

The words struck upon the young man's ear like a knell; but, ashamed to expose his weakness to the jeers of his companions, he sat out the feast, plying himself with wine even more liberally than usual, in order to drown his intrusive thoughts; till, in the gloom of a winter's morning, he mounted his horse to ride home. Some hours afterward, the horse was found, with his saddle and bridle on, quietly grazing by the roadside, about half way between the city and Mr. B————'s house; while, a few yards off, lay the corpse of his master!

16

In the year 1746, A gentleman of the name of Dorrien, of most excellent character and amiable disposition, who was tutor in the Carolina Colleges, at Brunswick, died there in that year; and immediately previous to his death he sent to request an interview with another tutor, of the name of Hofer, with whom he had lived on terms of friendship. Hofer obeyed the summons, but came too late, the dying man was already in the last agonies. After a short time, rumours began to circulate that Herr Dorrien had been seen by different persons about the college; but as it was with the pupils that these rumours originated, they were supposed to be mere fancies, and no attention whatever was paid to them. At length, however, in the month of October, three months after the decease of Herr Dorrien, a circumstance occurred that excited considerable amazement among the professors. It formed part of the duty of Hofer to go through the college every night, between the hours of eleven and twelve, for the purpose of ascertaining that all the scholars were in bed, and that nothing irregular was going on among them. On the night in question, on entering one of the ante-rooms in the execution of this duty, he saw, to his great amazement, Herr Dorrien, seated, in the dressing-gown and white cap he was accustomed to wear, and holding the latter with his right hand, in such a manner as to conceal the upper part of the face; from the eyes to the chin, however, it was distinctly visible.

This unexpected sight naturally startled Hofer, but, summoning resolution, he advanced into the young men's chamber, and, having ascertained that all was in order, closed the door; he then turned his eyes again toward the spectre, and there it sat as before, whereupon he went up to it, and stretched out his arm toward it; but he was now seized with such a feeling of indescribable horror, that he could scarcely withdraw his hand, which became swollen to a degree that for some months he had no use of it. On the following day he related this circumstance to the professor of mathematics, Oeder, who of course treated the thing as a spectral illusion. He, however, consented to accompany Hofer on his rounds the ensuing night, satisfied that he should be able either to convince him it was a mere phantasm, or else a spectre of flesh and blood that was playing him a trick.

They accordingly went at the usual hour, but no sooner had the professor set his foot in that same room, than he exclaimed, "By Heavens! it is Dorrien himself!" Hofer, in the meantime, proceeded into the chamber as before, in the pursuance of his duties, and, on his return, they both contemplated the figure for some time; neither of them had, however, the courage to address or approach it, and finally quitted the room, very much impressed, and perfectly convinced that they had seen Dorrien.

This incident soon got spread abroad, and many people came in hopes of satisfying their own eyes of the fact, but their pains were fruitless; and even Professor Oeder, who had made up his mind to speak to the apparition, sought it repeatedly in the same place in vain. At length, he gave it up, and ceased to think of it, saying, "I have sought the ghost long enough; if he has anything to say, he must now seek me." About a fortnight after this, he was suddenly awakened, between three and four o'clock in the morning, by something moving in his chamber, and on opening his eyes, he beheld a shadowy form, having the same appearance as the spectre, standing in front of a press which was not more than two steps from his bed. He raised himself, and contemplated the figure, the features of which he saw distinctly for some minutes, till it disappeared.

On the following night he was awakened in the same manner, and saw the figure as before, with the addition that there was a sound proceeded from the door of the press, as if somebody was leaning against it. The spectre also stayed longer this time, and Professor Oeder, no doubt frightened and angry, addressing it as an evil spirit, bade it begone, whereon it made gestures with its head and hands that alarmed him so much, that he adjured it in the name of God to leave him, which it did. Eight days now elapsed without any further disturbance, but, after that period, the visits of the spirit were resumed, and he was awakened by it repeatedly about three in the morning, when it would advance from the press to the bed, and hang its head over him in a manner so annoying, that he started up and struck at it, whereupon it would retire, but presently advance again.

Perceiving now, that the countenance was rather placid and friendly than otherwise, the professor at length addressed it, and, having reason to believe that Dorrien had left some debts unpaid, he asked him if that were the case, upon which the spectre retreated some steps, and seemed to place itself in an attitude of attention. Oeder reiterated the inquiry, whereupon the figure drew its hand across its mouth, in which the professor now observed a short pipe. "Is it to the barber you are in debt?" he inquired.

The spectre slowly shook its head.

"Is it to the tobacconist, then?" asked he, the question being suggested by the pipe.

Hereupon the form retreated and disappeared. On the following day, Oeder narrated what had occurred to Councillor Erath, one of the curators of the college, and also to the sister of the deceased, and arrangements were made for discharging the debt. Professor Seidler, of the same college, now proposed to pass the night with Oeder, for the purpose of observing if the ghost came again, which it did about five o'clock, and awoke Oeder as usual, who awoke his companion, but just then the form disappeared, and Seidler said he only saw something white. They then both disposed themselves to sleep, but presently Seidler was aroused by Oeder's starting up and striking out, while he cried, with a voice expressive of rage and horror, "Begone! You have tormented me long enough! If you want anything of me, say what it is, or give me an intelligible sign, and come here no more!"

Seidler heard all this, though he saw nothing; but as soon as Oeder was somewhat appeased, he told him that the figure had returned, and not only approached the bed, but stretched itself upon it. After this, Oeder burned a light, and had someone in the room every night. He gained this advantage by the light, that he saw nothing; but about four o'clock, he was generally awakened by noises in his room, and other symptoms that satisfied him the ghost was there. At length, however, this annoyance ceased also; and trusting that his unwelcome guest had taken his leave, he dismissed his bedfellow, and dispensed with his light. Two nights passed quietly over; on the third, however, the spectre returned; but very perceptibly darker. It now presented another sign, or symbol, which seemed to represent a picture, with a hole in the middle, through which it thrust its head.

Oeder was now so little alarmed, that he bade it express its wishes more clearly, or approach nearer. To these requisitions the apparition shook its head, and then vanished. This strange phenomenon recurred several times, and even in the presence of another curator of the college; but it was with considerable difficulty they discovered what the symbol was meant to convey. They at length, however, found that Dorrien just before his illness, had obtained, on trial, several pictures for a magic lantern, which had never been returned to their owner. This was now done, and from that time the apparition was neither seen nor heard again. Professor Oeder made no secret of these circumstances; he related them publicly in court and college; he wrote the account to several eminent persons and declared himself ready to attest the facts upon his oath.

Stilling, who relates this story, has been called superstitious; he may be so; but his piety and his honesty are above suspicion; he says the facts are well known, and that he can vouch for their authenticity; and as he must have been a contemporary of the parties concerned, he had, doubtless, good opportunities of ascertaining what foundation there was for the story. It is certainly a very extraordinary one, and the demeanour of the spirit as little like what we should have naturally apprehended as possible; but, as I have said before, we have no right to pronounce any opinion on this subject, except from experience, and there are two arguments to be advanced in favour of this narration; the one being, that I cannot imagine anybody setting about to invent a ghost-story, would have introduced circumstances so apparently improbable and inappropriate; and the other consisting in the fact, that I have met with numerous relations, coming from very opposite quarters, which seem to corroborate the one in question.

With respect to the cause of the spectre's appearance, Jung Stilling, I think, reasonably enough, suggests that the poor man had intended to commission Hofer to settle these little affairs for him, but that delaying this duty too long, his mind had been oppressed by the recollection of them in his last moments—he had carried his care with him, and it bound him to the earth. Wherefore, considering how many persons die with duties unperformed, this anxiety to repair the neglect, is not more frequently manifested, we do not know; some reasons we have already suggested as possible; there may be others of which we can form no idea, any more than we can solve the question, why in some cases communication and even speech seems easy, while in this instance, the spirit was only able to convey its wishes by gestures and symbols.

Its addressing itself to Oeder instead of Hofer, probably arose from its finding communication with him less difficult; the swelling of Hofer's arm indicating that his physical nature was not adapted for this spiritual intercourse. With respect to Oeder's expedient of burning a light in his room, in order to prevent his seeing this shadowy form, we can comprehend, that the figure would be discerned more easily on the dark ground of comparative obscurity, and that clear light would render it invisible.

Dr. Kerner mentions, on one occasion, that while sitting in an adjoining room, with the door open, he had seen a shadowy figure, to whom his patient was speaking, standing beside her bed; and catching up a candle, he had rushed toward it; but as soon as he thus illuminated the chamber, he could no longer distinguish it.

The ineffective and awkward attempts of this apparition to make itself understood, are not easily to be reconciled to our ideas of a spirit, while, at the same time, that which it could do, and that which it could not—the powers it possessed and those it wanted—tend to throw some light on its condition.

17

In the year 1785, some cadets were ordered to proceed from Madras to join their regiments up the country. A considerable part of the journey was to be made in a barge, and they were under the conduct of a senior officer, Major R————. In order to relieve the monotony of the voyage, this gentleman proposed, one day, that they should make a shooting excursion inland, and walk round to meet the boat at a point agreed on, which, owing to the windings of the river, it would not reach till evening. They accordingly took their guns, and as they had to cross a swamp, Major R————, who was well acquainted with the country, put on a heavy pair of top-boots, which, together with an odd limp he had in his gait, rendered him distinguishable from the rest of the party at a considerable distance.

When they reached the jungle, they found there was a wide ditch to leap, which all succeeded in doing except the major, who being less young active, jumped short of the requisite distance; and although he scrambled up unhurt, he found his gun so crammed full of wet sand that it would be useless till thoroughly cleansed. He therefore bade them walk on, saying he would follow; and taking off his hat, he sat down in the shade, where they left him. When they had been beating about for game some time, they began to wonder why the major did not come on, and they shouted to let him know whereabouts they were; but there was no answer, and hour after hour passed without his appearance, till at length they began to feel somewhat uneasy.

Thus, the day wore away, and they found themselves approaching the rendezvous. The boat was in sight, and they were walking down to it, wondering how their friend could have missed them, when suddenly, to their great joy, they saw him before them, making toward the barge. He was without his hat or gun, limping hastily along in his top-boots, and did not appear to observe them. They shouted after him, but as he did not look round, they began to run, in order to overtake him; and, indeed, fast as he went, they did gain considerably upon him. Still he reached the boat first, crossing the plank which the boatmen had placed ready for the gentlemen they saw approaching. He ran down the companion-stairs, and they after him; but inexpressible was their surprise when they could not find him below! They ascended again and inquired of the boatmen what had become of him; but they declared he had not come on board, and that nobody had crossed the plank till the young men themselves had done so.

Confounded and amazed at what appeared so inexplicable, and doubly anxious about their friend, they immediately resolved to retrace their steps in search of him; and, accompanied by some Indians who knew the jungle, they made their way back to the spot where they had left him. Thence some footmarks enabled them to trace him, till, at a very short distance from the ditch, they found his hat and his gun. Just then the Indians called out to them to beware, for that there was a sunken well thereabouts, into which they might fall. An apprehension naturally seized them that this might have been the fate of their friend; and on examining the edge, they saw a mark as of a heel slipping up.

Upon this, one of the Indians consented to go down, having a rope with which they had provided themselves tied round his waist; for, aware of the existence of the wells, the natives suspected what had actually occurred, namely, that the unfortunate gentleman had slipped into one of these traps, which, being overgrown with brambles, were not discernible by the eye. With the assistance of the Indian, the body was brought up and carried back to the boat, amid the deep regrets of the party, with whom he had been a great favourite. They proceeded with it to the next station, where an inquiry was instituted as to the manner of his death, but of course there was nothing more to be elicited.

I give this story as related by one of the parties present, and there is no doubt of its perfect authenticity. He says he can in no way account for the mystery—he can only relate the fact; and not one, but the whole *five* cadets, saw him as distinctly as they saw each other. It was evident, from the spot where the body was found, which was not many hundred yards from the well, that the accident must have occurred very shortly after they left him. When the young men reached the boat, Major R——— must have been, for some seven or eight hours, a *denizen* of the other world, yet he kept the rendezvous!

18

It will not be out of place, here, to mention the circumstance recorded in Professor Gregory's *Abstract of Baron von Reichenbach's Re-*

searches in Magnetism, regarding a person called Billing, who acted in the capacity of amanuensis to the blind poet Pfeffel, at Colmar. Having treated of various experiments, by which it was ascertained that certain sensitive persons were not only able to detect electric influences of which others were unconscious, but could also perceive, emanating from the wires and magnets, flames which were invisible to people in general; "the baron," according to Dr. Gregory, "proceeded to a useful application of the results, which is, he says, so much the more welcome, as it utterly eradicates one of the chief foundations of superstition, that worst enemy to the development of human enlightenment and liberty. A singular occurrence, which took place at Colmar, in the garden of the poet Pfeffel, has been made generally known by various writings. The following are the essential facts. The poet, being blind, had employed a young clergyman, of the evangelical church, as amanuensis. Pfeffel, when he walked out, was supported and led by this young man, whose name was Billing.

"As they walked in the garden, at some distance from the town, Pfeffel observed, that as often as they passed over a particular spot, the arm of Billing trembled, and he betrayed uneasiness. On being questioned, the young man reluctantly confessed, that as often as he passed over that spot, certain feelings attacked him, which he could not control, and which he knew well, as he always experienced the same, in passing over any place where human bodies lay buried. He added, that at night, when he came near such places, he saw supernatural appearances. Pfeffel, with the view of curing the youth of what he looked on as fancy, went that night with him to the garden. As they approached the spot in the dark, Billing perceived a feeble light, and when still nearer, he saw a luminous ghostlike figure floating over the spot. This he described as a female form, with one arm laid across the body, the other hanging down, floating in the upright posture, but tranquil, the feet only a hand-breadth or two above the soil.

"Pfeffel went alone, as the young man declined to follow him, up to the place where the figure was said to be, and struck about in all directions with his stick, besides running actually through the shadow; but the figure was not more affected than a flame would have been; the luminous form, according to Billing always returned to its original position after these experiments. Many things were tried during several months, and numerous companies of people were brought to the spot, but the matter remained the same, and the ghost-seer adhered to his serious assertion, and to the opinion founded on it, that some individual lay buried there. At last, Pfeffel had the place dug up. At a considerable depth was found a firm layer of white lime, of the length and breadth of a grave, and of considerable thickness, and when this had been broken into, there were found the bones of a human being. It was evident that someone had been buried in the place and covered with a thick layer of lime (quicklime), as is generally done in times of pestilence, of earthquakes, and other similar events. The bones were removed, the pit filled up, the lime scattered abroad, and the surface again made smooth. When Billing was now brought back to the place, the phenomena did not return, and the nocturnal spirit had for ever disappeared.

"It is hardly necessary to point out to the reader what view the author takes of this story, which excited much attention in Germany, because it came from the most truthful man alive, and theologians and psychologists gave to it sundry terrific meanings. It obviously falls into the province of chemical action, and thus meets with a simple and clear explanation from natural and physical causes. A corpse is a field for abundant chemical changes, decompositions, fermentation, putrefaction, gasification, and general play of affinities. A stratum of quicklime, in a narrow pit, unites its powerful affinities to those of the organic matters, and gives rise to a long-continued working of the whole. Rain-water filters through and contributes to the action: the lime on the outside of the mass first falls to a fine powder, and afterward, with more water, forms lumps which are very slowly penetrated by the air. Slaked lime prepared for building, but not used, on account of some cause connected with a warlike state of society some centuries since, has been found in subterraneous holes or pits, in the ruins of old castles; and the mass, except on the outside, was so unaltered that it has been used for modern buildings.

"It is evident, therefore, that in such circumstances there must be a very slow and long-continued chemical action, partly owing to the slow penetration of the mass of lime by the external carbonic acid, partly to the change going on in the remains of animal matter, at all events as long as any is left. In the above case, this must have gone on in Pfeffel's garden, and, as we know that chemical action is invariably associated with light, visible to the sensitive, this must have been the origin of the luminous appearance, which again must have continued until the mutual affinities of the organic remains, the lime, the air, and water, had finally come to a state of chemical rest or equilibrium. As soon, therefore, as a sensitive person, although otherwise quite healthy, came that way, and entered into the sphere of the force in action, he must feel, by day, like Mdlle. Maix, the sensations so often described, and see by night, like Mdlle. Reichel, the luminous appearance. Ignorance, fear, and superstition, would dress up the feebly shining, vaporous light into a human form, and furnish it with human limbs and members; just as we can at pleasure fancy every cloud in the sky to represent a man or a demon.

"The wish to strike a fatal blow at the monster superstition, which, at no distant period, poured out upon European society from a similar source, such inexpressible misery, when, in trials for witchcraft, not hundreds, not thousands, but hundreds of thousands of innocent human beings perished miserably, either on the scaffold, at the stake, or by the effects of torture—this desire induced the author to try the experiment of bringing, if possible, a highly-sensitive patient by night to a churchyard. It appeared possible that such a person might see, over graves in which mouldering bodies lie, something similar to that which Billing had seen. Mdlle. Reichel had the courage, rare in her sex, to gratify this wish of the author. On two very dark nights she allowed herself to be taken from the castle of Reisenberg, where she was living with the author's family, to the neighbouring churchyard of Grunzing.

" The result justified his anticipation in the most beautiful manner. She very soon saw a light, and observed on one of the graves, along its length, a delicate, breathing flame: she also saw the same thing, only weaker on the second grave. But she saw neither witches nor ghosts; she described the fiery appearances as a shining vapor, one to two spans high, extending as far as the grave, and floating near its surface. Sometime afterward she was taken to two large cemeteries near Vienna, where several burials occur daily, and graves lie about by thousands. Here she saw numerous graves provided with similar lights. Wherever she looked, she saw luminous masses scattered about. But this appearance was most vivid over the newest graves, while in the oldest it could not be perceived.

"She described the appearance less as a clear flame than as a dense, vaporous mass of fire, intermediate between fog and flame. On many graves the flames were four feet high, so that when she stood on them, it surrounded her up to the neck. If she thrust her hand into it, it was like putting it into a dense, fiery cloud. She betrayed no uneasiness, because she had all her life been accustomed to such emanations, and had seen the same, in the author's experiments, often produced by natural causes.

19

A circumstance fully as remarkable as any recorded, occurred at Odessa, in the year 1842. An old blind man, named Michel, had for many years been accustomed to get his living by seating himself every morning on a beam in one of the timber-yards, with a wooden bowl at his feet, into which the passengers cast their alms. This long-continued practice had made him well known to the inhabitants, and, as he was believed to have been formerly a soldier, his blindness was attributed to the numerous wounds he had received in battle. For his own part, he spoke little, and never contradicted this opinion.

One night, Michel, by some accident, fell in with a little girl of ten years old, named Powleska, who was friendless, and on the verge of perishing with cold and hunger. The old man took her home, and adopted her; and, from that time, instead of sitting in the timber-yards, he went about the streets in her company, asking alms at the doors of the houses. The child called him *father*, and they were extremely happy together. But when they had pursued this mode of life for about five years, a misfortune befell them. A theft having been committed in a house which they had visited in the morning, Powleska was suspected and arrested, and the blind man was left once more alone. But, instead of resuming his former habits, he now disappeared altogether; and this circumstance causing the suspicion to extend to him, the girl was brought before the magistrate to be interrogated with regard to his probable place of concealment.

"Do you know where Michel is?" said the magistrate.

"He is dead!" replied she, shedding a torrent of tears.

As the girl had been shut up for three days, without any means of obtaining information from without, this answer, together with her unfeigned distress, naturally excited considerable surprise.

"Who told you he was dead?" they inquired.

"Nobody!"

"Then how can you know it?"

"I saw him killed!"

"But you have not been out of the prison?"

"But I saw it, nevertheless!"

"But how was that possible? Explain what you mean!"

"I cannot. All I can say is, that I saw him killed."

"When was he killed, and how?"

"It was the night I was arrested."

"That cannot be: he was alive when you were seized!"

250

"Yes, he was; he was killed an hour after that. They stabbed him with a knife."

"Where were you then?"

"I can't tell; but I saw it."

The confidence with which the girl asserted what seemed to her hearers impossible and absurd, disposed them to imagine that she was either really insane, or pretending to be so. So, leaving Michel aside, they proceeded to interrogate her about the robbery, asking her if she was guilty.

"Oh, no!" she answered.

"Then how came the property to be found about you?"

"I don't know: I saw nothing but the murder."

"But there are no grounds for supposing Michel is dead: his body has not been found."

"It is in the aqueduct."

"And do you know who slew him?"

"Yes—it is a woman. Michel was walking very slowly, after I was taken from him. A woman came behind him with a large kitchen-knife; but he heard her and turned round: and then the woman flung a piece of grey stuff over his head, and struck him repeatedly with the knife; the grey stuff was much stained with the blood. Michel fell at the eighth blow, and the woman dragged the body to the aqueduct and let it fall in without ever lifting the stuff which stuck to his face."

As it was easy to verify these latter assertions, they despatched people to the spot; and there the body was found, with the piece of stuff over his head, exactly as she described. But when they asked her how she knew all this, she could only answer, "I don't know."

"But you know who killed him?"

"Not exactly: it is the same woman that put out his eyes; but, perhaps, he will tell me her name tonight; and if he does, I will tell it to you."

"Whom do you mean by *he?*"

"Why, Michel, to be sure!"

During the whole of the following night, without allowing her to suspect their intention, they watched her; and it was observed that she never lay down but sat upon the bed in a sort of lethargic slumber. Her body was quite motionless, except at intervals, when this repose was interrupted by violent nervous shocks, which pervaded her whole frame. On the ensuing day, the moment she was brought before the judge, she declared that she was now able to tell them the name of the assassin.

"But stay," said the magistrate: "did Michel never tell you, when he was alive, how he lost his sight?"

"No—but the morning before I was arrested, he promised me to do so; and that was the cause of his death."

"How could that be?"

"Last night, Michel came to me, and he pointed to the man hidden behind the scaffolding on which he and I had been sitting. He showed me the man listening to us, when he said, 'I'll tell you all about that tonight;' and then the man———"

"Do you know the name of this man?"

"It is Luck. He went afterward to a broad street that leads down to the harbour, and he entered the third house on the right———"

"What is the name of the street?"

"I don't know: but the house is one story lower than the adjoining ones. Luck told Catherine what he had heard, and she proposed to him to assassinate Michel; but he refused, saying, 'It was bad enough to have burnt out his eyes fifteen years before, while he was asleep at your door, and to have kidnapped him into the country.' Then I went in to ask charity, and Catherine put a piece of plate into my pocket, that I might be arrested; then she hid herself behind the aqueduct to wait for Michel, and she killed him."

"But, since you say all this, why did you keep the plate—why didn't you give information?"

"But I didn't see it then. Michel showed it me last night."

"But what should induce Catherine to do this?"

"Michel was her husband, and she had forsaken him to come to Odessa and marry again. One night, fifteen years ago, she saw Michel, who had come to seek her. She slipped hastily into her house, and Michel, who thought she had not seen him, lay down at her door to watch; but he fell asleep, and then Luck burnt out his eyes, and carried him to a distance."

"And is it Michel who has told you this?"

"Yes: he came, very pale, and covered with blood; and he took me by the hand and showed me all this with his fingers."

Upon this, Luck and Catherine were arrested; and it was ascertained that she had actually been married to Michel in the year 1819, at Kherson. They at first denied the accusation, but Powleska insisted, and they subsequently confessed the crime. When they communicated the circumstances of the confession to Powleska, she said, "I was told it last night."

This affair naturally excited great interest, and people all round the neighbourhood hastened into the city to learn the sentence.

20

A lady who had left the West Indies when six years old, came one night, fourteen years afterward, to her sister's bedside, and said, "I know uncle is dead. I have dreamed that I saw a number of slaves in the large store-room at Barbadoes, with long brooms, sweeping down immense cobwebs. I complained to my aunt, and she covered her face and said, 'Yes, he is no sooner gone than they disobey him.'"

It was afterward ascertained that Mr. P——— had died on that night, and that he had never permitted the cobwebs in this room to be swept away, of which, however, the lady assures me she knew nothing; nor could she or her friends conceive what was meant by the symbol of the cobwebs, till they received the explanation subsequently from a member of the family.

The following very curious allegorical dream I give, not in the words of the dreamer, but in those of her son, who bears a name destined, I trust, to a long immortality:—

"Wooer's Abbey-Cottage,
"Dunfermline-in-the-Woods,
"Monday morning, 31st May, 1847.

"Dear Mrs. Crowe: *That* dream of my mother's was as follows: She stood in a long, dark, empty gallery: on her one side was my father, and on the other my eldest sister Amelia; then myself, and the rest of the family, according to their ages. At the foot of the hall stood my youngest sister Alexes, and above her my sister Catherine—a creature, by-the-way, in person and mind, more like an angel of heaven than an inhabitant of earth. We all stood silent and motionless. At last *it* entered—the unimagined *something*, that, casting its grim shadow before, had enveloped all the trivialities of the preceding dream in the stifling atmosphere of terror. It entered, stealthily descending the three steps that led from the entrance down into the chamber of horror: and my mother *felt* it *was Death*! He was dwarfish, bent, and shrivelled. He carried on his shoulder a heavy axe; and had come, she thought, to destroy 'all her little ones at one fell swoop.'

"On the entrance of the shape, my sister Alexes leaped out of the rank, interposing herself between him and my mother. He raised his axe and aimed a blow at Catherine—a blow which, to her horror, my mother could not intercept, though she had snatched up a three-legged stool, the sole furniture of the apartment, for that purpose. She could not, she felt, fling the stool at the figure without destroying Alexes, who kept shooting out and in between her and the ghastly thing. She tried in vain to scream; she besought my father, in agony, to avert the impending stroke; but he did not hear, or did not heed her, and stood motionless, as in a trance. Down came the axe, and poor Catherine fell in her blood, cloven to 'the white halse bane.'

"Again, the axe was lifted, by the inexorable shadow, over the head of my brother, who stood next in the line. Alexes had somewhere disappeared behind the ghastly visitant; and, with a scream, my mother flung the footstool at his head. He vanished, and she awoke.

"This dream left on my mother's mind a fearful apprehension of impending misfortune, 'which would not pass away.'

"It was *murder* she feared; and her suspicions were not allayed by the discovery that a man (some time before discarded by my father for bad conduct, and with whom she had, somehow, associated the *Death* of her dream) had been lurking about the place, and sleeping in an adjoining outhouse on the night it occurred, and for some nights previous and subsequent to it. Her terror increased. Sleep forsook her; and every night, when the house was still, she arose and stole, sometimes with a candle, sometimes in the dark, from room to room, listening, in a sort of waking nightmare, for the breathing of the assassin, who, she imagined, was lurking in some one of them. This could not last. She reasoned with herself; but her terror became intolerable, and she related her dream to my father, who, of course, called her a fool for her pains, whatever might be his real opinion of the matter.

"Three months had elapsed, when we children were all of us seized with scarlet fever. My sister Catherine died almost immediately—sacrificed, as my mother in her misery thought, to her (my mother's) over-anxiety for Alexes, whose danger seemed more imminent. The dream-prophecy was in part fulfilled. I also was at death's door—given up by the doctors, but not by my mother: she was confident of my recovery; but for my brother, who was scarcely considered in danger at all, but on whose head, *she had seen* the visionary axe impending, her fears were great; for she could not recollect whether the blow had or had not descended when the spectre vanished.

"My brother recovered, but relapsed, and barely escaped with life; but Alexes did not. For a year and ten months the poor child lingered, and almost every night I had to sing her asleep—often, I remember, through bitter tears, for I knew she was dying, and I loved her the more as she wasted away. I held her little hand as she died; I followed her to the grave—the last thing that I have *loved* on earth. And *the dream was fulfilled.*

"Truly and sincerely yours,

J. Noel Paton."

21

Mr. A———— F————, an eminent Scotch advocate, while staying in the neighbourhood of Loch Fyne, who dreamed one night that he saw a number of people in the street following a man to the scaffold. He discovered the features of the criminal in the cart distinctly; and, for some reason or other, which he could not account for, felt an extraordinary interest in his fate—insomuch that he joined the throng, and accompanied him to the place that was to terminate his earthly career. This interest was the more unaccountable, that the man had an exceedingly unprepossessing countenance, but it was nevertheless so vivid as to induce the dreamer to ascend the scaffold, and address him, with a view to enable him to escape the impending catastrophe. Suddenly, however, while he was talking to him, the whole scene dissolved away, and the sleeper awoke. Being a good deal struck with the lifelike reality of the vision, and the impression made on his mind by the features of this man, he related the circumstance to his friends at breakfast, adding that he should know him anywhere, if he saw him. A few jests being made on the subject, the thing was forgotten.

On the afternoon of the same day, the advocate was informed that two men wanted to speak to him, and, on going into the hall, he was struck with amazement at perceiving that one of them was the hero of his dream!

"We are accused of a murder," said they, "and we wish to consult you. Three of us went out, last night, in a boat; an accident has happened; our comrade is drowned, and they want to make us accountable for him." The advocate then put some interrogations to them, and the result produced in his mind by their answers was a conviction of their guilt. Probably the recollection of his dream rendered the effects of this conviction more palpable; for one addressing the other, said in Gaelic, "We have come to the wrong man; he is against us."

"There is a higher power than I against you," returned the gentleman; "and the only advice I can give you is, if you are guilty, fly immediately."

Upon this, they went away; and the next thing he heard was, that they were taken into custody on suspicion of the murder.

The account of the affair was, that, as they said, the three had gone out together on the preceding evening, and that in the morning the body of one of them had been found on the shore, with a cut across his forehead. The father and friend of the victim had waited on the banks of the lake till the boat came in, and then demanded their companion; of whom, however, they professed themselves unable to give any account. Upon this, the old man led them to his cottage for the purpose of showing them the body of his son. One entered, and, at the sight of it, burst into a passion of tears; the other refused to do so, saying his business called him immediately home, and went sulkily away. This last was the man seen in the dream.

After a fortnight's incarceration, the former of these was liberated; and he then declared to the advocate his intention of bringing an action of damages for false imprisonment. He was advised not to do it.

"Leave well alone," said the lawyer; "and if you'll take my advice, make off while you can."

The man, however, refused to fly: he declared that he really did not know what had occasioned the death of his comrade. The latter had been at one end of the boat, and he at the other; when he looked round, he was gone; but whether he had fallen overboard, and cut his head as he fell, or whether he had been struck and pushed into the water, he did not know. The advocate became finally satisfied of this man's innocence; but the authorities, thinking it absurd to try one and not the other, again laid hands on him: and it fell to Mr. A——— F——— to be the defender of both.

The difficulty was, not to separate their cases in his pleading; for, however morally convinced of the different ground on which they stood, his duty, professionally, was to obtain the acquittal of both, in which he finally succeeded, as regarded the charge of murder. They were, therefore, sentenced to two years' imprisonment; and, so far as the dream is concerned, here ends the story. There remains, however, a curious sequel to it.

A few years afterward, the same gentleman being in a boat on Loch Fyne, in company with Sir T——— D——— L———, happened to be mentioning these curious circumstances, when one of the boatmen said that he "knew well about those two men; and that a very strange thing had occurred in regard to one of them." This one, on inquiry, proved to be the subject of the dream; and the strange thing was this: On being liberated, he had quitted that part of the country, and in process of time had gone to Greenock, and thence embarked in a vessel for Cork.

But the vessel seemed fated never to reach its destination; one misfortune happened after another, till at length the sailors said: "This won't do; there must be a murderer on board with us!"

As is usual, when such a persuasion exists, they drew lots three times, and each time it fell on that man! He was consequently put on shore, and the vessel went on its way without him. What had become of him afterward was not known.

LEONAUR

ALSO FROM LEONAUR
AVAILABLE IN SOFTCOVER OR HARDCOVER WITH DUST JACKET

THE COMPLETE FOUR JUST MEN: VOLUME 2 *by Edgar Wallace*—*The Law of the Four Just Men & The Three Just Men*—disillusioned with a world where the wicked and the abusers of power perpetually go unpunished, the Just Men set about to rectify matters according to their own standards, and retribution is dispensed on swift and deadly wings.

THE COMPLETE RAFFLES: 1 *by E. W. Homung*—*The Amateur Cracksman & The Black Mask*—By turns urbane gentleman about town and accomplished cricketer, life is just too ordinary for Raffles and that sets him on a series of adventures that have long been treasured as a real antidote to the 'white knights' who are the usual heroes of the crime fiction of this period.

THE COMPLETE RAFFLES: 2 *by E. W. Homung*—*A Thief in the Night & Mr Justice Raffles*—By turns urbane gentleman about town and accomplished cricketer, life is just too ordinary for Raffles and that sets him on a series of adventures that have long been treasured as a real antidote to the 'white knights' who are the usual heroes of the crime fiction of this period.

THE COLLECTED SUPERNATURAL AND WEIRD FICTION OF WILKIE COLLINS: VOLUME 1 *by Wilkie Collins*—Contains one novel 'The Haunted Hotel', one novella 'Mad Monkton', three novelettes 'Mr Percy and the Prophet', 'The Biter Bit' and 'The Dead Alive' and eight short stories to chill the blood.

THE COLLECTED SUPERNATURAL AND WEIRD FICTION OF WILKIE COLLINS: VOLUME 2 *by Wilkie Collins*—Contains one novel 'The Two Destinies', three novellas 'The Frozen deep', 'Sister Rose' and 'The Yellow Mask' and two short stories to chill the blood.

THE COLLECTED SUPERNATURAL AND WEIRD FICTION OF WILKIE COLLINS: VOLUME 3 *by Wilkie Collins*—Contains one novel 'Dead Secret,' two novelettes 'Mrs Zant and the Ghost' and 'The Nun's Story of Gabriel's Marriage' and five short stories to chill the blood.

FUNNY BONES *selected by Dorothy Scarborough*—An Anthology of Humorous Ghost Stories.

MONTEZUMA'S CASTLE AND OTHER WEIRD TALES *by Charles B. Cory*—Cory has written a superb collection of eighteen ghostly and weird stories to chill and thrill the avid enthusiast of supernatural fiction.

SUPERNATURAL BUCHAN *by John Buchan*—Stories of Ancient Spirits, Uncanny Places & Strange Creatures.